THE FAVOR

AMELIA SHEA

Amelia Shea

This book is a work of fiction. The names, characters, places and incidents are products of the writer's imagination, or have been used fictitiously and are not to be construed as real. Any resemblance to real persons, living or dead, actual events or organizations is entirely coincidental.

Copyright © 2020 by Amelia Shea
All rights reserved.

The unauthorized reproduction or distribution of this copyright work is illegal. No part of this book may be distributed, reproduced, or stored in a retrieval system, or transmitted in any form or by any means, electronic, mechanical, photocopying, recording, or otherwise, without express written permission of the publisher.

Dedication

For Chrissie, whose positivity is contagious and inspires me each and every day.

Chapter 1

"Five minutes tops, I swear." It was a lie. One of several she had told her mother in the last ten minutes of their conversation. She glanced at her clock on the dashboard and sighed. *Eleven minutes.*

Her foot tapped on the gas slowly, her gaze drawn to the speedometer. Maybe she could get there in fifteen. But unless the car grew wings, a five-minute arrival wasn't happening.

"Where are you?" Suspicion laced her mother's voice. Of course it did. The woman had known her for the past twenty-six years.

She bit her lip. This was why lying wasn't good for her. She could never seem to keep up with her lies. "Okay, so I might have underestimated when I said five minutes. It's probably gonna be about twenty."

Her mother cleared her throat, which was never a good sign. "So you lied."

"No," she snapped. Admitting the lie would give the woman leverage. "Underestimated. You know I've always sucked at math." She tightened her grip on the steering wheel and pressed her foot on the gas pedal.

Cheyenne could hear the heavy sigh and knew what was coming even before the words were spoken.

"This is why you should move closer."

She silently groaned. *Not this again.*

"Remember the Parkers from down the street? They're moving and renting out the house. I can get the information from Carol." The enthusiasm in her tone was evident. "And we have plenty of bars around here you could work at." Her mother gasped. "Oh, I have a great idea. Let me reach out to Lenny and see if he's got any shifts available."

Lenny was her uncle. He owned a dive bar on the outskirts of town. The same place her mother had forbidden her to go due to the seedy location. *Now she wants me to work there?* Obviously, the woman was desperate to have her back home.

Her mom had always been overbearing, but it seemed as Cheyenne got older, it had gotten worse.

"I'll call him now."

"Mom, no." Cheyenne gritted her teeth. "I have a job, and a home, in Blacksburg."

The same job and home she'd had for the past four years, though her mother liked to ignore that fact.

"But it's so far. Don't you miss it here, being with us?"

Cheyenne clamped her lips. *Don't answer!* It was a loaded question with no right answer. If she said no, she'd feel the wrath of her mother. If she said yes, her mom would have her moved back home in a day. Lose-lose situation. Though she would never admit it to anyone except Macy, her mother was the reason she lived almost two hours away from her hometown. Eighty miles proved too far for a "surprise" visit. *No way am I moving back.* Cheyenne had it good, and she kept her mom at a safe but long distance.

"Mom, we can talk about this when I get there, but I gotta go. Driving on the cell is so unsafe. See you in a few." She clicked End and then tossed the phone onto the seat. She didn't miss the sound of her mom calling out before she hung up. Cheyenne would deal with her in person. She snorted while envisioning the one-sided conversation.

She fiddled with her radio and turned back to the road. Monthly dinners were a must, and as usual, she would arrive late. The two-hour drive was good for her. It gave her time to gear up for the inevitable. *Why aren't you dating? I was married at your age.* Why were mothers so hellbent on diminishing their daughters' life choices? *Or is it just my mom?*

Cheyenne hadn't been a scholar like her older brother. She opted to work, as opposed to going to college after high school. Her resumé was filled with waitressing and retail jobs, which wasn't exactly rave-worthy material. However, she had her own place and paid her bills on time, usually.

Her newest endeavor was bound to be her claim to success when it finally got off the ground. She and her best friend, Macy, had started an online shop. They had visions of someday opening up a storefront. It was a dream set in the future. A fantastic vision, though. Cheyenne smiled, seeing it in her head.

A boutique-style set-up. Gorgeous, trendy-chic clothes lining the outer walls, all color coordinated, of course. Shoes lining the floor underneath with shelves above for hats. The center floor plan was her own little creation. Three circular tables, all offering one-of-a-kind, handmade jewelry. Along the back wall, home furnishings, candles, and oils. She drew in a breath and could almost smell the scents. *Almost.*

Currently, they were stuck working out of their cramped apartment. If their calculations were correct, they had another five years before their dream was even remotely possible. *Five friggin' years.* Cheyenne slumped in her seat, allowing the weight of disappointment to settle in. She sighed.

The apartment. Yet another source of her stress.

Her best friend and roommate, Macy, had lived there most of her life. When her mom moved out after getting married, Cheyenne moved in. It wouldn't have been Cheyenne's first choice of places to live, but the timing played out perfectly. For a while, it was great. Until about two months ago, when her courtyard became the meeting ground for some local assholes. Cheyenne, Macy, and a few other women had made complaints to the landlord. As of yet, they hadn't been heard, and if they were, they were blatantly ignored. It had started out more bothersome than anything else. However, in the past few weeks, it had escalated. They seemed to become more brazen with their taunting and sexually aggressive comments. For a threesome asshole brigade, they were fairly smart, only targeting women late at night when witnesses were scarce.

Between asshole thugs, dealing with her mother, and her dream job out of her immediate reach, Cheyenne felt the weight of it all. She needed to focus on the good. *Oh, shut up!*

"I need a distraction," she muttered.

And just like that...she got one.

The sound of a roaring engine had her glancing in her mirror. Coming up on her left was a leather-clad man with a gray beard and dark sunglasses. He had a big black-and-silver motorcycle situated between his legs. She clucked her tongue. *Where's your helmet?* By law, her state didn't require it, but for safety purposes, he should be wearing one, she thought. *Shut up, Miss Goody-Good and enjoy the view.*

She leaned forward, taking a longer glance, a small smile playing on her lips.

This wasn't an uncommon occurrence in Blacksburg and the surrounding towns. The Ghosttown Riders Motorcycle Club had taken up residency years ago, long before she moved into town. While they usually stayed under the radar and shied away from the town festivities, it wasn't unusual to see a few driving around. There was a certain shock to her heart every time she caught a glimpse of one. Maybe it was the badass vibe or the long hair and tats. Whatever it was, it always seemed to grab her attention. And today was no different.

The corner of her mouth curled. She sat up straight and split her vision between the lane and watching the motorcycle on her left. The road was empty beside her car, and the bike was gaining speed and pulling up on her side.

Is it just me, or do all women perk up from the sound of a rumbling engine? There was something about men on motorcycles that gave her cause to sit up straighter, jut out her breasts, and check her hair. If given enough time, she would have added a sweep of gloss on her lips. She gauged his speed as she glanced in the mirror. She also took in his appearance. If she had to guess, he'd be old enough to be her dad. Somehow, it didn't deter her excitement. She casually glanced over as he passed. His gaze was trained on the road in front of him.

Nothing. Really?

She slouched in her seat. It was disappointing. Her love life had tanked a year ago when she walked in on her boyfriend banging a coworker. *Her coworker.* It was disastrous and ugly and took a heavy toll on her self-esteem. Cheating was, and always had been, her deal breaker.

She was due for a boost of self-esteem, but she wasn't going to get it. Not from this guy.

He sped in front of her, and she caught sight of the three-piece rocker. *Ghosttown Riders.* She released a silent sigh. They were notorious in her area. On occasion, she had piqued the interest once or twice from a club member, but nothing more than a lingering glance. A hell of a lot more than this guy had given her. *He's old enough to be my dad.* Even that blaring fact didn't diminish her disappointment. *Not even a look?* He wasn't exactly her dream guy at forty years her senior, but he could have thrown her a bone with a simple glance her way.

I'm pathetic.

She glanced down at the clock, ignoring the biker ahead. She needed to make up some time. She pressed harder on her gas pedal. Not for the benefit of catching up to biker man, but to dodge the wrath of her mother for being later than usual.

She rounded the bend and let off the gas. The steep decline

would give her enough speed, and making the sharp turns through the valley was suicidal at anything more than sixty. She remained in her lane and caught a flash from her left again. A sleek, dark blue sedan was coming up on her fast. She widened her eyes. This car was going way too fast. *Definitely not a local.* The massive hill and harsh turns were enough to slow most drivers down, but not this one. She flickered her hazards in hopes of giving some warning, but it wasn't heeded—the car passed her faster than the motorcycle before her.

She caught a quick glimpse. It was a man, probably not much older than her. His cheeks were hollowed, and a fairly large bump protruded on the bridge of his nose. As he passed, she noticed a prominent, raised scar rippled down his forehead, and his dark hair was pulled into a ponytail at the nape of his neck. She twisted her lips. *A pink hair tie?* She chuckled, half wondering if he even realized how absurd he looked.

She kept her gaze glued to the car, glancing down at the license plate. *Yep, out of towner.* She should report him as soon as she got to her mom's house. People like him had no place on these roads, driving like an asshole. She watched the motorcycle in the distance as the sedan caught up to him. She waited for the brake lights on the car to shine, but it never happened. Instead, it shifted to the right on the curve.

"Slow down," she muttered, completely fixated on the car swerving dangerously close to the motorcycle.

Her heart pounded, watching the scene unfold. Cheyenne gripped her steering wheel. "Oh, my God."

She gasped as the sedan sideswiped the motorcycle into a tailspin across the road.

She sucked in a harsh breath again, not fully believing what she saw. "Oh, my God. Oh, my God!" she screamed as her body shook.

She'd never been witness to a car accident. It was horrific as it played out in slow motion right before her eyes. The motorcycle shot out from under the biker and careened over the embankment. She stared in horror as the man slid across the asphalt, nearing the same direction of his bike.

Her hands shook as she grasped the wheel tightly, and her heart raced. The biker had come to a halt, barely reaching the guardrail. Her first instinct was to lean over and feel for her phone in her handbag. Her gaze was glued to the scene in front of her.

She raced forward, slamming on her brakes as she pulled to the half shoulder, about fifty feet from the biker lying on the road. She threw the car into Park and jumped out, leaving her door wide open. She sprinted to the man who was face down on the asphalt. He was dead. He had to be. There was no way even a superhero could have survived the wreck. The pounding of her heart was blazing through her eardrums. She stopped about ten feet away. He wasn't moving. She bit her lip and scanned the road. It was just her and him. *What do I do?*

Help him. She froze, wondering where the voice had come from. It took only a second to recognize it as her own. She rushed forward.

As she neared, she slowed down. Blood was everywhere. *Oh God.* She stopped short of his body. Her quick perusal would forever be ingrained in her mind. She'd never forget this. His hands were bloodied to a pulp. The flesh was so raw it looked like ground meat. Her stomach curled as she inched forward. This man needed a doctor, a surgeon. Oh God, he needed a miracle if he had any chance of surviving. None of which she could provide. She drove her hands through her hair, tugging sharply at the ends. *I don't know what to do.*

Help him.

Cheyenne dropped to her knees, her body visibly shaking. She spread her hands out and reached forward, hovering over his back. Should she try to roll him over? What if his neck was broken? She remembered the basic rules of driver's ed. *Do not move the body, or you may cause more damage.* She glanced up the road. It was completely desolate. But he was lying in the middle of the lane. If a car came, he might get hit if the driver couldn't see him. *I should move him. No, don't move him.* She squeezed her eyes shut. A dark dread spread through her body. "Oh God, what do I do?" she muttered.

Nothing could have prepared her for this. She glanced up and over her shoulder. There was no one to help; it was all on her. His only hope was her. She gulped a breath and flinched when she heard a faint, pained grunt. She leaned closer but refrained from touching him.

"You-you're okay," she stammered. It was another bald-faced lie. He wasn't okay, not even close to okay. It was a miracle he was even alive. She reached out but still didn't touch him. *What should I do?* Another faint moan forced her to place her hand gently on his back, not applying any pressure. "Just try to stay still. I'm going to call for help." She swallowed the lump in her throat, forcing out another lie. "You're gonna be okay, just hang on." He made no further sound, and his body was still. Had she just heard his last breath? *Oh, my God.*

She scrambled to her feet and ran to her car, lying over the driver's side to grab her phone. Her hands were trembling so hard, the simple task of dialing was nearly impossible. She kept her gaze on the man in the road. The two rings seemed to take forever.

"9-1-1, what's your emergency?"

"We need help, send an ambulance to Route 417, the Belgium Road exit, and fast. This guy...oh God...it's bad." Her words were rushed and possibly incoherent. Tears threatened her eyes. "It's so bad," she uttered, barely able to get the words out. She drew in a breath, and her face heated.

"Ma'am, I need you to calm down and tell me what happened."

Cheyenne shook her head. "I don't know. A guy on a motorcycle got sideswiped by a car, and he's messed up really bad, please just send someone."

"Before or after the Belgium exit?"

"Uh...." She scanned the deserted highway. *Think.* She had a horrible sense of direction. She knew landmarks, not mile markers. "Before, I think. The exit before the Dairy Cup and Grandview's garage. He's in the center of the right lane. There's so much blood."

"Okay, ma'am, I'm dispatching now."

Cheyenne straightened from the car when she saw a shift in his leg. "Should I move him?" She glanced over her shoulder to the empty road.

"No, don't move him, the ambulance is on its way."

"Okay, just…" She gulped. "Please hurry, it's really bad." Her eyes welled, and she clasped her mouth with her hand.

"Hang tight, they are on their way."

She nodded and clicked the phone, tossing it onto her seat. The ambulance would get there and fix him up. She sucked in a breath and sighed in relief. Help was on the way. She slowly stepped closer and squinted her eyes. *Oh, thank God.* She caught sight of the biker moving slightly, as though he was trying to roll over. She rushed forward and skidded to a stop inches away from him. He was on his side and a bloodied mess. She'd never seen so much blood. Even in movies, there hadn't been quite as much blood as the scene in front of her.

"Don't move. The ambulance is on its way, okay, just try to breathe easy, help's coming." She recited her words twice—once for his assurance, and another for hers. She bent down, dropping to her knees, carefully avoiding contact but remaining close to him. Her hands hovered over his side, unsure of how to help him. When he shifted, she gently guided him back to the ground.

Her breath hitched when his face came into full view. A thick stream of blood dripped down his head, over his eyes, and down his cheek. She followed the source and had to draw in a deep breath to combat her nausea. The deep gash across his temple and hairline was an open laceration displaying jagged flesh. So much blood poured out of the wound, it looked black rather than red. His body jolted forward, and she clasped his hand when he started to swing.

"Please, just calm down, I don't want you to get more hurt, please." His hand squeezed hers in a very faint motion, and she pressed her free hand against his shoulder, easing him back. He didn't resist. He could hear her. *This is good, talk to him.* His hand moved slightly, and one eye peered open.

She strained a smile in hopes of calming him and leaned closer. "Just hang on, okay?"

His lips moved, and his tongue laved his bottom lip. His words were gravelly between his coughs. "My bike."

He was concerned over his bike? She glanced over toward the embankment. She hadn't seen it but didn't need to. The drop was about a hundred feet. The chances his bike was intact were slim to none. She clamped her lips, squeezing them together tightly.

"They'll get your bike once they fix you up, just hang on, please." She sighed and whispered, "Don't die on me." She couldn't be sure if the plea was for the man or God. She'd never witnessed anyone die, and she didn't want to. He groaned and moved slightly as his hand gripped tightly against hers. She moved closer, swiping her hand against his forehead. "Just breathe for me, okay? Nice and steady." She wiped the fallen hair strands from his eyes. "You're gonna be okay, I promise. Just need you to hang on." She cradled their clasped hands against her chest and forced a smile. He stared back at her with a dazed glimmer, but the corner of his lip curled.

She tightened her grip on his hand as a way to will him to stay strong.

His lips twisted, and she leaned closer. "Cops." It came out soft but strangled.

Was that a request? She was sure the cops would come along with the ambulance.

"Yeah, they'll come, and don't worry, I have a good memory. I can identify the car and the license plate of the driver." Her mind drew a blank, except for the Illinois license plate. She couldn't remember the tag number. *Shit.* For the first time, she realized the car never stopped. She was so focused on the biker, she didn't even know if the car had at least slowed down. It certainly hadn't stopped, and there was no mistake he'd hit him. Maybe the driver called nine-one-one too. *How could he not stop?*

The man stared back at her, and his head shook slightly. His lips moved, but his words were mumbled. She leaned in to hear him better. With only a few inches separating them, she got a good look at the biker. She had been right about the age assessment. He was probably in his sixties, his face weathered and lined with deep wrinkles. His eyes were a soft brown and currently pleading.

His lips moved, and she blinked. "What?"

"Take it," he said and then sucked in a sharp breath. His pain was so raw she could almost feel it. She waited for his breathing to settle. It didn't. "My stomach." He coughed, spewing up a wad of blood. She swallowed her breath and the bile threatening her throat.

"Take it."

His short responses were choppy and mumbled, but she understood the gist of it. She glanced down at his tattered clothing, which had been ripped to shreds from the wreck. She lifted his leather vest. Her hand shook as she maneuvered beyond his blood-soaked T-shirt. A crumpled wad of what was she assumed was originally a manila packaging stuck out from the front his pants. The sirens caught her attention, and she looked past her car.

She grazed her hand over his forehead and wiped away the beads of sweat. "The ambulance is here," she whispered with a faint smile. "You're gonna be okay."

A hard squeeze to her hand had her angling closer, only inches away from his bloodied face. "Take it." He gasped a breath. "No cops."

This man was asking her to take and hide a package from the cops? *Oh hell no.*

She shook her head and pulled away slightly, but his eyes drew her back.

He hinged forward slightly and grimaced. She eased her hand against his shoulder.

"Don't move, help is coming."

His bottom lip trembled, and his eyes were at half mast. "Your name?"

She blinked and drew in a breath. "Cheyenne."

The corner of his mouth curled as he tightened his clasp on her hand. "That's pretty."

Even in the most horrific and dramatic experience, she smiled. It was a sweet compliment, especially coming from someone in such obvious pain.

"I'm Mick." His lips meshed together as if he was gearing up to say something but losing the battle. "Please, Cheyenne." He gulped and struggled for breath. "Just take it."

Somehow, the exchange of names had changed something. He was Mick, and she was Cheyenne, and she had to do what he'd asked. Maybe it was the desperation in his tone. His last words were a plea to her. She drew in a breath and stared back at the man. If he did survive, it would be a harsh and painful recovery. It was a big if too. Her eyes teared, bracing some of the pain he must have been feeling. Without giving it another thought, she grabbed the envelope and shoved the crumpled package down the back of her jeans and untucked her shirt to cover it.

"No cops, I promise."

The corner of his lip curled slightly, and she smiled back. "Ya gotta hold on, Mick, okay?" A tear streamed down her cheek, and she swiped her shoulder against her face to wipe it away.

He slowly nodded incoherently. His lips meshed together, opening and closing. He struggled and then moaned. "Meg." His eyes were trained on her until his lids slowly lowered, and he whispered again. "Meg."

She held on tight to his hand but felt his grip loosen. *Oh God, no.*

The stammering from behind was what tore her gaze from him. It had all happened so fast. Two police officers, accompanied by an ambulance, raced over to them, and things got crazy. She reluctantly released his hand when she was pulled away, but her gaze never left him. There was so much chaos and loud screaming from all around. All Cheyenne could do was stand by and watch. She curled her arms around her stomach and said a silent prayer. *Please, don't let him die.*

The voice sounded from far away, even though they were a mere three feet from her.

"We're losing him."

"Pulse is faint."

Cheyenne stepped back, making room for the gurney rolled out in the middle of the highway. Maybe it was shock, but she felt frozen, watching the paramedics try to revive him. The man lay silent and still. *No, not the man. Mick.* Her eyes teared and quickly streamed down her cheeks.

He's not gonna make it.

THERE WAS AN ACCIDENT...HE *didn't make it.*

Trax had gotten the call about twenty minutes ago. It was one he wasn't prepared to receive. A life-changing call.

Mick was gone.

There were few details, or maybe there were more he missed. He zoned out, trying to wrap his head around the news. He wasn't sure how long he had stood in his garage, silently gripping the phone. Could have been minutes or hours. Grief had an odd way of making time stand still.

Mick is dead.

It wasn't the first time death had knocked on his door. Trax was the only surviving member of his immediate family. His younger brother had died at the age of thirteen. He'd been hit by a car while riding his bike home from school. An accident, horrific and life-changing, but an accident. It was his first experience with loss and grief. It wouldn't be his last.

A few years later, it was his mom. She'd been sick for a month or two, refused medical assistance, and continued to smoke two packs a day. By the time she gave in and saw the doctor, it was too late. Stage four lung cancer took her a few months later. His father hung on but eventually succumbed to the pain of losing his kid and wife. He drank himself to death. Trax couldn't blame him. So much grief in such a short time was enough to make anyone throw in the towel.

Then there was Trax, the lone survivor.

If anyone should know the heartache and be able to grasp it, it was him. Yet, there he was, completely blindsided by Mick's death.

Mick. His brother. His friend. His mentor. The man who had vouched for Trax when he prospected with the Ghosttown Riders nine years ago. *Gone.*

The short drive seemed longer than it had ever been. He pulled into the side lot of the clubhouse. He was one of three motorcycles pulling in. He dismounted and then hurried inside. When he'd gotten the call from Rourke, he'd had few details. Mick was on his way back from a pickup and had been hit on the highway. He died on the scene.

It was surreal. He'd just spoken to him in the morning. They had plans. They were meeting up for drinks at the strip club. After all, Trax owed Mick. It was Trax who was supposed to make the pickup. Mick offered when Trax had mentioned being backlogged on some repairs.

A favor, which ultimately cost Mick his life.

The somber greeting he received when he walked in only confirmed the truth. Mick was dead, and the entire club was feeling it. Nadia, one of the club girls, walked over to him, tears streaming down her cheeks. She fell into his chest with a sharp sob. He curled his hand around the back of her neck.

She sniffled, and her muffled voice was strained. "I can't believe he's gone."

The Favor

Trax did his best to comfort her, but he wasn't generally good with crying women. "Where's Meg?"

Nadia glanced up, tears rimming her eyes. "Home. Me and a few of the girls are gonna head over now."

Trax nodded. Meg was Mick's old lady. They'd been together for years, and of all the old ladies, Meg was his favorite. She was a surrogate mom to him, though she was only about twenty years his senior. Both Meg and Mick had taken him on when he started prospecting. They gave him a safe place and became his family, just as the club had.

A sharp pain speared his chest. *Meg.* She was beyond devoted to her husband and the club he loved. This was going to wreck her. He closed his eyes and willed himself to pull his shit together. He'd let the guilt sink in later when he was alone. For now, the only thing he could do was be there for Meg and his club. He steadied his breathing and glanced down at Nadia.

"You tell her I'll be there soon. Need to check in with Kase." He squeezed her shoulder and then released her, making his way into the back. All the brothers were gathered as he entered the room. The usual jovial crew was destroyed by this loss. It would be a hard one for the club. Mick was one of the oldest and most loyal members. He lived and breathed Ghosttown Riders. He was what most brothers strived to be. *What I strive to be.*

Years ago, when Trax showed an interest in becoming a member, it was Mick who took him under his wing. A lot of men were drawn into clubs with promises of partying and women. Not Trax and not Mick. It was the brotherhood that Mick spoke of. The solidarity of the members, the unity, and the loyalty drew Trax in. The Ghosttown Riders wasn't just an MC. It was a family of brothers who had each other's backs and would stay true until their last breaths.

Until Mick's last breath. He gritted his teeth and clenched his jaw. He would mourn Mick properly with his brothers. Then, when he was alone, he'd allow himself to truly grieve.

Kase, the president of the Ghosttown Riders, stood in front of the members while Trax angled his way in the back to Rourke and Gage. Both men lifted their chins in acknowledgment and aimed their attention back to their president.

"Details are still coming in." Kase dropped his gaze to the table. Losing a member was always hard, but Mick had been especially close with Kase. "Officially, all we got now—" he drew in a breath "—he was coming home from the pickup, and a car sideswiped him."

Trax cleared his throat. "Unofficially?"

Kase's scowled deepened. "I had a prospect go to the scene and take pictures, knowing the fucking cops wouldn't be sharing all their information with us." Kase grasped his neck. "Mick was slammed with enough force to throw him off his bike and send it over the side of the road."

"Know the driver?"

"No. The driver took off." Kase paused and scowled. Trax was sure he was sharing the same suspicions as his president and the rest of his brothers. Mick was hit with deliberate force, and the driver took off. *Fuck.* Kase clenched his jaw, scanning the brothers. "Another car coming up from behind witnessed it, called nine-one-one and stayed with him until the ambulance showed."

"He able to give a description?" Rourke asked from next to him.

Kase gazed up. "She. It was a woman." He sat back in his chair and clasped his hands at his waist. "Waiting on Carter to get more, but for now, it's all we got." He eyed the room. "Officially. Unofficially, don't think I gotta say, something doesn't sit right with how this went down. I want everyone riding in pairs from here on out."

No one would argue with the logic. It was a safety measure. The club had run rough for years, dabbling in activities on the other side of the law. Mostly, drug transporting and loans with an extreme interest. The money had been great, but the risk weighed them down. Too many members, including Trax, had done time. A few years ago, they set their sights on going legit, but their past held a lot of grudges. It was a thought crossing the minds of every member in the room.

It could possibly be a fluke accident. Maybe the car who hit him didn't realize. Possible, but not likely. They had enemies. Trax settled in against the wall, staring down at the floor. Retribution was common among clubs. The way it played out with Mick—driving alone, quiet road, coming back from a pickup? *Fuck.* They should have seen it coming. He closed his eyes, trying his best to control his anger. And his regret.

"Mick deserves a big send-off," Kase said. "And we are gonna fucking give him one." He glanced around the room. "We fucking clear?"

Trax merely nodded while some of his brothers spoke up with cheers. He wasn't there yet. He couldn't celebrate Mick while he was still mourning the loss. Trax remained in the room as others made their way out to the bar.

Most members had left, leaving just a few men.

His VP, Saint, moved through the room in silence, which was usually how he moved. As he passed Trax, he gripped his shoulder in a tight squeeze, and Trax gazed up.

"This isn't on you." Saint narrowed his eyes. "We'll find out who set this up and carried it out," he paused, "but this isn't on you. You feel me?"

Trax jerked his chin. The assurance did nothing to relieve any guilt he was feeling. This was *on him*. He was scheduled for the pickup. He should have been on that highway, not Mick. Saint lingered a second longer before slapping his shoulder and then making his way to the door.

"I'll make the calls." He left the room without explanation. There wasn't a need for it. They all knew what he meant and who'd he'd call. The chapters would want to know, show their solidarity and support, and everyone would want to pay their respects to Mick. He'd garnered a reputation as being a good guy among all the members.

Trax started toward the door when Rourke came to his side.

They left the room and made their way through the hall in silence. As they entered the bar area, the room was flooded with people, yet it was eerily quiet.

"Driving out to Meg's?" Rourke asked, keeping in step with Trax as he headed to the door.

"Yeah." Trax pushed the door open and then descended the stairs.

"Saint's right, man. This ain't on you."

Trax halted mid-step, staring at the parking lot. He swallowed the knot in his throat and bowed his head. "It was my ride." He shook his head, feeling the weight of the guilt as if it were a thousand bricks on his back. "It shoulda been me."

"But it wasn't," Rourke said, hovering over Trax. He rested his hand on his shoulder, tightening his grip in a comforting squeeze. "This is not on you," he muttered, releasing his grasp and then making his way to his bike.

Trax followed without saying another word.

Chapter 2

"Wait a minute, back up. You took it?" Macy's eyes widened, and Cheyenne averted her gaze. *This is a fucking mess.*

Cheyenne had spent the last thirty minutes rehashing the accident to her best friend, Macy. Saying it out loud and reliving it all over again left her trembling by the time she stopped talking. It all happened so fast. She'd been on autopilot when it was going down. Now, given time to actually have it all replay in her head, she was rocked to the core. Seeing the car swerve right into the motorcycle as if it were deliberate had her stomach rolling in waves. Then watching the bike fly up into the air and over the embankment. Retelling the story had the same effect as watching it firsthand. Nothing hit her as hard as seeing the poor man sliding at least thirty feet down the asphalt. All the blood and his open wounds. Her stomach churned. It was tragic.

Mick.

"Chey?" Macy snapped her fingers.

Cheyenne blinked twice and turned to Macy. "What?"

"You took the package?"

Cheyenne nodded, biting her bottom lip. "Well, yeah." She

twisted her fingers and pulled up her knees to rest her chin. "I had to."

Macy's eyes grew wide, the size of saucers. "What's in it?"

Cheyenne shrugged and whispered, "I don't know."

"What do ya mean, you don't know? You didn't look?" Macy jumped up from the couch. "Where is it? Let's open it."

Of course, Macy's brain would take her to entertain her curiosity. She wasn't the one who had witnessed the horrific accident. *So much blood.*

"Chey?"

She shook her head, trying to rid her memory of the image.

"No, we are not opening anything." She licked her dry lips. "Look, they probably took him to Glenview General or Blacksburg Memorial. I'm going to go to both until I find him and give it back. I already tried calling, but unless you are family, they don't give out any info."

"I think we should look."

"No," she snapped. He'd been so adamant about her taking it, it must have been important.

"Let me get this straight. You are going to walk around with a package you got from a biker of a gang who gave it to a total stranger in complete desperation because he didn't want the cops to find it. But you won't look inside?" She whistled and raised her brows. "And they say I'm the dumb one?"

"Macy, I..."

"You could very well be toting around a pound of crack in your pocketbook, Chey. You know what that'll get ya?" She cocked her brow and folded her arms. "Three squares a day and a hideous orange jumpsuit."

Cheyenne hadn't given much thought about what was in the envelope. But now, having time to think, he'd been adamant about the cops not getting it. It was a red flag. What if it was drugs, and she somehow got caught with it? Would the police even believe she didn't know what was in the envelope or that it wasn't hers? Her stomach churned. What if they didn't? Beads of sweat formed on her upper lip, and her skin prickled. She glanced up at Macy.

"You think it's drugs?"

She rolled her eyes. "Well, it sure as hell isn't a grocery list. Seriously, we have to look for your own safety."

She squinted at Macy. She had a point, but there was no denying Macy's intrigue. Her concern was half safety and the other half pure nosiness. Either way, Macy was right. She had to know what she was dealing with.

"Fine." She walked back to her room, grabbed her bag, and headed into the living room where Macy was practically bouncing on her toes. *Make that three-quarters intrigue.* She grabbed the large tattered envelope, which had been folded in half. She slowly unraveled it to the opening. Oddly enough, it wasn't sealed. She peeked inside and gasped at the contents. Nausea rolled her stomach, and a large chunk rose up her throat. *Oh hell.*

"What is it? Drugs?" Macy asked in a high-pitched screech.

It wasn't drugs, but the sight made her stomach flip and heat rise over her skin. She swallowed hard and flicked her gaze to Macy. She could feel the blood draining from her face. Her head got light, and she swayed slightly. She tried swallowing, but her throat felt raspy and dry. *This is bad.*

"Take it out."

She shook her head to the point of pain in her neck. There was no way she was reaching into the envelope and touching anything inside. Cheyenne blinked and tried to center her vision on something in the room. She felt dizzy and light. Holy shit, she might just pass out. She pushed the envelope into Macy's hands and fell into the chair, which did nothing to relieve the nausea.

"Oh, my God!" Macy shouted and quickly dropped the envelope. "It's a finger, like a human finger off of someone's frickin hand."

Yes, it was. A dirty, bloodied human finger. She took deep

breaths through her nose in hopes of combatting the vomit rising from her belly. She closed her eyes, resting her head against the cushion of the chair. Inside the envelope was a finger and a wad of cash. She was so fixated on the body part, she didn't focus on the cash, but if she had to guess, there were hundreds of dollars.

"Chey, you okay?" She felt cold hands grasp her cheeks. The coolness had her opening her eyes, looking straight into Macy's.

"It's a finger."

She nodded. "Yep."

"Maybe it's fake." It was a long shot, but she'd grasp at anything right now. A human finger in an envelope? It was like a scene from a movie. Things like that didn't happen in real life. Did they?

Macy snorted. "No, I'm pretty sure it's real, and so are those fifties."

"Oh God." She needed to think. She was in possession of a body part and more cash than she'd ever seen in her life. This was bad, so bad. "I need to call the police." She pushed Macy's hands away and reached for her bag, but the second she moved, her head got heavy, and she fell back against the chair.

She licked her lips and tried once again to swallow. "I'm gonna be sick."

"Okay, slow down." Macy bent, grabbed her purse, and tossed it behind her. "Chey, we need to think about what we are going to do."

What they were going to do? Why was that even a question?

"What do you mean? I need to call the police and report this, Mace. It's a fucking finger."

"I know. just hear me out, okay?" Macy's tone softened.

Cheyenne nodded, eyeing her friend.

"Okay, if you call the police and give them the envelope, they're gonna know you didn't give it to them yesterday. It looks sketchy, Chey. This guy asked you to take it, and you did, concealing an obvious crime." Macy raised her brows and held up her index finger. "Strike one. Right now, our fingerprints are all over the envelope. They could turn this on us."

She scrunched her eyebrows. "What? Why the hell would they?"

Macy sighed, rolling her eyes.

"Ghosttown Riders run this place. You don't think they got cops in their back pocket? Come on, girl, you're smarter than that. You've seen those guys riding around. You know they're up to no good. You ever see one pulled over?" She raised her brows but didn't wait for an answer. "No."

They were the local motorcycle club. Most people, like Macy, scoffed at the term "club." Macy claimed everyone knew what they really were. *Gang.* Cheyenne wasn't sold on them being full-fledged criminals like her best friend. She would randomly see them drive through town. They kept to themselves, never bothering anyone. Every year they did a charity run. Macy said it was bullshit. Cheyenne thought it was a kind gesture. They didn't have to do it, yet they did. She had never actually come across one in person until yesterday, though she had garnered a few glances from a member or two at the bar where she was a waitress.

"So, what are you suggesting, we just toss it in the trash and forget about it?"

"Noooo…like I said, our prints are on it, Chey. If the cops find it, we're screwed."

She dropped her head back against the cushion. This was a clusterfuck. She should have never stopped. The second the thought reached her mind she shook her head. If she hadn't stopped, he surely would have died on that road all by himself.

"So, what do we do?"

Macy drew in a breath. "Give it back to him. We'll find out where he is, go to the hospital, and return it like you planned."

Cheyenne shot up and cocked her head. "Knowing there's a finger in it? This guy was probably the one to cut it off, and you want me to give it back to him." She sighed. "I should have never stopped."

She folded her arms and glanced down at the floor. *Liar, you saved his life by stopping. Did I?* There had been so much blood, and he'd been in such bad shape when the ambulance stopped, she had to wonder if he even made it.

"What's done is done, but yeah, I think you should give it back." She scooted next to her on the chair and draped her hand on her back. "I'll go with you. We'll just drop it off and leave. Maybe we can just leave it with the nurse or something, watch her take it into the room, and jet outta there. We don't technically have to see him, just make sure he gets it."

It sounded like a solid plan. They would just leave it for him. Then she could put it all in the past.

"Okay."

Yeah, we'll just drop it off. She'd never have to actually see him. Not him. Mick. His bloodied face and mangled body came at her as if he were an apparition standing in front of her. The cut along his head was so deep the blood almost appeared black. Even the road seemed drenched in his blood. No matter how hard she'd try, she'd never rid her mind of the sight.

Macy moved to get up, and Cheyenne grabbed her hand. She opened her mouth, and her lips clamped. She was losing her shit with the vision of him lying in the road. "There was so much blood, Mace." A tear escaped from her eye. "I've never seen anything like it." Cheyenne sniffled. "It was horrible." Macy immediately sat, taking Cheyenne into her arms for a tight hug. Cheyenne remained in her best friend's embrace for quite some time. She needed it.

"Let me get my bag. We'll do it now and be done with it." With a tight squeeze, she released Cheyenne and got up.

She nodded, staring down at the envelope Macy had dropped onto the floor. *Pull yourself together.* So much for being a good Samaritan. She slumped down on the couch and swiped it up. This much cash and a body part?

She sucked in a breath just as she heard the knock. She

whipped her head toward the door, and Macy appeared from the small kitchen.

"Who is it?" she mouthed.

Cheyenne's eyes widened, and she shrugged, holding tight to the breath she had just gasped. She watched Macy inch near the door, but her stare was on Cheyenne. They were overreacting. Someone knocking on their door was not unheard of.

"Yeah?" Macy shouted.

"I'm looking for Cheyenne Wilcox."

Her back straightened. *Oh shit.*

"Who's asking?"

"Detective Ross from the Blacksburg PD."

Macy gasped, and her mouth dropped open. Cheyenne shot up from the couch and immediately dropped her gaze to the envelope. Macy shook her head and mouthed again. "Hide it."

"Where?" she whispered in complete panic mode.

"I don't know." They both frantically looked around the room until the detective knocked again. Macy pointed to the couch. "Under the cushion."

Cheyenne followed her instructions and patted the cushion down before standing back up.

"Yeah, um, what do you need? Chey already talked to the cops."

A soft masculine chuckle echoed past the door. "This is extremely awkward. Would you mind opening up?"

Cheyenne nodded, and Macy unlatched the door and stepped back as she opened it. The detective stood in the doorway, taking up most of the space.

"Hello." His smile reminded her of a cop on TV, welcoming but suspicious. Of course he was suspicious. Everything they'd just done screamed they were hiding something.

Macy grinned and reached out her hand. "Hi, I'm Macy."

"Pleasure, Macy." His gaze shifted, and his smile grew. "You must be Cheyenne?"

Cheyenne nodded and took the hand he offered. She pulled

back and wiped her hand on her jeans. Her palms were so sweaty there was no way he would miss it.

"I'm sorry to bother you. I just have a few more questions about the accident, if you don't mind?"

She squirmed where she stood. "Sure, but, um, I told the officer at the scene everything."

He nodded and pulled out a Blackberry. "Yeah, I got the info, and I appreciate you giving us everything. But the driver of the car? You didn't see him?"

She had been honest when she'd been questioned at the scene. With everything going on, and all the police and ambulance, her mind was shady to details. She couldn't remember the man. It wasn't until now his face appeared in her head. It was a grainy resemblance, one she might not be able to describe, but if he stood in front of her, she'd be able to pick him out.

"Not really."

He eyed her and tilted his head. "What do you mean? Did you catch a glimpse of him, maybe?"

"Umm…" She lifted her gaze to Macy, who stood behind the detective. She shook her head. They must not have been flying under the radar because the detective immediately glanced over his shoulder.

Macy smiled and shook her head and swatted the air in front of her face. "Damn fruit flies."

His stare stayed on her for a second before returning to Cheyenne. "Anything you can give me on the driver would be helpful."

"I'm sorry, I didn't get a good look. It all happened so fast, ya know."

He eyed her and nodded slowly. She got the distinct feeling he wasn't completely buying her explanation. He pulled a card from his pocket and then handed it to her. "If you think of anything, no matter how small, please give me a call."

She snatched it from his hand. "I will." She followed him as he made his way to the door. "Um, what hospital is the man on the bike at?"

He turned around and furrowed his brows. "Why?"

She shrugged. "Just thought I'd send him flowers or something."

His gaze shifted from Cheyenne to Macy and landed back on her. His back straightened, and he drew in a breath. "He died on the way to the hospital."

"What?" she whispered. He'd been in bad shape when they'd loaded him into the ambulance, but according to the EMT, he was still breathing. Tears threatened over the rim of her eyes. She'd never watched someone die. She sniffled and wiped her cheeks. It was silly to cry for a man she didn't know, but she couldn't help herself.

"Cheyenne?"

She glanced up and quickly wiped her cheeks with her sleeves. Her bottom lip trembled.

His eyes softened. "It was good of you to stop. You helped him."

She nodded as her tears streamed down her cheeks. "He died."

"Yeah. But he didn't die alone."

No, he didn't.

She tried to smile, and the detective held his stare on her. "Think of anything, call me." He closed the door behind him, and she was left staring back at Macy.

She wiped her eyes again and laughed without humor. "I don't know why I'm crying, this is stupid."

Macy grabbed her hand and held it to her chest. "No, it's not." She pulled her in for a hug, and Cheyenne embraced her tightly. She knew nothing of this man, except for his name, the envelope, and he must have had a woman named Meg, but her heart broke anyway.

Macy walked her to the couch and pulled her down, and sat next to her.

"Why were you shaking your head when he asked about the driver?"

Macy rubbed her back. "I don't know. I just had this feeling, like if you gave a description and the guy found out, he'd come for you. It's stupid. I guess I just got freaked out. I mean, you said yourself, the car seemed to be aiming for the motorcycle, and then the driver just takes off? It doesn't sound like an accident to me."

The thought hadn't even occurred to her until now. What if the driver got a good look at her or her car? It may have been far-fetched, but this was obviously intentional, and with all murders, witnesses were the downfall.

"I'm a witness." She drew in a breath. "God, I didn't even think about that."

"This whole thing is crazy, Chey, but there's no reason to freak out, right? I mean, what are the chances the guy even saw you?"

She had a point. It all happened so fast, and the driver never looked over at her.

"Now what do I do?"

Macy hugged her against her side, and they fell against the cushions. What the hell was she supposed to do now? The cops knew her name. What if the driver found out and came looking for her? *Oh hell…*

TRAX PULLED up in front of the clubhouse. He usually parked in back with the others, but the police cruiser in the spot out front left no time. He pulled up next to it, immediately turning off the engine, climbed off his bike, and headed inside. It wasn't unusual for the police to pay them a visit. But he knew exactly which cop car it was, and he was eager to get inside and hear what information he had for them.

Mick's death had hit the whole club hard, but for Trax, it was different. Mick had been his mentor, his sponsor into the Ghost-town Riders. Losing him was like losing a father, a man he respected and looked up to. The loss ripped him in ways he didn't know were possible.

When he'd gotten the call yesterday, he'd spent the twenty-minute ride to the clubhouse in denial. It had to be some fucked up joke, or at the very least a mistake. It was neither. Mick was gone, his old lady, Meg, was now a widow, and the club was forever changed.

It wasn't the first time a member had died or been killed. In his nine years as a brother, he'd been to plenty of funerals, but never an intentional death. The grief and rage the whole club was feeling was a deadly combination.

He made his way down the hall in long strides. The somber mood in the club took a backseat to the anger streaming through each member. This would be handled internally by them, but with it being in the public, they'd have to break one of their biggest rules. They had to speak to the cops.

Trax took in the scene playing out in front of him. There were several brothers at the bar, but no one was partying. Trax made his way into the room slowly, taking it all in. Kase was facing off with the lead detective.

"I want her fucking name."

Trax rounded the side and stood next to Rourke.

The detective glanced over as Trax folded his arms and stared back. Carter Ross was considered a friend to the club. Officially, for outside purposes, they were enemies, but in truth, he and Kase, along with the club VP, Saint, had known each other for years. Carter helped out when he could, and the club returned the favor. Although it seemed this time, Carter was not lending a hand.

He lifted his chin in greeting and then turned back to Kase. "She didn't see anything. Trust me, Kase, this girl gave us everything she knew. We got a few leads we're looking into, but you won't get much from her anyway. She never saw the driver."

Kase's face hardened. "I wanna hear it from her myself. What's her name?"

Carter shook his head. "Can't do it."

Kase's back went rigid, which put all the men on high alert. They'd be forced to jump in if things went south during this meeting. Having a brawl with the local cops would bring on too much heat for the club. It was bad enough they were on the radar with Mick's death.

"Do I need to remind you who the fuck you are talking to? Got a lot of shit on you, Carter."

The detective's back straightened.

"And I've got just as much on you and the club. Do I need to remind you who *you're* talking to, Kase?"

Trax had to give him credit. Carter had a set on him to go head to head with Kase. Not many men dared.

"Don't like being threatened."

"Neither do I." He drew in a breath. "Look, I gave you what she gave us."

Trax stepped forward. "Then what's the problem us talking with her?"

Carter turned to Trax. "She went over the details of what happened and never once wavered, Trax. You won't get anything from her that she didn't already give us. You guys hunting her down isn't gonna change the information, but it will scare the shit out of her." He paused, taking in a breath. "She stopped, Trax. Did more than most people would have. Let her be."

She did. This woman who had witnessed what had happened to Mick pulled over and called the police. While most would have just called it in, she stopped. From Carter's account, she was holding Mick's hand when they got there, trying to comfort him. The thought of him being out there hurt and alone ripped him apart. It had also become a compounding heartache for Meg. She was inconsolable. The small detail of how the cops found Mick and the mystery woman was the only saving grace for his widow. At least he didn't die alone.

Kase took a drag of his cigarette. "You find the package?"

Carter shook his head. "I took everything from the hospital. It wasn't there."

The missing envelope had been on everyone's mind. *Where the hell was it?* It was a sure-fire link to the club and all its members. It was also a guaranteed prison sentence if it found its way into the wrong hands. The run was a pickup of cash on a past due loan from the club. The *borrower* had fled a few times in the past until they used their muscle to prove, mainly on those closest to him, no one runs from the Ghosttown Riders. Trax wasn't proud of the tactics used, but everyone who took money from them knew the risks. Loan runners were treated to another reminder that no one fucked with them. If Trax had to guess, the missing package included a limb, which would be easily traced back to the club. *Fuck!*

Kase scowled at Trax and then questioned Carter again. "You think she lifted it?"

Carter snorted. "Not this girl. She actually teared up when I told her Mick died. Stay away from her, all right? She stopped, comforted your brother as he died. Pay her back by leaving her alone. The least you can do, man. A girl like her, seeing what she saw, the memory will play over in her head for the rest of her life. Don't make it worse."

He had a point. Though they didn't know who she was, Carter was clear on the type of person she was—civilian, innocent. Hell, she'd been on her way to her mother's house for dinner when Mick had died. They needed to let it go. It wasn't his decision, though. It was Kase's as president.

"I'm going. Just think about what I said." Carter turned and walked out of the club. Silence invaded the room. They were waiting on Kase to say something. He glanced around at the members, stopping at Trax. Kase wasn't a man who took orders well. Very rarely did he have to as president.

"You want us to keep looking for her?" Rourke asked.

Kase shifted his gaze to Rourke. They had been trying to get her info from anybody who might have leads. The only problem was no one was talking—not the police, not the ambulance crew, nobody. They were tight-lipped when it came to the identity of the Good Samaritan.

"I want that girl," Kase said and turned heel back down the hallway. It was done, their president had spoken. Whether Trax agreed or not, it didn't matter. When Kase gave an order, it was followed.

Chapter 3

The rumble of the engines was loud and vibrating. Even half a block away, she could feel the tremors on the road, which intensified her anxiety. She sat silently, the same as she had been doing for the past hour. She'd never seen so much leather in her life. Or motorcycles.

She craned her neck to watch the next batch of riders. A wave of twenty or thirty bikes would pass by, then minutes later, another wave would come through. The streets were lined with men, women, and even a few children. It almost looked like a parade, but it wasn't. It was a funeral.

The plan of returning the envelope had been foiled majorly. She'd made the decision a few days ago. Not one of her better choices. She had spent the last few days weighing her options, and Macy's. They were both involved now. Going to the police with the envelope would have been the most sensible choice. It was a no brainer. But something held her back. There had to be a reason Mick had been so adamant about her taking the package. A further inspection of the envelope showed, along with the decaying body part and cash, a few documents. Neither she nor Macy could make anything out of it, but the one thing they agreed on was it was meant for the club. It cinched her decision. She would just return it to the Ghosttown Riders.

Then her mind changed again.

Cheyenne glanced up into her rearview mirror as another group drove down Main Street. Blacksburg hadn't seen this much action in years. Since then, the news had picked up the story. Their small town had been inundated with news cameras and motorcycles. To anyone not involved, it was intriguing, but not for Cheyenne. The police had visited her apartment again. They were digging deep with their investigation. She rehashed the story of what happened, omitting the obvious envelope part. She kept that piece of information to herself. If she admitted she had it now, it would raise suspicion on why she never turned it over from the beginning. Detective Ross seemed nice enough and genuinely concerned, but his questions were leading. He flat out asked if she'd taken anything from the scene. A question he hadn't asked earlier. She vehemently denied it, but he gave her an uneasy feeling.

He instructed her not to talk to the press for her own safety and assured her that her name would not be released. She was also specifically instructed not to approach the club. The officer's words replayed over in her head.

"These are not good guys, Cheyenne. They tend to take matters into their own hands. It's best that they don't know who you are."

She agreed.

That was yesterday.

Now she sat in the convenience store parking lot, watching the procession of bikes at the local funeral home. All the preconceived notions and ideas she had about the club were slashed as she watched the men somberly embrace one another. Women in tears, even small kids holding tight to the hands of the adults.

They may be outlaws and criminals, but what she saw now was nothing more than a group of people in complete sorrow for losing their friend. It made them seem more human, not cold-blooded killers or criminals, but a family who had lost one of their own.

She had struggled with her decision to not turn over the envelope. It was as if she had Mick's last dying wish in her hands. He didn't want the cops to have it. She glanced over to the passenger seat. The envelope lay there like a fork in the road, daring her to make the right decision.

"Tomorrow," she whispered, never taking her gaze off the envelope. "I'll do it tomorrow."

THE MOOD in the clubhouse was a vast contrast from earlier in the day. The funeral was a time to reflect, to comfort one another for a fallen brother. Now they were celebrating his life with booze, music, and half-naked women filtering throughout the club. He leaned back, watching the show play out in front of him. Strippers on the stage, men drunk everywhere, some fucking in the corner, a train forming at the pool table.

He groaned, dropping his head back as Val suctioned over his cock, taking her mouth to the root of his dick. With his cock shoved down her throat, she licked his balls. He closed his eyes, thankful for the distraction and release. Right now, all he wanted to do was come down her throat and relieve some tension. Think of anything but his fallen brother. He gripped her hair and angled her down farther. She gagged slightly, and he eased off.

He gave her no warning except the tightening of his fist through the strands of her bleached hair. It wasn't soft like silk, which for some crazy reason pissed him off. The coarse hair was almost brittle in his hand. He wrenched his hand back and gripped the couch. He was seconds away from coming.

Her moan vibrated over his cock, sending a pulsing shock over the crown of his length. It was her thing. She did it every time. *Fucking A, it was the perfect end.* But that was just it, the end. It was a mere distraction to keep his grief at bay.

Without the distraction, his thoughts would be brought back to Mick. *Shit.*

He stood, ignoring her stare, and zipped up his jeans. He needed to get out of there, away from everyone. He needed the escape of the road. Val dropped onto the couch where he had been sitting. Her red nails trailed down his jeans, and he glanced over.

"Was it good?"

"I came, didn't I?" He smirked and cocked his brow. His tone was teasing and light.

Val twitched her nose and chuckled. He smiled and lifted his chin. "See ya later."

He hadn't made it a foot away when her hand clasped into his. She jolted up and pressed her breasts against his chest.

"I don't think you should be alone. Not tonight." She batted her lashes, and Trax sighed. *Fuck me, I shoulda known better.* Val wasn't just a club whore happy with the life. She had an agenda. She had been working her way through the brothers, waiting on someone to make her an old lady. That someone wouldn't be him.

She clasped her hand around his waist and smiled. "I could come home with you?"

He was shaking his head before she even finished talking.

"Why not?"

"I don't bring anyone home." He leaned closer. "You know that."

"But..."

His jaw tightened, and he pinned her with his stare. "No."

He pulled away, forcing her to release her hold, and walked around her. He had made it clear to every woman in the club. He was only interested in a good time. He wasn't looking to take on an old lady. He'd tried once before, and it had been an epic fail. He still saw rage whenever he envisioned his wife bent over their couch with some guy from work fucking her. Fucking cunt had been cheating on him as he made his way into the club. She'd begged him to forgive her, promised it would never happen again. He revenge fucked half the club whores before Ariel was able to work her way back into bed. Their whole marriage and relationship had been a sham, but he'd been too young and blind to see it at the time. Then he got locked up. It wasn't until after he was released that he smartened up.

He'd been a fool when it came to Ariel. He wouldn't make the same mistake ever again.

He was almost to the bar when she appeared in front of him, glaring. She folded her arms, and he could see her anger building. What the hell did she expect? Did she really think giving him head when he was mourning the loss of Mick would get her into his bed? He snorted and drew in a breath. *Yeah, that's exactly what she thought.*

"You're an asshole and…." She shouted loud enough to gain some attention from those around them, pissing him off. Who the hell did she think she was? This was his fucking club, and he was not about to take any shit from her, especially tonight.

He grabbed her wrist and held it tightly in his grip. Hard enough to get his point across, but not enough to hurt her. She obviously hadn't understood when he'd told her he wasn't looking for anything more than a good time. But he'd make it clear right now.

"Yeah, I'm an asshole. You knew it before you dropped to your knees, ya knew it while swallowing my cock, and you know it now. You knew exactly what was gonna happen because it's the same fucking thing that happens every time we fuck or you suck me off." He stepped closer and growled, causing a slight hitch in her breath. "But you coming at me like this, especially today? I don't need you feeding me some bullshit line about me being alone and pretending you give a shit about me. I'm about as special to you as the last brother ya banged a few hours ago." Trax paused, eyeing her carefully. "You want old lady status? You look somewhere else 'cause it ain't happening with me. And just so we're clear. You working whatever angle you can to get in my bed for your own fucking agenda? That makes *you* an asshole, sweetheart."

Her cheeks turned a dark shade of pink. She pulled her hand away and righted her shirt, covering up her tits. She turned quickly, not saying a word, and sauntered over to Gage. He walked to the bar and took the empty stool to the right of Rourke. His brother glanced up, shaking his head.

"The bitch ain't worth the trouble. Don't know why you mess with her. She's a pain in the ass."

"She's Gage's problem now," Trax smirked, slapping his friend on the back. "Gotta give her credit, she knows how to suck dick."

"So do the rest of the slits in here."

He had a point. The girls who hung around the club knew the score, and they knew what was expected of them. It was their choice to be there. He glanced around the smoky, dimly lit room. Most of the girls who hung around were there for a good time. He actually enjoyed the company of quite a few even beyond the sex. But then there were a few like Val. He'd chalk the latest experience to a lesson learned.

He'd been ready to go even before he'd walked through the door. He wasn't feeling the celebration, didn't sit right with him, though it was what Mick would have wanted. He knew his longtime mentor and friend would slice off his balls if he could see him now, wallowing in the loss. He turned to Rourke and got up from his stool, not even bothering to touch the beer placed in front of him.

"Heading out." He slapped Rourke on the back.

"Home?"

Trax took another glance around the room. He wanted to celebrate Mick, but not this way. "Nah, think I'll take a ride."

Rourke lifted his chin and then his drink, finishing it off before pushing off the stool to face Trax. "Need to take a piss. I'll meet ya outside."

He walked through the throngs of people. It was always amusing to watch Rourke walk through a crowd. They split in two groups as if he parted the Red fucking Sea. For a man like him, no words were necessary. People just got the hell out of the way.

Trax headed toward the back of the club. He was just beyond the threshold of the hall when he felt someone behind him. Glancing over his shoulder, he saw Gage in step with him. Just a look was all he needed to know Gage was ditching the party to celebrate and honor Mick with him, Rourke, and a ride for their fallen brother.

He pushed open the door and caught their vice president rolling up and parking near the back. Trax made his way down the stairs with Gage following close behind.

Saint removed his helmet, draping it over his handlebar, but remained seated as they headed his way.

"Didn't think you were coming?" Gage said with a tease in his tone. "You here for the beer and BJs?"

Saint was notorious for ditching most club parties. Even when he did make a rare appearance, he never participated in the girl action, much to the dismay of the women. His life was a lot different than most men in the club. He had a few tattoo shops he owned, a bunch of lucrative side gigs, and a young kid. Trax often wondered why he never gave up the club but was thankful he didn't. His disposition was eerily opposite of Kase. While Kase ruled with fear and his mouth, Saint was quiet and cunning. They were the perfect set to run the club.

Saint stared back at him, not acknowledging Gage's question. Trax wasn't surprised. Saint was a man of very few words, but when he did speak, everyone listened. Mick once told Trax that Saint was the smartest man he'd ever met, and the deadliest.

Trax mounted his bike parked next to Saint's and glanced over. "Taking a ride, heading up through the valley, maybe out to Ghosttown."

Saint nodded, and the corner of his mouth curved. "Mick's ride."

Ghosttown had been the original home to the Ghosttown Riders. Years later, when Kase took over as president, he'd moved the clubhouse to Blacksburg. But nothing could tear Mick away from Ghosttown. It was aptly named as there were only a handful of residents to the small town.

"Yeah. You in?"

Saint grabbed his helmet and then started up his engine. He was in. A few minutes later, Rourke came out, and they took off. This was what it was about, what it had always been about.

The ride.

Chapter 4

She had spent the last two days engulfed in research on the Ghosttown Riders. It was a fail. If anything, the only real information she had gotten was there was no information. No social media outlets or website. The images she came across were all posted by others in an almost investigative style. They certainly weren't advertising for membership. *Who the hell doesn't have a Facebook page in this day and age? A motorcycle gang.*

She pulled up alongside the curb directly across the street. The area was fairly residential, and without the dragon and crossbones donning the building, it might appear to be a bike shop. The garage bay doors were down. Maybe she should come back another time. Maybe they were closed.

Do motorcycle clubhouses close down? Were there hours of operation? Again, useful information that would have been helpful in her predicament.

Several motorcycles lined the front of the building along with a few parked on the street. She silently counted. Seven bikes for seven bikers.

Her cell pinged, and she was tempted to ignore it. But she didn't. She grabbed her phone and snorted when she saw the text.

Macy: Are you dead?

Cheyenne: Yes, I'm dead.

Macy: LOL Have you gone in yet?

Cheyenne: If you wanted all the details, you should have come with me.

Macy: Uh…hello…working here. Our store isn't going to happen on our looks and charm.

Cheyenne chuckled. Too bad for them. Opening up their dream shop took more cash than either one of them had. Luckily, Macy was the brains and currently the higher revenue for their future endeavor.

Cheyenne: I'm going in now.

Macy: Text me when you're out. If something goes wrong…can I have your laptop?

Cheyenne: Bitch.

She tucked her phone into her bag and got out of the car. She drew in a deep, shaky breath. She couldn't remember the last time she'd been this on edge. She shook her hands, trying to calm her nerves, and then wiped her palms down her jeans.

"It'll be fine," she said and straightened her shoulders. She draped her satchel bag over her chest, leaving her hands free. She had seen a television special about female safety. *Always be ready to start swinging.* That was not exactly what it said, but it was how she'd interpreted it.

She crossed the abandoned street. For the first time since pulling up, she realized there were few cars in the quiet, seedy section of town. It was off the beaten path, and the clubhouse was surrounded by businesses that had gone under and never been replaced. It made her wonder if the club had driven them out. She scanned the street, gripping tightly to the strap of her bag. It really was a shithole. A place where people minded their business and looked the other way. *Great.*

She weaved through the bikes and then stopped at the large metal door. The dent in the center looked as if someone had been thrown up against it. This was getting worse by the second. She wiped her moist forehead with her sleeve and inhaled a deep breath.

"Calm down," she muttered.

She scanned the outer wall, looking for a bell. Nothing. She drew a deep breath and raised her hand to knock. Her knuckles scraped against the door, and she flinched back when it suddenly swung open. A tall, thin man with a black goatee scowled down at her.

His gazed dropped, perusing her body and back up without losing his furrowed brows.

"Party's at nine." He stepped back and started to close the door. She reached out, slamming her hand against the hard wood.

"Wait."

"What?" he snapped, and she dropped down a step.

"Um...I'm not here for a party." She cleared her throat and straightened her shoulders. She may have not been feeling it, but she needed to act the part of confident. "I'd like to speak to the person in charge."

He stared at her, giving no indication he'd heard her.

She licked her lips and forced a smile. "Please."

He cocked his head to the side as if she spoke another language. He moved forward, and she stepped back, stumbling on the concrete step. He peered at her and then down the street. He was suspicious, and she couldn't blame him. She might as well have been wearing a clown costume she was so ridiculously out of place.

"Who are you?"

"Cheyenne Wilcox."

"And you wanna..." He left the question open and smirked.

"Speak to the person in charge?" Her confidence dwindled. She had the feeling he was about to burst out laughing at her. Instead, he lifted his chin and stepped away from the door, widening it for her entry. She slowly walked in and stopped just inside the door.

"C'mon."

She followed him down a short dark hall. This was a bad idea. The hallway opened up into a large room, light rock music playing in the background, and three large men seated at the bar. The man behind the bar looked over at her, his eyebrows quirked, and then he grinned.

"Early entertainment? Nice job, prospect."

One of the men seated at the bar turned in his stool, grinning while the other two glanced over their shoulders. She did a mental calculation. Three seated at the bar, one behind, and the guy next to her. Another tidbit she learned from the special on TV—know your surroundings and those in it.

One by one, her gaze traveled the faces of the men staring back at her. The blond man seated and the guy behind the bar shared the same smirk as they glanced down her body without a bit of shame. She jerked her gaze to the huge man next in line. Where the other two showed a glimpse of interest, this man glared at her. His features were harsh and sharp. His lips tightened. *Look away.*

She blinked and bit her lip, eyeing the last guy at the end of the bar. He stood, resting his hip and arm on the bar. *Oh!* Her face flushed. He was a welcomed contrast to the guy sitting next to him. His ball cap was tugged low over his forehead and shadowed his face but didn't hide his dark eyes, which were currently aimed at her. His lips, surrounded by a thin, neatly trimmed beard, were full. *They look so soft.* Her cheeks heated, and she dropped her gaze down his chest, avoiding eye contact. *Wrong move.* If she thought his face was a distraction, his body wasn't helping the blush on her cheeks. She perused the length of his stance, taking in his height and build. Sexy, rugged, and definitely strong if his bulging biceps were any indication. Her heart pounded. Both arms displayed an array of tattoos, but she was too far away to make them out. *Where else does he have tattoos?* Her gaze lingered over his black T-shirt, outlining his curved pecs. *Definitely on his chest, I bet. Who cares! What the hell am I doing?* This was hardly the time to be checking out men, but her gaze had a mind of its own. Of all the men in the room, he was by far the best looking. She lifted her gaze back up and caught the slight curl of his lip when he cocked a brow.

Her tense lips trembled, and heat rose over her breasts, causing a reaction. Her nipples tightened. She forced a smile while she racked her brain, trying to remember if she was wearing a padded bra. She watched as his smirk turned to an amused smile. She sucked in a breath and immediately averted her gaze to the man next to her.

"Nah, man, she's here to…" He glanced down at her. "…speak to the person in charge." His repeated words were laced with sarcasm as if he mocked her. She flickered her lashes, feeling the heat rise from her chest to her cheeks. She dared another glance up, specifically aimed at the dark-haired man at the end of the bar. He tilted his head and smirked. Her bottom lip quivered as her cheeks burned up. *Why the hell am I blushing?*

"Who the hell are you?" The growl came from the large man next to the current object of her fascination. Her entire body flinched, and she jerked her gaze a few inches to the left. He was big and obviously aggravated with her presence. His dark eyes pinned her in her spot, and she sucked in a hard breath.

She swallowed the knot in her throat and pointed to her chest. "Me?"

Of course you, jackass.

His facial expression tightened, and his scowl grew deeper. If not for the harsh glare he threw at her, he'd be handsome. *Maybe.* It was hard to tell from his contorted features. "Yeah, you. I know everybody else in this fucking place."

She caught the faint chuckles from the opposite end of the bar but didn't look.

She gulped. "I'm Cheyenne Wilcox."

"Wil*cox*?" The blond-haired man seated next to him laughed. There was a humored tone on the second syllable. She refrained from rolling her eyes. It wasn't the first time she'd been teased about her name, but it had been a while. It seemed this man channeled his inner middle-schooler.

She straightened her shoulders and knitted her brows. "And you are?"

The blond grinned, obviously amused. "I'm Gage." He hooked his thumb over his shoulder toward the man behind the bar. "That's Dobbs." The man laughed and mockingly waved at her.

Cheyenne forced a smile, feeling as if she was the butt of an inside joke.

Gage chuckled and gestured his chin to the left. "The big guy is Rourke and," he smiled and wiggled his brows, "Trax is the one you been eye fucking since you walked in."

Her mouth fell open, and her heart actually stopped. He did not just say that? *Uh, yeah...he did.* Her face heated, and her eyes widened in complete shock, though Gage didn't seem fazed. Her gaze darted to the man on the end. *Trax.* His lips pressed together with only one corner quirking up into a sexy half smile.

"All right, now that we got the introductions done, get naked and dance for us. If we like what we see, we'll get the prez."

What?

She gasped and stepped back again, landing her into the man who let her in. His hands came to her arms, but she tore away from him, glaring back at him. This was a new fear. She moved forward, away from him as a sinister roar of laughter rang through the room. *Oh hell, this is worse than I thought.* What had she gotten herself into? Panic rose in her chest, and her leg twitched as she moved closer to the wall. There was a chance she could dart past the guy who let her in and make it out the door. *Right?*

Gage stood, making his way toward her. He towered her by more than half a foot. He had to notice her fear, but if he did, he didn't care. "Babe, don't be shy." He glanced down her body. "I like what I see already."

"Back up," she demanded. "Or I will scream."

He grinned and looked over his shoulder. "Guys, we got a screamer."

She wasn't sure what it was that sent her over the edge, but her mouth opened, and she released a high-pitched shriek, which echoed in the room. Her eardrums vibrated from the sound of her own scream.

It had gotten all their attention. Gage jumped back, and the screeching sounds of stools echoed in the dark room. The room stirred in silent chaos with Trax stalking toward her. Somehow, he didn't seem as appealing this time. When her back flattened against the wall, she quickly reached in her bag, fumbling for her mace.

"Fuck, gun," a masculine voice shouted, and suddenly she fell onto her side and was tackled to the ground, her hand still half in her bag. She gasped as pain rippled through her arm from his hand squeezing her elbow.

"Stop," she screamed. Her hand released the mace, and she tried to pull away, but he lay over the top of her, his legs caging her down tight.

"What the fuck is going on?" The sharp bark sounded from across the room.

She peeked up past Trax, who had her pinned to the floor, to see a tall man with long hair tied at his nape and a beard to match, glaring down at her. "Who the fuck is she?" He pointed down at her.

"Fuck if I know. Crazy bitch comes in, we think she's here to party, and she fucking loses her shit, reaching for a gun, Kase," Rourke said, shaking his head.

"I don't have a gun. It's mace," she panted, breathing heavily from the weight constricting her chest.

A whip of air ruffled her hair, and she turned to the guy who had laid her out. Trax was now hovering over her, which gave her a chance to breathe deeply. Did he realize she struggled for a breath? The corners of his eyes crinkled in a sharp squint.

"Oh, what a fucking sweetheart. You don't wanna kill us, just fucking blind us. Good to know."

She lowered her head to the floor, relieving the tension in her neck and putting as much space between them as possible. His dark hair curled around his ears, and his face was days away from a shave. His eyes were darker than his hair, almost black.

"Um, I can explain."

"You fucking better. And talk fast, bitch." He leaned in with a menacing scowl. "'Cause I'm losing patience."

Long gone was any softness she'd seen earlier. Never in her life had she been spoken to in such a cruel and volatile manner. Not even her meanest boyfriend had ever called her a bitch. Well, not to her face.

"You don't have to be rude," she muttered, mostly to herself. He angled his head to the side and scowled. She held his stare and licked her lips nervously. His silence was only increasing her fear.

"Trax, get off her."

Almost immediately, his weight lifted, and she sucked in a deep breath. She slowly turned onto her side and caught his gaze on her. He made no attempt to help her, and she scrambled to get up. She wiped the wispy hairs flying in her face and stared at the barrage of men all dressed in leather and jeans. It was like something out of *The Outsiders*. *So, this is what Cherry felt like.*

"Fucking speak."

She gasped. She had barely gotten up, and already the large man yelled at her. She shifted her gaze to the long-haired man.

"I...um...are you in charge?"

He stared at her and looked around the room at the men who she noticed seemed to calm a bit and were now amused by her question.

"Can't fucking read?" He pointed to his chest, and the patch read President. He shook his head, twisting his lips. "Ain't got time for this. You either tell me what the fuck you want or get the fuck out. Getting my dick sucked is the only concern I got, and seeing how you fucked that up, either talk and get out or take her place and drop on your knees."

Her mouth fell open, and she was speechless. This was how this man talked to people? She was doing him a favor, possibly all these men, and this was how she got treated. She retreated a step and opened her mouth to speak, but the words wouldn't come out.

"Out." He turned around.

She had had enough. This was bullshit. She was trying to help them.

"You are very rude." The man halted and turned slowly. The men in the room all locked their harsh glares on her. She should be scared, and honestly, she was, but her anger trumped her fear. Before he could say another word, she stepped forward. Mainly because she needed ample access to the door. A clear line to the right and she'd be outside.

She drew in a breath. "I was trying to do the right thing, which is probably the wrong thing, but most likely the right," she pointed, "for you."

"Meth head?" Gage snorted.

She whipped her head in his direction. "I'm not on drugs. Look, I was just trying to…oh. Forget it."

Why would she even bother at this point? They didn't deserve anything. In a matter of minutes, they had offended her, spoken rudely to, and accosted her. She glanced around, taking in their smug amused expressions. Now they had resorted to mocking her. She shook her head in utter disgust. It didn't pay to be nice.

"Just forget it," she whispered.

She started to the door, and the man who'd let her in stepped aside, giving her a clear path. A few more steps, she'd be down the hall and out of there. She stopped at the edge of the hallway and turned back. She should have kept her mouth shut and kept walking, but something inside her, the part that had been mocked and ridiculed in the past, would not allow it.

"I actually felt bad for all of you. I thought losing your friend was hard enough, and maybe coming here and returning the package might," she shrugged, "I don't know, give you solace. Ya know, I didn't come here for thanks or anything else, but truth be told," she folded her arms and gritted her teeth, "I didn't have to stop. God knows the other car didn't. I didn't have to call 9-1-1 or wait with him until the ambulance got there. But I did it because it's who I am. Nice." She scowled and shook her head in disgust, turning her head and aiming her gaze at Trax. "Not like you jerks."

She immediately turned to the door, acutely aware of the tense air and the silent room. She pulled back her shoulders and felt a warm rush of pride. It wasn't often she stuck up for herself, especially outnumbered in a room full of alpha men. She smiled as she pushed open the steel door. *Score one for the underdog.*

The air smacked her face at the same time she felt a hard grip wrap around her forearms. *Oh fuck.* She thrashed her arms, swiping at the man grabbing her. "Get off me!" She watched the door slam shut. Her panic set in, and her racing heart threatened to explode. She cocked back her head and felt the instant pain shoot through her neck when she connected to his head.

"Fucking cunt." He didn't release her or even loosen his grip. That stunt had made him enraged. His large hands covered her stomach, tightening his hold, and she cried out when his finger dug into her ribs. She was lifted and brought back to the main bar where all the men stood.

Trax stalked over toward her, and from the look on his face, she was fucked. His jaw squared, and she read the rage on his face. Why the hell didn't she just leave quietly?

"I-I'm sor..." Her stuttered apology was cut short when she realized his harsh glare was aimed over her shoulder.

"You better not have fucking hurt her." He was seething, all his anger directed at the guy who grabbed her.

"Her? Trax, she fucking clocked my nose. Bitch could have broken it."

"Let her go before I *do* fucking break it," he snapped, reaching for Cheyenne's wrist, tugging her next to him. Her chest brushed against his arm, and he pushed her behind him. "Told you to bring her back, not fucking hurt her, asshole."

Now this guy was being her savior? What the hell was going on? His hand was still holding her in place, but his thumb glided over her pulse in a soft caress. The move should have calmed her, but it didn't. There was too much anger and rage circling the room. Though it was no longer aimed at her. She peeked past his arm to see all eyes now on the man who manhandled her.

He held up his hands in surrender. "Sorry, man."

"Fuck your apology." He lunged forward, but Rourke stepped in front of him, blocking him. She wasn't sure why she did it, but she reached out and gripped the back of Trax's shirt. The last thing this day needed was a bloodied brawl. Her knuckles grazed his back, and he froze.

Kase stood next to Rourke. "She's fine. He fucked up." He glanced over Trax's shoulder, meeting her stare. "You're the girl?"

She tightened her grip on his shirt and nodded. He drew in a breath and scanned the room before stepping back.

"Bring her in the back."

Panic set in, and she shifted her gaze around the room. Her grip on Trax's T-shirt tightened, making it awkward when he turned around.

"I don't wanna go in the back." Her voice trembled with each word.

The corner of his mouth curled, making his face soften. He reached around to his back and unraveled her fingers from his shirt. She yanked her hands away and drew them between her breasts, twisting her fingers. A small internal alarm sounded in her head. She was officially in survival mode. She shifted her gaze, accessing her best escape route. She must have taken longer than she should have. Trax stepped forward, grasping her hand, tugging her past the bar and down another hallway. She barely had time to react. As they moved forward, her attention lowered to their hands intertwined. The rough callouses rubbed against her palm. She should have been pulling away, but instead, she moved closer. It was a strange pull, a warming in her belly. When was the last time a man held her hand? Without thinking, she grazed the pads of her fingers over his knuckles. They were a bit rough as most men's hands were, yet it only increased her desire. She tightened her grip and meshed her palm against his. *I miss hand holding.* He led her into a room and leaned around her to slam the door closed.

She realized her mistake. While she was mesmerized with hand holding like a middle schooler with her first crush, she was being carted away to a back room. *Alone.*

It was a large room, but not what she expected from bikers. A long conference table sat center in the room with matching chairs around the table. The only man who was seated was the president, Kase.

I'm screwed. She jerked her head, taking in the men who all watched her intently. She silently calculated how many steps it might take to get to the door and bolt. She eyed the men again. Four versus one. *I'm so screwed.*

She backed up but hadn't realized she was still holding hands with Trax. He tightened his clasp and pulled her closer, leading her to a chair situated across from Kase.

She noticed not all the men from the bar had come in. Actually, aside from Trax and Kase, only Rourke and Gage were in the room.

"Sit." Kase motioned to the chair.

Whatever was happening was not good. She scanned the room again before making a rash decision. She wouldn't go down without a fight. She yanked her hand from Trax.

"No." She rushed to the door, only to be blocked by Rourke. His palm slammed against the wood door with a cracking echo. She jumped back.

"When he tells you to sit, you sit," he said with a snarl, and her heartbeat responded in pure fear. Her bottom lip trembled, and she backed away.

She curled her arms around her stomach. "Why are you doing this? I helped your friend. Doesn't that count for anything?"

"Sit," he growled.

"I don't want to. Please, I just want to go home." The shakiness in her tone matched the shiver of her body. She shook in fear, as though she were locked naked in a freezer. Her hands clutched the straps of her bag so tightly her fingers were losing circulation.

Trax stalked forward. She gasped and stepped back, landing into the wall with no retreat. His gaze met hers, and he halted only a second. His hand moved in slow motion, wrapping around her upper arm gently and pulled her forward to the chair.

"Just sit. Let's get this squared away, and then you can go." He lightly pushed her arms, and she sat, never looking away from him. There was a change in his face, a softening in his eyes. Even his voice changed to a low, calming murmur.

He moved away to take his stance between Rourke and Gage. They may have changed from angry and aggressive to curious, but it did nothing to calm nerves. If ever there was a time for a panic attack, this was it. Her heart pounded in an erratic rhythm. She clutched her bag and flicked her gaze over the men. With her sitting, their presence was more frightening.

"Been looking for you."

She jerked her gaze to Kase. "Um…" She licked her lips. "You're gonna let me go, right?"

He slowly nodded. "When I've heard all I want to hear. Now, tell me what happened."

She nodded and inhaled deeply, blowing out the uneven breath. "I was driving down Belgium, and your friend passed me. A few minutes later, another car came flying up. Ya know the big turn?"

He nodded.

"Yeah, well, he didn't slow. Anyway, the car and your friend were pretty far away from me, but I saw the car swerve into the bike. He must have lost control from the turn and speed." She glanced up to their dark, glaring faces. "It happened really fast.

The bike went flying over the embankment, and Mick slid down the pavement."

"Mick?" Kase asked, raising his brows.

"Yeah." She swallowed a breath. "He told me that was his name. Anyway, by the time I got there, he was lying across the asphalt..." Images of the biker, bleeding, made her gulp. He must have been in so much pain. "I called 9-1-1 and waited until they got there."

"What did ya do?"

"Um...well, uh, I didn't move him, but he rolled over, and I just kinda held his hand until the ambulance got there. Ya know..." She peeked up. They were staring so intently she dropped her gaze to the wooden table. "Just talked to him, telling him to hang on and help was on the way. As soon as they got there, he closed his eyes. I thought maybe he passed out, from shock?" She sniffled, not even realizing until that moment tears streamed down her face. Reliving the scene was heartbreaking, knowing the outcome.

"You the last thing he saw?"

She turned her head to Trax and shrugged. "Maybe." If what the police had told her was right, then she must have been. She peeked over at the men, carefully watching them. Behind the stone masks, she could almost see some semblance of pain.

"I'm really sorry for your loss." It was said to all of them, but she was staring at Trax.

"Why'd you stop?"

She stared back at him, not quite understanding his question. "What?"

"Why stop? You could have called 9-1-1 from the car."

She cocked her head to the side, not fully understanding what he asked. "I wouldn't just leave someone hurt on the side of the road. I stopped because I wanted to help. What if another car came along and didn't see him?" She shuddered at the thought.

The men shared a look among themselves.

Kase shifted in his seat, resting his forearms on the table. "Why'd you come here?"

She swallowed the lump in her throat and glanced down at her bag on her lap. She reached in and felt the tension explode. All the men shifted forward, and she froze. "He gave me something." She felt for the package, eyeing the men, afraid if she looked away, they'd attack. She grasped the package and slowly lifted it out of her bag. She placed in on the table in front of her.

"Son of a bitch," the low, gravelly voice uttered. She couldn't be sure who said it, but Gage smirked.

Kase leaned forward, grabbing the package and opening it up to peer inside. A small smile crept on his lips.

"That what I think it is?" Trax asked.

Kase nodded. From their reactions, they were obviously happy with her bringing it back. She sagged her shoulders in relief. She might just make it out alive after all.

"You take this from him?"

"Yeah, well he told me to. He was pretty adamant I take it. I planned on going to the hospital and returning it, but then the detective told me he passed away." She tightened her lips.

"Why not give it to the cops?"

"He asked me not to." She shrugged. "I didn't want to get in trouble."

"You look inside?"

"No," she lied.

Trax raised his brows, and all signs of softness diminished. "Bullshit."

"Look, I've watched enough shows to know if a biker gives you something when you mention the police are coming, it's probably not good. I thought of bringing it to them, but what if they thought I was involved or something? Too many innocent people in jail as it is. I didn't wanna be one of them."

Trax's laugh echoed in the small room. "You think the cops would believe we'd be involved with you?"

What the hell is that supposed to mean? Was is it weird she was insulted? As if the thought that any of them would have an interest in a woman like her was absurd? She clasped her hands on her lap, biting back her small twinge of anger. She pursed her lips and squinted at Trax.

His brows knitted together in confusion. "What?"

She furrowed her brows. "You don't have to be mean."

Trax flinched and widened his eyes. He seemed taken aback by her comment.

This man was a jerk. Her eyebrows furrowed as she stared back at him. "Look, I was just trying to do the right thing. I brought it back when I didn't have to. A simple thank you without the insults would be enough."

"That wasn't an insult, sweetheart." He smiled, seemingly amused. "Just don't think the cops would suspect our club would be involved with you."

She gritted her teeth and tightened her lips.

He laughed and looked at the men before turning back to her. "What did I say?"

She sighed. "Again, with the insults." She tossed her hands into the air. "I get it. None of you would ever have an interest in me. Now, please stop."

Trax's mouth fell open, and he grinned while the others chuckled. She eyed them.

Gage burst out laughing. "I'm pretty sure Trax meant the cops wouldn't think *you* would ever be interested in hanging with *us,* honey. Trust me," his gaze dropped to her breasts and slowly up to meet her gaze, "you would always be welcome here." He winked and smiled.

She darted her gaze to Trax, who smirked.

"Oh." Well, that was kind of nice. *Wake up!* She turned to Kase. "Can I go now?"

"No. You see the driver?"

"Wait, you said I could leave."

"When we're done with you. See the driver?'

She sighed. "No. I gave a description to the police of the car and the license plate, but I couldn't remember the tag number, just the Illinois plate. He passed quickly and never stopped, so I didn't see him. Or her." She shrugged, focusing on the scraped up wooden table in front of her. She was not about to get more involved than she already was. The cops would find the guy, they always did. There was no need to put herself in danger. She glanced around the room. *Well, more danger.*

"What kind of car?"

She stared up at the ceiling. She was never good at identifying cars. "Dark blue sedan, I think." She bit her lip, dropping her gaze to Kase. "Not new."

"A *not new* blue sedan. That's your fucking description?" Kase's face reddened, and he slammed his fist onto the table, sending her jolting back into her seat. "You just described fifty percent of every car around here. What the fuck am I supposed to do with that?"

She pursed her lips, unable to hold back her anger. What the hell did he expect? It had all happened so fast; she hadn't paid much attention to the kind of car. He should be thanking her, but instead, he yelled and belittled her. "Yeah, sorry I couldn't get the make, model, and friggin' VIN, but I was kinda distracted watching a bike and man fly through the air."

His laugh was humorless and nasty. "You better watch your mouth with me."

It was a fair warning. These were not the type of men who appeared to easily forgive or let things slide. But a person could only be pushed so far before they snapped. She'd had enough.

"My mouth? Are you kidding me?" She pushed up from her chair and leveled him with a narrow glare. "I didn't have to come here, get treated like a friggin' stripper, taunted, accosted, and now berated. You think this is how I wanna spend my day? Hostage in a dark, dank room with bikers breathing down my neck? Well, it's not."

He remained silent as he watched her. Her outburst of confidence dwindled under his stare.

"You keep your mouth shut about this." It was an order, and one she had no intention of breaking. If this was the last time she ever saw these men again, it would be too soon. They never even thanked her. She wasn't expecting a grandiose show of appreciation, but a simple *thanks for being with him* or *thanks for stopping* or at the very least, *thanks for returning our illegal contraband*, would have been nice. She got nothing.

Let it go and get the hell outta here.

"If I was going to say anything, I'd have given this to the cops." She snorted. "Besides, who would I tell?" She sighed and scanned their expressions. Nothing had changed. "Can I go now?"

Kase jerked his chin toward the door.

She got up from her seat and turned to the door, giving Trax one last look. It was a shame, really. He was the only one to show her a sliver of kindness, and if circumstances had been different, she wouldn't have minded meeting him. Ironic. The first man to pique her interest in months and he was untouchable. They lived in two different worlds.

He dug his hands into his pockets and sighed. Maybe he thought the same thing. She smiled and bowed her head.

"You need something, let us know."

She glanced over her shoulder, looking to Kase. "What?"

"The club owes you. You need something, you make it known."

The club owed her? She scanned the room, trying to understand exactly what that entailed. They all stared back at her but gave no indication they would elaborate on what Kase meant. She flicked her gaze to Trax, who remained fixated on her. Her chest expanded, making room for her fast pumping heart. She quickly averted her eyes, glancing back at Kase.

"Like what?"

He stared at her. "You need something done, you let us know."

"Like a favor?" Her question seemed to amuse the room, and her cheeks heated.

What could she possibly need from these men ever? They were scary, intimidating, and obviously not law-abiding citizens. She'd count herself lucky to never cross paths with them again. Except maybe one.

Wait a minute. A thought popped into her head. It was the perfect solution to an ongoing problem. It may not be the best way to handle it, but she was at a loss. When would she ever get the opportunity? The idea of calling on these guys for anything else was absurd.

She turned back around and smiled. "Okay, I know what I want."

Kase cocked his brow.

"So, I live over at the apartments at McAllister. The ones by the tracks?"

He gave no acknowledgment that he knew what she was talking about, but everyone knew the building. She peered to the rest of the men who looked on with curiosity.

"Anyway, I have these neighbors, three guys. Well, not neighbors exactly, I don't even think they live there, but they hang out at the entrance a lot." She raised her brows. "Like every night. They're assholes, always saying shit to the women, ya know, like catcalling and being extremely vulgar." She paused, half wondering if what they said would be deemed intolerable by these men. "I work at Muller's bar on Quincy and don't get home until after two in the morning."

The room was doused in silence. Was she even getting her point across?

"They scare me. There's three of them, one of me, ya know? And I seem to be their favorite victim."

A sharp growl sounded from across the room. She jerked her gaze to Trax, Gage, and Rourke. Their tight features made her think maybe she had gotten through to them. She couldn't be sure who made the sound, but judging from Trax's scowl, she'd bet it was him.

Gage stepped forward. "You want us to kill them?"

She gasped in shock. They paid favors with murder? She frantically shook her head. "What? No, of course not. I just thought maybe you could." She shrugged. "Ya know…."

"Beat the shit out of them?" Trax snapped, confirming it was definitely him who growled. She ignored the swirling butterflies in her belly.

She cleared her throat. "No. But can you talk to them, or I don't know, show up and scare them or something? Get them to back off. I don't think they're dangerous, but, um…" She stopped short and stared down at the floor.

"What?" Trax asked

She shrugged, slightly embarrassed at admitting her own fear. "Like I said, I get home late from work after dark, so do a few other girls. And they just seem to be getting more aggressive lately…I don't know…"

"They hang there every night?"

She nodded.

Trax stared back at her. "We'll take care of it."

"Yeah?" She grinned with a wave of relief. "Thanks." She hoped she got the chance to see it when these guys showed up.

She turned to leave and walk toward the door. The quicker she got out of there, the better. None of the men said a word. She stopped in the hall, looking back through the door and smiled.

"I really am sorry about Mick." She didn't wait for a response and rushed down the hall through the bar, ignoring the shifting stools and stares. She made a beeline for the door, pushing it open, and the sunshine on her face had never felt so good.

She was never stepping foot in that place ever again. *Never.*

TRAX WAITED by the edge of the door. He'd been waiting on Kase to emerge from the meeting for the past hour. While the rest of his brothers were drinking, drugging, and fucking, he was waiting like a bitch for the boss.

This was not how his day was supposed to pan out. He'd gotten the call early in the morning. They were driving out on a run in an hour. Completely fucked his day. He was scheduled to work on two bikes he'd promised by the end of the week. While most all the members held outside jobs from the club, Trax had his intermixed. His talent for building and repairing bikes had made him good money, and having the freedom to work from his personal garage, he was able to make his own hours. It was fucking perfect. But he still had deadlines, which were currently being screwed by the last-minute run.

He didn't even have the chance to get off his bike when he met everyone at the clubhouse. They took off on their five-hour journey. According to Rourke, it would be a two-night stint. Two days behind schedule meant he'd be in his garage twenty-four seven when he got back. His customers would understand the delay. And if they didn't? Tough shit. The club always came first.

The work wasn't his biggest concern. The run also interfered with his promise to the brown-haired beauty from the other day. He'd spent too much time with her face in his head. Nothing had surprised him more than when she'd walked into the club. She'd stood out like a rabbit surrounded by a pack of hungry wolves. Yet, she'd stayed with a purpose. He knew what outsiders thought of the club, and he knew the stigma he had when he wore his cut. The Ghosttown Riders had their wild and rough reputation to not only other clubs but to everyone around them. They struck fear in everyone they crossed paths with. It took a lot of courage and strength to walk into the clubhouse. It took something else to set aside her own fear and stay true to a man's last dying wish. A big fucking heart.

He folded his arms and sighed heavily, giving a scowling glare to the redhead making her way to him. She curled her lips, her tongue poking out, licking the bottom lip and curving around to her mouth. She was hot. Stacked the way he liked it—tits, ass, and curves. A week ago, he would have taken her in the back to one of the bedrooms without even getting her name. He waited for it.

Just a spark of desire or want. *Nothing.* Now, had she been a stunning brunette with long wavy hair and dark eyes with lashes for fucking days? A pouty lower lip that jutted out when she smiled, making her nose crinkle and turn upward? If she had soft tiny hands that fit into his like a fucking glove.... *Fuck!* She was not Cheyenne, not even close. He drew in a harsh breath, silently berating himself for letting Cheyenne invade his mind. She stopped an inch from his chest. She stood waiting on him for something. He knew what she wanted, but she wasn't getting it.

She reached out her hand.

"Don't touch me unless I tell you, and I'm not fucking telling you." His tone was harsh and venomous, exactly the way he intended. She shied away slightly, proving she wasn't quite the seductress club whore she thought she was. With wide eyes, she glanced to the bar. He followed her gaze to see Gage grinning like a fucking idiot.

He must have sent her over. Fucking Gage. He gave him the finger and turned back to the girl in front of him. She stared up at him as if waiting for instructions. He had neither the desire nor the patience to deal with her, but there was something in her face. It held him back from telling her to fuck off. Some women were made for the club life. This girl in front of him was not.

Usually, he would tell a woman to fuck off and be done. The words couldn't pass through his lips, though. He shook his head. "I'm not interested."

She seemed to breathe a sigh of relief from the way her shoulders sagged, and her face eased. She nodded with a small smile. "Sorry."

"No need to be sorry."

She quirked up her lip and turned, heading back to the bar and a waiting Gage who would gladly take his place between her legs.

The door to the office opened, and the three men emerged. Trax pushed off the wall and waited. Kase said a few words before coming over to him.

The Favor

"Everything settled?"

Kase eyed the room and gave a quick nod of his chin. "Yeah, they're in. Had to give more than I wanted, but they got a bigger reach and more garages. We're gonna let them think they got the better deal." Kase smirked. "Five fucking years in the making and the shit's all coming together." Although it was rare, Kase was letting down his guard a bit. There was no denying the tinge of excitement.

It had taken some time, longer than predicted, but Kase was making it happen and staying true to the club becoming ninety percent legit.

It had been a hard sell to the club five years ago when Kase brought the idea to the table. The vision itself was brilliant and would prove to be lucrative for all. However, in order to get to where they wanted to be took an immense amount of sacrifice from the club as a whole. All earnings went directly to the club. No one got paid, including Kase. The members were forced to live purely on their side jobs, which made for hard times for some, especially those with families. Finally, it was all coming full circle, and they were close to reaping the benefits.

The plan came in two parts, the first being their relocation. They were heading back to where it all began. Ghosttown. It was a prime spot for them since it had been their home at one time. The desolate area was also key. Most clubs had clubhouses, but they would have a whole town. In the past years, they were able to purchase all the available property throughout the entire town. While the square footage of the town was in abundance, the residents were not. At last count, the population was forty-six. Kase had big plans for the town and made it so when it started to boom, the club would be in complete control. It was a slow process to not bring any attention to themselves. They had a close friend of the club form an LLC and purchase the properties sporadically on their behalf.

Phase Two would solidify the cash for the club. Over the past five years, they had pooled all their money and purchased all the inventory from auto parts stores and companies who'd gone under. At the cheap cost, they were able to stock a huge inventory as well as set themselves up with cars to stock for their junkyard. They'd started to venture out to Mexico and Canada, almost doubling their stock in the last year. When Kase's vision finally unfolded, most doubts had been banished.

Getting buyers was the easiest out of all the parts to the plans. Other charters hopped onboard to buy their parts solely from the club at a fraction of the price, and with access to the junkyard, it was a deal no one could turn down, and they didn't. *Fucking brilliant.*

"You talk to Cade?"

Caden was Kase's brother and the final link in the plan. He owned and operated a fairly large trucking company in Turnersville, the neighboring town to Ghosttown. Partnering up with Caden meant getting the trucks at their disposal, being able to make the deliveries themselves, and charge the other chapters. It was yet another income for the club. It was a win situation for everyone, but they needed Caden on board.

"Still working on little brother, but he'll come around."

"Why's he holding out?"

Kase clenched his jaw. "Pride." Kase lifted his chin. "He started his company from nothing. He did that shit all on his own, worked his ass off." Kase side eyed Trax. "He's got a lot of shit on his plate." Kase snorted. "And that stubborn motherfucker would rather go under than ask me for help. He needs this deal with us, and he fucking knows it, and that shit is eating at him." He glanced around the room. "But he'll do it."

Trax had known Caden for years. He considered him a friend, but this was the first he'd heard about him falling on hard times. It shouldn't surprise him, though. A man like Caden, same as Trax, did what they had to do without complaint. Kase stepped forward. Trax gripped his arm. Keeping his president from pussy wasn't a smart idea, but he wouldn't be able to relax until he talked to him.

The Favor

Kase looked down at his hold and then back up to Trax. He released Kase and stepped forward, keeping his voice low. "Who'd ya send for the girl?"

She was the real reason he was aggravated by the last-minute run. It had little to do with the bikes he needed to work on and more to do with the girl. Fucking Cheyenne. Even thinking her name had him balling his hands. He was set to take the lead on *the favor,* as she called it, until the run took precedence.

He had spent the last two days with thoughts of her clouding every fucking moment. The way she came in, the story she told. Even in the face of one of the most notorious biker clubs, she hadn't backed down. She ran, yeah, but kept on fighting. He liked it, respected it, and could not get her goddamn face outta his head. Especially her eyes, long lashes filtered around almond-shaped, soft brown eyes. *Innocent and so fucking pretty. The last thing Mick saw before he died.*

Kase furrowed his brow. "What girl?"

Trax crossed his arms and narrowed his eyes. Kase knew what girl. He was merely fucking with him. Originally, after she'd showed up, Kase had put another member on task to take care of it, but Trax insisted he be the one to handle it. He may have come off a little too eager by the looks he got from the other brothers. Kase didn't bother to ask, assuming it was for Mick, knowing how close they were. That had something to do with it. What Trax failed to mention to Kase or anyone else was the burning desire to beat the shit out of anyone who messed with that woman.

He felt an unrealistic possession over her, knowing she was the one who'd tried to save Mick, and there was something about her face, almost angelic, that made Trax feel it all through his blood. Fucking everywhere. When she'd walked into the club, she'd gotten all the guys' attention, but for Trax it was different. She wasn't his usual type, yet he hadn't taken his gaze off her. He was accustomed to the club girls who threw themselves at him, wore next to nothing, and had the dirty talk patted down to a science. But Cheyenne? She was sexy without trying. She stood in the middle of the club, fully clothed, stammering her words and giving off a thick nervous energy. He just could not tear his eyes away from her. When her gaze had lingered longer on him than any of the other guys, he'd hardened under her stare. The blush on her cheeks when she'd realized she'd been caught staring was one of the hottest looks he'd ever seen. *Fuck!* It had been a long time, so long he couldn't remember, seeing a woman as beautiful and sweet as her.

Kase lifted his brows. The fucker was gonna make him say her name.

"Cheyenne."

A nasty grin crossed his face. "Right. Cheyenne. You remember the bitch's name, huh? Ain't like you to remember their names, especially the ones you don't fuck."

"Gonna spend the night busting my balls?"

Kase laughed, lighting up a cigarette and taking a long drag. "I'm interested in pussy, not your balls. Sent the prospects."

"They go yet?"

Kase shifted his eyes. It wasn't often his president looked surprised, but the look on his face had Trax almost regretting the question. *Too fucking eager.* Kase watched him and pulled out his phone. Bringing it up to his ear, Kase gave a quick smirk.

"Yeah, you get it done?"

Trax was showing his cards when it came to Cheyenne. He didn't give a fuck. He waited as Kase stood silent.

"Any problems?" Kase paused. "Good." He clicked his phone, shoving it back into his pocket. He took another drag. "Done. They won't be a problem for...*Cheyenne.*" The way he said her name made it clear Kase was on to him about his interest.

Trax nodded but held back his thanks. He waited for the ribbing, but it never came. Kase swung his arm over Trax's shoulders, tugging him toward the bar.

"Pussy time."

Trax spent the rest of the night drinking and partying with his brothers. They would be there for the next forty-eight hours.

While he watched the entertainment and enjoyed it, he didn't partake in all the offerings. For the first time in years, he refused the free pussy being offered. Something that did not go unnoticed by his brothers. He could take the teasing, but he wasn't giving in. None of these women were who he wanted sliding between his legs.

That face. *Cheyenne.* The woman was fucking with his head.

Chapter 5

"So much for keeping your word," she muttered as she made her way through the path leading up to her apartment. There they stood, same as they had for the past few days. Each night she anticipated the three thugs gone, but every night they stood around spewing vulgar obscenities while she walked past. She tried not to engage with them, though she had plenty she wanted to say. Men like that were usually harmless. They just wanted to get a rise out of her and look cool in front of each other, like a pissing contest. However, some men weren't all talk, and that was what she truly feared. If cornered, she doubted she could get past the three of them.

She dropped her head and walked. She avoided eye contact in hopes she could slip past them undetected.

"Well, look who we got here. You're my favorite."

She groaned and sidestepped from his approach. "Shut up."

"Ooooh...she speaks today." The cackling had the hairs on her arms rise. "Been waiting on you, sweet tits."

She shuddered and shook her head. It was never good to tug the tail of the tiger, but she spoke before she could think. "Don't you have jobs you should be at?"

"My only job is making you scream." He laughed and reached

out to touch her arm. She backed away and yanked her hand away as if it were burned.

"Don't you dare touch me," she snapped. They were getting bolder. She considered turning around and going back to her car. The last thing she wanted was to be trapped in the hall with these men. She had already stopped using the elevator weeks ago. She feared they'd slide in, and she'd be trapped. That was no way to live.

"Playing hard to get?" He laughed and turned back to his friends. "I like 'em feisty."

She glanced up to see the light in their apartment. Macy was home. She would just rush past them and get inside. She made a move, but the one who was taunting grabbed her around the waist and pulled her to the side of the building. *Oh fuck.*

The side unit had a dark alley where the garbage was kept. It was the perfect scene for an assault. *Oh God.* She thrashed her legs, but it did nothing to slow him down. As she saw the entrance grow farther away, she opened her mouth. *Scream!* Before she could make a sound, another one came up and clamped his hand over her mouth. His eyes peered back into hers, and he smirked.

His hands wrapped over her waist, sliding one up to her breast, and she flailed her lower arms. This could not be happening. Tears streaked down her face from sheer panic. Deep inside the alley, even if someone heard her, it would take time to figure out where she was. He threw her down, and they descended on her as if she were prey. She screamed, but one of them kicked her ribs, and she jolted back on a pile of something. She had never been hit before. The pain was much worse than she could have imagined. She gasped, trying to inhale, but fresh air was not reaching her lungs.

One of them leaned forward, laughing, grabbing her breasts in a painful squeeze. She tightened her fist and swung, but missed any contact until she thrashed again and connected with his chest. It only infuriated him, and he slapped her jaw. The sharp, throbbing sting raced through her mouth up her cheek to her pulsing temple. A warm rush of liquid filtered from her nose. Oh God, she was bleeding. She gripped the gravel, trying to crawl away, but hands pawed at her, flipping her over to her back. She braced and locked her eyes shut before seeing an open palm come down across her face. A sharp sting on her cheekbone burned.

Her shirt ripped, and the cool air wafted against her stomach. There was pain, and she began to feel disoriented. How was she supposed to get away if she didn't know where to go? She pried open her eyes and fought back as best she could. She thrashed her legs when she felt cold skin at the zipper of her jeans. *Oh God, no.*

A loud thunderous bang sounded from the alley. She didn't know what it was or where it had come from, but it halted all movement from the men attacking her. She was still pinned down, but the guy on top of her looked down the alley. *Now, move now!*

She thrust her chest forward and knocked him back. She scrambled to her feet but immediately dropped to her knees from the sharp pain piercing her ribs.

"Oh fuck."

She whipped her head to the side, expecting them to descend on her again. Instead, she found all three men staggering away from her, and their gazes fixated down the dark alley. She followed their gaze, but a dumpster blocked her view.

"What did I tell you boys about coming in my alley?" The voice was deep and gravelly. "You need a reminder to stay away again?"

Cheyenne darted her gaze up to the men who were slowly backing away. They remained silent, but even in the dark, she watched their faces pale. Another loud whack echoed through the alley. The guys turned quickly and ran the opposite way.

Beyond the dumpster, a shadow appeared.

Through her glassy eyes, she looked up. He was not at all who she'd envisioned scaring away her attackers. He was tall but so very thin as if he hadn't eaten in weeks. His cheeks were hollowed and gaunt. Her gaze dropped to his clothing, which was tattered and filthy. He was long overdue for a shower, as in weeks overdue. It was hard to tell his age, but he couldn't have been much older than her, and he was obviously homeless. She wiped her eyes but made no move to get up. She noticed a large pipe in one hand and a knife in the other. It wasn't huge but big enough to do damage.

The mystery man made no movement toward her but angled his head to meet her gaze. *Oh shit*. Her heart raced, and her stomach turned. She sank back against the wall, wondering if her savior was going to attack her.

"You okay?" he croaked, coming forward with the light shining on his dirt-smudged face.

She nodded, fighting against the knot lodged in her throat.

He looked down the end of the alley. "They're gone."

She followed his gaze to the empty alley and then back to him. "Can I get up?"

The corner of his eyes crinkled. "I would if I were you. We got rats bigger than your head out here."

She slowly eased her body off the pavement. Every part of her back ached. She would probably have bruises lining up her spine. She stumbled forward, and the man inched back. She peered up at him and grabbed the torn remnants of her shirt and covered her breasts.

Her tears welled up. So much adrenaline now that she was left with what could have happened. If he hadn't come along... She refused to finish the thought. Her body shook, and she gulped a breath. "Thank you," she whispered.

He glanced away and shifted on his feet. "Go on. I'll follow you until you get inside."

She didn't even bother telling him it wasn't necessary. It was. She trembled as she made her way down the dark alley, glancing back at the man who remained armed with his knife and pipe three feet behind her. Here was a man who owed her nothing, and he came out willing to protect her. He had a knife, but there were three of the guys, two of them most definitely bigger than the slight man. He put himself in danger to help her.

When she reached the side of the building, she dug in her purse, pulled out her wallet, and turned back. She only had a ten and a few singles. It wasn't much since she rarely carried cash. She turned back and jutted her hand to him with the money.

He glanced down and twisted his lips. "Don't need your money."

"Consider it a thank you."

"You already thanked me."

She wiped her hand over her face and started to cry. Her body shook from everything that had just unfolded, and the panic over what could have. "Please, just take it." She reached out and stepped toward him, begging. "Please."

He slowly took the money from her hand, his eyes weary. He didn't say another word and turned around, heading back to the alley. Did he live there?

"Hey," she yelled.

He halted, glancing over his shoulder.

Cheyenne forced a half smile. "You think they'll come back?"

His lips tightened, and he gave her a slow nod.

Her heart sank to her stomach. *Great, just great.* They'd be back, and probably out for vengeance. It didn't take a genius to figure out who they'd be looking for. She stepped back and made her way to the front door. No signs of the men. She walked half a step up and broke down again. She should have moved when she had the chance last month. The only thing stopping her was Macy's unwillingness to leave the apartment. She liked it there. She'd grown up in the building and knew most of the residents. When a tiny house had come up for rent, she'd begged Macy to come with her, but she'd declined.

Anger outweighed her fear, and her blood burned. She was frustrated with Macy for not moving, and mad as hell at those guys for attacking her. Hell, she was even mad at the homeless guy for putting himself in danger to take up for her. She wouldn't have even been in this situation had those bikers kept their word. They promised her. They owed her.

"This is their fault." she snapped.

She buttoned up what was left of her shirt and then swiped the blood from her nose. Her left eye was already swelling and making her vision slight. Her best decision would have been to go upstairs, get cleaned up, and try to forget the night. She balled her hands into fists as her nails bit into her palms. *This was their fault.* She clenched her jaw, grinding her teeth. She had too many emotions swirling through her mind in the last twenty minutes. Now, she was left with unfiltered anger and juiced up on pure adrenaline.

She backed up and stormed to her car. The Ghosttown Riders were going to hear exactly what she thought of them and their fucking favor.

THURSDAY NIGHTS WEREN'T USUALLY the big parties, but this one had gone from twenty to forty people in the matter of an hour. Trax sat at the bar with Gage and Rourke for the past thirty minutes. He was tired, and the last place he wanted to be was the club tonight.

The last couple of weeks had been shitty. The loss of Mick was proving to be harder than he'd thought. The man was his mentor, brought him in, taught him everything he knew. He had just seen him in the club hours before he died.

He lifted his beer to his lips, trying to drown out the sounds of the music. They had just gotten back from a ride out for three days up to Culpepper, and he had agreed to one beer before heading home. He glanced at his phone to check the time.

The club was still on edge. The heat was definitely on them since Mick's murder. It was no accident, and everyone knew it. The brothers rode in pairs, something they never did before, but for safety purposes, it had to be done. Kase's orders.

"Val." Gage nudged his arm.

He glanced over his shoulder to see the blonde walking toward him. He turned back around and sighed. His previous encounter with her was enough for him to learn his lesson. The last thing he needed was more aggravation.

"Hi, baby." She purred and curled her hand over the nape of his neck.

He shifted in her direction and smirked, the scent of her flowery perfume burning his nostrils. "Did I say you could touch me?"

She smiled. "No." She thought he was teasing her. He wasn't.

"Then get your fucking hands off me." He growled and rolled his shoulders. She took the cue and slid her hand off his neck. But she didn't go away. She leaned on her elbow, jutting out her tits. It was a new tactic.

"I thought we could hang out?"

"No."

"Oh, c'mon..."

He narrowed his eyes. "Back the fuck off, or I'll have you thrown out on your fat ass."

"You don't have to get nasty, Trax." The sound of a familiar voice to his left had him jerking his neck. Meg was scorning him with her gaze. A reprimand from her held a little clout among the brothers. She was Mick's old lady, a woman he'd grown to respect.

"Honesty, Meg, that's all I'm giving."

"Kinder, Trax, that's all I'm suggesting." He pursed his lips to keep from smiling. Her throwing his own words back in his face was something Meg was known for doing. Of all the old ladies, Meg was his favorite. She kept her nose out of club business, was sweet on most of the girls, even the ones who practically threw themselves at Mick. An offer he never once indulged in.

He once asked Mick how Meg could even tolerate it, and his answer was simple. "Told me a long time ago. If I wanted to be with other women, it was my choice. Never wanted me to be with her outta obligation. If I wanted the free pussy, I was more than welcome to it."

The admission shocked Trax. A lot of men took what was offered, even with an old lady at home, but he hadn't heard of their women okaying it. "Really?"

"Yeah, said if I wanted to fuck other women, then I should. But if being with others was my choice, then she would make her own. Didn't want to be with someone who didn't want only her. I never wanted anyone but her. You got a good woman…you do anything and everything to keep her. Sticking my dick in some skank for release isn't worth what I'd lose. Besides, no woman here or anywhere can come close to Meg. So, there's no concern. I got it all, don't need nothing else."

With Mick's words and Meg's playing in his head, he turned to Val. "Back the fuck off." He smiled. "*Please.*"

"Asshole." Meg giggled.

Val turned but abruptly stopped, staring at the door. "Oh wow." Her tone was hushed.

He glanced up at her, and her eyes were wide. He followed her stare to a tiny woman standing a few feet away. *What the hell?* She was an absolute wreck. Her clothes were torn and disheveled, her shirt torn down the center, hanging on by only a few buttons, giving way to her bra. Bright red, inflamed scratches lined her chest near her neck. Her hair was a mess, strands sticking out from what he thought was a bun. Dark lines streaked down her face, her eyes were red-rimmed and glassy, and there was dried blood under her nose. Even beyond the mess, he knew those eyes. A light brown shade. *Fuck.*

He swiveled in his seat and bolted up. "Cheyenne?" His voice was low.

Meg rushed toward her, but Cheyenne immediately backed away, scanning the room until she locked her gaze on him. Her face tightened and hands balled. He watched in shock, and her whole body trembled.

"You!" She pointed at him. "You fucking liar." Her tone was strangled, but there was no hiding the rage behind her words.

Trax stalked toward her, but she met him halfway. Getting a closer look, his heart skipped a beat. There was no way of denying she'd been fucked up and attacked. His heart pounded against his chest, but he remained still, not fully comprehending what stood in front of him.

"What the fuck happened?" Gage asked, standing shoulder to shoulder with him.

Her gaze jolted to him, and she unleashed her fiery anger. "You lied, that's what happened. I asked you for one thing." She held up her finger, which shook. "Something you said you owed me, and you couldn't even follow through. One fucking thing after what I did for you all."

"What the fuck is going on?" Kase emerged from the backroom, snapping his jeans and pulling up his zipper. Nadia followed and gasped when she caught sight of Cheyenne. She cupped her mouth. Trax understood the shock on all the women's faces. It was obvious this woman had been beaten.

"Fuck you, fuck all of you. Why offer to do something if you aren't going to do it?" She pointed to her face and whipped her head, glaring at Trax. "See me, take a good fucking look because this is your fault, you son of a bitch. I helped one of yours, held his fucking hand while watching his brains practically pour out of his fucking skull, and you can't make good on one promise to help me out. Fuck you, you piece of shit." She scanned the room waving her hand. "All of you, fuck you all." The tears streamed down her face in dark lines he attributed to makeup. Her eyes were bloodshot, and one barely opened.

In a hundred years, he'd never forget the sight of her in front of him. This vision would haunt him, he knew it. He stepped closer, but she darted to her left, knocking into another brother who braced her arms. She was like a rabid animal and skittered away to the center of the room. They had fucked up, and it was breaking him.

"Mick?" Meg's voice caught his attention as her lips curved into a frown, and her eyes welled. The last thing she needed to hear were the details of her husband's death. Making the ID of his body was hard enough once he was cleaned up, but Cheyenne giving her the gory details was too much.

Trax lunged forward, grasping Cheyenne's arm lightly. He needed to get her out of hearing distance from Meg in case she shared any more details. She thrashed, and he tightened his grip to keep her from leaving. His intent was to shut her up, not hurt her. She screamed out in a pained cry.

"Get off me. You're hurting me." She tugged her arm and cried out again. He wasn't sure if it was shock or pure adrenaline meltdown that had her yelling. Whatever it was, he needed to get her in the back and to calm down.

"Get her in the back—now," Kase shouted.

Trax pulled Cheyenne against his chest in hopes of guiding her to the back. He gingerly locked his arms around her and carefully tried to guide her down the hall.

"Wait, this is her, the one who stopped for Mick?" Meg rushed forward behind him, holding his waist.

"That's me. The moron who helped the poor guy who was fucking bleeding out in the road. I should have left him, and then I wouldn't be here with you fucking assholes. I should have just let him die alone." Her voice was strangled and on the verge of menacing. This was not the girl who walked in there a week ago. This girl was scared and venomous, fear and anger taking over and spewing her words. She wanted them to feel the same pain that was reeling through her own body.

Meg rounded his back.

"Sweetheart," he warned. Something had happened to Cheyenne, something bad, but he was not going to let her words strike Meg.

"Did he say anything?" she begged in front of Cheyenne.

He watched Cheyenne curl her lip. "Who the hell are you?"

Trax tightened his grip around her in warning. He jerked her to his chest, glaring down at her. "Don't." He wasn't sure what Cheyenne would say next, but he wouldn't let Meg take the brunt of anything. She'd been through too much already. Cheyenne was hurt, and he would find out what happened to her, but there was no fucking way he'd stand by and let her disrespect Meg. He narrowed his eyes at Cheyenne, who stared back with a glimpse of confusion. He whispered, "She's been through enough, don't fuck with her." He watched as Cheyenne's anger sobered and she furrowed her brows.

"I'm his wife."

Cheyenne's face paled, and her snarking lips curved into a frown. "Meg?" she whispered, and her struggling subsided. Trax felt her relax into his back, and he held her weight to keep her from falling. Her reaction to Mick's widow and knowing her name struck him as odd. He peered down, watching her lips tug down into a somber frown. How the hell did she know Meg's name?

"Trax, get her in back now," Kase commanded with a low snarl. Trax pushed her forward past Meg who trailed behind them. Her body had loosened, and she easily walked ahead of him, not even reacting to the way he tightened his grip on her. All the anger and fight seemingly left her body.

"Wait, let me talk to her. Please, Trax."

"She doesn't know anything. Anything she says will just upset you." He watched as one of the women wrapped her arms over Meg's shoulders, trying to calm her. Trax glanced over his shoulder to see Meg trying to rush past the group surrounding her. "Meg, stop."

"He said your name." The soft whisper came from the woman he held bound. His gaze dropped to her. She leaned over, looking back at Meg. Her face was soft, and her eyes were the sincerest he'd ever seen a woman look. She smiled and nodded. "The last thing he said before he closed his eyes was your name."

Meg started to cry, a sight that broke Trax's cold heart. The tears streamed down her face, and she nodded, mouthing, "Thank you," to Cheyenne.

"Trax," Kase shouted, and he quickly moved her forward into

one of the empty rooms. The men followed him, and when he breached the threshold, he released her. She darted forward into the corner with her head hung low.

She curled into the wall as if to blend into it. She was like a wounded animal, scared and broken.

Gage, Rourke, and Saint followed him inside. Kase came into the room, slamming the door shut with so much force Cheyenne trembled again, sinking deeper into the corner. Her legs gave out, and she slithered down the wall, her face shielded by her hands.

"What the fuck happened to her?" Kase barked.

"She came in and started yelling about us lying and shit. I'm still gonna go with my gut and say meth head," Gage said and then snickered. His friend was known for making light of fucked-up situations. This time it wasn't welcome.

"Are you looking at the same girl I am? Do you see anything fucking funny about this situation?" Saint glared as he watched Gage sober up, his lips flattening. He glanced over at Trax and lifted his chin in her direction.

Trax moved toward her. His steps were heavy, and her head jerked in his direction. With her eyes the size of saucers, she bolted from the floor, scurrying to the opposite corner of the room. She tugged tightly at the opening of her shirt. With all the chaos, it took him a minute to realize she was panicked and now trapped in a room with five large, intimidating, virile men. Her mind could only be going in one place.

He slid off his cut and grabbed the hem of his shirt, pulling it off.

She wept. "Oh God, please no." Her sobs grew louder, confirming what she thought was going to happen to her. Her arm struck out, and he saw her shaking. The pure terror in her tone struck Trax in a way he'd never felt. A possession and need to protect her filtered through his body.

"Shhh... relax, not gonna hurt you, you have my word." It was rare for Trax to even care about soothing anyone. If they were scared of him, fuck them, it was their problem. With her, he wanted her calm, not afraid. The whole scene was fucked, and seeing her scared to the point of panic ripped at something inside him. The woman who'd taken up residence in his head since he'd laid eyes on her was not the girl shaking in front of him now.

She snorted in disgust. "Your word means nothing."

He had tried to forget her, block her brown eyes and sweet body from his mind, but he couldn't. Seeing her like that enraged him. He barely knew this Cheyenne, yet he felt a strong possession over her. As though she was *his*.

He kneeled down, pulling lightly at her arm. She struggled, her words coming out as a stutter. "P-please don't do this. I-I'm sorry I came here, just let me go, I won't come back, I promise." Her words were mumbled by her erratic breath, tears streaming down her face. She was begging. "I-I promise."

"Relax," he whispered. "Not gonna hurt you, Cheyenne, okay?"

She watched him with zero trust in her eyes. *Good.* She shouldn't trust him or anyone else. He wasn't going to hurt her, in fact, he'd kill anyone who tried to step near her at this moment, but trust needed to be earned. Something the club had obviously failed on.

"I'm just gonna cover you up, sweetheart, okay?"

He smoothed the hair away from her face. It was soaked from tears. He was not a gentle man, but he paid close attention to how he handled her. He collared the shirt, putting it over her head and lightly drawing her arms through the sleeves. She didn't help him but didn't fight it, either. She was on high alert. His white tee engulfed her, reminding him of how small she was.

When he reached for her legs, he expected a fight. He was wrong. Her body was limp, and if not for the sound of her breaths, he'd think she had passed out.

"I'm gonna get ya off the floor now."

He lifted her dead weight and hooked the chair leg with his foot, pulling it closer to him, and set her down.

He bent down to her eye level and gently gripped her chin.

The eyes staring back at him were void of the fight she'd possessed earlier. Was she in shock? With her now centered in the room, unmoving, he and the rest of the men were able to see exactly how hurt she was. He sucked in a harsh breath. Dried blood covered the edges of her swollen lips, nose, and scattered over her face. The markings of a handprint shadowed her cheek. He gazed down her body. The beginnings of red and purple bruises on her wrists and forearms were a sign she had been held down.

"Christ." He recognized Saint's faint murmur.

The heat running through his body was almost too much to bat down. If they'd raped her, they wouldn't live to see morning.

"Fuck," Rourke whispered in a deep breath. He understood where his brother was speaking from.

He cupped her jaw. "Who did this?"

"Now you care?" She whispered so low, if he hadn't been as close to her, he wouldn't have heard it.

"Yeah, now I care. Tell me." He stared at her, willing her to answer, but she just gazed back without an emotion. "The guys from your place?"

Her bottom lip trembled as she tightened her mouth. "You said you'd scare them away." A lone tear fell down her cheek, and he caressed it away with his thumb. He left his hand lingering over her jaw.

Trax looked over at Kase and snapped, "You said it was done." He rarely took an accusing tone with Kase. As president, his word was never questioned. Trax didn't care. Someone had fucked up, and Cheyenne had paid the price for it.

"Fuck." Kase opened the door, yelling for the prospects. The three newest filed in and stopped by the door. Trax could see something was off with the younger two. They kept glancing at Cheyenne with a look he read clearly. Regret.

"You do what I told you on Tuesday?"

"Yes, sir. Talked to them myself. Told 'em to back off."

"Yeah, well, they didn't get the message," Trax snapped.

"I-I don't...."

Kase pushed the three guys out of the room before they finished.

This would be handled, but first, he needed to take care of Cheyenne.

"I'm gonna get ya cleaned up, Chey." Trax lifted her into his arms. He was surprised when she willingly allowed it without a fight. He passed Rourke and Gage, who stepped aside. But Saint came to stand in front of him, his gaze on Cheyenne.

"This wasn't handled. I'm personally going to make sure we rectify this, okay?" He was speaking to Cheyenne, but even Trax was surprised. Saint was a man of few words, and to have him speak to her, who he barely knew, was out of the norm. Saint hadn't been around when the promise had been made to her, but his vow was spoken with such conviction. This would be handled, even if Saint had to do it himself. When Saint gave his word, it was gospel.

She glanced up and nodded. Saint gave her a rare smile and gestured Trax toward the door.

Kase opened the door. "Where ya taking her?"

"My room." He moved down the hall. The music had started back up, but the usual voices and shots and laughter were non-existent. This night had taken a shitty turn. He pulled out his key, unlocking the door, and carried her to the bed. He hadn't been in his room at the club in a few weeks. He used it mainly for fucking. Since buying his house two years ago, he rarely slept there at night. But he never brought the girls home. He was in talks about giving it up for another member since the clubhouse only had ten bedrooms. Tonight, he was thankful he still had it. He placed her on the bed, and she immediately scurried to the edge.

"Can I please go home?"

He turned back to see her huddled with her arms wrapped around her waist. Until he knew exactly what had happened and she was no longer in danger, she wasn't going anywhere. He took this as his personal mission. She had been owed a favor from the club. A favor she'd earned in Mick's memory. He didn't think lightly of that, and she would be repaid. But first, he needed answers.

"I'll get ya home, I promise." He carefully watched her gaze shoot from the floor to him and glance around the room.

"Can I sit next to you?" He couldn't remember the last time he'd asked permission from any woman to do anything.

Her gaze flicked up to him. "If I say no, will you stay where you are?"

"Yeah."

"No," she blurted and then dropped her chin to her chest.

He smirked. "Okay." He folded his arms and leaned back against the door. "They attack you?"

She nodded, nibbling on her mouth.

"When did they start showing up again?"

She blinked and tilted her head. "They never stopped. They've been there every night. I guess they don't scare easily." She snorted and wiped her eyes with her sleeve. "If you guys showed up and told me not to come around again, I'd probably move to another state."

Their reputation was known far and wide as being one of the more violent clubs around. For their warning to go unheeded made Trax suspicious. The last-minute ride out had had the prospects delivering the message. A message that apparently was not understood. It would be handled by him this time, and it would be made clear Cheyenne was under his protection—she was untouchable. He stepped forward, and her eyes grew to the size of saucers.

"Now can I sit next to you?'

She shook her head.

"Okay." He stepped forward again until he stood in front of her. The fear he saw ripped at his heart. A heart that had gone cold so many years ago. He squatted in front of her, putting them at eye level. She shifted back, tightening her grip on the edge of the bed.

"Did they rape you?"

She scanned his face. Her eyes welled, and a shot of adrenaline spiked up to his chest. He would fucking kill them, but not before he made them suffer. His repeated words came out in a menacing tone. "Did they rape you?"

She released the bed, wiping her tears from her eyes. A slow shake of her head. "No, but not because they didn't try." She drew in a breath. "Some homeless guy scared them away. If he hadn't come along..." Her body shook, and Trax couldn't resist it any longer. He slid up next to her on the bed, swinging his arm across her back, and pulled her into his side.

She came willingly and nestled her face against his chest. He couldn't remember the last time he'd served as comfort to a woman, but if she was willing to accept it, he wanted nothing more than to hold Cheyenne. He leaned closer, his nose skimming her hair, and breathed in her scent.

"Trax," she whispered. It was the first time she'd said his name.

"Yeah?"

"Can you please take me home? You owe me, right? That's what I want. I just wanna go home," she whimpered. He pulled her closer. He expected a little resistance, but she curled into him, needing someone, anyone. Her hands curled into her chest, and her moist face brushed against his bare skin.

"I'm gonna get ya home, okay? Need ya to trust me, Chey. No one's gonna hurt ya."

"I just really wanna go home." She shook against his chest. Her tears ripped him apart. He slid his hand over her back soothingly. His hope was to put her at ease. He'd make sure she got home safe, but first, he needed to handle other things.

"I'm gonna clean ya up, Chey." He hugged her closer to his side before he released her and made his way into his bathroom. He got a clean washcloth and soaked it with warm water. He grabbed a dry hand towel and did a sniff test, making sure it was clean.

He found her as he'd left her, huddled on his bed with her head drawn down. He squatted in front of her, bringing the cloth to her lip. She winced, and his hand stilled. The last thing he wanted was to cause her any more pain.

"Sorry," he whispered.

"It's okay, it's just really sensitive." She glanced up, and the corners of her lips curled slightly. "Thanks for doing this."

She thanked him? After all she'd gone through, she remained sweet. Those motherfuckers were gonna pay for what they did to her. He'd personally see to it.

He gave a sharp nod and continued to carefully wipe the dried blood from her face. He couldn't remember a time when he'd cared for a woman he hadn't been involved with. There was something about her. She felt like his, and it broke him up inside knowing she'd been hurt. Not only had the club made her a promise, but he personally felt responsible. She'd trusted his word, and he'd broken it. Had he known the outcome beforehand, he would have defied Kase's orders for the run and handled it himself. Then she would have been safe. He scanned her bruising cheeks, swollen eyes, and the tear in her lip. His shoulders tensed, and his breath shallowed. He'd let this happen to her. He tossed the rag to the side and then clasped his hands in hers.

"Need to go talk to the guys. I'm gonna lock the door behind me. Need anything? Food, drink?"

She raised her brows in question. "To go home?"

He smiled. Even bruised, battered, and seemingly defeated, she still had spirit. "I'll be back in five."

She scanned the room, hugging herself. She was scared. He couldn't just leave her by herself. He opened the door, spotting Gage at the end of the hall. "Gage, get me one of the girls."

His eyebrows cocked up. "Now?" From his expression alone, Trax knew where his brother's mind had gone. He couldn't fault him. When a brother requested a girl, it usually wasn't for anything but sex.

Trax sighed and rolled his eyes. "To sit with her. I need to talk to the prospects."

Clarity struck, and he jerked his chin. "Right, sorry. Nadia, come hang with her for a few."

Nadia appeared and sauntered toward him. She was usually with Kase, but she wasn't his old lady, so she made the rounds. She'd even warmed Trax's bed a few times. She wasn't so much like the others. She was great in bed but never looking for more. She was usually gone before he woke up in the morning.

She stepped in front of him and smiled. "I'll be nice, I promise."

Trax didn't doubt it. Where some girls were nasty and bitchy, Nadia usually treated everyone with kindness. He opened the door, but a flash of red caught his eyes down the hall. Meg rushed to the door, ignoring his head shaking.

"I'll sit with her."

"No."

"Why not?" she pleaded with red-rimmed eyes.

"Because you've been crying enough tonight, don't need you more upset, Meg."

"I won't."

He shook his head and glanced down at her when her hand rested on his stomach. "And I won't upset her either if that's what you're worried about."

It struck him as odd she would make that assumption. He didn't doubt Meg wouldn't do anything to upset Cheyenne.

Nadia giggled. He turned his head and glared. "What the hell was that for?"

She shrugged and smiled. "Heard the guys talking about *the one who got under Trax's skin*, he didn't even partake in the pussy party at the club." She peeked into the room and then back to Trax. "I'm guessing that's her, huh?"

He didn't answer, which turned her smile into a grin. He would address the men later about their gossiping like bitches.

For now, he had other business to deal with. Nadia tapped his arm. "Let Meg go in."

Meg stepped up with a plea. "Please."

He looked between both women. Either one would be his top choice. He trusted them, but out of the two, he'd prefer she be with a woman he hadn't slept with. "Fine."

Meg walked in, going directly to the bed and sitting next to her. Her gaze drew to him.

"Meg's gonna hang with you while I'm gone. Okay?"

She nodded, and her lips formed a tight line, eyeing Meg and Trax. "Okay."

Meg put her arm around Cheyenne, tugging her into her side. "We'll be fine, Trax. Go do what ya have to do."

He reluctantly closed the door and walked down the hall with Nadia following close behind. "So, is it serious?"

"Is what serious?"

"You and her?"

He stopped and turned back to Nadia, who smiled and practically bounced on her toes. "Nad, I just met her."

She grasped his waist. She'd always been a touchy type of person, especially with those she liked. "Yeah, but I sense something."

He laughed. "Ah, fuck me."

"She seems sweet, and we already know she's loyal, sticking with Mick the way she did. She's unbelievably gorgeous, Trax, as if you didn't know."

He'd have to be fucking blind not to notice.

"You done?"

Her smile faltered, and her tone lowered. "You need someone sweet, Trax. Always so serious, you need a little light and sweet. This world is too dark without a little light."

He leaned in closer and smirked. "I get all the sweet I want when I want it."

She rolled her eyes and narrowed her gaze. He turned to head out back where the brothers had gathered. But Nadia wasn't done just yet.

"That's pussy." She'd caught his attention, and he glanced over his shoulder. "You need more, you deserve more. Your ex jaded you." She pointed to his door and narrowed her gaze. "Don't let her slip away, Trax, because someone will come along and take her sooner than you think. Hell, half the brothers are eyeing her as old lady material."

He spun around. "Who the fuck is looking at her?"

A Cheshire cat smile curved on Nadia's lip. "What does it matter? You just met her, right?" She winked and sashayed around him. She'd hit a nerve, exactly what she had intended to do.

Gage watched as Nadia passed and then looked back to Trax. "What do ya need?"

"The prospects."

Gage gathered the boys and followed them out back into the lot behind the clubhouse. The surrounding buildings were all vacant, with the occasional bum lurking. They'd made their presence known when they'd moved in seven years ago. Most people hightailed it out of there, except for a few who kept to themselves.

John, Mikey, and Joe stood in front of him with Gage on the right and Rourke standing on the left. Kase and Saint lingered behind, allowing Trax to run the show how he saw fit. As one of the lead brothers, Trax was given more clout than others.

"When did you talk to these guys?"

John stepped forward. "We rode out Tuesday like Kase instructed. These guys are just local punks, Trax. I scared them off."

"No, ya didn't, fucker. You see her face? You didn't scare dick." Rourke growled, and John stepped back.

"You guys with him?" Trax asked, carefully eyeing their response and demeanor.

"Yeah, they were with me."

Trax stepped closer, butting his chest against John. "Wasn't asking you, asshole."

"Mikey, you were there?"

"Yeah."

Trax noticed the way his gaze flicked to John. Someone was lying. Trax lifted his chin, and Rourke grabbed John by the collar, pulling him back into the clubhouse.

"Rule number one as a prospect. Don't fucking lie to me."

Mikey sighed and glanced over at Joe. "Okay, we went with him, but when we were walking up to the apartment building, John told us to head back to the bikes. Said he knew these guys and he'd settle everything. I said we'd go with him, but he insisted that him being the longest prospect, he had seniority."

"Prospects don't have any fucking seniority, even over each other," Kase barked.

"Look, I thought he was handling it. I didn't think the girl would get hurt. I trusted he knew what he was doing. I thought we were being loyal to our brother."

"None of you are fucking brothers without a patch. Your president gave you a direct order, and you let another fucking prospect override him, asshole," Trax snapped, sending both men flinching backward. They knew they'd fucked up.

Joe stepped up. "He said he'd handle it. When he came back, he said they wouldn't be a problem. Mikey and I wanted to wait until they left, 'til she was back in her place, but John said he didn't want to miss the party."

"We fucked up, Trax, I get it now. But it won't happen again, I swear. Me and Joe want this, man. We'll do whatever it takes."

Trax dragged his hand through his hair. Those motherfuckers should be booted out and banned for life. He'd known them since they started prospecting six months ago. They hustled for the club, did everything that was asked. Trax didn't believe in second chances for prospects usually, but it wasn't his call to make. He glanced over his shoulder to Kase and Saint, who remained silent.

"Your call," Trax said.

Saint pushed off the wall, making his way to stand in front of Mike and Joe. "You wanna stay, you start over today. We erase those six months you put in. You still wanna prospect?"

"Yeah, fuck yeah, man. We screwed up. We'll take our punishment."

Saint eyed Trax. It wasn't often a vice president would ask permission from a member, but Saint was not the average VP. Trax nodded, knowing these were good guys who had made a mistake. He was willing to extend a second chance.

Saint turned back to the prospects. "This is happening 'cause Trax is allowing it, do you understand?"

They nodded.

"He's showing more mercy on you than most brothers would. If you fuck up again—" Saint lowered his voice. "—you will answer to me. Do you understand?"

Mike and Joe shuffled on their feet, giving short nods.

He nodded, and the guys went back inside, passing Rourke, who still had John in his grip. He pushed him forward, and the prospect stumbled. He righted himself.

"You are seconds away from losing the prospect patch. Fucking truth or I take it, we beat the shit out of you, and ban you from not just the club but the fucking city."

"Okay, I know them." He gave up the truth a lot quicker than Trax had expected.

"Who?"

"The guys from the apartment. I went to school with them. They're not bad guys, just thugs, man. Told them to back off, they said they would."

Trax ground his teeth. "You see her fucking face. You call that backing off?'

"Look, I'm just saying, we don't know this girl, but I know the guys." He scanned the men surrounding him and shrugged. "If they did that, she probably had it coming."

He barely finished the sentence when Trax's fist descended across John's jaw, snapping his neck back. The prospect stumbled, but Trax caught his shirt before he fell. He punched his stomach so hard pain shot through his arm. The guy keeled over, and Trax brought up his knee, slamming it into his face and feeling the crunch of his nose. John shouted. Trax dropped him to the ground and stomped on his back.

"Motherfucker, *you* had that coming." Trax backed away and watched the sorry excuse for a man roll over, grunting in pain. Not one brother moved. They looked on with disgust at the prospect. He was officially out. There wouldn't be any second chances for John.

"We'll clean this piece of shit up. Go, man." Gage slapped him on the back, and Trax walked through the door into the house. He ignored the stares from his brothers. They'd get the story tomorrow in church. Right now, the only priority he had was getting back to Cheyenne. He unlocked the door and then opened it to see Meg watching TV with Cheyenne snuggled into his bed.

Meg took in the sight of his bloodied hands. "You good?"

He nodded and jerked his chin to the bed where Cheyenne lay cuddled into his pillow. "Give you any problems?"

Meg smiled and glanced over at her. "She's a sweet one for sure. Spent ten minutes apologizing to me for her attitude." Meg rolled her eyes and smirked. "Girl gets the hell beat out of her and damn near raped, and she's thinking about me and my feelings." Her eyes teared up, glancing back at Cheyenne with her bottom lip trembling. "Said Mick fought hard thinking of me. She said she knew the way he said my name that I was the last thought he had before closing his eyes." Her breath hitched as a tear fell down her cheek. "I needed to hear that."

Trax stepped a foot closer, wrapping his arm around Meg's shoulders and pulling her in for a hug. Her body shook against his chest, and he clung on to her harder. Meg put up a hard front for the club. Brave and strong, but deep inside, she was dying without Mick.

"The only saving grace was he didn't die alone. It may not have been me, but she held on to his hand, giving him comfort."

"Yeah." It was all he could say without getting choked up. Mick was a huge loss to the club, but more for him than any other member. She squeezed Trax into a hug and let go abruptly, stepping back. She wiped her eyes and smiled.

"You need to make sure she's safe, Trax, for Mick."

"I will."

Meg smiled, a small glimmer in her eyes. "I know you will." She reached up, kissing his cheek, and jerked her head to the bathroom. "Go get cleaned up. She wakes up and sees your hands, she'll probably freak out."

He cleaned up quickly, and when he came out, Meg had left. The glimmer from the TV shined over her, snuggled under his covers. A gentleman would have left her alone and found somewhere else to sleep.

Trax undressed, keeping only his underwear on and climbed into bed with her. The moment he settled, she turned her body, draping her arm over his chest. She snuggled into his side while he lay frozen. This girl was traumatized enough. If she woke up tangled in the sheets with him, she was liable to freak the fuck out and slit his throat.

She curled into his shoulder, resting her face in the curve of his neck. The slow puffs of air tickled him, but he resisted the urge to move. Her fingers dug into his side, her leg crossed over his thigh, and she curled into him. This girl was like a cat. He should have untangled her limbs from his and found another place to sleep for the night. Instead, he wrapped his arm around her back, lifting his hand to feel her hair between his fingers. Even in a tangled mess, it was silky and soft. He dropped his arm to her back, gently pulling her closer.

It had been so long since he'd lain in a bed with a woman and hadn't fucked her, it seemed strange. Comfortably and soothingly odd. Any chance of him leaving the bed were shot down the second she curled into his side. He hoped to God she didn't wake up. He wanted her in his bed and in his arms, where she was safe.

He turned, resting his face against the top of her head, his hand caressing her back. She was different from most women he'd been with, including his ex. Ariel hadn't a pure bone in her body. But Chey? She was loyal and fierce and so damn sweet. This woman would be his downfall, he feared. Or she could be *his* saving grace.

Chapter 6

Cheyenne stirred in the warmth of the sheets. The soft bed was nice, but the straining ache of her body was making it impossible to fall back asleep. She slowly peeked open her eyes. The room was the same from last night. It was dark and unfamiliar. She craned her neck slowly. *Trax.* His eyes were closed, and he was only a breath away from her. Her heart raced. His lips were parted, and she was entranced by his mouth. His lips were definitely soft. She inched closer, wondering how he tasted. *Probably like morning breath, so get outta the goddamn bed.* She squeezed her eyes shut. Of all the things that had happened last night, her focus should not be on Trax and his enticing lips.

Her body stiffened as she tried to calm her breathing. What the hell was she even doing in bed with him? She inched away, making slow movements. The last thing she needed was for him to wake up. His hand on her back fell to the mattress as she sat up. His bare torso evenly rose with a steady heartbeat. He was definitely fast asleep. The perfect time for a getaway. If she could only stop ogling him, she could get out of there without him waking. Her gaze traveled down the contours of his abs. *I knew it.* How could she have missed it last night? He was heavily tatted. A large mural was colored into half his chest, wrapping around his shoulder and down his arm. She'd had boyfriends in the past with decent bodies, but nothing quite like Trax. Strong muscles outlined his pecs and abs. She wouldn't even know how to go about getting her stomach to look as defined as his. She followed her gaze down and caught sight of his dark gray briefs.

She felt a twinge of disappointment, knowing she'd spent all night in bed with him and all they did was sleep. *Snap out of it, moron.*

She jutted up onto her hands and knees and bit back a groan. Her aching muscles served as a reminder to last night's events. She slowly crawled to the edge of the bed. She was fully clothed, but someone had removed her socks and sneakers. She scanned the floor. Aside from ashes, a few receipts, and a thong in the corner near the dresser, her sneakers were not there. She sat back on her feet and perused the room.

It wasn't huge but definitely roomy. It was certainly larger than her bedroom in the apartment, though not nearly as lived in. Aside from a dresser, nightstand, and the large bed centered in the room, it was barren. It didn't have any special touches to it. No pictures or knickknacks, though Trax didn't come off as a knick-knack type of guy.

She got up and stepped onto the floor with her back to the bed. One last look proved effortless. Wherever her sneakers were, she couldn't see them. Her pocketbook hung over the back of the chair. She made her way to it, taking careful, quiet steps not to wake him up. She needed to get out of there.

She grabbed the bag and turned around. She screamed, falling back into the chair and almost losing her footing. The quick move had her wincing from the pain shooting up her back. She gasped for a breath as she stared into his eyes. Somewhere along her quiet quest to sneak out, he'd gotten up and sat on the edge of the bed, watching her. His arm rested against his thighs, and he cocked his head.

"Leaving?"

She nodded in a shaky tremble. "Yeah."

His gaze darted down her frame. "Barefoot?" The corner of his mouth curled. He seemed less scary when he smiled.

She licked her lips, and his gaze immediately dropped to her mouth, losing any ease he had. His jaw tightened.

"I can't find my sneakers."

He leaned forward, reaching to the floor, and tucked his hand under the bed. Seconds later, her sneakers appeared. She inched forward, thinking he would hand them to her, but instead, he left them between his bare feet. The thought of getting too close to him was slightly freaking her out. The idea she had slept with him all night was surreal. Aside from being sore, it had been one of the best night's sleep she'd had in weeks.

She walked toward him and leaned down to grab her sneakers, but his hand cupped her jaw, and she was frozen in her spot. His finger grazed over her bruised cheekbone. "We should have put ice on that. It hurt?"

Yes! It was achy before but tolerable. Now, with him rubbing the raw skin, it felt as if it was on fire. She winced from the pressure on the spot. "A little."

He nodded and shifted his thumb over her lips. She watched his gaze drift to her mouth, and for a brief second, she thought he might kiss her. How absurd was that? A total stranger kissing her, and what was even crazier was, she was pretty sure she would have let him. His gaze flicked up to hers. His eyes were so dark, without the sunlight in the room, she could have easily mistaken them for black. Being this close gave her the opportunity to really see him. Her original assessment of *gorgeous* had been on point.

"Never thanked you."

She tilted her head, curving it deeper into his hand, and though not intentional, she liked it.

"For Mick."

There it was. The long awaited and now unexpected gratitude. Her face heated.

"Oh, um…you're welcome."

His mouth curled again, but this time it was a full grin. His eyes glimmered, and the corners crinkled. "Would have stopped for anyone, I'm guessing." His head shook in amusement, but she wasn't sure why. "Even a damn dog, huh?"

She pulled back slightly, and his palm slid across her jaw. "Of course, wouldn't you?"

His smiled faded, and she wished she had kept her mouth shut because his eyes darkened again, and he scowled. "No."

She straightened her back and watched as he got up and paced across the room. "Get your stuff, and I'll walk you out."

She refused to acknowledge the short wave of disappointment. She was leaving. She sat on the bed and bent over to grab her sneakers from the floor and yelped. A sharp pain shot through her ribs, and she eased up slowly. Oh God, did they break a rib last night? She grasped her side and drew in a deep breath.

"You okay?"

She kept her eyes aimed at her shoes. "Yeah." How the hell was she going to get them on if she couldn't even bend down? Before she could strategize a plan, Trax appeared in front of her, bent down on his knees, and untied her laces. He dug inside, pulling out her socks, and she watched in complete awe as he put them on her feet. His touch was gentle. She peeked through her lashes as he reached for her sneaker and guided her foot. He did the other sneaker and then tied her laces. *A Ghosttown Rider tied my shoes.* She felt a giddy bubbling in her chest. *So sweet.*

He sat back on his heels and glanced up with his dark-eyed gaze set on her. She flattened her lips and shifted on the bed. Under his heated stare, her pulse raced.

"T-thank you," she stammered, unable to control her breath.

The corner of his mouth curled. He rose but remained bent over at eye level. "You're welcome."

Kiss him, just do it!

She blinked at the voice screaming in her head. He chuckled. *Oh, my God, did I say that out loud?* She watched him straighten and turn slowly, walking to the opposite side of the room.

She took even breaths before standing and faltering her steps. She heaved her bag over her shoulder and stood silent. The whole mood shifted. She waited for him to put on his boots and grab a T-shirt from the dresser. The muscles on his back contracted as he lifted the material over his head. She'd never given much thought to a back being sexy but watching the muscles tighten and flex, she was getting slightly turned-on. He turned to the side, giving her a half view of his abs. Damn. Even from the side view she was getting, she could see the lines cut into his skin. She sucked in a breath and smirked. Too bad she couldn't snap a quick picture because Macy was going to think she lied when she described this later to her best friend.

"You get a good look?"

Her gaze darted up to meet his. *Oh shit.* She turned her head to the door. "Sorry."

A soft chuckle sounded from behind, and she squeezed her eyes shut as her face heated. *Breathe, girl, breathe.* This was embarrassing. Her skin prickled. There was no way of hiding her blush. She pried her eyes open and glanced next to her. Trax stood a foot away, staring at her.

"Sorry."

"You said that already."

She gulped. "You have nice abs." Her face burned hotter. *Shut up!* His lips spread into a wide grin.

"Glad to hear ya think so."

She looked everywhere in the room but at him.

He snorted. "C'mon."

She followed him out of his room and down the short hallway. All the doors were closed, and it was eerily quiet. The hallway opened up into the bar area she remembered from last night. The lights were lowered, giving a soft glow in from the window. She thought they were heading to the door, but he rounded the tables and walked down another hallway. She stopped just at the doorway.

"Umm...I'm parked across the street."

He glanced over his shoulder and stopped. "Had one of the guys move you to the back last night." He pointed toward the front door. "They'll tow you if you park overnight."

"Oh." That was sweet of him.

They passed two doors and down to the main steel door. He pressed in a code and then pushed the door open. She skirted by him and turned. "Thanks." She rushed down the steps and expected to hear the door close, but it didn't.

"Go straight home." It was an order.

She glanced over her shoulder. "Actually, I'm gonna stop at the police station and fill out a report." She strummed the strap of her pocketbook. "With them getting so aggressive, I think it's best if I report it, ya know?"

"No."

She jerked her gaze to Trax, who was scowling. "What?"

"I'll handle it, don't report it. Just go home."

She snorted, and his face hardened. *Don't piss him off, idiot.* Cheyenne forced a smile. "Look, these guys obviously don't scare easily, and while I appreciate the gesture, I think I need to go to the police. I mean, chances are they'll come back and I-I…" She clamped her mouth shut and glanced away. So much for being a strong, badass woman. She sighed and looked back at Trax. "I'm scared." She hated to admit it, especially to someone like him who'd probably never been scared of another human being before.

The door slammed closed, and she stepped back as he descended on her. His steps were heavy. She leaned back when he gripped her forearms and leaned forward. "Nothing to be scared of. I will take care of them."

"No, really, it's better this way, I'll just…"

His body pressed against hers, and her heart raced. His breath fanned over her face. "Chey, I'm gonna take care of this. You got *my* word. Nobody's touching you again. Ya got me?"

He said it with such conviction, she had no option but to believe him. She couldn't recall another time where a man had been so adamant about protecting her. Her belly warmed, and an ease strummed through her blood.

"Okay." His head dipped closer, and she sucked in a breath.

"No one," he whispered in a demonic tone that sent shivers through her body.

His hands released her, and she quickly spun around.

She walked toward her vehicle with him following. The lot had only a few motorcycles parked and her car at the rear of the clubhouse. She gulped a breath, wondering how she had even had the courage to walk in last night. Adrenaline had a crazy way of warping the mind.

She unlocked her car from her key fob and then turned when she reached her door. Her body was still aching, and she moved slowly.

"Well, um....thanks." Her face flushed. *Thanks for what?* Not killing her when she'd stormed his clubhouse and told him and everyone inside to fuck off? Thanks for letting her sleep with him? *Desperate much?* This was beyond awkward, and his stone-cold stare was not helping.

He stood a foot away with his hands shoved into his pockets, his biceps bulging from the seam of his T-shirt. God, he was sexy. It was probably the last thought she should be having after the night she had, but maybe she was just crazy. She pursed her lips.

"Bye."

He stared again, not saying a word. *Awkward.*

She grabbed the handle and opened it. When she stepped inside the car, his hands gripped her waist, pulling her back out and propping her against the open door. It all happened so quick she didn't have time to register exactly what was happening. He moved forward, his chest butting against hers, his hand sliding up her back, cupping her jaw and angling her head up. His lips were on hers before she could even think of what he was doing. Her eyes widened, focused on his, which were closed. His tongue plunged past her lips, dipping into her mouth, warm and wet. She was having flashbacks to her first kiss where she'd stood frozen against a wall as her date kissed her. Back then she didn't know how to kiss, right now, she was struck with shock. His chest pressed against her body, sending her shoulder blades into the rim of the door. Every part of him was laid flat against her. *Kiss him back, you dumbass.* His tongue circled around hers, and his lips moved over hers with such precision she couldn't even think.

She'd been kissed before, but usually she knew what to expect. Trax was unpredictable and amazing and gifted when it came to her mouth. His hand slid down to her neck, tightening as his thumb flexed into her pulse. There was no way of hiding it now. He could definitely feel her pulse racing.

This kiss alone had her rethinking her decision to get out of his bed. Right and wrong played a fierce game of Mortal Combat in her head. She leaned in closer, curling her hand around his waist. His growing erection dug into her stomach. *God, why did I leave his bed?* His tongue swiped along the shell of her lips, and an immediate twinge of pleasure heated her lower half. *Just from a friggin' kiss?*

His fingers dug into her back, giving way to a small tug of separation. It was ending a little too soon for her liking. When his lips shifted away slightly, she clawed her fingers into his waist and moved forward, pressing her lips against his. It was a bold move, one that could have gotten her rejected, but it didn't. He released a soft groan, and she took it as an invitation. Her tongue swept inside his mouth. Her skin tingled in pure delight when his hand drove into the back of her hair. She fiddled her fingers under the hem of his shirt, caressing up his sculpted muscles over his bare skin. He was so warm. The skin-to-skin contact deepened the kiss.

To any passerby, they'd appear to be a couple in desperate need of finding a room. She shifted her lips, rubbing her core against his straining cock. She was struck with immense regret that she'd left his room so quickly. If she had stayed, no doubt they'd both be naked at this point. Her tongue swirled slowly against his, and the moisture in her panties was on the verge of embarrassment, but she didn't care.

She felt him pull back again. He rested his forehead against hers. Her breath was erratic and fanning his face, which should have embarrassed her, but her mind was too set on kissing him again.

"So soft," she whispered in a daze.

"What?"

"Your lips."

His lips slowly perked up, and his eyes crinkled. He was obviously amused by the compliment. *Just one more kiss.*

She jutted forward, but his hands around her neck prevented her from getting any closer.

She glanced up through her lashes. The corner of his mouth curled. "No cops."

She furrowed her brows, not understanding what he'd said. One second, they were in the midst of an orgasm-inducing kiss, and the next, he told her not to see the police. She regained control of her breathing. She had the distinct feeling she was being dismissed. She licked her lips and gave a sharp nod.

When Trax stepped away a foot, Cheyenne turned, got into her car, and grabbed the door, closing it.

Too much had happened last night and this morning to process it all. She glanced over and watched Trax heading back into the clubhouse. Did he really think a kiss would sway her decision of not going to the cops and leaving her safety in his hands? She snorted, turning the key in the ignition, and felt the heat drape over her cheeks. That was exactly what he thought.

He thought right.

As she passed the police station on her way home, she slowed down but couldn't bring herself to stop. Hopefully, he'd live up to his word.

TRAX SPENT the better part of the day in his garage. He had several bikes lined up for work. Luckily, none too difficult. He'd gotten behind in the last few weeks and needed to catch up. There were a few he'd have to take down to Rourke's shop. He had a fully stocked tool assortment, but a few he lacked.

He grabbed a rag, wiping the sweat from his chest and then tossing it onto the chair in the corner before starting up the bike. The engine purred just as he wanted. He shut it down and glanced up as Rourke pulled in. The garage was set back from the house, giving him a long driveway. It was the selling point on the house, which wasn't much to speak of, but it was his. At one point, he'd shared it with his wife, but he made sure when things ended the cheating bitch was left with nothing of his. Ariel had fucked him in ways he was still recovering from.

"Hey."

Rourke dismounted slowly and jerked his chin. Of all the brothers, Trax was closest with Rourke. Their shared love of all things mechanical made a friendship easy when they'd met eight years ago. Rourke had been on Trax's ass to come work with him down at the shop, but Trax enjoyed the freedom of working from his own garage.

"You alone?"

Trax smirked and glanced at his house. Unfortunately, he was. Now, had the kiss lasted a minute longer, things might have been different. He might be locked in his bedroom, making Cheyenne's toes curl and fucking her into unconsciousness.

Nadia had been on point last night with her comment. Since meeting Cheyenne, he hadn't been with another woman. He hadn't had the desire. And everyone had taken notice it seemed, even Rourke.

"Yeah."

Rourke nodded and made his way into the garage, inspecting Trax's latest work. He bent at his knees, getting a closer look at the engine.

"Any word from Kase about Mick?"

Rourke shook his head, engrossed in the bike, but answered him. "Nothing yet. He thinks your girl is the key, though."

Trax didn't bother correcting him when he referred to Cheyenne as his. She may not realize it, but everyone around him did. Cheyenne was very much his.

"He's not gonna let up, thinks she knows more than she's saying." Rourke stood to face Trax. "I agree with him."

Trax was onboard with their assessment also, but pushing her last night was not an option. When she'd made mention that Mick had called out for Meg, it was new information, something she hadn't shared with them. Cheyenne hadn't given the whole story, and he needed her to. He circled the bike, grabbing a wrench from his toolbox.

"Kase send ya out here to give me a push on it?"

Rourke snorted. "Nah, haven't seen him today, but we both know him. It's coming."

Trax was well aware when Kase wanted something done, it got done. It was what made him a great leader to the club. It also made him a relentless hardass when shit wasn't done on his timeline. He'd give ample thought on how to proceed with Cheyenne. They needed the information, but for now, there was a more pressing issue.

"I'm going tonight. You in?" He didn't bother explaining. After last night's debacle with Cheyenne, everyone knew it would be handled by him as soon as possible. It was a priority over everything else.

"Yep. Gage is coming too." He sighed and chuckled. "Saint offered up his services if we need a fourth."

Trax bent down in front of the bike and slowly glanced up at Rourke, who was obviously amused. "Really?"

While all members participated in club issues, and most enjoyed the frequent brawls, Saint rarely participated. He had a lot to lose if shit went south. Saint was a scary and deadly motherfucker but never flaunted it. He was surprised by the offer.

Rourke cocked his brow. "He didn't like how shit went down

with Cheyenne. Made it known last night after you went to your room. Not often ya see the president knocked down a peg, but Saint was all over Kase's ass about fucking up with the prospects."

Trax would have liked to have been there. Kase was president. Everyone followed his orders, with the exception of Saint. The man did what he wanted, when he wanted, and answered to no one, including the club president. There was an unspoken respect between Kase and Saint that allowed it. It was rare for Saint not to back Kase, but it seemed he'd missed the show last night.

"Made it clear he wants it done tonight, and asked me to pass along he'd be around if we needed him."

"It'll be done tonight. If they don't show, I'll wait there every fucking night until they do." He tossed the wrench into the box and then wiped his hands down his grease-stained jeans. "I think we should be good, just the three of us. We'll meet up around nine at the clubhouse."

"All right. Kase wants everyone in tonight. He's got the final word on the move."

Trax snorted and shook his head. "We're really doing this, huh?"

"Looks like it. A few brothers already scouted out which properties they want." Rourke cocked a brow. "Heard Saint called dibs on one."

Years ago, Kase brought to the table the idea of moving the clubhouse and all their business out of county lines. It was a step back to where the club originated. Ghosttown. There was a reason for the name. The current population was about forty-six people at last count. It was set about twenty miles from Turnersville, leaving it accessible to civilization but far enough away to fly under the radar.

The club had more of a criminal element years back. Most members had done time, some longer than others. Saint and a few others were the only ones who hadn't. Unfortunately, Trax couldn't say the same. He'd done eighteen months and made it his life's mission to never go back. Kase turned the club around, moving to more legit jobs and businesses. Not to say all things were on the right side of the law, but nothing that would catch any of the guys hard time.

Their new endeavor had been five years in the making. For it all to work out, patience was a necessity. The club was always being watched by the law and rival clubs. They needed to fly under the radar, which meant taking their time. With so much time passed, not many believed it would actually happen. Even Trax had had his doubts. Not to say he didn't believe in Kase's vision, but as each year passed, his doubt grew. But Kase lived up to his word.

Going legit didn't necessarily mean the club had to show their cards. Aside from their meeting, not a word was spoken about what they were doing. Wives, friends, and family were kept in the dark. With the exception of two key players outside the club, no one knew a thing.

"You gonna make the move?"

Rourke shrugged. "Maybe. Got my sister and niece, so I need to see where they're at, but I'll keep a room at the clubhouse. You?" He lit a cigarette.

"Don't know yet." The idea of Ghosttown appealed to Trax, but he hadn't committed to moving just yet.

"Well, it ain't set yet anyway. The plans Kase's got for the compound gotta be approved. He's planning a run up there." Rourke smirked. "Town meeting, introduce ourselves to Ghosttown."

Trax laughed. "Wouldn't miss the Mayberry shit show for anything." He could only imagine what the small, tight-knit town would think of the club taking up residency.

He spent the next hour bullshitting with Rourke before he took off to go check on Meg. They'd taken turns checking in on her.

He made his way inside his house and washed up in the bathroom. In a few hours, he'd meet up with the guys and then head over to Cheyenne's place. Thinking of her only intensified his anger, setting him up for what would go down tonight. It also set him up for making his move with her. Never, since he'd ended it with his ex, could he envision himself settling down again. He'd resigned himself to the idea of being on his own. Cheyenne had him rethinking everything. His incessant need to protect and his desire to curl up with her in his bed again was changing his view.

It had taken every ounce of control he had not to grab her and drag her back to his bed this morning. Though he didn't think she would have objected. For as alpha as he was with most aspects of his life, especially his relationships, he needed to do this on her terms. If time was what she required, then he would give it to her. If the morning encounter was any indication, he wouldn't have to wait too long. He got off on her not wanting to end their kiss. It was almost a demand when he tried to end it the first time around. She was feeling him as much as he was feeling her if that was even possible. Trax was stepping into new territory with Cheyenne. She wasn't part of his world, but she would be. He had to figure out the how of going about it. Unlike the girls from the club, she wasn't a good-time girl or looking to snag a member for old-lady status. If he had to guess, when Cheyenne fell for a man, she was all in for him. He wanted to be that guy. Their rocky start would surface a trust issue, which would only be compounded by last night's event.

He glanced up, taking a long look in the mirror. Aside from the club, he never needed to prove anything to anyone. He was who he was, and if people didn't like it, they could fuck off. He drew in a deep breath. Except her. Trax was set to prove to Cheyenne she could trust him with everything.

Chapter 7

She cupped her mouth as she yawned while turning into the lot of her building. The day had been too long. She should have taken a nap as soon as she'd gotten home in the morning, but she'd been riddled with too much energy. Her body had felt like a live wire, unable to settle and on the verge of catching flames. All from one kiss? The kiss. She hadn't realized how much she'd wanted it until his lips had touched hers. Then she was done. *Ah, this guy.* He was all wrong for her. Yet, everything felt right when he'd soothed her after her meltdown in the club. The way he'd approached her, reassuring he wouldn't let anyone hurt her. The crazy part was she actually believed him.

Trax had been in her head the entire day and well into her shift at the bar. She found herself staring at other men while working and comparing them to him. There was no comparison. She couldn't ever remember being so attracted to a man.

Maybe she had it all wrong. When it came down to it, Trax protected her. He'd cared for her in his room. Hell, he'd had someone sit with her so she wouldn't be alone. Those were good-guy traits, not bad. He'd spoken sweetly with concern and vowed to take care of the problem. And he was friggin' hot. If she spent too long thinking about his abs, her body heated with a prickled tingling all over her skin. Why shouldn't she pursue something with him?

He belongs to a motorcycle club who obviously dabbles on the other side of the law. Perfect example—the severed finger. The club's desperate need to find the driver meant they were seeking retribution, which probably meant more than just a scolding. Trax was rough, possibly dangerous, and in the end, no matter how much he apologized, he hadn't lived up to his word about taking care of my issue with the guys from my apartment.

Her shoulders sagged as she trudged through the parking lot. It was two in the morning, and she needed to get into bed, close her eyes, and forget about the sexy biker who was all wrong for her.

Cheyenne scanned the dark path illuminated only by the broken street lamp. She gripped the mace tightly in her fist. Shit. She hadn't been prepared for them to show up tonight. It seemed even a knife-wielding homeless man couldn't scare away these assholes. They were gathered toward the corner of her building. She glanced over at the stairs, considering her odds of making it to the door if they decided to come at her again. The odds weren't in her favor. She stopped about ten feet away, contemplating her next move. She could turn around, call the police, and wait in her car, but what would that get them? A ticket for loitering at most. She should have reported their attack on her, but instead, she'd taken the word of a man who'd broken his promise before. *Not a smart move, moron.*

Although his track record hadn't been good, she'd actually believed Trax when he'd said he would handle it. She snorted at her own stupidity. How she could put trust in a group of bikers was beyond her own comprehension.

She drew in a deep breath and glared at the three men who'd yet to acknowledge her appearance. *No, I will not run.* She straightened her shoulders and dug into her bag, pulling out her keys. She wouldn't be blindsided this time. She positioned the key between her fingers as a makeshift knife and propped her index finger on the mace.

She walked confidently and hurried to the steps. She was a few feet away from the stairs when they caught sight of her. *Shit.* They laughed at something and didn't notice her at first. Damn her timing. She double-stepped to the entrance. She was so close. But not quick enough. The tallest of the three sprinted in front of the steps, blocking her.

"Look who we have here, boys." His sinister cackle drove a shiver over her body. *Oh God.*

"Move now, or I'll call the cops."

The corner of his mouth curled, and he stepped toward her. Her immediate reaction was to step back, and when she did, another one wrapped his arms around her waist, confining her arms to her sides. She opened her mouth to scream, but the guy in front of her shoved his dirty hand over her mouth. She thrashed as she'd done the night before and kicked out in hopes of making contact. Her effort was fruitless. The man holding her started toward the alley. *De ja vu.*

They made it just past the threshold of the alley—the space drowning in darkness. She moved her mouth in hopes of biting the disgusting hand. She felt the skin between her teeth and clenched hard. He yelped and yanked his arm away. But only for a second before she watched his balled fist aim straight for her face. Pain shot through her cheek and eye. It felt as though she'd been sliced open on her cheekbone.

"Big fucking mistake, cunt."

Panic set in, and she grasped against the man's legs in a last-ditch effort to get free. If she pinched him hard enough, maybe he'd be forced to let her go.

"Get your hands off her." The voice echoed in her ears. It wasn't a loud scream or shout. The words were slow and sinister. It was the most beautiful sound to her ears as her relief set in.

The guy in front of her blocked her view, but his hand fell from her mouth. Both perpetrators were now staring down into the darkness of the alley. She couldn't see who they were looking at, but from their faces, they knew they were fucked. She, on the other hand, knew exactly who the graveled, deep voice belonged to. Her heartbeat grew faster even as her body sagged in relief. Cheyenne was abruptly released. She lost her footing at the sudden release and dropped to her knees.

The guys quickly scurried away toward the end of the alley. Loud footsteps pounded past her. Pressure gripped her waist, and she jerked her head to see Trax lifting her off the ground and turning her toward him. His face was hard in sharp edges. He was furious. His hand grazed over her cheek. He was in a trance filled with anger and rage. His nostrils flared, and he clenched his jaw. She didn't know him well, but she recognized the look. He was ready to explode.

Her thoughts from ten minutes ago had been completely diminished. His touch, tender and gentle, was a complete contrast to his rigid and fury-ridden body.

She didn't even think before bringing her hand to his face, cupping his jaw. Her fingers caressed his stubbled cheeks. "I'm okay." She nestled closer, strumming her thumbs against his cheeks. "I'm fine, Trax." She tried to calm him down but seemed to be having the opposite effect.

Her words only seemed to anger him more. He pulled her against his chest, his lips slamming against hers. She was completely caught off guard and gasped. The last thing she'd expected him to do was kiss her, but his mouth moved over hers in a desperate flurry. His tongue slid past her lips and tangled with hers. She lost her breath from his tight grip holding her. The kiss was hard and powerful, as if he needed it. This was his confirmation that she was okay. His mouth devoured hers while her fingers softly caressed his face in contrast.

The background sound of grunts and groans seemed to pull him out of whatever trance he'd been in during their kiss. He shifted her into the curve of his chest to glare over her shoulder, the anger blazing back into his eyes.

"Trax," she whispered, and his stare jerked to her. She leaned in, kissing his lips softly. "Really. I'm okay."

Something shifted in his face, and he gazed down at her lips again before separating their bodies, and then grabbed her hand and pulled her deeper into the alley. As they closed in on the three guys, she noticed only one was still standing; the other two lay motionless on the ground. The largest and scariest of the bikers, Rourke, dragged a bloodied guy toward them.

"Saved you one." He pushed the guy forward, and she recognized him as the one who'd held her and dragged her into the alleyway.

It all happened so fast. One second Trax held her hand, and the next, he pounded on the guy. He took a swing, catching his jaw, and the guy stumbled back, landing hard on the ground. Trax stalked over, reaching down, lifting him as if he weighed nothing, and punched him in the stomach, forcing the guy to heave forward with a string of blood flying from his mouth. The beating was so violent she stepped back. He landed another punch, and the guy flew to the ground, not moving.

He stood over the guy and looked across his shoulder at her. "You want me to finish him?"

She widened her eyes. Finish him could only mean one thing. She slowly shook her head. She didn't want anyone to die, and she certainly didn't want Trax to get in trouble, which was probably going to happen anyway, considering they'd just beat the shit out of these guys.

He watched and waited. Maybe he thought she would change her mind. She wouldn't. He looked back at the three guys on the ground, bending over and lifting the slumped body of the man he'd just beat. "Thank her. She's gonna let you live, asshole." When the man didn't say anything, Trax gripped him by the throat, sitting him up.

She watched in horror as the guy glanced over at her and mouthed, "Thanks."

Trax slammed him back to the ground and stepped over his

legs. She'd never seen someone get the shit kicked out of them in real life. Her hands trembled as he approached her. If he noticed her fear, he ignored it and grasped her wrist, pulling her into his chest before glancing over his shoulder.

He jerked his chin. "Get rid of them."

Her eyes widened, and her heart raced. *Get rid of them as in hide the bodies? Oh God, this is bad.* Trax gave her no time to utter a word. His hand slid around her waist, and he led her to the front of the building and in through the main doors. They walked in silence up the stairs. His breathing was heavy, echoing through the halls.

When they made it to her door, she turned to face him. "They're not gonna kill those guys, right?"

Trax tilted his head. "You told me not to. You change your mind?" The corner of his mouth curled, and she sensed he teased her.

"No," she blurted. "But you said get rid of them, so…"

Trax moved closer, pinning her against the door and cupping her cheeks. "Rourke and Gage will probably take a few more shots, then make it known they are never to come anywhere near your building, or you, again." His thumb slid over her bottom lip. "They'll never come back, I promise."

"Thanks."

Trax leaned closer, his lips softly skimming hers. "You're welcome." His gaze trailed her face, and his small smile faded. "Let's get ya cleaned up."

She turned and walked through the door.

Cheyenne scanned the small apartment to find a man standing in the kitchen, playing on his phone. Jason, Macy's boyfriend, had become a fixture at their place in the last two months. She was still trying to figure out what her best friend saw in him. He was decent, but he had a habit of talking down to Macy, which infuriated Cheyenne.

Jason looked up from his phone, and his face paled. "What the hell happened to you?"

She sighed. "A little altercation."

"You're bleeding." His voice was so loud she flinched and backed into Trax, who grasped her hips.

She immediately reached for her face, not realizing she'd been bleeding.

"Who's bleeding?" Macy walked out from the hall in her pajamas, her hair in a towel. It only took a second for her best friend to stop in mid-step. Her mouth fell open, and she covered her lips with her hand. Cheyenne hadn't seen what she looked like, but from Macy's horrified face, she could imagine. Macy's gaze darted over her shoulder and widened. She rushed forward.

"Oh, my God, what happened?"

Cheyenne met her halfway in the living room and reached out, taking Macy in for a hug. "I'm fine, Mace. It looks worse than it really is, I swear."

"Really, 'cause it looks like you got the shit beaten outta ya." Macy pulled away and narrowed her eyes. "Now will you call the cops?"

Trax cleared his throat. "It was taken care of."

Cheyenne glanced over her shoulder, expecting only to see Trax, but the other men, Rourke and Gage, stood behind him.

"Who the hell are they?" Jason asked.

Cheyenne watched the scene unfold. Trax walked in followed by Rourke and Gage, who closed the door behind him. Trax turned to Jason.

"We're none of your fucking business. Get your shit and get out." He jerked his head to Macy. "You too."

"I live here, asshole," Macy snapped, and Cheyenne grasped her arm as she moved forward. Her best friend was tinier than her, but unlike Cheyenne, she had no filter and no fear.

"Macy," she whispered.

Macy jerked her head. "What? He can't come in here and tell me to leave my own fucking home. Does he really think with you looking like you do," she raised her brows, "I'd leave you alone with him and his gang?"

"Club." The deep graveled voice came from Rourke, who stood next to Trax. It was said with a warning, which sent shivers down her spine.

For all her confidence and spunk, even Macy took a step back from Rourke. She turned her head and met Cheyenne's gaze. A slight twinge of fear laced her pupils.

"You," Rourke growled, sending a quiver through her body. He was talking to Jason. "Go."

Cheyenne didn't know Macy's boyfriend well, but she expected some kind of argument, or at the very least some plight that he was staying. Instead, he nodded and tucked his phone into his back pocket and turned to Macy. "You guys gonna be okay?"

What? Was he seriously leaving? She was stunned speechless, watching him make his quick escape past the bikers. She glanced over at Macy whose eyes were set on the door with her lower lip jutted out. They had been friends for years, and Cheyenne could read her friend better than most people. Macy was pissed.

"What a fucking douchebag." Her lips twisted as she stared at the closed door.

The silence of their small apartment was short lived when Gage burst out laughing. Cheyenne watched his face spread into a grin, and he slapped Rourke on the back. "Fucking pussy." He jerked his chin to Macy. "His girl's got a bigger set of balls than him."

"Shut up," Macy said, and Cheyenne gripped her arm to keep her from moving.

"Both of you shut the fuck up," Rourke said, and immediately the room was swept into silence. Although Gage had a smirk on his face.

When Trax stepped closer, she and Macy stepped back in unison.

"Just saved your ass and now you're afraid of me." He glared directly at Cheyenne.

She tightened her lips and shook her head. He was right. Had he not been there, there was no telling what would have happened. This time he stayed true to his word. She relaxed slightly, and she let go of Macy's arm. He watched her intently and jerked his head to the couch. "Sit down."

Cheyenne moved slowly. He motioned to Macy, who glanced up suspiciously.

"Go get her something to clean up her face."

Oddly enough, Macy followed his orders and rushed down the hall. His gaze fell over her cheek, and she could only assume it was where the blood had been. When she had been slapped, it had felt as if her skin had been ripped open. She sighed and curled into the couch, tearing her gaze from Trax.

"You set them straight?"

Cheyenne glanced up again, but Trax was talking to the men.

Rourke nodded, glancing over at her before turning back to Trax. "Protection of the club. They know."

She had no idea what he meant, but Trax seemed to be appeased with his statement.

Trax folded his arms, jerking his chin toward the hall. "She knows about everything?"

He was referring to Macy.

Cheyenne shook her head. Hopefully, she could keep Macy out of whatever was happening with them. Unfortunately, Macy was not on the same page. She came back from the hall at that exact moment.

"Yeah." She snorted. "Finger and all."

Trax's jaw tightened, and his stare shifted to Cheyenne. "Thought you didn't open the envelope?"

"Shit," Macy said in a hushed tone.

Cheyenne gulped, scanning the faces of all the men and shrugged. "We may have peeked inside."

His brows furrowed, and his eyes darkened. This was not good. She sat up and moved closer to Macy when she took a seat next to her. She watched his glare shift with every move she made. She took a breath, wiping her sweaty palms down her jeans.

This was not the same man from last night, or even a few minutes ago. His whole demeanor took a turn, and all his softness was a thing of the past. She couldn't fault him, really. She had lied to him. He'd spent last night and tonight comforting her and trying to make things right, and she'd returned the favor by lying to his face. As odd as it was, he seemed almost offended, as though she'd broken his trust.

"We looked," she said, trying to gauge his reaction. He was giving her nothing, except his continued venomous glare. "B-but, I never showed anyone but Macy. No one else knows, and they won't. We aren't going to say anything. You have my word."

"Your word don't mean shit," Rourke snapped.

Macy piped in. "She's super trustworthy."

Rourke's glare immediately turned to Macy. "Your word means shit too."

Cheyenne glanced over at Macy, expecting to see the same fear she felt. The corner of Macy's lips curled as she stared back at Rourke.

"You're very tall."

What the hell was she talking about? They were in a dire situation, with three angry bikers who could possibly kill them, hide the bodies, and be eating pancakes by sunrise, and she was making small talk. She didn't really think Trax would do anything to harm them, but how well did she really know him?

"How tall are you?"

Rourke didn't respond, and the others seemed just as perplexed by her question.

"I'm only five-three, so most people are taller than me, except for kids, but you, man, you have to be at least, what, six-five, six-six?" She shrugged and chuckled. "You probably outweigh us by over a hundred plus pounds, and well, let's be honest, one punch to the temple, and we'd be well on our way to the pearly gates." She cocked her brow. "Do you really think we are gonna say anything, knowing you know where we live and who we are and we are well aware of what you all could do to us if we opened our mouths?"

Gage chuckled. "She's got a point, man."

Macy pointed at Gage. "See, he gets it. We aren't gonna say anything to anyone. And really, besides a finger and some cash, we don't know shit. Look, believe it or not, and I'm sure you can't tell by our apartment, but we have pretty decent lives. We aren't looking to jeopardize it."

Trax seemed to be resolved by her speech. *Thank you, Macy.* Cheyenne breathed a sigh of relief. It was short lived. The thing about Macy? She never did know when to stop talking, as she proved with her next admission.

"And as for the guy driving, she barely saw him. I mean, brown hair, brown eyes, and a scar down his forehead?" She shrugged. "That could be anybody."

Oh fuck!

Trax jerked his head and stepped forward. "You said you didn't see him." He lunged forward, grasping her arm in a tight hold and yanked her up against his body. She reached out, about to lose her balance, and gripped his chest. Her heart spiked, and her lower lip trembled as she shook her head.

"I-It was so quick I didn't get a great look, I swear."

"Yeah? 'Cause the description she just fucking gave was pretty detailed."

Macy shot up and wedged her hand between them, pulling on Chey's arm. "Let go of her, asshole," she shouted, and Trax gripped her wrist.

"Rourke."

Suddenly, Macy was gone, and he pulled her into him again, his eyes furious and black as night. "You fucking lied to me." His guttural tone made her skin prickle. "Now, you got two choices. You can either give me the details and I let you go, or you can fucking lie again, and I can send your friend in the bedroom with Rourke and Gage, and you can sit here while she screams. Your fucking choice."

What? Oh, my God. She had watched enough movies to sense what he referenced. She shook her head in complete panic mode and caught sight of Macy's pale face. "No, um, I'll tell you. I only saw his face, but it was round, like maybe he was heavyset, and his eyes were brown, dark like yours." She bit her lip, racking her brain. Her heart racing almost made her breathing shallow. Her sweaty palms glided together as she twisted her hands against his chest. She glanced over her shoulder at Macy. The panic she saw on her friend's face brought her to tears. *Fucking think!* She closed her eyes, trying to see him in her mind.

"He had a beard, but only around his mouth and chin, and his nose was large or offset, like maybe he broke it once or twice." Her eyes burned and even closed tightly, she could feel the moisture. "His hair was brown, longer, maybe shoulder length and thin, like scraggly."

"The scar?" His voice sent her heart racing.

Think.

"It was red and raised, I think from his hairline over his left eye and down into his eyebrow. Maybe even into his lid."

A tear escaped down her cheek as she stared back at him. He wasn't looking at her. His head was cocked over his shoulder. Gage and Rourke stared back at him with expressions she couldn't understand. Trax turned back and leaned into her space.

"I find out you know more, and you aren't saying? I'll come back." He narrowed his eyes. "And they'll come back. You hear me?"

Another tear escaped as she nodded. He released her, and she staggered back against the couch. Trax turned and walked to the door with the other men following. As the door closed, she jerked her head to the wall and saw Macy staring back at her.

"Looks like you're finally getting your wish." She sighed and leaned against the wall. "We are fucking moving."

NO ONE SAID a word as they made their way to the bikes and back to the clubhouse. Trax was too hyped up and riddled with guilt to utter a word. That was a fucking shit show and not how he had planned to spend his fucking night. By now, he was supposed to be balls deep in her pussy, making her scream for God. Instead, he'd left her on the verge of pissing her pants with fear. Never in his life had he been so ashamed of how he had treated another human being as he was at this moment. *Fuck.*

They pulled into the rear driveway and parked near the door, blocking the few cars lined up in the spots. It only added to his frustration. He dismounted and didn't wait for the others to follow. The party was big tonight, with a mass of bodies shuffling around the bar. He stopped and glanced around, looking for Kase.

A soft hand slid up to his bicep. "Hey, Trax."

He ripped his arm from her hold and glared down at the topless blonde. "Touch me again, and I'll have your ass thrown out." He was pushed forward, and Gage's voice rang in his ear. "Back corner."

Trax followed the direction and saw Kase sitting at a table. Nadia was on his lap with her legs spread wide. No need for a look to see what was shoved between them. Sensing their arrival, Kase glanced up, and his serene face immediately tightened. He stood, moving Nadia to the side, and made his way into the back.

Trax didn't know if Rourke or Gage had given him the heads up, but Kase knew something was going on. They filed into the room, and the last man closed the door.

"What's the problem?"

"She saw him," Gage said, taking a seat at the table. "Gave a pretty detailed description." Gage cocked his brow. "My guess, it's Gallow."

Kase jerked his head to Trax. "She fucking saw him? Bitch said she didn't see shit."

Trax clenched his jaw at his reference to her. He cleared his throat. "Yeah, she saw him."

"And she just gave this up now? Why the fuck didn't she say anything before?"

Trax shrugged, gripping the back of the chair in front of him. Cheyenne had no reason to trust any of them. Maybe she figured if she gave up the driver, he'd come looking for her. It was a thought that hadn't crossed his mind while he'd threatened her and her friend. God, the look on her face played over in his head as he gripped hard on the wood.

"So, the cunt just up and admits she saw him and gives full disclosure. Why now?"

Gage raised his brows. "Trax was pretty persuasive. Turns out nothing gets little Chey talking like a threat to her friend."

Trax's blood boiled, and he shifted his glare to Gage, who merely raised his brows. "Fuck you. I said what I had to say."

"I know, man, you got the info." He raised his brows and nodded. "Well done, brother." Sarcasm riddled his tone.

Kase slammed his hand onto the table. "I don't give a shit what you had to say. Need you to get her inside here. I want her to see him before we carry this shit out. Girl is a fucking moron to begin with. Don't need her pinning Mick's death on someone without her taking a look at him and identifying Gallow."

Gage laughed. "Good luck with that. Those two are probably on a plane to fucking Tahiti right now." He eyed Trax. "Or the fucking cops."

"Fuck," Kase snapped. "What the hell are we dealing with here, Trax?"

Rourke stepped forward. "She won't talk, neither will the friend. Too fucking scared." His growl was menacing. "Trax made sure of it."

Kase nodded. "Tomorrow night. Get her in here."

Trax's body tightened. "No, she's outta this. She gave us Gallow, I'm not bringing her in here."

Kase turned slowly, eyeing Trax. He'd never told his president no in the past. Kase scowled.

"The fuck you aren't. I want her ass here."

"Why? She gave us all she had."

Kase tilted his head and sneered. "I want her here, Trax. If she's not, I'll bring her in myself." Kase charged out the door, and Trax was left with Rourke and Gage.

Gage stood and passed without a word. Trax turned, following him out but stopped when Rourke stepped into his path. They'd been tighter than most of the brothers along with Gage. No man, other than Mick, did Trax respect and trust more than Rourke. Trax had fucked up tonight. Threatening women was not his usual MO.

"Don't ever threaten her friend with me again, brother."

"Wasn't planned." Trax had no reasonable response. What he'd done was unacceptable. He drew in a breath, feeling the weight of his guilt. "Needed her to talk, man. You saw her."

Rourke glared. "Yeah, I fucking saw. Know what else I fucking saw? A girl scared outta her mind, thinking I was going to fucking rape her."

Trax stalked forward. "I never said rape."

Rourke's brows furrowed, and his eyes darkened. Trax knew the look. "No, you didn't say it." His jaw tightened. "But you knew damn well where her mind went. Where Macy's mind went."

Trax slowed his breathing, rallying in his anger, which now was directed at himself. It was a fucked-up move, especially after what Cheyenne had gone through being attacked two nights in a row.

Rourke stared him down. "You ever hold a woman who is shaking, on the verge of passing out from fear? I did tonight." He turned to the door but looked back. "You ever scare her again like you did tonight and use me to do it? I'll fucking kill you, brother or no brother."

He'd fucked up, and he understood where Rourke was coming from, but a heated possession ran through his blood. Cheyenne didn't need protection from him. No other man would stake any claim to her but him.

"Cheyenne ain't your concern, Rourke."

His brows furrowed. "Not talking about Cheyenne." He walked out of the room, and Macy popped in his head. While he wasn't proud of what he'd done, his only concern and regret had been how Cheyenne felt. He gave no thought to how Macy would react. But Rourke did.

In all the years they'd been brothers, this was the only time he could ever remember Rourke taking up for a woman. He fucked them but never so much as mingled or talked with them, and when it came time to have one's back, he never stepped in.

Until tonight. Until Macy.

Trax leaned against the wall, resting his head back and closing his eyes. His behavior was unjustifiable. He'd allowed his desire to find Mick's killer surpass his human decency. The look in her eyes and in Macy's was wreaking havoc in his head.

It was unforgivable.

Chapter 8

Cheyenne fumbled with her car keys while resting her head against her shoulder, holding the phone in place. This was a disaster. Oversleeping was usually reserved for people who woke up in the morning, not her. How she had slept through her alarm set for four thirty in the afternoon? She skipped the last step on the walk and was barely able to recover, curling her ankle and cursing. "Dammit."

"Hello?" Her boss had just picked up.

"Jess, oh God, I overslept, stupid cell phone alarm." She fingered her key ring, yanking it from her bag. "I'm on my way right now, I'll be there in…"

"Slow down, Chey, and relax. I got Paige to cover your shift."

She stopped and gripped the phone. "But I can be there in twenty minutes, and I'm only…" She glanced at her phone, and her stomach dropped. "Two hours late."

Jess laughed. "Yeah, I figured when you hadn't come in something came up."

"Ah hell, I'm sorry."

"Girl, not a big deal. You been working for me three years now and never been late or called out. Made a call to Macy when ya didn't show. She told me you had a rough night. Not gonna ask, but you get to take time off, Chey."

Rough night was an understatement. She sighed, and her shoulders slumped. She should have listened to Macy's voicemail.

"This is...damn, I'm sorry."

"Chey, baby, I get it. Calm down, go back to bed, or better yet, get out and have fun. You work too much anyway. It's probably my own fault, giving you such a kickass place to work."

Cheyenne smiled. Working for Jess was awesome. Being a waitress at a bar was certainly not her life's ambition, but it was perfect for this stage. It allowed her the days, usually, to fill orders for her and Macy's side business. All their extra cash went into savings for their future storefront.

"You sure I can't come in and relieve Paige?"

"Trust me, she was ecstatic getting a night shift, you know, tips and all. She'd probably be pissed if you show up and take it away from her now. Go do something fun. Boss's orders. I'll see you tomorrow night."

"All right. Later, Jess."

"Bye."

She clicked her phone and stood a few feet from her car. Do something fun? She couldn't remember the last time she did anything fun. With Macy out with Jason, there wasn't an option for a girls' night. Most of her other friends worked at the bar with her or had husbands and kids.

She swung her keys from her finger, eyeing her car. It was a shame to just go back inside when she was already dressed and ready to go out. She cocked her head back and forth and scanned the car coming into the lot. It pulled into a vacant spot at the end.

She caught sight of a figure a few feet away and gasped. Parked two spots down was a motorcycle with a familiar man draped in a leather cut. His gaze was directly on her, though he made no move to get off his bike. She was pretty sure she could make it back to the building before he could, but then again, she thought she could outrun the guys from last night too.

"Shit." She ducked her head and turned her back. Why the hell was he there? She'd given him everything. Damn, she should have gone to the police last night the second they'd left. Her finger twitched against her keys.

Her best bet would be to get into her car and leave. With a full tank of gas, she could drive for hours.

Go now! She rushed to her car, glancing over her shoulder, but stopped. His motorcycle was parked in the spot, but he was nowhere to be seen. She jerked her head to the left. Nothing. Where the hell had he gone?

"Hey."

She jumped forward as her heart lunged into her throat, and she gasped for a breath. His hand landed on her arm, and she instinctively ripped it from his hold, swinging around and losing her footing. She spread out her arms for balance, but it was too late. She felt herself falling back and braced for impact. Her hands darted down to the ground on her sides, but her ass made contact first with the gravel.

"Fuck." Trax rushed forward, but she scurried back on her hands and legs, essentially doing a crab walk.

"Stay back," she snapped. It was meant to sound authoritative but came out more like a desperate plea. He immediately halted and raised his hands. His eyes narrowed, and his gaze locked on her stare. She drew in a breath and licked her lips. "I'll scream if you come any closer."

Something happened. His eyes drew down to the ground, and his head shifted across the lot. It was impossible to miss his hushed curse. It seemed to be directed more to himself than her. Trax rested his hands on his hips. He wasn't looking, but she was. Like a hawk with prey, she refused to look away. If he was going to do something, she wanted to see it coming.

"Not gonna hurt ya, Chey."

Her heart pounded so heavy her breathing labored. She swallowed the lump in her throat. "That's not what you said last night."

His gaze darted to hers. The corners of his eyes crinkled, but not from smiling. His tense lips pursed. "I fucked up last night. That's why I'm here now."

She snorted and crawled back another inch on her hands and feet. "I don't need an apology. I just need you to go away and leave me alone."

"Fuck, let me just help you up." He approached her, and she panicked. She scrambled to get up without giving him her back, which was impossible. His hands gripped her forearms, and she struggled, but her strength, or lack of, was no match for his. He lifted her as if she weighed nothing. "Relax, I said I'm not gonna hurt ya."

That was rich, coming from a man who'd threatened her less than twenty-four hours prior. How could she have been so damn stupid?

She pulled her arms from his hold, but he didn't let go. "Yeah, and I'd believe you 'cause you're so damn trustworthy. Get your hands off me." Her tone raised to a high pitch. Surely, anyone would back away, not wanting to garner unwanted attention. Trax tightened his grip and leaned forward.

"I'm sorry for last night. You pissed me off."

She raised her eyebrows. "Oh? Is that the new standard? Someone pisses you off, and you threaten them with bodily harm." She leaned closer. She wasn't sure where all her courage came from, but she went with it. "Good to know. Now, can you please get your fucking hands off me?" She twisted her body in hopes of loosening his grip. His eyes darkened, but he released her and stepped back. It was a small gap of separation. If she tried to run, he'd only have to reach out, and she'd be locked in his hold again.

She drew in a breath and scanned the lot. *No one. Damn.*

"Chey?"

She slowly glanced at him again suspiciously.

"I was a dick last night."

She squinted her eyes. "Understatement."

He sighed and his jaw tightened, but his chin dipped in a shallow nod. "Yeah, it is. I got no right to ask you to hear me out or forgive me. The way things went down, the shit I pulled?" He inhaled. "Unforgivable, and I know it."

Cheyenne bit her lip and shifted on her feet. This was not at all what she had expected. Not knowing how to respond, she remained silent and watched him.

"Look, I don't expect you to understand, but this thing with Mick." He paused, seemingly conflicted with his choice of words. "It's on me. Losing him…" Trax dropped his head, hiding his face, but he couldn't mask the sorrow in his voice. Taking on another's pain wasn't something she was accustomed to feeling, but it was so raw with Trax. His voice changed saying his name, and his throat bobbed. She hadn't fully grasped the magnitude of Trax's loss until now. *Do not feel bad for him, Chey.*

"Finding the person who went after Mick is what I gotta do, for the club, for Meg." He glanced away. "For me." She lifted her hand, reaching toward him, but quickly pulled back and tucked it into her pocket. Comforting Trax after everything he'd put her through last night was not a smart decision. However, he didn't seem like the same man.

His gaze lifted back to her. "I fucked up last night when I heard you really saw the guy. My head just went to you standing in the way of finding him. Like you picked a side," he paused, "and it wasn't mine."

Why the hell was she feeling compassion and a sense of guilt here? Probably because the man in front of her had saved her ass last night. And while his tact was appalling and horrifying, she could understand it better. She now knew where his head was at. It didn't excuse his behavior from last night, but at least she understood why he acted the way he had.

And he saved my ass last night.

"Would they have hurt Macy? Your guys?"

Trax flinched and released a soft curse. "No, Chey, I swear. Even if I asked them to, which I wouldn't have, they never would have hurt her, I promise ya. I get the persona that comes with the club, and I was an asshole, but we don't hurt women." He dragged his hand over his face. "Caught a lot shit for pulling that stunt. I deserved it. It was fucked up."

There was no denying his sincerity. Given a better understanding of why he'd done what he'd done, Cheyenne could bring herself to forgive him. A strange part of her desperately wanted to forgive him.

"Look, I only saw him for a few seconds." It was a cop out. She could have given him the details, but she kept her mouth shut. After opening the envelope, she'd realized the situation was well beyond a routine car accident. She didn't want to be involved any more than she already was, which was too much.

She sighed. "I was scared. I don't have an entire club backing me, Trax. It's just me, and if this guy finds out who I am, then what?"

"I get it." He nodded.

"Do you?"

"Yeah, but here's what you don't get. Wouldn't let ya get hurt. What you did for Mick, the least I can do is keep you safe."

She snorted at the irony of his statement. "Newsflash, Trax, I got hurt. The favor, remember?" She intended it as a joke, but he obviously found no humor with it.

His face tightened, and his jaw locked. "I remember." His gaze scanned her face, mainly her right side where the bruises were still visible. She shifted her feet, feeling oddly exposed under his stare. His gaze hardened, and there was a glimmer of something harsh. Regret maybe? She sucked in a breath when she recognized the look of guilt. *Shit!* It wasn't his fault his guys fucked up, and he did fulfill his promise of keeping her safe, eventually.

This whole situation was screwed up, and she was set to be done with it.

"Look." She licked her lips. "You got what ya needed. I don't have anything else to share, I swear. But if I think of anything else, I'll reach out, okay?"

He stared back at her, giving her no indication of what he was thinking. Why wouldn't he just leave? She sighed and walked toward him, giving a large berth between them. Right now, all she needed was to go back to the apartment, lock her doors, and rid her mind of everything about Trax and his club. It was the sensible decision. He was the last person she should get tangled up with, even if the thought of being with him had her breath hitching. No, tell him to fuck off and walk away. She bit her lip, unable to move. She didn't want to. Why couldn't she just leave? If he were a simple man, it would be easy. Trax seemed to have too many sides to him. One minute, he was aggressive and threatening. A side she could rationally walk away from. However, when he was gentle and kind, she felt her own resistance. *God, be a total dick or a good guy, not somewhere in between.*

He moved forward but didn't touch her. "Take a ride with me?"

She jerked her head. He couldn't possibly think she'd go anywhere with him. Could he? "No way." She continued to the steps, feeling his presence close behind her.

"There's a view over in Eagle Hill I wanna show you. Come on." He started off through the lot. She halted, realizing he expected her to follow him.

"I just said no, Trax."

He glanced over his shoulder and smirked. "You wanna see it, babe, trust me. Come on. Gotta get there before the sun sets."

She channeled her inner four-year-old and stomped her foot. "I said I'm not going."

He smiled. *Damn his smile.* This guy was almost too sexy to resist. *Almost.* She wasn't going anywhere with him. She folded her arms, taking her strong stance. She would not cave just because a hot biker wanted to take her on a ride on his motorcycle. Such a cliché. Let some other twit be enamored by him and his friggin' leather. It wasn't going to be her.

"But you want to. Trying to think of a million reasons not to, but deep down, you wanna come with me."

Come with me. Those three words meant more than one thing, and she knew it. He'd probably said it to a dozen girls, and they'd all fallen for it. He was a beautiful man. Take away the harsh leather and the brooding scowl, which only added to his sexiness, and she was left with dark eyes, a square jaw, and cheekbones to rival any cover model. *Damn.*

She shook her head but remained quiet. She didn't trust herself if she opened her mouth. His lips pursed together in a tight smile as if he knew what she was thinking. He raised his brows, and she got the sense he was amused. Trax shoved his hands into his jean pockets and stretched his neck, taking a deep breath before making his way to her. This time she didn't back away.

"Wanna tell me why?"

She stared at him. "Are you seriously asking me that?" She mimicked his stance of shoulders back and hands in pockets. His gaze trailed down her body to her waist, and the corner of his mouth curved.

"I said I was sorry, Chey." He sounded so sincere with his light tone. *It's a trap, don't fall for it.*

"Sorry doesn't cancel out everything. You threatened me and Macy last night, not to mention you manhandled me."

"Did I hurt you?"

"Well, no but…"

He stepped closer, leaving a foot-length gap between them. "I was pissed, I'll admit it, but even with a heart full of rage, I'd never hurt you. I knew exactly how tight my hold was, enough to scare you but not to hurt you."

She raised her brows. "So scaring me is okay?"

"I needed answers. Doesn't make it right." He cocked his head to the side. "Not willing to forgive me?"

She sighed. She had forgiven him a few minutes ago. Forgiveness was one thing, taking off with him was another. She dropped her gaze to the concrete and toed the loose gravel in the lot. Staring into his dark eyes was not a smart option. She'd cave because deep down in her reckless heart, she really did want to take the ride with him. She gazed up through her lashes and laughed without an ounce of humor.

"Why me? Why are you so interested in taking me for a ride, Trax?"

He shrugged, and the corner of his mouth curled. "I like you."

She snorted. "You don't even know me."

He bridged the gap between them, and her heart raced, pounding erratically. Without even touching, his body did something to her. "You're fucking gorgeous, sexy as hell."

"Trax…"

He gave her no time to finish her sentence. His hands wrapped around her waist, pulling her gently against his chest, and she went willingly. His head bent toward her ear. "You stopped to help some guy you didn't know. A guy most people wouldn't even have called in for. But you stopped, held his hand." His breath heated over the shell of her ear, and he whispered, "Wasn't there, but knowing you, and yeah, Chey, I know you. Bet you talked to him in your sweet voice, telling him to be strong and hold on. Bet the sound of your voice comforted him until his last breath." His tone changed to a solemn whisper. "The night those fuckers messed with you, and you came into the club with fire ready to torch our asses, fucking fearless. All the shit you've gone through, and you're still standing." His nose skimmed across her jaw until his forehead rested against hers. "That's what I like, Chey."

God, why was he doing this to her?

"Come with me," he whispered.

She closed her eyes, trying to resist. *No. No. No!*

His lips grazed the shell of her ear. "Please."

Am I even considering this?

He chuckled. "Yeah, you are."

Her face heated, and she squeezed her eyes tighter. *Shit, I said that out loud. Real smooth, Chey.*

He pressed a slow, soft kiss against her lips. "You're thinking too much. Just come with me."

Her eyes flicked open, catching sight of his cheek and hair curling around his ear. "Promise me it's just a ride, no killing me and hiding the body so my family has nothing to bury?"

He stilled and pulled away a few inches. He tilted his head and pursed his lips. "You watch a lot of crime shows, huh?"

"Maybe."

He nodded and smiled. "I promise to take care of you. No one's gonna hurt you, including myself. Fuck, you just keep adding shit to the list."

"What list?"

"Shit I like about you."

Well, that was kinda nice, in a very odd way. She drew in a breath and bit her lip.

"Okay, I'll go."

He grinned and reached out for her hand, but she stepped back. "Give me your driver's license."

He flinched, and his brows furrowed. "What?"

She drew in a breath. "Give me your license. It has your name on it, right, with your address?"

She expected him to decline or even a bit of hesitation, but Trax gave neither. He reached into his back pocket, opened his wallet, and pulled out the plastic square, handing it to her. She didn't miss his smile either. She grabbed it quickly and looked down. Derrick Traxon.

She smirked. "Derrick?"

His eyes crinkled. "Yeah." He shifted on his feet, crossing his arms over his chest. "You got my info, Chey. Would I give it to you if I was gonna hurt ya?"

She sighed. "Probably not." She bit her lip and stared at him. A thought popped into her head, and she reached into her bag for her phone. She pulled up her boss's name and texted, telling her she was going out with a guy and snapped a picture of his license in the text. She could have sent it to Macy, but she had the feeling Macy would not approve of this date.

She got an immediate reply from her boss. *Damn, girl, he's freakin' gorgeous. Have fun. Wear a helmet and a condom.*

Chey chuckled.

"We good now?"

She glanced up at Trax, who was clearly amused by her safety measures. Cheyenne nodded and gave him back his license. He snagged her hand and stepped away, pulling her with him toward his bike across the lot.

HE'D HAD women on the back of his bike before. He didn't hold the spot sacred like some of his brothers had. It was a fucking ride, not a status symbol. It didn't mean shit. Until now. Only with one other woman, his ex, did he have the feeling of wanting a woman on his bike to actually mean something. Cheyenne was awkward, not holding on to his waist as tight as most women would have. She made a point of scooting back so her legs didn't lie against his.

Fuck no, he wasn't having any of that. He wanted her pressed against him. He'd shifted gears purposely to force her against his back. By the third time, she seemed to get the message, not bothering to readjust herself. Somewhere along the ride, she moved her hands from his shoulders to his waist. Fucking perfect.

The ride was too short for his liking. He could get used to her arms wrapped around his waist. Preferably naked, but he wouldn't complain about this either. As he skirted the hill, she clung to him, her fingers digging into his leather. The view would be worth it, but the ride wasn't for the faint of heart. He took the turns slower than usual to keep her calm. He could tell without looking each time she looked over the cliff. Her arms would tighten around his stomach, and she'd move her head closer to his shoulder. He smirked. He'd bet his next paycheck her eyes were glued shut.

It was late in the day, and the sun was setting. They wouldn't catch the whole view, but even the partial was impressive. He pulled into the open, empty lot and then turned off the ignition. He was prepped to tell her how to get off when her hands came to his shoulders, and she dismounted. He released the kickstand and steadied the bike before swinging his leg over the seat and straightening. He watched as she unstrapped the helmet and then shook her hair out. Her hand drove through her dark locks and stopped in mid-strand.

She twisted her lips. "Oh, that sucks."

Trax smirked. "Knots. Gotta tie it back next time."

She gave him a side glance. "How do ya know there will be a next time?"

Such a smartass. He grasped her hand, threading his fingers through hers, and tugged her into his side, bringing his mouth down to hers for a kiss. He was quick, not giving her any chance to pull away. When he pulled back, her cheeks were heated, and she remained silent.

"Come on." He kept hold of her hand. Holding hands? Who the fuck was he? He couldn't remember the last time he held a woman's hand. Even back with his ex. She wasn't big on affection in public, at least not with him. Cheyenne was different, though. She seemed to tighten her grip with the pads of her fingers sliding over his skin. He caught the faint caress over his knuckles. The innocent touch shot straight down to his dick.

"How far is it?"

"Just up the bend."

They walked a few more yards, and the woods opened to the view over the skyline. He traveled a lot with the club, had taken more than his share of road trips, but nothing compared to the view of the canyon.

"Wow, this is amazing." Her tone was pure awe, and she released his hand, moving closer to the edge. He mirrored her steps in case he needed to grab her. The drop was deadly. He waited for her to say something, but she stood, gazing out at the view, a serene smile spread across her lips. She shifted and moved to the ground, taking a seat close to the edge. She patted the spot next to her, glancing up. He sat, resting back on his hands while she sat straight with her legs crossed.

"I'm surprised they don't close the park."

"They do, babe."

"When?"

"About an hour ago."

She jerked her head. "How'd we get in, then?"

"Back entrance. They leave it unlocked for the night ranger."

"So, are we trespassing?" Her face paled. "Are we breaking the law? Oh God, can we go to jail for this?"

Her face was too amusing, and he couldn't contain himself. He laughed, shaking his head. "Yes, yes, and maybe, but chances are we'd get off with a warning." He leaned closer. "Afraid of doing time?"

Her eyes widened. "Uh, yeah. Can you imagine me in prison? They'd eat me alive."

Trax scoffed. "You're tough. You'd survive."

She snorted and then giggled. "No way. I'd probably wind up someone's bitch and cry in a corner the whole time."

Trax watched her face. She was weird but in a highly amusing way. "You'd find out what you're made of in jail. I'm thinking you'd surprise yourself."

"Talking from experience?"

Trax looked out over the mountains. For some, going to jail was a badge of honor. Not him. He wasn't proud, but it was part of the life he chose.

"Have you been to jail?"

Ignoring her wasn't an option, he guessed. He turned to her and saw how her easygoing face had transformed. Small lines marred her forehead, and her eyes were intently stuck on him.

"Yeah, couple years ago. Did eighteen months."

Her bottom lip dropped open, and she whispered, "What did you do?"

"Transporting drugs."

She leaned back. "You do drugs?"

He smirked. "Nothing hard, but yeah, I smoke some weed, on occasion. Not why I got time, though. The club was transporting across state lines."

"Oh." She twisted her hands in her lap. "I guess to sell, right?"

He nodded.

"What was prison like?"

"It fucking sucked. Just like you imagine but a hundred times worse. Fights, murders, rapes, everything you see on TV, it fucking happens. You're a fucking caged animal in there, got people telling you when to eat, sleep, and shit. Eighteen months felt like eighteen years." He sighed. "But I had Mick and Rourke with me. We survived." He turned his head and winked. "You would too."

She snorted and laughed. "I don't wanna test your theory." She bunched up her legs and rested her arms on her knees. "So, you and Mick were close, huh?"

"Yeah. He brought me into the club, mentoring shit. He was a good guy."

She rested her head on her arms and smiled. "I bet he was. He had kind eyes." She nodded. "And as much as it was only a short time when I was with him, I knew he was someone who was going to be missed. I'm really sorry you lost him, Trax."

Her compassion stabbed him in a part of his heart he'd thought was locked up and cold as ice. He hadn't opened up to anyone about his loss for Mick. His brothers knew, Meg knew, but everyone let him do it alone because that was how he was. And here was this stranger, trying to get inside with her sweetness. He stared back at her, and her smile grew.

"He'd probably get a kick out of us together, enjoying a sunset. Don't ya think?"

He would. He'd be saying, *she's too good for you, so you trap her down before she realizes it, man. Knock her up if you have to, but do not let this one go.* Trax laughed and leaned forward, taking her lips for a kiss. He hadn't planned on it being anything more. Not even an hour ago, she'd been in fear for her life with him. If he wanted her, and he did, he'd have to do something he'd never done before. Take it fucking slow.

He cupped her jaw with every intention of pulling away, but it seemed she had a different idea. Her legs collapsed over his, and she leaned into the kiss, twisting her body to line up against him. Her tongue curled around his, and the heat from the kiss shot straight to his cock. He couldn't remember the last time he'd wanted a woman as much as he wanted Cheyenne.

She hooked her leg over his lap and straddled him, deepening the kiss in the process. His hands trailed down her back, grabbing her ass. Fuck, she was perfect. A soft moan emitted through her lips. The sound alone got him harder, and when she rubbed her jean-clad pussy against his length, he found it hard to hold back his own groan. Not fucking her wasn't an option. He needed to be inside her. He hooked his arm around her waist and turned, flipping her onto her back. It was smoother than he'd expected. Her hands were everywhere, a soft but urgent caress on his neck, over his shoulder, and through the back of his hair.

He felt himself losing control. His free hand grasped her breast, squeezing and getting the response he wanted. Her chest heaved into his palm, begging for more. Through her padded bra, he could barely feel her breast, and certainly not her nipple. Why women bothered with it was beyond his comprehension. Bras should be fucking outlawed. Her fingers frantically moved past his chest, down to his cock. Even through his jeans, he felt the touch as she rubbed her palm over his length. Damn the fucking seam. Her hand fumbled with his snap, desperately trying to unsnap it.

He grabbed her wrist and broke the kiss, turning his head to the side. Her heavy breath fanned his ear in short pants.

"Why'd you stop?"

He glanced down at her and cursed himself. Seeing the heat and desire in her eyes was hard to resist. "Not gonna fuck you on the dirt."

If it had been any other chick, he would have been balls deep, not giving a shit if she had dirt in her ass crack or rocks jamming into her back. Taking Cheyenne that way wasn't happening. He reluctantly pulled away, standing and reaching out to take her hand. He didn't miss the blush across her cheeks. She might have taken his stopping the wrong way. She clasped her hand into his but stared down at the ground and dusted off her backside with her free hand.

It had been forever since he'd seen a woman blush. There was a sweet innocence to it he rarely saw from the women at the club. Cheyenne wasn't hard or jaded. He'd need to keep that fresh in his mind. She wasn't like the others.

His cock strained against his jeans painfully. *Fuck!* He adjusted his stance, but it did nothing to relieve the pressure in his pants. She pulled her hand, but he tightened his grip. She peeked up at him through her lashes, shyly. Just the look of uncertainty had him about to go back on his word. Kind of. He wasn't gonna take her in the dirt. She deserved better.

There were other options, and he was going to fucking take one.

He stepped into her space, and her eyes widened. Eyes way too big for her face gave her a cartoonish, sweet look. He hooked both arms around her waist and lifted so her feet dangled. He immediately took her lips as he walked to the spot, he'd eyed a few seconds ago. When her back came against the tree, he lowered her to the ground and steadied her on her feet, never breaking away from the kiss. He unsnapped her jeans in record time and hooked his thumbs, pulling her them down her legs along with her panties. He broke the kiss to lift her legs and removed the pants.

She gasped, and he glanced up. If she told him to stop, he would. He'd hate every second and fight against every instinct to take her, but he'd stop. What he saw wasn't hesitation but heated desire. She swiped her bottom lip with her tongue.

She watched him now that he was at eye level with her exposed pussy. The corner of his mouth curled, and he inched forward, dragging his tongue over her lips. Her body twitched, and he licked her clit as her hips pushed forward. It was a plea for him. He'd never shied away from going down on a woman, he enjoyed it, but something about the way she looked at him—it excited him in a way it never had before. His cock grew harder as he tongued her pussy, hearing her panting and soft moans. He could make her come in less than a minute, but having her come all over his dick was too tempting. He flicked her nub vigorously.

"Trax." His name on her lips came out a breathy hush. He sucked her sensitive bead between his lips and grasped her thighs, feeling her tremble. Her hand curled into his hair. He half expected her to yank at his locks. Instead, she weaved her fingers through, giving Trax his own slight tremor.

He couldn't remember the last time he'd gotten so worked up to fuck a woman. It was always available and became a routine. With Cheyenne right now, he felt the true effects of wanting her so desperately his cock ached against his jeans. With a parting flick of her clit, he stood.

He barely had time to unsnap his own jeans when her hands pushed his away, and she fisted the seam of his pants and ripped them open. He quickly snagged his wallet to grab a rubber before she shucked down his pants, exposing his cock. Her hand wrapped around his length and tugged.

"Fuck." He groaned, and his head fell against his neck. He knew once she got her hands on him, it would be heaven, but nothing prepared him for the sheer ecstasy. Her palm was silk against his rigid cock. She jerked him slowly, a little unsure and awkward, making the sensation all the more powerful. He managed to rip open the wrapper just as her thumb slid over the crown of his cock. *Oh fuck, that felt good.* He nudged her hand away and sheathed himself in record time.

This would not be a long fuck. He'd be lucky if she came. He grabbed her thighs to hoist her up. She wrapped her legs around his waist, and he lined up his cock against her pussy. Her lips grazed his neck, licking and sucking, and he shoved his face against her neck, her hair tickling his nose, and he cocked his hips forward, sliding inside her with a groan. She was so wet, there was no hesitation as he slid deep inside her. Her walls tightened around his dick.

If she wanted this to last, she'd have to stop doing that. It felt too good. His hands curled over her ass, giving her a rough squeeze. It was a warning that went unheeded. She clasped his cock in a strangling hold. He had to move. He slowly withdrew and took his time, her hips in sync with each shift of his cock. She tightened her walls again, and he groaned with a small chuckle. "You keep doing that, and I'm gonna fucking come."

Her lips trailed over his cheek, and she whispered, "Isn't that the end goal?" He smiled and gripped her waist, digging his fingers into her flesh through her shirt.

"Want you to come with me." He licked her neck, fixating on her pulse. She moaned and curled her arms over his shoulders.

For as good as it felt, he wanted her naked, wanted to touch every inch of her skin with his hands and lips. He thrust forward in a sharp move, and she cried out. "Ahh, yeah. Right there."

He smiled against her neck. "There?" He thrust again, and her head fell back against the tree. He kissed her neck, licking a line up to her ear. "Yeah, there's the spot."

She moaned as he slid inside her again. "Trax."

Just the sound of his name on her lips was too much. He wanted to play with her, but his desire to come was greater. He rocked against her hips, feeling the tightening of her walls as her breathing labored, matching his own. His cock drove inside her, pounding her against the tree. For all the women he'd had, not one could compare to taking her in the middle of the woods. He pounded deeper and felt the tightening in his balls as he thrust forward and heard her moan so loud it echoed around the valley.

It was a sound he knew for sure. Her body trembled against him, and she hugged his shoulders, almost trying to crawl over him. He gripped her waist and fucked her until he locked into her pussy and came. Fuck. He jerked his cock once more and finished himself off.

Their breathing was rapid and pressed up against her chest, he felt her heart beating. It mirrored his own. She didn't say a word but hugged him closer, and he fell into her against the tree. It was an awkward position, but one neither of them was willing to break.

Against a tree was better than in the dirt, but he still wanted her in his bed. Over and over and over. This was not a one-time deal. This was the least likely woman to end up in his bed, in his house, or on the back of his bike, but it was happening. No fucking doubt about it. He was doing something he swore years ago he'd never do. Trax was claiming a woman again, and this time it was forever.

He caressed from her waist down her hip and under her thighs. He didn't miss the shiver and soft moan. He clutched her thighs, slowly lowering her legs to the ground. She was bound to be shaky and unsteady on her feet, so he carefully took her weight. She leaned against the tree with her head bowed. *Oh, hell no.*

There was no room for hiding. He clasped her neck in his palm and angled her chin up to face him. This was a sight he'd lock away in his memory. She was completely flushed with a dazed, lazy look in her eyes. He didn't wait for her to say anything. He pressed his mouth against her, kissing her intimately and slow.

She may have felt shy, but she returned his kiss with as much passion as he was giving. When she shivered again, he figured it had less to do with the kiss and more to do with being half naked on the ridge. The temperature had dropped, and the wind picked up. He reluctantly pulled away and bent down to retrieve his pants. Before she could do the same, Trax grasped the hem on her jeans around her ankles and lifted them. He dressed her and zipped her pants. He caught her dazed stare when he snapped her button.

The corner of her mouth curled. "Thank you."

"Welcome." He clasped his hand in hers, and they headed to the bike silently.

During the ride back, he sensed she tried to figure out how this would play out. She was too quiet, but she wrapped her arms around his waist and plastered her chest against him. Maybe she was just cold, or maybe she wanted to be close to him. He hoped for the latter.

He pulled up in front of her building and then shut off the engine. She gripped his shoulders and dismounted. They stood close as she removed her helmet.

She handed it to him with a shy smile. "Thanks for the ride." Her cheeks burned red, and he smirked.

He stored the helmet in his saddlebag and then reached into his pocket, pulling out his phone.

"Gimme your phone."

She eyed him suspiciously but reached into her bag.

"Put your number in mine, and I'll do the same."

He caught the small shock as her eyes widened, but she did what he'd said and then returned his phone. She teetered on her heels and stepped back.

"Okay, well, I should go in."

He nodded and waited. Most women would at least try for a kiss, but Cheyenne seemed too shy. She gave him a small wave and turned toward the stairs. He leaned forward, quickly grabbing her hand before she could get farther, and yanked her back against his chest. She gasped.

"Not gonna give me a kiss?"

"Oh," she gulped. "I didn't know...think..." She stumbled over her words, which was one of the cutest fucking things he'd ever seen. He smirked and decided to put her out of her awkward misery.

He took her lips, much to her surprise, and kissed her. His

hand released hers and curled around her waist, pressing her body against his chest. His tongue tangled against hers. She may have not been ready for it, but from the way she kissed him back, she had wanted it.

He considered blowing off tonight's meeting. If they didn't stop soon, he'd be dragging her up to her apartment and staying the night. Maybe two. When her hand curled around his neck, his muscles tensed. Her touch was soft. Softer than anything he'd ever felt.

She retreated slowly but leaned in again with a light kiss, then another. *Sweet.* Horny, sexy, bold, and aggressive were the women he usually spent time with, but never sweet. He realized he'd been missing out most of his life.

"You need to go before I throw ya on the back of my bike and take you to my bed," he said against her mouth. He felt her lips twitch.

"Yeah, I should go before I let ya."

He kissed her, and she stepped away. She drew in a breath and turned. He watched her walk up to the building and then get inside before he reversed. He glanced over his shoulder and caught sight of her in the doorway, looking at him.

He smiled the whole way back to the clubhouse.

Chapter 9

Cheyenne didn't have much faith Trax would actually call. She had hoped. Even considered calling him the next morning but didn't. *Desperate much?* Was it really desperate if he was the one who insisted they exchange numbers? He could have driven off without even a goodbye, something she'd considered on the ride back last night. If anything, he seemed to be stalling to spend more time with her.

"Stop obsessing," she shouted.

She took a deep breath and pulled up her computer. She had seventeen orders to fill and get shipped by the end of the day.

They had started the small business two years ago, getting connected to a few local vendors and starting up a site where they sold merchandise. Mostly candles, essential oils, and handmade jewelry. In the last few months, they had acquired a few pieces of clothing, which changed the game for them. They'd finally started to make a decent profit. One step closer to their storefront. *A small step.*

The living room looked like a war zone of products, boxes, and packing supplies. She had a hard time finding her phone when it rang. She leaned across the carpet and grasped it under a packing slip. She answered without looking, assuming it was Macy.

"I'm halfway done, but we're low on boxes, so you need to stop at the supply store on your way home." She grabbed a signature tag and the tie backs. "Oh, and I'm working tonight, so I'll get what I can done and shipped, but you need to do the rest when you get home." She sighed. "I'll get it to the post office in the morning."

The masculine chuckle on the other line had Cheyenne pulling the phone from her ear and scanning the caller. *Oh, my God.*

"One date and ya already making me your bitch boy?"

Her heart raced against her chest. She released a nervous laugh. "I thought you were Macy. Sorry."

He chuckled. "So, I don't have to stop at the supply store on my way home?"

She smiled at his teasing. "Not unless you want to get on my good side."

A soft growl had her shifting on the floor. The sound shot straight to her core.

"Oh, I want to get on all your sides, Chey." His tone suggested the naughtiest implications. Her cheeks heated, and her skin puckered in goosebumps.

She bit her lip. Macy loved to point out that Cheyenne had no game when it came to men and flirting. Her best friend was right. She scratched her head, thinking of a sexy rebuttal. She drew a complete blank. Luckily, Trax didn't make her suffer.

"What are ya doing?"

"Um, orders. I have a small business with Macy."

"Really? Thought you worked at the bar."

"I do, for now. But we're hoping it takes off. We want to get a store eventually, but for now, we sell out of the apartment."

"What do ya sell?" He laughed. "Sex toys?"

She laughed and shook her head. "Not even close. Some clothes, candles, jewelry. We have oils too, but not the ones you're thinking of."

"Ahhhh...you know me better than I thought."

It had been a while since she'd gotten giddy over talking with a man. She curled her knees up to her chest.

"What are you doing?"

He sighed. "Waiting on Rourke outside the clubhouse. Taking a ride up north for a few days."

Her heart plummeted. It was disappointing. She must have misread his call, or she was just jumping to conclusions. She thought for sure he'd wanna see her. She brushed away the hair from her cheek, hooking it over her ear.

"Well, have fun." She rolled her eyes. It was a lie. She actually hoped he had a horrible time and spent the days missing her. It was an irrational thought. Sex against a tree with a virtual stranger did not constitute a relationship. For all she knew, he'd left her the other night and went to the club to be with another woman. God knows, there wasn't a shortage of scantily clad beautiful women to take care of his needs. Probably more well-versed than Cheyenne.

He snorted. "Unlikely." He paused, and she heard the mumbling banter in the background. "Gotta go."

"Okay." Her shoulders slumped. Trax was not good for her ego, and neither was her insecure mind.

"When's your next night off?"

"Thursday."

"Good, I'll be back by then. I'm taking you out."

She straightened her back from her hunched position. "You are?"

He snickered. "Yeah, I am." His voice lowered. "One taste was not enough, Chey."

She clamped her lips. How the hell was she supposed to respond? Macy would have an awesome sexy comeback as would the girls from the club. Cheyenne, however, was a mute. She crinkled her nose. *Think of something.* She bit her lip. *Will I get my own taste this time?* The question shocked her mind. She'd never said anything like that to a man. She swallowed her breath, hoping the words would come out in a sexy purr as opposed to stuttering gibberish.

"Later, babe."

She squeezed her eyes shut. It was a lost opportunity. *Damn it.*

"Bye." She clicked the End button and then tossed the phone onto the carpet. She leaned back and lay down, covering her face with her hands.

Epic fail.

TRAX SCANNED HIS GARAGE. He was so fucking far behind with work. He was finally back from the three-day excursion up north. It had been a complete waste of time. The deal wasn't settled, and now his repairs were backed up. He'd be eating and sleeping in the garage for the next week to get caught up.

The balance between the club business and his money-making business teetered. It left little time for much else, which for once, didn't sit well with Trax. Adding Cheyenne into the mix was going to spread him real thin. It was worth it, though. He'd spent the better part of the run thinking of her and texting her. She'd been silent until the first night when he'd texted her. From then on, she'd send him random shit.

It became obvious, and he had to put up with a ribbing here and there from the guys. They were especially relentless went he got up to answer her call. He didn't give a shit. He'd take anything they sent his way just to hear her voice.

His phone rang twice before he wiped his hands and answered.

"Done." It was Rourke, and the one-word answer was all he needed.

"Fuck," he snapped, tossing the rag against the bike he worked on. "Told ya I didn't want this."

"Hands are fucking tied with this, man. Kase wanted it done."

Kase had brought up bugging Cheyenne's place during the

run. He was convinced she was still holding out. With enough members on board, he didn't get much of a say. Rourke had his back, but it still was only two against the rest of the club. Even Saint, who was usually the voice of reason, went along with Kase on it. His one stipulation was it be placed in the living area only; no bedroom or bathroom.

"You know this will come back to bite me in the fucking ass."

Rourke laughed. "No doubt, brother."

"Fuck." He ran his hand over his hair, tugging at the ends.

This would end badly if she ever found out. Bugging her place proved the mistrust the club had, and he was outnumbered with the decision. It was out of his hands. He could mention it to her, but it would have been a betrayal to the club. It wasn't even a consideration. *But betraying Cheyenne is an option?* Fuck, his balance was completely off with her in the picture.

"She coming tonight?"

"Yeah."

He'd talked her into meeting him at the club later on. She was hesitant, and he would have preferred to bring her himself, but they had a meeting before the party. Having her exposed to the club without him with her was not how he wanted her first party to go down. He'd be lucky if she didn't bolt after five minutes of the debauchery.

Kase had insisted on talking with her again. Trax would be at her side, hopefully putting her at ease. None of her past experiences with the club had ended well, but he'd make sure nothing went down. He'd have control of how Kase spoke to her this time. Hopefully, once Kase heard her description, he'd take out the bugs and she'd never find out. It wasn't the way he wanted this to go, but he had no choice.

"All right, see ya later."

"Later," Trax said and tossed his phone. It pinged just as it hit the chair in the corner. He grabbed it and smiled when he caught the name.

Chey: *What does a girl wear to a club party?*

Trax laughed and started to type.

Trax: *Nothing, if I'm lucky.*

Chey: *Not happening.*

Trax: *Whatever ya want, babe. But we like to lean toward the less is more concept at the club.*

He waited.

Chey: *I bet you do. LOL You sure ya can't pick me up?*

Trax sighed. She was nervous, and it struck him in his usual stone-cold heart. The meeting was mandatory. He couldn't miss it. He must have taken too long because she responded before he got the chance.

Chey: *It's okay.*

Trax: *You'll be fine, Chey. You tell the prospect at the door you're there to see me, and he'll let ya in.*

Chey: *Ok. See ya later.*

He shoved the phone into his back pocket. A bad feeling crept inside his gut. He shook off the premonition and got back to the bike he had been working on.

Chapter 10

"Grow some balls, Chey." She parked in the lot across from the clubhouse. She had made mistakes in her life, some bigger than others, but this was definitely on her top five. She should have demanded he pick her up.

It wasn't like her to balk at meeting a man somewhere. Usually, it was a first-date requirement of hers. There was nothing worse than wanting to bolt from a horrendous date and knowing they drove. She'd made the rookie mistake a few times. This wasn't different circumstances. She'd never had a date that began at a motorcycle clubhouse.

"God, shut up and go in already," she muttered. This wouldn't be the first time entering the club by herself. If anything, she should be more at ease now. At least she was invited tonight. She glanced up at the building. *Put your big girl panties on and go inside so Trax can rip them off.* She shook her head with a sharp snort.

She drew in a breath and got out of her car, chanting "You can do this," the entire walk up to the door. She knocked softly without getting an answer. The music pounded through the solid wall. She knocked again and moved down a step when the door swung open.

The long-haired man grimaced and scanned the area behind her. "What?"

She swallowed her breath. "Is Trax here?"

"Why?"

She flinched at his tone. Who was he to ask any questions? She was invited. A simple yes or no would have been cordial and sufficient. "Why?"

He stepped forward, sending her down another step. "Yeah, fucking why?"

"Um...h-he..." Why was she stuttering? "He asked me to come?"

The corner of his mouth twisted. "Yeah, and can you come on command?" His gaze traveled down her body. "Like to see that."

She furrowed her brows. *Asshole.* "If he's here, can you just tell him Cheyenne is here."

His gaze stopped at her breasts but not from ogling. He seemed almost frozen. His gaze darted up to meet hers, and his face tensed. "Shit, get in here." He stepped inside, widening the door for her to enter. She put a wide berth between them. This man made her nervous. She turned to him once she'd made it inside the hallway. He jutted his chin toward the bar. "He's back there."

She nodded and walked down the hall but halted when she heard her name.

"Don't tell him I was fucking around with you, all right? Wouldn't have done it if ya told me who you were."

Her brows furrowed in confusion. "Okay, I won't." She turned again, not understanding why Trax would even care.

When she breached the hallway, all thoughts stopped as she scanned the room. It was packed with people, mostly half-dressed women and obvious bikers. She'd never seen so much leather or exposed flesh in one place. Finding Trax was going to be like searching for a needle in a haystack. She surveyed the dimly lit area.

So, this is what live porn looks like? A topless woman was on her knees, giving a blowjob to one man standing and jerking off another who sat at the table. *What the fuck?*

When the man receiving head glanced over, she quickly jerked her body in the opposite direction. She'd never considered herself a voyeur, but then again, she'd never witnessed people engaging in sexual acts in public.

She fiddled with her fingers, feeling the heavy stares aimed at her. Where the hell was Trax? The dim lighting made it difficult to see. It also didn't help they all wore similar attire. A small group parted, and she raised onto her tippy toes at the same time as her stomach dropped.

Trax stood at the bar, his arm hooked around the waist of a petite blonde. It seemed fruitless for the woman to even be wearing a shirt. Her neckline was non-existent, and her breasts were dangerously close to popping out. The woman was curled into his side, and when she turned her head, smiling, she whispered something into his ear. Cheyenne felt a heated fury course through her blood. It only intensified when he laughed and tugged her in closer as his hand dragged lower down just above her ass.

She stood frozen with her stare glued to his hand. She should have expected this, should have at least suspected he wasn't a one-woman man. Everything she had with him since the moment they'd met had been hot and cold, right and wrong, legal and illegal. There wasn't a normal or average to any of their interactions. She'd been a fool to think that beyond sex Trax would want anything more. All the signs pointed to something like this happening. Yet there she was, blindsided by the pure disappointment. She would have preferred anger and rage over the emotions swirling through her body now. Screaming and throwing things would've released pent-up anger. But hurt and betrayal cut deeper. It lingered without outlet.

"So stupid." She clamped her lips, realizing she'd said it out loud.

What had she expected? This wasn't a nice guy who wanted to

date her, meet her family, spend nights in bed watching movies with her. Her face heated, and she jerked her gaze to the dirty floor. *Stupid.* She contemplated her options. She could march up to him and cause a scene. *It wouldn't be the first time, girl.* She could scream, shout obscenities in hopes of embarrassing him, and possibly even throw a drink in his face. Where would that leave her? She'd get the same outcome, looking like a deranged maniac. No, she wouldn't make the same mistake twice. *I could just leave.*

She sighed, turning and coming face-to-face with a familiar person.

"Hey, babe, you made it."

"Uh, yeah, but I'm not feeling well, so I'm gonna go." She stepped to the side to pass Gage, but he mirrored her movement, which struck her as odd. She moved again with the same result.

"Shit, that sucks. Trax know you're here?" He glanced around the room, but she had the sneaking suspicion he knew exactly where Trax was and who he was with.

That was humiliating. Her eyes burned, but she refused to give in to her tears. She smiled, her bottom lip twitching, and shook her head. "No, but I really gotta go. I'll call him later. Bye." She rushed past him and walked to the hall. The guy who let her in came into sight, and she took a relieved breath. Just a few feet to the exit. She had just breached the hallway when a strong hand wrapped around her forearm. She whipped her head around and stared back at Gage. He smiled, but it didn't quite reach his eyes. A sense of immense dread wafted her body.

"Come here, Chey."

She tugged her arm, but he had a tight hold, and she found herself being dragged through the room nearest the wall. No one even glanced her way, though she doubted anyone would have helped, even if they had. She recognized the hall near the back exit, and Gage gave a quick knock to the door at the end and then opened it, ushering her in before him. It had all so happened so quickly.

There were two men sitting at the pub table and another

standing. All familiar faces but none of them comforting. What the hell had she gotten herself into now? She locked gazes with Rourke, whose back was against the wall. His stare was a usual glare, but his chin dipped in acknowledgment. It was the most he'd ever engaged with her, aside from their initial meeting.

"Want me to get Trax?" Gage asked from behind her.

The man at the table shook his head and stared back at Cheyenne. Kase. *Oh shit.* She gazed to his left. He'd been the one to assure her the men at her apartment would be taken care of. She remembered because he'd seemed so sincere. *Saint?*

The door latched behind her, and she whipped around to see Gage lean against it. He smiled, but it did nothing to calm her nerves. She was now locked in a room with four bikers. Holy hell, she was dead.

"Kase?" Rourke said. Cheyenne immediately looked over. He stared at his brother with a harsh grimace. "Trax should be here."

Kase lit a cigarette, eyeing Cheyenne. "No." He leaned forward, taking a drag, letting the smoke filter around his face. There was nothing comforting about this man. Aside from his handsome yet rugged good looks, there was nothing endearing about him. She twisted her hands in front of her and tried to even her breath. *Don't panic.*

"Saint?" Rourke said.

"She'll be fine. You have my word," he replied. She didn't put much faith in his statement. Why wasn't Trax allowed to be there?

She glanced over to Rourke. He was hard to read with his scowl locked on his face. But if she had to guess, his aggravated sneer was for his president and not her. She squinted in hopes he'd read her plea for help.

"Get over here, need you to look at these and tell me if you recognize the guy in the car."

She winced from his harsh tone, and her lower lip trembled. "I didn't get…"

"Shut the fuck up with that shit. Now, get your ass over here, or I'll come get you." He narrowed his eyes. "If I gotta get up? You're not gonna like it."

Cheyenne rushed forward, tripping on her own feet, but caught herself, straightening her chest. She peeked at the pictures lined up on the round table. She leaned in, not wanting to get too close, within touching distance of Kase. Not that it mattered. Hell, she was locked in the room with him.

"You see him?" Kase asked.

She eyed each picture. The third one looked similar to her description, but it wasn't the same guy. The hair was shorter and a lighter color than the man who'd struck Mick. The scar was off too.

"Which one?"

Cheyenne jerked her head up to meet Kase's stare.

"He's not here."

"Look again." It was a command, and she followed it, even knowing none of the pictures were the guy she had seen.

She shook her head. "None of these are him."

She jumped back before his hand made contact with the table. Kase slammed his fist down and shot up from his seat. "The fuck he isn't. Point him out, bitch, or I will beat the ever-loving hell outta your ass."

A feral snarl came from across the table. "Kase," Saint warned.

Her heart dropped to her stomach, and her body trembled from head to toe. She felt the blood draining from her face. She was getting light-headed. She held her hands out in front of her, virtually surrendering. "I don't see him, I swear." She pointed to the third picture in. "He kinda looks how I described him, but it's not the guy." Her breath hitched, and she licked her lips, stumbling on her words. "I mean, the scar was down from his scalp to his eyebrow, and it was thick like it was raised. I remember because it looked kinda gross, not like that guy's. And, and his hair was darker, a bit longer." Tears welled in her eyes. Maybe she should have just said it was the guy, but chances were something bad was going to happen to him, and she couldn't live with naming the wrong man. It wasn't right.

A tear seeped past her eyelid, and she pleaded, "I don't know what you want me to say, but it wasn't him."

Kase rounded the table, and she skittered back against the wall. Rourke rushed forward but didn't come in between them. She was definitely on her own. Before he could reach her, Saint spoke out. "Kase, hold up." Cheyenne stared at Saint and watched his face twist, turning his attention to Kase, who was only a few feet away from her.

"You know?" Kase asked.

The man shifted his gaze to Cheyenne. "You said the scar was raised? Was it red?"

She sucked in a breath and shrugged. "Maybe pink. I only got a really quick look."

He seemed more sympathetic to her situation than the others. He nodded. "I think I may know who it is."

"Who?" Kase snapped.

Saint sighed and glanced over to Rourke, ignoring Kase. "Get her out to Trax and walk her to him." His face softened when he turned to her. "Thank you, Cheyenne."

Rourke grasped her arm, and she immediately yanked it out of his reach. "Don't touch me." She curled her arms around her waist and widened the space from them all.

She turned toward the door as Gage opened it and darted through. Her legs were jelly, but she didn't slow down. She heard the faint shout over the music. "Chey, Trax is at the bar."

She didn't slow down. If anything, she picked up her pace to a jog, knocking into a woman, but not even bothering to look back. The main door was opened, and she ran out and across the street, not even looking at possible cars coming. She needed to get out of there. She stumbled to a stop at the curb, scanning the lot. *Where the hell is my car?* In the spot where she remembered parking, it was empty. She gripped her hair at her temples. "You've got to be kidding?" *Someone stole my fucking car?*

"Chey, c'mere." The voice was familiar, and she jerked her gaze to the front door. Gage stood on the concrete porch, waving her over to him. She gasped and turned heel, running through the lot and around the store. Her feet pounded the pavement as her heart threatened to beat out of her chest.

The only way she was stopping was if someone tackled her.

HE RESISTED the urge to check his phone for the tenth time. It'd been a long time since he'd waited on a woman. It was a foreign feeling. Maybe she wouldn't show after all. The idea bothered him more than he was willing to admit. He had sworn to himself he wasn't gonna go down that road again with any woman. Yet, there he was, waiting on Cheyenne.

Most of the guys who belonged to his club were single. For the ones who had wives and girlfriends, less than half were faithful. He never understood why they shacked up if they were gonna cheat. It had never been his style.

He lifted his beer to his lips and took a swig. When he felt a hand on his back, he turned.

Meg hopped onto the stool next to him. "Waiting on someone?" She winked and lifted her hand, getting Nadia's attention.

"Beer, Meg?" Nadia leaned on the bar, giving Trax an amazing view down her shirt. The girl was stacked, and he'd enjoyed everything she had to offer a few times. For as beautiful as she was, he wasn't interested, though. Not anymore. Only one woman he wanted to catch that view of.

"Yeah, sweetie, thanks." Meg turned to Trax. "So?"

He raised his brows.

Meg rolled her eyes, and playfully punched his arm. It was her thing; she'd done it all the time. "Is she coming?"

He shrugged. "Said she would."

Meg grinned. "I like her."

Trax smiled and snickered. He didn't need her to tell him. He was well aware of what Meg and Nadia thought of Cheyenne.

Nadia placed the bottle on the bar, looked up at him, and winked. "Me too."

Trax took another swig of his beer. The last thing he was going to do was chime in that he agreed with them. Hell, his balls were on the verge of shriveling in this girl talk.

"Can I give you some advice?" Meg said. He slowly cocked his head. He loved Meg, but her advice on women was unnecessary.

"Ain't a virgin, Meg."

She chuckled, followed by Nadia's giggle. "I can confirm it, Meg. Trax knows what he's doing." She winked again, and he smirked.

"I wasn't talking about sex." She swiveled her seat and faced him. "I remember the first time Mick brought me to the club." She narrowed her eyes. "He had enough sense to pick me up and not make me walk in alone."

He sighed and opened his mouth, but her hand struck out, slapping his arm again. "You'll know better next time. Now listen. I was scared shitless, thinking 'I like this guy, but his club? No way.' I only came 'cause I wanted to be with Mick. This was back when Jack was president, and things tended to be a bit wilder." She smirked. "No offense."

"Orgies on the bar?"

Meg rolled her eyes. "Fucking first time here. Surprised I didn't go running for the door. Actually, I probably would have had Mick not been holding my hand with a vise grip. The whole scene was intimidating, Trax. From the guys, to the women, my first thought was, I don't belong here. This life isn't for everybody, but it was the one Mick chose, and he made it known he wasn't gonna give it up."

Neither would Trax. He'd been through a lot with these men—prison, wives, jobs, death, they were brothers in the truest sense of the word. Not a man he trusted more than the ones who wore the patch. Giving it up for anyone wasn't an option.

"So, your advice is what? Don't get involved with her?" Saying it caused a tightening in his chest. It was absurd for him to have this reaction about letting Cheyenne go. He barely knew her. Yet, the mere thought of not being with her struck deep. She was the first woman to make him consider long-term plans.

"No. Listen." She paused. "You have to bring her in slowly. Make her see why you love it, show her. You can't expect for her to fall in line 'cause this is your life. She's gotta see why this is special to you. Then you gotta show her you two can have a life that doesn't include the club. Something for just the two of you. You want her forever, she's gotta know while you wouldn't give up the club, she's just as important."

Trax snorted. "You got me married off now?"

Meg cocked her brow. "You will marry that one, Trax. You can sit here and deny it, but I'll be saying, 'Told ya so, asshole,' when you're standing at the altar. Mark my words."

"I think you're gonna marry her too, and have babies. Oh God, Trax, you gotta let me babysit." Nadia grinned, turning to Meg. "They are gonna make the cutest babies, right?"

"Oh, fuck me," Trax said, downing the remainder of his beer, listening the women laugh at his expense.

Meg headed home ten minutes later, and Trax was left checking his phone and glancing back at the door. He'd give her five more minutes, and then he was calling. He threw back a shot when he felt a hand on his shoulder. He turned to see Gage with Rourke standing close behind. The looks on their faces was not a good sign.

He slammed the glass onto the bar, turning to face them.

"What's goin' on?"

"Cheyenne," Rourke said before looking away.

"What? She's here?" His gaze immediately scanned the room.

"Was."

Trax jumped from the stool. "Was? What the fuck are you talking about?"

Gage cursed, resting his hands on his hips and dropping his

chin. "Saw her walk in. She looked pissed seeing you with Nadia, was high tailing it outta here when I stopped her."

Fuck me! There weren't many women he was affectionate with besides Meg, but Nadia was one of them. It wasn't anything more than a few casual fucks in the past and liking that Nadia wasn't a bitch like most women who hung around the club. She was the only woman he'd banged who never tried to stake claim on his dick. She was a touchy-feely type to begin with and never shied away from Trax. But obviously, it didn't sit well with Cheyenne. He couldn't blame her. If some guy was all over her, Trax would have ripped his limbs from his fucking torso.

"Where is she?"

"Well, here's where it gets a little fucked." Gage forced a smile and shifted to Rourke, who stood stone-faced, staring at Trax. "Brought her in the back to see Kase."

Trax stepped forward, bumping his chest against Gage, raging red fury running through his blood. "Without me?"

"I was gonna come get ya, man, but..."

"No fucking buts, asshole, you should have never fucking taken her back to Kase. That was my fucking place, Gage, not yours." Trax shoved his brother, forcing him to step back. Rourke set his hand on Trax's chest.

"Told Kase we should get ya, brother. He said no." Rourke stepped in front of Trax, blocking Gage. "Nobody hurt her, didn't even touch her, but she was scared. When Kase let her go, she took off through the lot."

"On foot?"

Rourke solemnly nodded. "Turks moved her car to the back lot like you told him earlier. She went out and panicked when she didn't see her car and took off."

Gage came around Rourke's side. "I was gonna go after her, but Rourke said we should let you handle it. But Trax, man, I never hurt her, and neither did any brother in the room. Wouldn't let that happen to her, man. I fucking swear on Mick's grave."

Trax was enraged. He could barely see anything but drawing

blood from a brother, mainly Kase. They'd had a plan. He would explain shit to Cheyenne, he would ease her into looking at the pictures and identifying the guy. It was the plan they'd set up in the meeting earlier. He would be next to her so she wasn't fucking freaked out, and these assholes fucked it all up. Now, she was running scared.

"She could be at the station, giving a fucking report right now or fucking hit by a car. What the fuck were you thinking?" Trax couldn't remember the last time he'd been so enraged. He was seconds from making someone pay for this fuck up with his fists.

Trax pushed through Rourke and Gage, making his way to the end hallway. He'd find her. His brothers better fucking hope he found her, or it would be their heads he'd come for. He was just at the exit when Kase stepped out from the back room.

"Need you to get Rourke and Gage."

Trax halted. Every bone in his body tensed, and he slowly turned his head to Kase. He would have loved nothing more than slamming his fist dead center into Kase's face. He could almost envision it. He snarled. "Fuck you."

Kase grabbed his arm. Trax turned fast, and with all his weight and built-up rage, pinned his president against the wall with his forearm against his neck. Kase didn't so much as flinch, but Trax could see the fury beyond his calm.

"I told you how I wanted it to go down, and you fucking ignored that shit. Fuck you, Kase."

"Move your fucking arm." Kase narrowed his gaze.

A whispered curse. "Oh fuck."

Trax leaned closer, shoving his arm deeper against Kase's neck. "I did what you wanted, got her down here, and this is how you keep your word to me, brother?" His lips twisted on his last word and spewed with venom.

"Trax, I'll give you one more warning. Back the fuck up," Kase said.

Saint appeared next to Trax. "Let him go."

Trax whipped his head toward his VP. "Can't believe you let shit go down this way."

Saint cocked a brow. "She was never in danger from us, and you know it."

Trax twisted his lips tensely. "But she didn't fucking know it, Saint."

"Gonna give you fair warning. You got two seconds to back the fuck off," Kase warned.

His threat only fueled Trax's rage, and he pressed deeper against Kase's neck. Trax wasn't about to back down, but the choice was made for him when Rourke hooked his arms and pulled him away. He whispered, "Pull it back, man, you don't want this."

Kase straightened but made no move forward. Sucker punch was not his style. Rourke loosened his grip, and Trax yanked his arms from his hold, spinning around and glaring at him. There weren't too many people he trusted more than the men standing in front of him, but he took it as a personal betrayal.

"You couldn't come and get me, asshole?" Trax shouted.

Kase drew in a deep breath, eyeing Trax with a harsh glare. "*We* fucking decided." His statement was interrupted by Rourke, who stepped forward.

"No fucking *we* about this." He pointed between Kase and Saint. "You guys decided, not us. Me and Gage wanted to get Trax. Asked fucking both of you and got shot down." Rourke shook his head in disgust.

It didn't calm Trax down, but at least he had Rourke backing him in this fucked-up scene.

Kase snarled. "You got a problem with how I run my club?"

Trax stepped forward, but it was Rourke again who spoke first. "The way you handled his girl? Yeah, I gotta a fucking problem, Kase. She was scared out of her fucking mind, and you fucking fed off that shit."

Saint moved forward. "Let's all calm down, all right?" He

turned to Trax. "We could have..." He paused. "We should have handled it with you here."

It was too late for an apology or regrets. The damage had been done.

"Everybody get in the office, and we'll sort this shit out," Kase said.

The last thing he intended to do was go anywhere with Kase. His only mission was to find Cheyenne. He backed up as his brothers watched him.

He turned to Kase. "You fucked up." He pointed at him and held his stare before throwing the side door open and rushing to his bike.

She couldn't have gotten too far, and for the sake of his brothers' lives, she better be in one piece when he found her.

Chapter 11

"I need to exercise more." Cheyenne heaved her bag over her shoulder. The weight caused her shoulder to throb. "And I need to clean out my purse." She'd always kept everything in there. "Great, now I'm talking to myself." She scanned the streets. It was quiet but eerie. It wasn't the worst section of town, but not her first choice to walk alone in. Most of the retail shops had closed for the night. The lights streamed through the street in a soft glow. The only light coming from an opened business was the corner diner at the end of the road.

If she had to guess, she had at least two more miles to go before she was home. She considered calling a cab or Uber, but the thought of stopping had her reconsider. She was going to kill Macy when she got home. The girl was forever forgetting to charge her phone. All seven calls had gone straight to voicemail.

A car came down the road, and oddly, slowed as it got closer. She double stepped and glanced over. It was too dark to make out the driver and passenger, but from the profile, they were men. Oh hell. She kept forward but glanced back to see brake lights at the corner. If they made a U-turn, she'd book it again. Her legs trembled at the thought. No more running.

She noticed the single light before she heard the roar of the engine. As it got closer, she realized the men in the car were the least of her worries. She moved closer to the building in hopes of blending but quickly realized the motorcycle was slowing down.

Shit.

She darted between the cars and crossed the street. Her feet pounded the concrete, and she quickly rushed into the corner shop. The bells jingled over the door, and she stopped at the entrance. She tried to catch her breath while scanning the small diner. There were only a few people, and a waitress approached.

"Are you okay?"

Cheyenne shook her head. "No, some guy is following me." She was on the verge of tears. There was only so much she could take before she broke down. The waitress rushed toward her.

"Okay, calm down, come in the back with me, and I'll call the police." She took Cheyenne's hand, weaving her through the tables, and headed toward the swinging doors of the kitchen. "Jim, lock the doors." Chey noticed a heavyset man rush to the doors before she was ushered into the back. They walked through the kitchen and into a small room. It must have been a break room.

"Okay, just sit tight here, and I'll call the police, okay?" She cupped Cheyenne's jaw and gave her a soft smile. It was motherly, though the waitress couldn't have been more than five years older than her.

All she could do was nod. Finally, she'd deal with the cops. It was something she should have done from the very beginning. If she had, she wouldn't be on the verge of a heart attack in the tiny room.

"I'll get you a tea to calm your nerves. Stay here, sweetie."

Cheyenne took a seat in the corner and slumped down. *Breathe, just breathe. It's almost over.* She closed her eyes, resting her head back against the wall. As soon as the cops arrived, she was going to tell the detective everything. Every little detail of what happened, including the description of the driver. Maybe there was some kind of protection they could offer against the club. *Her mom*. She'd go stay with her mom for a while. Not the most convenient or pleasant experience, but anything was better than this.

Breathe, just breathe.

"Here you go, sweetie."

Cheyenne opened her eyes to see the waitress at the small table, placing the mug down and smiling. Cheyenne started to smile, but her gaze shifted over the woman's shoulder. Trax stood between the doorframe, staring down at her. Two deep lines embedded his forehead, and his jaw squared.

She shot up to her feet. "Are you serious? Oh, my God, you let him in?"

The waitress looked confused, shifting her attention between Cheyenne and Trax. "He can help you. That guy chasing you won't step foot near this place knowing Trax is here."

Cheyenne balled her hands and pointed over the waitress's shoulder. "He's the one chasing me."

"What?" She jerked her head to Trax. He continued to stare at Cheyenne. "Is that true?"

His gaze never faltered from her. "No."

Cheyenne gritted her teeth.

"Deb, give us a minute here."

Cheyenne's eyes widened when the waitress turned to leave. "Wait, don't leave me alone with him. Please tell me you at least called the cops for me?"

Deb glanced at Trax and then back to Cheyenne. "Trax told me he'd take care of it." She slipped past Trax and left.

"You all right?"

Cheyenne glared his way. "No, I'm not all right. Christ, do you have everyone on your payroll?"

He shrugged, leaning against the frame and folding his arms. "Just about."

"God, I need to move far, far away." She paced in a small circle, not giving him a second glance. She totally understood the mindset of a caged animal and the incessant pacing.

"How come you didn't come to me as soon as you got to the club?"

She snorted. "You looked busy with your hand on some chick's ass."

"Nadia."

She halted and lifted her gaze. "I don't care what her name is."

He smirked and cocked his brow. "All right."

"For the record, you inviting me to your club to hang out is pretty fucked up since you've already got a girl. That makes you an asshole, just so you know."

"She's not my woman."

Cheyenne snorted and forced a laugh. "Whatever, it didn't look like it."

"We're close…"

Cheyenne raised her hand. "I don't care."

Trax pushed off the wall and ambled forward. "Yeah, you do, otherwise you wouldn't be saying shit to me right now. Was waiting on you, hanging with her and whole lot of others you seemed to miss. Didn't have my hand on her ass, and if I did, didn't notice it. I was waiting on you, Chey. Not interested in anyone else."

She squinted, eyeing him carefully, and twisted her lips.

"Yeah, I'm sure you are a one-woman kind of man." She rolled her eyes.

His brows furrowed.

"You can fucking think what you want. Never touched another woman while I was with Ariel until I caught her fucking cheating on me. Not fucking once." He sighed, and his jaw tightened. "I don't know what the fuck you think you saw, but I got nothing going on with anyone but you." He paused. "So, don't stand here like you know dick about me, 'cause you don't."

Cheyenne dropped her gaze to her feet. Why the hell was she feeling guilty? So what if he'd never cheated? It didn't make him a saint. *But he claimed me as his. Yeah, then he threw you to the wolves.*

The Favor

He set her up with his club. No matter what he'd said now didn't change the fact, when she'd needed him, he hadn't been there.

She tried her best to hold back her tears, but the night's events were catching up to her. "You're right, Trax, I don't know anything about you. I thought I did, but I don't have a clue who you are or what you are capable of." She sniffled. "But I know me. I know that what you did tonight is something I'd never do to anyone." Tears fell down her face. "You set me up."

"Chey, I didn't," he whispered. "The only way I was letting shit go down tonight was if I was there. Made that clear to the club. Didn't want you scared."

She shook her head and wiped her face with her sleeve.

"Never planned for it go down like this."

Don't fall for it. It didn't matter what he intended. All that mattered was how it went down.

"Yeah, well it did." She sighed, needing for this night to be over. Needing everything with Trax to just be over. "Can I leave or what? 'Cause this whole 'you and your club holding me in small, dark rooms for interrogation' is getting old."

She tightened her grip on her bag, staring down at the floor. Could this night have gone any worse? Probably not. First seeing him with another woman, then being scared shitless by his friends, and then her car was stolen. Her shoulders sagged, and she groaned. "My car." She said it more to herself than him. She needed her damn car. How was she gonna get to work? She slumped against the wall.

"It's at the clubhouse."

What? She jerked her head and straightened her back to stand. "It is? Are you sure?"

He nodded. "Earlier, I told Turks, the guy at the door, to move it to the back when you got there."

That didn't make any sense. She swung her bag in front of her and reached in. Her finger looped through the key ring, and she pulled them out. She glanced up, confused. "My keys are right here."

Trax shifted uncomfortably and folded his arms with a blank stare. "We got a master."

"Wow, professional car thieves too. Not much you boys can't do." She snorted in disgust. "Fine, whatever, I need to call a cab to get it." She eyed him with a squinty stare. "Don't follow me."

His lip twitched. "I'm heading back to the club, so let me give you a ride."

"No, I'll call a cab."

"Don't trust me?"

"Are you seriously asking me that? Do I look like a fucking moron to you?"

"Babe, you're getting awfully heated for me asking an innocent question."

"There's nothing innocent about you, Trax," she spewed.

He shrugged and smirked as if he was amused. "Probably not." He turned and walked to the door. "Come on."

Oh hell, no!

"I'm not going anywhere with you." She folded her arms, fully prepared to wait until he left before exiting the small break room.

He snickered when he glanced over his shoulder. She had a sudden urge to punch him in the face. So fucking cocky. She watched him lean out from the room and shout for Deb. The waitress appeared in the doorway next to Trax.

He looked over at Chey and smiled. "Tell her she's got to leave."

What? *He can't do that.* She shifted her gaze to Deb, who looked extremely uncomfortable and shifted on her feet. The waitress gave her a sympathetic glance and mouthed, *"Sorry."*

Every bone in Cheyenne's body tightened, and her back grew rigid. She could imagine what she must look like to both of them staring back at her. If steam could have shot from her nose and ears, it would have. She didn't move.

"Deb?"

She cleared her throat. "You have to leave now." There was a reluctance in her tone.

Cheyenne heaved her bag over her shoulder and stomped past both of them. Luckily, they shifted out of her way because she was prepared to plow through them. She treaded heavily all the way past the kitchen, tossing the doors open and slamming them against the wall. There were only a few people in the diner, but all of them turned to watch her. She whipped around to face them, watching Deb and Trax emerge from the kitchen.

"I will never eat here again. And I will be leaving a one-star review on Yelp!" It was a lame statement, but it was all she had.

She pushed the door open with force and stormed out. She only made it a few feet down the sidewalk before she was halted by Trax's firm grip on her arm. She tugged away from his hold, but he refused to let go.

"Get off me."

"Chey, baby, calm down."

"Don't tell me what to do, and do not call me baby," she shouted, continuing her effort to get his hand off her arm. She tried to pry his fingers, but it was impossible. "Terms of endearment are meant for people you like, and you certainly proved you think nothing of me."

"Chey." It was a plea.

"No." She pointed in his face with her free hand. "You hurt me tonight, and I don't like you anymore." It was juvenile but honest.

His face softened, and he stepped closer but didn't pull her into him. "Please, just let me take you back to the club to your car. Don't like the idea of you riding alone in a cab."

"A hell of a lot safer than being around you." She twisted her lips.

He sighed and pulled her into his chest. "Please, let me take ya." His hand grazed her hair away from her eyes and slid down her cheek. She tried her best to ignore the shiver rolling over her skin from his touch. "Then you can go, and I won't bother you again."

He was lying. She could feel it. She glanced down the empty road and bit her lip. If she called a cab, it would probably take about twenty minutes. Waiting in the diner was no longer an option, thanks to him. She could try calling Macy again. However, she'd still have to go to the club, and he'd be there, probably waiting by her car.

She slumped her shoulders in defeat. "Fine. But you are not allowed to talk to me. I mean it, not one word."

He held on to her for another second before nodding, releasing her arm and walking to his bike. He kept glancing back at her as if watching her to see if she was going to bolt again. The thought had crossed her mind, but what was the point, really? Most likely he could outrun her. She was so damn tired, it was time to throw up her white flag.

THIS WAS NOT how he had planned for the night to go down. Chasing, fighting, and now kidnapping. Just another eventful night in his life. He was surprised he'd even gotten her onto the back of his bike. He was prepared for at least one more chase down Main Street, but she surprised him when she followed him to where he was parked. She made no effort to hide her unhappiness with the situation. She barely held on to his waist during the entire ride. All the small tricks he'd used the other day hadn't worked this time. He finally settled into the fact that if he continued shifting gears to get her closer, it might backfire with her falling off the motorcycle. He was learning Cheyenne was quite stubborn when she was pissed off.

They had been driving for fifteen minutes before he turned onto his street. He knew the second she realized he wasn't taking her back to the club. Her body shifted, most likely from her looking around the neighborhood.

He'd bought the house three years ago. While he enjoyed his time at the clubhouse, he was getting tired of the late-night parties and the lack of privacy. Sometimes he needed his space, and this place was perfect. It was close to the club, and it had a detached two-car garage, perfect for his bike, the one he was restoring, and his truck. It also served as his garage for repairs. The house wasn't anything special. It was a small cape that needed work, but it had a new roof, and structurally, it was sound.

He pulled into his driveway, past the house, and into the backyard where the garage was. He angled his bike and turned off the ignition. He geared up for what he knew was about to happen. He waited for her to get off, but she didn't. He glanced over his shoulder and was met with a harsh glare.

"You lied to me."

"No, technically, I changed my mind. But since you told me I couldn't talk to you, I couldn't mention my change of plans."

She narrowed her gaze. "I knew you were lying."

He chuckled. She was so damn cute with her scrunched face. "And yet ya still got on my bike."

"Yep, makes me an idiot. You must be so proud, proving I'm a moron."

"I don't think that, Chey."

She huffed and dismounted, whispering under her breath, "Yes, you do."

He would have rather had her screaming and berating him than feeling as if he thought she was stupid. It couldn't be further from how he saw her. Aside from her beauty and kind heart, she was smart. He knew it from talking to her and listening to the way she spoke to others.

He got off his bike and then stalked toward her just as she removed her helmet. He clasped his hand through hers and squeezed. She had no idea what she meant to him. In such a short time, he'd decided a life without her wasn't happening. He'd take any means necessary to not let her get away. *I can't lose her.*

"I don't think you're stupid. I tricked you, and for as shitty as it is, I'm not apologizing. That makes me an asshole." He lifted their enclosed hands and brushed her jaw with the back of his hand. "But it sure as fuck doesn't make you dumb. Ya got me?"

Her eyes softened slightly, but she seemed to catch herself and turned away from his touch. He liked that. She wasn't willing to forgive and forget. It was good. It showed she had fire and wouldn't take his shit. He pulled her toward the garage, dropping her hand to open it.

"Wanna show you my bike."

It was a project he had been working on for months. It may have not seemed to be anything special to some random woman, but it was important to him. And he wanted to share it with her.

She didn't respond to him, but when he lifted the garage door, she walked in without prompting. He flicked on the lights, illuminating the old garage. His truck took up half, but his motorcycle covered the remainder. He'd been working on it for half the year. Scattered parts covered the workbench, with the frame of the bike set in the center of the floor.

"It doesn't have wheels."

He glanced over as she circled the frame. Her brows furrowed, giving an adorable, confused stare. She bent down and leaned closer. "Or an engine."

He chuckled. "Working on it."

"You're making your own motorcycle, like from a kit?"

He scoffed, "Fuck, no. I'm rebuilding it."

"Oh." She glanced up at him. "Why? You already have a bike."

"No such thing as too many bikes, Chey."

She tightened her lips in a flat line and stood. "This is what you do in your spare time, like a hobby."

He snorted, wondering if she was trying to insult him. Rebuilding a bike wasn't a fucking hobby, it was a passion. Her tone was curious, which made him smile. He was sharing, and she was accepting it.

She nodded before he could answer. "I get it. I like to paint."

He pursed his lips. He was trying to win her over, not start another brawl with her. He'd let it slide, her comparing painting to his bike.

"What do ya paint?" He smirked. "Fruit?"

She rolled her eyes and walked around his garage, scanning all his tools. She slid her hands across his wrench seated on the bench. "No, mostly people. I'm actually not good, though if you ask Macy, I'm the next Picasso." She smiled, still looking at his tools. "But I enjoy it, kinda like volleyball." She sighed and turned to face him.

The corner of his mouth curled. Like volleyball? What the fuck did painting and volleyball have in common? Her nose twitched, and he grinned. She was definitely different.

"Volleyball?" he asked, spiking up his brows.

Her lips puckered, shifting to the right. "Uh-huh. I suck at volleyball." She smirked. "But I love it."

"Good to know. Make sure I don't pick ya for my team if we ever have a tournament."

"Smart move on your part." Her gaze wandered. "So, why am I here?'

"Wanted to show you my place."

Trax had a firm rule of not bringing women to his house. He had a room at the clubhouse, which had served the purpose of fucking. Allowing a woman into his home, it was sacred and a rule he never broke. Until her.

"Why?"

'Cause you'll be spending most of your nights here. He refrained from saying it out loud. If anything, it would get her running again. That would probably be it. He wanted her there. Not only in his bed but on his couch watching TV, in his kitchen eating dinner and, more importantly, breakfast. He just wanted her there. "Come on."

She walked toward him and out the bay doors. Trax moved his motorcycle inside and then closed the doors. He walked through the yard and up the back steps with Cheyenne following. He'd expected more resistance, but she followed his lead. He'd love to know where her head was at.

He hadn't planned on bringing her there, but after what had gone down, and Meg's voice ringing in his head, he wanted to lay it out for her. His place wasn't anything special, but it was his. He led her through the kitchen into the living room, flicking on the lights and settling into the couch. He stared up at her when she stood at the edge of the room, looking around.

"Not impressed?"

She jerked her gaze and furrowed her brows. "With what, your house?"

He nodded.

"It's nice. Nicer than mine." She shrugged. "I thought you lived at the clubhouse?"

"I got a room but don't use it too much. I like my space."

"Oh."

He watched as she peered around the small room. It wasn't much, but he'd bought it a few years ago.

"Gonna stand there all night?"

"Will I be here all night?"

"Yeah." There was no sense in lying to her. She shook her head and took a seat across from him on his recliner. He noticed she sat on the edge with her hands clasped together on her lap, looking extremely uncomfortable.

"Don't wanna sit over here?" He patted the cushion of the couch, and she narrowed her eyes.

"I'm fine here."

He smirked, loving her resistance. Again, there was the fire he liked.

"So, what now?"

It was a loaded question, and he couldn't resist.

He shrugged. "We could fuck?" It was intended as a joke to lighten the mood.

Her face tightened, and she gritted her teeth. "I'm not having sex with you anymore."

"No?" He leaned up and rested his elbows on his knees. "I thought you liked fucking me. I mean, you seemed to enjoy it when I was inside you. The panting and moaning, screaming out my name when you came all over my cock? Hmmm…guess I read it wrong, huh?"

Her face turned the brightest shade of red he'd ever seen. He tried to fight against the smile creeping over his lips, but he was doing a sorry ass job at covering it up. Her harsh frown was evidence of that. While he was amused by the back and forth, she was not.

"This is funny, huh?" She nodded impassively. "I get why. You nailed me against a tree, proving I'm nothing but an easy lay. Then you have me show up at your club while you're screwing around with another girl, probably to prove the point again that I was an easy lay."

Trax balled his hands, feeling his anger build. Everything she'd said was complete bullshit. Before he could say anything to dispute it, she continued.

"And while you're feeling up some chick, I get dragged into a room, the door locked behind me, and forced to identify a man I barely saw. When I couldn't do it fast enough or correctly, I was then threatened with bodily harm. I believe your president's exact words were, 'I'll beat your ass.' Hmmm...he's a charmer, that one. But I mean, yeah, I get it. You scare the hell out of me, threaten me, and then send me on my way." She snorted. "Oh no, wait, no, you felt the need to stretch your muscles and prove what a badass you were by following me into the diner, forcing me to get on your bike under false pretense and keep me in your house like a prisoner. Reminding me again how completely fucked up I am for believing any word that comes out of your mouth."

Ah, fuck me.

Listening to her and watching her as she went on her tirade, it all became clear. Clearly fucked. Seeing everything that went down through her eyes made him feel like a complete asshole. The plan of bringing her to his house to get closer to her had totally backfired. Her whole speech pretty much summed it all up.

She sighed and nodded again with resignation. "You know why I stopped for Mick?" She turned her head and stared back at him. His jaw twitched, but he didn't move a muscle; he couldn't.

Everything she'd just said had put him into a rage. Not because it was bullshit, but because in her eyes, it was the absolute truth.

"I stopped because, well..." She paused, twisting her hands together and glanced back up at him through her lashes. "I couldn't not stop. I didn't even think of any consequence that might happen as a result of pulling over and helping him. I saw someone hurt and in need of help, and I just acted without thought." She licked her lips. "I've never seen someone bleeding like that, and his gashes and cuts, not even every scary movie I saw, could have prepared me for that scene. For all the fear running through me, and there was a lot, I didn't leave him. I couldn't. He was in so much pain, his face did nothing to hide it, and I just kept thinking, 'Please don't let him die.'"

He'd been witness to a few motorcycle wrecks, all gory and awful, something that had stuck with him. It was part of the life, it happened. But it wasn't her life, not something she signed up for. If she hadn't stopped, who knows how long he would have been out there by himself. He most likely would have died alone on the empty road.

"With one decision, my simple life got thrown upside down." She huffed a breath in disgust. "You and your club thinking I deserve all the shit you've handed me."

He was willing to hear her out, but she'd gotten that part wrong.

"No one thinks that. Not me, not the club, no one." He stood, wanting nothing more than to take her into his arms and hold her. The only thing holding him back was her. "I'm so fucking sorry for how this all played out, Chey."

Her eyes welled, and she drew in a breath. She wiped her hands down her jeans and stood. His gaze followed her every move.

"Ironic, huh? If I had to do it all over again, knowing how my life would be catapulted into shit," she paused, narrowing her eyes, "I still would have stopped." She turned, and he caught her wiping her cheeks with her sleeve. She wandered down the hall, and he heard the door latch and lock, forced into place. The hall only provided three options. His bedroom, a spare bedroom, or the bathroom.

He dragged his hands over his face. *I don't deserve this girl.* A better man would allow her time, offer her a ride to the club to get her car, and promise never to bother her again. And keep the fucking promise.

Chapter 12

"What a waste of good makeup." She dragged the tissue under her eyes, cleaning up her smudged mascara and liner. She'd made a point of wearing extra makeup tonight. It was a fruitless effort. Everything about tonight had been useless. She snagged a few more tissues and blew her nose. She cringed at her reflection in the mirror, with her red eyes and blazing red nose. She was an ugly aftermath crier. It would take at least another twenty minutes to get her blotchy face back to normal. Who cared, anyway? She tossed the tissues into the trash and then washed her hands before unlocking the latch and opening the door. The hallway was dark, but she would have to have been blind to miss Trax leaning against the wall with his arms folded over his chest. Even in the dim lighting, she could see the curve of his muscles bulging from the hem of his shirt.

His stare was thoughtful, any remnants of humor gone. The corner of his mouth curled, and he drew in a breath. "I'll take you home or to the club, your choice."

Good, this was good. "The club so I can pick up my car." She glanced down at the floor and mumbled, "Thanks."

"I wanna show you something." He stopped abruptly and lowered his voice. "If it's all right?"

This was a different Trax. She had the feeling if she'd said she wanted to leave immediately, he would have taken her. The ball was in her court. For everything that had happened tonight, she still held a little faith in him. Or maybe it was wishful thinking.

"Okay."

He pushed off the wall and reached out, taking her hand in his and intertwining their fingers. *The hand holding again.* With him, it seemed to be her downfall. It was such a simple sign of affection, yet her belly swirled every time their fingers intertwined. She glanced down and couldn't stop her smile creeping up her lip. He led her down the short hall and through a doorway. The room was small and cluttered with cardboard boxes on one wall and a small old desk in the corner. The walls were a pea-green color and completely bare. He let go of her hand and leaned across the desk, grabbing a frame. He stared at it before handing it to her.

She recognized the bar in the club and the two men standing in front of it. They were dressed with their leather vests and smiling at the camera. A younger Trax was the man on the right. The man on the left?

Cheyenne smiled and peeked up. "You and Mick?"

He nodded. "Day I patched in."

She smiled, tracing her finger over the glass. "You look happy."

"I was." He stepped toward the desk again, moving a box from the top down to the floor. "Meg took the picture and framed it. She's got the same one at their place, except it's hanging on the wall." He fumbled with another box, setting it on the floor before sitting on the desk, staring back at her. "I knew I wanted in from the first time I hung out with them. Me and Mick, we just got each other. He knew me better than my own family. Took me in, all the mentoring shit, vouched for me. Prospected for thirteen months until that day." He pointed to her holding the frame. "Finally, a brother. I belonged to something."

She clamped her lips closed, not knowing what to say. The last thing she'd expected from Trax was for him to open up to her.

"Stood up as my best man when I got hitched."

She glanced up. He'd mentioned he had been married, but him talking about it surprised her. He smirked and lifted his chin. "He offered me five hundred bucks not to marry her." Trax laughed, shaking his head. "Saw something I didn't, and fuck, was he right. Stood at the altar, watching her walk down the aisle with Mick in my ear, saying, 'There's still time, brother.'" Trax folded his arms over his chest and gave a sad smile. "Good advice I shoulda taken."

"You must have loved her, though, right?"

He shrugged. "I was twenty-two, getting regular pussy. So, yeah, where I was back then, I loved her. But she wasn't loyal. Found out she was fucking around a month into my stint in prison. She stopped visiting." He scanned her face. "When a weekly is all ya got, it becomes the only thing to look forward to. It keeps ya going. She took that from me."

She averted her gaze from his stare and glanced down at the picture again. Mick and Trax. It seemed so strange that a man she only knew for a mere ten minutes, she felt a connection to. Maybe it was the way Trax spoke of him. She glanced up again at Trax.

"It must have been hard."

He raised his brows and nodded.

"I got word from those close to me she had guys in and out of our place. Got any idea how that fucks with a man's head? She sleeping with guys in my fucking bed while I was locked up." He shrugged. "Made her wait, though. Wasn't divorcing her while I was on the inside."

"Why?" Wouldn't he want to be rid of her?

"Wanted to see her face when I handed her the papers. Did it at my homecoming party." He winked. "Meg's got a picture of that too." He laughed, and Cheyenne snickered. It was a picture she'd love to see.

She leaned a step forward, handing him the frame. "Bet that one isn't hanging on her wall."

Trax grabbed the frame and smiled. He had such an amazing

smile, though she rarely saw it. It softened his face, making him seem less dangerous. There was a part of her that wished she could just forget everything that had happened between them up until that point and have a do-over. *Well, not everything.*

"Why are you telling me all of this?"

His smile faded, and he scanned the room. Cheyenne wasn't sure if he was looking for something or just avoiding the question.

"I don't know." His eyes softened as he pointed toward the door. "I guess you pouring out your soul back there reminded me of what a bastard I am, and for once, it bothered me." His head bowed. "Swore I'd never fall again." He looked up with a tense face. "Made a vow to myself, no woman would ever get in here." He rested his hand over his heart and smiled. "Then you showed up."

She sucked in a breath and gulped.

"Trax."

"I can't change the past. Everything that happened." He paused. "It happened. In my world, shit gets real, it gets fucked up." He tilted his head. "It's messy, sometimes dirty, it's the life I chose. It's who I am." He pushed off the wall but made no move toward her. "Tell me what I gotta do."

"What?"

"I got my life with the club, and I got you. I don't wanna give up either." He shoved his hands into his pockets. "So, tell me what I gotta do to keep ya both."

What the hell could she say to that? She fumbled with her fingers, unable to answer. Could it be so simple? She would just list her requirements? Hell, what requirements?

"You want me to take you home?"

She flicked her gaze to meet his stare. She shook her head without hesitation.

The corner of his mouth curled again. He was so damn sexy when he did that. Could she really forget all that had happened and move on with him? He cleared his throat and stood, straightening to full height. "Come here."

Her eyes popped open, and she staggered back slightly. If she went over there, she knew exactly what would happen. She'd go to him, he'd kiss her, and they'd be horizontal in ten seconds flat. *Think, think.* As bad as she wanted him again, she was getting caught up in all of this. Having sex with him again was a distraction, but it wouldn't change anything that had happened tonight, and she'd still be left in the same position. Or would she?

Tell me what I gotta do to keep ya both.

"Chey." He growled and dared her gaze to meet his. "Come here, please."

Her eye twitched, and she blurted, "You come here." She didn't even know where her voice came from.

He stalked toward her and didn't stop until his chest bumped against hers. His hands gripped her hips, and his neck bent, kissing her without hesitation. This was probably the worst choice, but she kissed him back. How could she not?

She was barely aware of everything around her. The only thought taking up space in her head was him. He kissed her with so much passion and desire she was set to combust. She tangled her arms against his, grasping at his back as he thrust his body against hers, and they fell into the wall. She could barely breathe, but tearing her mouth from his was not an option.

Her back fell flat against the wall as his chest meshed against her. How could she forget everything that had happened? *Because he'll do what it takes to keep you.* His admission was a game changer. He wanted to be with her as much as she wanted to be with him. They just needed to find their happy medium.

His tongue swirled against hers, and she moaned a hot breath into his mouth. He groaned and angled his hips, drawing his erection against her core. This would play out like it had against the tree. Or so she thought.

Trax ripped his lips from hers, breathing heavy and resting his forehead against hers.

"I'm sorry." He panted, and her hands spread across his back, urging him forward, but he remained an inch away. "Need you to forgive me."

"I do." She wasn't sure what she agreed to at that point and didn't care. She wanted him. She leaned forward, just wanting his lips against hers, but she had to tell him. "Don't hurt me again, Trax," she whispered, tucking her chin and avoiding his eyes.

He gripped her jaw in his hand and pulled away, forcing her to look at him.

"I won't let it happen again."

Only time would tell if he'd keep that promise. But she was prepared to risk it.

She nodded and moved closer. "Okay." He held her back.

"Chey, I mean it. What happened? You being scared and alone." His gaze crossed over her features, and she settled against the wall. "I won't let it happen again."

"Trax…" she whispered.

He kissed her lips and then bowed his head. "I'll protect you. You can trust me, Chey."

It was then it hit her. This was so much more than sex and passion. He vowed to her. He'd given in to her. That was a game changer in everything she'd thought she knew about him.

"Okay," she whispered.

He held back and eyed her. "Give me the words. Tell me you trust me to keep you safe. Say it. I gotta hear it."

"I trust you."

He lifted her against his body, and she was aware they were moving. She was so focused on him and his beautiful lips she didn't realize they had moved to his room until she was laid down against the soft mattress.

She watched through hooded lids as he slid down her body, removing her pants in a swift motion. How the hell did he do that?

He peppered light kisses over her bare thighs, tracing his lips up to her pussy. Maybe it was her need for him, maybe sheer desire, or maybe it was his confession and vow, but every touch seemed electrified. Her skin burned for his touch in a tingling fire. She lowered her hand to the back of his neck when his lips pressed against her core.

It was all too intense. She shifted her hips, but his hands on her hips locked her in place. She stretched her tight muscles and angled her neck, digging her head against the mattress. She gasped as his tongue circled directly over her clit, giving her a sensation that tensed every muscle in her body.

It was obvious he knew his way around a woman's body. She sent the thought to the back of her mind. She would focus on being the recipient of his gifted mouth. She pushed her hips forward, and his flicking tongue sent her over the edge into a beautiful euphoric state.

When he rose from his knees, he gripped the hem of his shirt, ripping off the material in a quick swoop, revealing his chest. She immediately shot up, reaching for him. His mouth lowered and took her in a deep kiss. She fumbled with the snap to his jeans and hooked her thumbs, dragging them down his body.

His groan echoed through the bedroom when she grasped his cock, stroking his length slowly. She eyed his cock, and unabashedly licked her lips. Finally, she would get her own taste. He must have sensed where she was going and gripped her shoulders, gently pushing her back.

His voice was raw and course. "Your mouth on me right now will end badly for you, sweetheart." He choked out a laugh when she tightened her grip on his dick. "Fuck."

She smirked. It was empowering to be in control. She leaned forward, but in a swift move, he flipped her onto her stomach. She giggled when he playfully slapped her ass, and his mouth whispered against her ear, "Bad girl, Chey."

She glanced over her shoulder. His lips twitched, clearly amused by her disobedience.

"I don't wanna come off as just a taker and not a giver." She cocked her brow.

"Oh, you're gonna give me exactly what I want." He growled,

and the head of his cock lined up between her folds. She arched her back and pushed toward him, reeling in the sensation as he entered her slowly.

From behind had never been a favorite of hers. The position left an awkward intrusion instead of what she felt now. Her face planted against the mattress, and his hips rocked into her ass. She felt every inch of him deeper inside her core. His hands caressed her back, causing a shivering pulse. It was electric.

She pushed against him, taking what little lead she could. His hands gripped her cheeks, and he thrust inside her, taking his time and making every move curl her toes. His chest lined up against her back, and one fist landed near her head. His other hand slid her hair away, caressing over her damp skin, and he kissed her neck. She shrugged and moaned. His tongue flicked over the curve of her neck, and she moaned from the sensation. She wasn't sure what that spot was, but it sent all the feels over her body. She smiled and turned her head, reaching back to kiss him.

"Feels so good."

He rocked deeper inside her and swiveled his hips, landing on a spot she was sure was the mythical G-spot. She'd called bullshit on the mystery spot for years. She was convinced either everyone lied or she just didn't have it. Now the truth sent her hands into fists, and she gasped for air. Trax proved he'd found her golden ticket.

He chuckled against her neck. "Looks like I found your sweet spot, Chey."

She moaned, knowing nothing coherent would come out even if she tried. Her arms shook from the slow build up, and she remained still against his steady pounding. If he lost his rhythm, she might be driven to tears. She was on the edge of an amazing orgasm. This would be a first for her. Two in one night? She bit her lip to the point of pain, riding the sensation.

His pace quickened, and her orgasm went from a slow intro to a cosmic explosion. She opened her mouth, panting, unable to control her breath. "Oh God."

His hand cupped her jaw, and he kissed her while she moaned desperately in his mouth. Slow and steady was a thing of the past as he fucked her hard and fast, sending the bed slamming into the wall. It was reckless and frenzied, and by far the best sex she'd ever had.

His cock jolted deeper into her core and stilled. Even with the condom, she felt him pulse inside her. He groaned against her lips. She stroked his tongue as his body trembled against hers.

Perfect.

THE LIGHT PEEKING through his cheap blinds wasn't what woke him up. It was the soft caress on his abdomen, drawing circles over his skin, and her warm breath fanning over his neck. The last memory he had before he'd passed out was Cheyenne curled into his side, completely drained from fucking. Her soft snore and complete contentment in his arms was what had eased him into sleep.

It was surprising they had slept the entire time in the same position, but there she was, snuggled into his side. It was all new territory for him. Women had tried to make a one-night stand into something permanent, but it wasn't what he was looking for. Or maybe they hadn't been the right woman. Here, with Cheyenne, it all felt right.

She curled deeper into his chest and sighed with her fingers digging into his ribs as though she held on, not wanting to let go. He fucking liked that. It should have scared the shit out of him. A self-proclaimed bachelor who made it known he wasn't looking to wife up or take on an old lady. *Now, fucking look at me.* Getting off on just having her snuggled in bed with him. His hand tightened on her back, pulling her closer.

"Morning," she whispered.

"You sleep good?"

"Yeah. I like your bed."

"Good 'cause I like you here, and you're gonna be spending a lot of time in it."

She giggled and cocked her head up. Her hair was a mess, strands sticking in every direction, smudged makeup, and a small crease in her cheek, probably from sleeping against his chest. *Beautiful.*

"You sound pretty confident, Trax. How do ya know there will be a next time?" She smirked, and he drew his brows tightly to the center. There would be a next time and a time after that. She was fooling herself if she thought this wasn't happening again.

"I made ya come twice, babe. There will be a next time."

She smiled and then dropped her face into his chest so quickly he almost missed the pinkening of her cheeks. His hand engulfed the back of her head, scratching her scalp, and she purred like a cat.

Her head popped up so quickly, she surprised him. He stared back at her, watching her eased face tense.

"So, we should have ground rules?"

He cocked his brow. "Rules?" What the hell was she talking about? She must have read the confusion on his face.

"You do know what rules are, right? I mean, I get they don't usually apply to you, but I have a few." She wiggled her brows. "Wanna hear them?"

Trax choked out a laugh. "This I gotta hear."

She propped her arm up, lying over the side of his chest. It would be hard to concentrate on these rules with her tits pressing against him, but he'd humor her.

She lifted her finger. "One. You can't kidnap me anymore."

The corner of his mouth curled. If she'd stop running from him, it would be an easy one to follow. She drew up a second finger.

"Two. If I'm in your bed, then you can't be with other women."

He nodded, holding back a laugh. "So, no threesomes? Is that what you're telling me?"

She narrowed her eyes, and before she could say anything, he pulled her in for a kiss. His mouth pressed against her lips, and though she was a bit resistant, he breached her lips, sliding his tongue inside. He hugged her close and shifted to the right, sending her onto her back with him caging her in.

He broke the kiss and smiled down at her. "Only one woman I wanna be inside of, and as soon as she gets done with her list of fucking rules, I plan on being there."

He expected her to smile or laugh. Instead, her lips turned down, and her forehead creased. "I'm serious, Trax." She licked her lips, and her gaze dropped down to his neck. "Don't cheat on me."

"Eyes up here, Chey." He waited for her to glance up. He'd be a dick not to understand her concern. His lifestyle allowed for women at his disposal. There were quite a few brothers who gave into temptation and cheated. It wasn't rare. It happened all the time. But he wasn't one of them.

"Don't want anyone else in my bed."

She squinted. "Or against a tree?'

He barked out a laugh and dropped his face into her neck. This woman. He kissed her under her ear, leaning back, so she saw his eyes when he answered her and knew the truth. "You, Chey. All I want, anywhere." He leaned closer and whispered, "You."

She stared back at him, searching for what he assumed was deception. He gave her that. She could look into his eyes for the next fucking hour. She wouldn't find any deceit. Her hips twitched, and he maneuvered between her legs. He was hard as a steel rod, rubbing against her warm core. She needed to wrap up this shit.

"We good or ya got more 'cause…" he shifted his cock to glide against her pussy "…not sure how much longer I can hold out, baby."

She smirked, dragging her hands down his back with her nails scratching against his skin. "One more." She smiled, but it didn't reach her eyes. "Don't trick me. If you wanna know something, just ask me, but don't invite me to the club just to get information."

He all but halted and froze. It was never his intention to try to con her. "It wasn't supposed to go down the way it did last night. You were there 'cause I wanted you there. Now, I won't lie and say I wasn't gonna show you the pictures of the guys to find out who did this to Mick, but you weren't there as some kind of con."

"I felt tricked," she whispered.

His finger lined the side of her head, and he leaned in. "It was fucked, and I am sorry shit went down without me there, Chey. Won't happen again, you got my word."

His lips pressed into hers, and he moved against her core, sliding his cock against her clit. Her breath grew heavy in his mouth. Fuck, he had to wrap up, but she felt so damn good. And wet. Her tongue swirled around his, and when he slid down to her entrance, it was too much to resist. The crown of his cock breached her lips, and he thrust inside her.

The only way he was stopping was if she told him to, but she grasped his back, pulling him deeper inside her. The last time he'd gone bareback with anyone was his ex, and even then, it didn't feel this good.

Her lips pulled from his mouth, and he thought she'd tell him to get a condom, but instead, her lips trailed over his neck, licking and sucking his skin. She felt so right, so fucking perfect. His hips kept a steady sway, and she moaned against his neck.

He would not be lasting long if she kept making those sexy sounds each time he moved. His body completely engulfed her in smooth strokes. Sex with her a was game changer for everything in his past. Usually, it had been a means to an end. Coming being the end goal. With her, he tried to hold out, completely lost in their connection.

He was too close to chance it, and he shifted to his knees and sat back, pulling out of her and taking his cock in his fist. The sight of her tits and her hands, sliding up her rib cage and cupping her breasts, was too much, and he jerked himself all over her stomach in a sharp groan.

When he opened his eyes again, she stared up at him with a small smile playing on her lips. "That was hot."

He snorted and leaned across the bed for a blanket, wiping her clean before tossing it onto the floor. This wasn't over. Even being with her only twice, he knew she hadn't come. That was unacceptable. He shifted down the bed, and her eyes widened. He didn't give her any time to speak or possibly protest. He dropped his head between her legs and licked her clit, getting the reaction he wanted.

"Oh, God." He would have preferred to hear his own name, but he'd settle for her gasping for the Lord instead. Her hips shifted forward, wanting more, and he sucked the nub between her lips. Her pelvis drove against his mouth, and he continued his assault.

Then the doorbell rang. He paused for a second. Who the fuck was at his door that early in the morning? Her legs locked against his head, caging him. It was a non-verbal command. He would have laughed if not for the mouthful of pussy. When he shifted to his stomach, her hand drove into his hair.

"No, no, please don't stop."

The desperation in her voice was almost comical. Little did she realize, nothing could stop him from making her come. He ignored the bell when it sounded again and continued to get her off, rapidly sliding his tongue over her clit and hearing the panting in short breaths. Stopping would be cruel, she was so close. Hell, not that it mattered, even if she were hours from coming, he would stay there until he got her off.

Her fingers twisted in his hair, and she tightened her grip as her hips moved against his mouth. He felt the minute she came as her body tensed, and she moaned his name past her lips.

"Trax, please." It was breathy and half incoherent, but he

heard it. Her hips spasmed, and she gasped when his mouth covered her core, pressing his lips against her sensitive bead. Her hand pushed against his head, tearing him away from between her legs.

"Too sensitive." She breathed heavily, and his lips curled as he glanced up at her. She was completely spent with her eyes closed and her mouth open in the shape of an O.

His phone rang as he climbed up the bed and laid next to her. He sighed. Whoever was at his door wasn't leaving. They were just trying a new tactic to get in touch with him. He sat up, leaning over her, and grabbed it. As he shifted back to his side of the bed, she grabbed his neck and pulled him down for a kiss.

"Thank you," she said and slumped against the mattress. He chuckled, sensing she might pass out again.

He brought the phone to his ear. "What?" he snapped.

"Open the fucking door, asshole. It's freezing out here."

Trax sighed. "Why didn't you just use your fucking key?" Both Gage and Rourke had a spare to his house. It wasn't uncommon to find them crashing on his couch after a late night. Gage more so than Rourke.

Gage laughed. "Was gonna, but Rourke said with how fucking raged you were last night, you might shoot our asses if we just come in."

He huffed and threw his legs over the side of the bed, searching for his jeans. It made sense. While being with Cheyenne may have distracted him from the shit last night, he hadn't forgotten. Thinking of it now, he harbored the same anger.

"Use the key. I'll be down in a few." He clicked his phone and then tossed it onto the bed before leaning forward and grabbing his jeans from the floor. He kept silent and glanced over at Cheyenne, who was clearly passed out. It was better that way. He had the feeling winning her over into feeling good about the club wasn't something that would happen any time soon.

He shoved his phone into his back pocket and walked out of his room. He heard Gage's and Rourke's hushed tones as he got closer. The house was small, and most conversation could be heard from any room. He walked out to find them in the living room, Gage on the couch and Rourke standing by his front window.

"Mornin'." He stretched his arms over his head, hearing the crack in his back. Sleeping with a woman nestled into his chest was new for him, and so was the ache in his neck. It would take some getting used to but definitely something worth doing. He folded his arms over his chest and stared at his brothers.

"Good night?" Gage chuckled and wiggled his brows.

"You come over here to ask me how my night went? Thinking this isn't a social visit, man, so let's get on with it."

"Still pissed?" Gage asked.

Trax narrowed his eyes. "What do you think?"

Rourke stepped into the center of the room and cocked his head toward the hallway. "We got the party coming up on Friday. Kase wants her there."

"Why?"

Rourke stretched his neck and scowled. "Saint thinks he might know who it was. Actually, he's pretty sure he'll be there on Friday. Wants Cheyenne to ID him."

"Send me a picture, and I'll check with her."

Before he could finish his sentence, Rourke shook his head. "Kase wants her there."

Trax ground his teeth. Getting Cheyenne to agree to go back to the club was a long shot, and even if he could conquer the feat, he wasn't sure he wanted her there. This thing with her was different from anything he'd had before. He'd almost lost it once, and he wasn't sure he could risk it again. Not even for the club.

If he brought her in, he wanted all the information. He hadn't fully gained her trust, but he wasn't about to lose the little she did have.

"Who ya looking at?"

Rourke tightened his lips in a straight line. "Neither one is saying. Something about accusing the wrong person." Rourke sighed in frustration. "Think about it, man. The only people coming on Friday we got close ties to. It's fucked thinking one of them took Mick out."

"Shit." That was bad. Having an ally being the one to betray the club would be a hard pill to swallow for all of them. They had too many enemies to begin with.

"Just make sure she's there," Gage said, rising from the couch and centering himself between him and Rourke. Of all three, Gage had been the most laid-back, often discounted because of it. Too many had taken his easy-going demeanor and counted out his lethal side. He'd bared witness to that mistake once or twice.

But Trax didn't appreciate the order.

"I'll think about it."

Gage cocked a brow and smiled. "Kase wasn't asking, Trax."

Trax snorted and balled his hands. "Don't give a fuck what Kase wants."

"You should 'cause if you don't bring her in, he'll send us back to come get her."

Trax steeled his chest and stepped forward. "Are you threatening me?"

Gage shrugged. "Take it however the fuck you want, brother. Threat? Friendly advice? A mere suggestion?" Gage grinned. "Whatever gets her ass down to the club."

Trax stepped forward, and Gage held his ground. One punch to the jaw would send him flying. Gage was strong, but Trax was stronger, and they both knew it. "You like playing bitch boy for Kase?"

Gage curled his lip and snickered, glancing over his shoulder at Rourke. "Bitch boy? Is that what he called me?"

Rourke tensed but gave no reaction. Trax hadn't expected one. Gage sidestepped Trax, coming to stand next to him, only an inch away. Gage nodded and smirked. "Not a bitch boy, Trax. Just being a brother, something I signed up for, following the lead of the man I voted in as my president. A president who would do anything he could to find the people with blood on their hands."

He lowered his voice. "The blood of his brother, my brother, and in case you forgot, your brother."

Trax felt the slow burn rise in his chest. His back straightened, and his hands clenched. Gage had struck a nerve. There was no one more loyal to Mick than him, and for it to be questioned threw Trax into a wild, vengeful fury. He slowly turned to Gage, who inched back a step.

Rourke pushed Gage back and blocked him from what would have been a bloody wrath.

"Brother, you got the missing link locked up in your room." Rourke pointed over Trax's shoulder. "She saw him, man. She knows. And she's the only one who can ID him." Rourke rarely showed emotion, but Trax saw the deepening glimmer of pain in his eyes. "I get what you got with her, I get it, man. And if there was another way to do this, I'd have your back." He pressed his finger against Trax's chest. "For you, I'd go head to head with Kase if there was another option. But there isn't." He lowered his voice. "We owe it to Mick."

It was a hard, blasting truth. There was no other option, and they all owed Mick his vengeance. *Mick.* The man who'd stepped in to be Trax's only ally when he'd had no one. The man who'd showed him nothing but love and loyalty. Guilt crept in like a burning log, sparking in his chest. Trax stood in the way of Mick's justice. It was a no-win situation for him. If he followed through with what the club wanted, he'd be going back on his promise to her.

"I gotta sacrifice one for the other."

Rourke gripped his shoulder. "No." He tightened his grip. "Ain't nothing gonna happen to her. I'll give you my fucking word, brother."

"Like last time?"

Rourke closed his eyes and sighed. It was fucked up what had happened last night and rocked his trust in not only Kase but all the brothers.

"Listen to me, Kase was wrong, he knows and so does every

other member. This thing with Mick has everyone on edge, and it wasn't handled as it should have been."

Trax glared at him.

"No one's denying it, man, not even Kase. He knows he fucked up, misjudged what you got going with Cheyenne. That's on him, and he will make amends."

Trax shrugged off Rourke's hands. "Yeah, okay."

"Trax." Rourke furrowed his brows. "He knows, and he'll fucking fix this with her. Those are his words, not mine. But don't you forget, you ain't no fucking angel in this." He jerked his chin to the hallway, indicating where Cheyenne was. "You wanted this handled a certain way, didn't work out, but you taking hands to the president or any fucking brother, it goes against everything we are. So, man the fuck up, own the fuck up, and let's get Mick some fucking justice."

Truth. Rourke just unleashed on his ass nothing but the truth. Trax gazed down at the carpet. It had been all handled wrong from the very beginning.

"She's at my side the whole time."

Rourke gave a sharp nod. "Done, man."

"I'm not fucking around, Rourke."

Rourke nodded. "We'll have her flanked—you on one side, me on the other. Giving you my word, ain't nothing happening you don't want, and if Kase has a problem with it, he can take it up with you." He nodded. "And me."

"AND THERE IT IS," Cheyenne muttered as she crept back to the bed. She had spent the last ten minutes with her ear pressed against the door. She folded her leg and sat on her foot, allowing the other to dangle off the bed. He had been given a choice, and he'd made it.

Club 1, Her 0.

She was a fool for thinking it would have turned out any

differently. Of course, he would do what the club wanted. He'd made it clear how important it was to him. It was his life. And she wasn't.

Who was she to him anyway? Sure, they were great in bed and being with him last night, just talking, definitely sparked something other than arousal. He seemed so damn sincere when he'd spoken of protecting her and asking for forgiveness. *And I fell for it.* She liked him too much. It would end badly for her. She shook her head and nibbled on the inside of her mouth. The club would win every time. No matter what she thought she meant to him, the club would always come first.

She jerked her head when she heard the floor creak. The knob turned slowly, and he stopped in mid-step. He smiled, but it didn't quite reach his eyes. She raised her brows.

"Hi."

"Thought you'd still be sleeping."

She clamped her lips together to form an awkward smile. He had to know she'd heard everything. Maybe he expected her to just volunteer to go into the club. That wasn't happening. She was done with the Ghosttown Riders.

Trax eyed her as he came closer, dragging his hand through his hair and gripping at the back of his neck. "So, listen…"

"I don't want to," she blurted, not even sure where the assertive voice came from. It didn't even sound like hers. She stood and shook her head. "And you can't make me, Trax."

She inhaled deeply, but it was shaky on the exhale. Could he make her? Would he be willing to drag her down to the club even if she refused? She had no clue because, honestly, she didn't even really know Trax, and the small admission not only scared her but saddened her. She was getting involved and attached to a man she didn't even know.

His hand dropped from his neck down to his side. She couldn't read his face to get an idea of what he was thinking. The corner of his mouth curled, and he crossed his arms, rocking back on his heels. She was surprised when he burst out laughing. The corners of his eyes crinkled, and he heaved forward, releasing a hearty laugh. His eyes moistened, and his teeth gleamed from his open-mouthed smile. Cheyenne couldn't help but smile back, even though she couldn't see the humor in the situation.

"I don't get it. Why are you laughing?"

Trax wiped his cheek and then shoved his hands into his pockets. He stared at her with such ease. "Wasn't lying when I said Mick woulda liked ya. But that there, 'You can't make me?'" He chuckled. "Definitely something his old lady woulda said." He lifted his brows. "Actually, I'm pretty sure she has said that when I've been around."

"How did Mick respond?"

Trax shrugged. "Meg don't wanna do something, nobody alive can make her do it. Mick knew and wouldn't have even tried."

Cheyenne gazed down at the floor. She didn't know Meg well, but she didn't seem like the type to be told what to do.

"Wouldn't do that to you either, Chey."

She jerked her head up. His eyes softened, and he lifted his finger, calling for her to come closer. She stepped toward him, and before she could reach him, his arm circled her back and her breasts crushed against his chest. His mouth descended on her, taking her lips for a sultry, warm, arousing kiss. She gripped his neck, not wanting it to end too soon. She loved kissing this man. His teeth playfully nibbled her bottom lip before he grazed his tongue along the seam of her mouth. If he was trying to convince her by seduction, it may have been working.

He pulled away slightly, peppering soft kisses to her lips and then resting his forehead against hers. "Won't make ya do anything. Ever." He held her stare, and she had the feeling he wouldn't, but she also knew he wasn't done speaking. "I know you heard us, right?"

She nodded. Lying was useless.

"So ya heard Rourke say it. You're the only person who can help us find the guy who killed Mick."

"Trax." She sighed. What he'd said might be true, but the

thought of going into the club again had her heart racing and fear spiking.

"Not knowing who he is or why he did it leaves us all in danger. What if he comes for me next?"

Oh hell! Now he was using guilt? She pulled away, but he refused to let her an inch away. His fingers dug into her back.

"Please, Chey, nothing's gonna happen, I swear to you. Where I go, you go. You'll never be alone with anyone. We need ya to help us, baby."

"You're not asking me to look at a picture, Trax. You're asking me to be in the same room as him. Telling me to point my finger and say, 'He's the guy who killed Mick.' Do you have any idea the danger that puts me in? Or does that not even matter to you and the club?"

"I would never let anything happen to you, and neither would the club, I promise."

"Yeah, well your track record sucks on keeping me safe." She folded her arms. "I'm not sure I believe you."

His eyes darkened, and he released his hold over her. She inched back toward the bed, not liking the glare he sent her.

He snarled, and his lip curled. "You think I'm lying. All the shit I said to you last night, you think I lied?"

"I don't know, Trax." She drew in a breath. "Your club means everything to you, and I'm just some girl you got tangled up with due to circumstance."

He flinched and settled back against the wall. "Is that what you think?"

She shrugged. "I don't know what to think."

The silence lingered in the room. She peeked up through her lashes but couldn't get a read on what he was thinking. His head fell back against the wall, but his gaze remained on her.

"First time I saw ya, when ya came into the club." He smirked. "You looked so outta place. You did this weird, nervous shift on your feet and scanning the guys. I thought, 'What the fuck is a woman like this doing in our club.' We've had pretty girls there but none compared to your beauty. If I had gotten ya in my sights riding down the road, I woulda stopped just to look at ya, Chey."

She bowed her head as her cheeks heated. He was not allowed to be sweet right now.

"Then I tackle your ass." He snorted. "Not the best first impression. Hell, any other woman would have called the cops on the spot. Not you, though. You came in, scared as hell, but gave the info to the club. Then ya shocked the shit outta me."

She glanced up, and his lips curled.

"Know what ya did?"

She shook her head.

"You gave your condolences." He drew in a breath with a small smile. "You're surrounded by bikers, in their club, handing over something ya know ain't legal. You get insulted, accosted, mocked, and berated, and still, ya say, 'I'm sorry ya lost Mick.' You may not have realized it, but you gained the respect of every man in the room when ya did that."

He sighed, pushing off the wall and strolling to the bed. He sat on the opposite end, much to her disappointment. "Everything I said last night was true. I wanna be with you, even if I don't deserve ya, and I probably don't." He glanced over. "I'd protect you with everything I am, Chey. I'm not choosing the club over you. I just can't let what happened to Mick go."

He sighed, staring back at her in silence.

"But I won't try to force your hand on this. Whatever you decide, I'll back it against the club." From where she sat, she could only see his profile. He took a deep breath and stared up at the ceiling.

There was more to the story here. She could feel it. He held back. She crawled across the mattress and saddled up next to him, grasping his hand. He clasped his fingers through hers and tightened his grip when he glanced over.

"What aren't ya telling me?" she whispered.

"It wasn't supposed to be Mick." He paused and angled his head toward her. "I was scheduled to make the pickup."

"What?"

He nodded and stared straight. "It was my pickup. But Mick knew I was backed up with the bike repairs, knew I needed to get shit done, so he offered to do it." He sighed, and his shoulders sagged. "And I fucking let him. Guilt is a hard thing to carry." He turned his head. "Don't want you to feel guilty, though. I carry that shit. I wouldn't intentionally put it on you." He cupped her jaw and pressed his lips against her mouth, smiling. "Got a confession, I lied this morning."

Her gaze lifted, and he smirked. "I promised not to trick ya ever again. It was a fucking lie."

"What?"

"Yeah, planning on tricking you to one day fall in love with me."

"How long does it take for this plan to go into effect?"

"Why? Is it working?"

She leaned in with a soft kiss and whispered, "Yes."

He grinned and kissed her again, lingering on her lips and tugging her body against his. She could have spent the rest of the day cuddled up kissing him, but he broke apart and tapped her butt. "Got a few repairs I gotta do. Get dressed and come hang with me." He stood and walked to his dresser.

"That's it?"

He glanced over his shoulder.

"It's over?"

"Unless you changed your mind, yeah, that's it. I'll call Kase, tell him it ain't happening."

"Then what?"

He shrugged. "Like I said, I got a few bikes I gotta work on. Should only take a few hours. We can go grab something to eat now if ya want. Ya hungry?"

"So I say no and that's it? You're not gonna make me go to the club, even though you know it can help the club?"

He sighed, crossed his arms, and leaned against the doorframe. "Thought we covered this. Not gonna make ya do something you don't want to do."

"And you're fine with that? You make the call and that's it. We're still gonna…" She clasped her lips, searching for the right word.

"Fuck?" His eyes flicked in amusement.

She glared back at him. "I was going to say date."

The corner of his mouth curled, and he pushed off the wall, stalking to her. He gripped her waist and tossed her onto the bed. She landed with a soft bounce, and he immediately straddled her body, reaching in and kissing her.

"Yeah, we're still gonna date." He chuckled and kissed her neck. "And God, I hope there's still gonna be fucking. My dick is hard just thinking about being inside you. All sweet, warm, and wet." He ground his cock against her pussy. Even with layers of clothes between them, moisture pooled between her legs.

"Trax." It came out as a moan, and he reamed against her.

"That's exactly how I want you to say my name when my cock is sliding inside you." His hands were over her breasts, tugging at her shirt.

"Wait."

He groaned and tweaked her nipple, sending chills straight to her core. She moaned as he licked her neck and twisted her nipple again. It felt so good, she was getting completely lost in her thoughts, and all she could do was feel.

"The bikes can wait. I want you naked," he whispered into her ear, and his teeth grazed her outer shell. He pulled away and tore off his shirt, tossing it across the room. She immediately pressed her hands against his pecs. This man's body was a dream. She dragged her nails lightly across his abdomen and down to the buckle of his jeans.

"I'll do it."

"What?" He froze.

"I'll go to the club, but only with you, and ya have to promise not to leave me alone with anyone." His admission about him being the intended target changed things. It changed everything.

"No, Chey." He swung his leg off her and fell against the bed. She angled up on her elbow. "Fuck." He covered his eyes with his arm.

"Trax. Just listen..."

He growled in obvious frustration. "You said no, and it's no. Not gonna change your mind just 'cause you're fucking about to come."

She leaned over, draping her chest over his and tugging at his arm to see his eyes. She smiled at his distraught face. "I want to and not because I'm about to come, which by the way, ya gotta do a little more work before I orgasm." She smirked. "You're good but not that good, Trax." He lifted a brow, and she continued. "It's like you said, I'm the only one who can help, and if this guy is looking to hurt the club, you could be next." Her heart raced in a panicked stutter. "I don't want you to get hurt."

"Hey," he whispered, grasping her jaw and bringing her closer. "No one's gonna hurt me."

"You don't know that. If it had been you instead of Mick that day, you'd be dead."

Her eyes welled. This sucked. She was getting too attached to him, falling for him. All the emotions she felt pointed to falling in love with him, and the mere thought of losing him sent fear racing through her blood.

"Chey." He stroked her face. "Stop, sweetheart. Not gonna get hurt." His features softened, and a small smile spread across his face. "Don't like seeing ya weepy, but gotta say, feels nice ya worrying about me."

"I do." She sniffled and silently prayed her nose wasn't running.

"And I'm telling you, ya got no reason."

But there was reason. As long as the man was out there, Trax wouldn't be safe.

"Then let me do it. I wanna go to the club."

He stared at her for a long while. He seemed to be contemplating. Maybe he was trying to figure out if she was doing it for the right reasons or not. Either way, she was going, and she would help them out if it meant keeping him safe.

He nodded and licked his lips. "I gotcha, Chey. Nothing's gonna happen at the club. I know you don't believe me, but that's one place ya never have to worry about whether you're safe or not. You are. And here too, you'll always be safe at my place, in my bed, anytime and anywhere with me. Ya got me?"

"Yeah."

Chapter 13

Cheyenne was seated in the middle of the living room, finishing up the last of the orders. The week had proved to be their best yet. A storefront was still a futuristic goal, but they were on their way. She leaned over, checking her phone.

"What's the matter? Lord Leather dodging your calls?" Macy snorted. "I'm not surprised."

Cheyenne turned toward the hall just as Macy made her way to the kitchen. Snark and sarcasm had been running rampant in the apartment the last week. Cheyenne understood her friend's reluctance with Trax, but Macy took it to new heights. She couldn't whisper his name without Macy going into a tirade about what she thought of him.

Her phone pinged, and she grabbed it.

Trax: *Pick you up at 9*

Cheyenne: *Yes.*

"Ugh." Macy groaned, gaining Cheyenne's attention. It was her plan.

Cheyenne sighed, and her shoulders slumped. *Here we go...*

"What the hell are you doing here, Chey?" Macy rested her

hands on her hips and cocked her head. It was easy to read her face—confusion and aggravation were hard to mask. Cheyenne reminded herself it was Macy's concern that caused her to be a gigantic pain in the ass when it came to her love life.

"I'm finishing up orders." She smiled up at her friend, who glared back at her. Cheyenne knew exactly what the question referred to, and it had nothing to do with their business.

"And him?"

Cheyenne rolled her eyes as she gathered the last of the packing slips and moved them to the kitchen table. The way she referred to Trax as *him*, as if she couldn't bear to speak his name. *I get it, Mace.* Trax wasn't Prince Charming. He wasn't from money, and he didn't have a white-collar job. Hell, he'd served time. No, he wasn't going to be someone's model version of the perfect boyfriend; she understood it. But Macy didn't know Trax. She didn't have a view into Chey's heart.

Telling Macy it was none of her business was not an option. Being best friends for so long had given her a right into Cheyenne's life and vice versa. It was best to handle this with care. Extreme care with a touch of vagueness. Telling her to mind her own business was not going to go over well at that moment, and the last thing she wanted was more confrontation with an already annoyed Macy.

She sighed, shrugging as she leaned back into the sofa. "I don't know." She would give her the bare minimum. After all, her relationship was really none of her business.

"You don't know? What the hell kinda answer is that?"

She snorted. "I don't know, I guess we're hanging out."

"Hanging out?" Macy's eyes widened, and her jaw tightened.

"Yes, and please stop repeating everything I say with a question." Cheyenne tucked her feet under her butt and sat up straight. "We're getting to know each other, so yeah, I guess dating." She could gauge the unhappiness in Macy's expression. "You told me to have fun." And Macy had, before the threatening incident. That had changed everything

"Yeah, fun as in having sex once, maybe twice if he was any good." She stepped forward and spread her arms in front of her. "Not date him. Hell, Chey, do bikers even date anyway?"

Cheyenne chuckled. Macy made Trax out to be inhumane.

"Yeah, I'm pretty sure it's in their bylaws they can date."

"Don't be cute. You know what I mean."

"Actually, I don't."

"Are you so naïve to think you are the only one," she held her hands up, giving her hand quotes, "'dating him'? Come on, Chey, you gotta know he's banging other girls. Is that what you want? To be one of his girls."

Cheyenne was taken aback. Was it necessary for Macy to make assumptions and shit all over her relationship she knew nothing about?

"You don't even know him, Mace. Judgmental, much?"

"No judgment here. He can do whatever he wants as long as he doesn't hurt you." She pointed at Cheyenne, and her face softened, the corner of her mouth curling. "I know you, Chey, you're too good to be one of his girls. You should be the only one for whatever guy you choose."

Cheyenne sighed, resting her head against the cushion. It was coming from a good place, which was why it was hard for her to be mad at Macy.

"He's not seeing anyone else, Mace."

She slowly sauntered to the couch, taking a seat next to Chey. "So, what, you date, have fun, then what? Gonna marry the biker and have little biker babies?"

"Shut up." Cheyenne snorted. Kids were so far from her mind it was comical. But her question wasn't so off. Cheyenne had always wanted to get married and have a family. She bit her lip, tearing her gaze from her friend. The club didn't seem family friendly, though she'd only been there three times. All disastrous.

"I'm serious. Can't count the times you told me what your end game looks like—husband, kids, vacations at the beach, house with a two-car garage and two-and-a-half baths." She cocked her brow. "Those are your words. Now what? You think he can give you the life you want? And even if he could, you want to spend your life with a man like him? Their lifestyle, how they make their money, Chey, it's fucking shady gangster shit. The things they do could land their asses in jail."

Cheyenne lost all traces of humor. She may not like it, but everything Macy had said held an ounce of truth. Trax made no secret that some of what they did was illegal, and while kids weren't on her brain now, they were in her future, along with a house and a husband who was not incarcerated. Her body sank into the couch as she released a deep breath.

"In this dream of yours, can you see yourself traipsing the kiddies to the prison for visiting hours to see Daddy? Look, banging a biker for a night? That's one thing, but making a life with him? Are you crazy? It's absurd. You really want a lifetime with a dirty thug and to spend your weekends schlepping his little biker babies to the prison to visit their dad, who is probably spending his time making drug deals or dropping the soap?"

Macy's rant was slightly ridiculous but not all of it. She couldn't even imagine something so horrible. Children at a jail, visiting their dad? What kind of life would she have with him? Certainly not the one she envisioned for herself. She clasped her hands together and stared at her chipped nail polish.

Macy wrapped her arm around her shoulders, tugging her into her side. "I'm not trying to shit in your Cheerios here, just wanna lay it out for you, Chey. I get it, ya like him, and this whole thing is new and wild, but eventually, the thrill of dating him will wear off. Then what? You deserve to get everything you want, and I just don't think Trax can give it to you."

She'd had enough. She pushed off the couch. "Let's get the orders done, all right?"

"Chey."

She'd had it and wasn't going to listen to any more. Her brain couldn't handle it. Neither could her heart. Through all Macy's ranting, some things rang true. It bothered her more than she wanted to admit. She spun around and held up her hand.

"I don't wanna talk about it anymore. Let's just get this done."

It seemed Macy would let it go, for now. It would come up again, Cheyenne knew.

THE ONLY SOUND pounding in his eardrums was the deep, hard breaths from his chest. He kept his focus on the corner wall and grasped his beer tightly just to remain in some sense of control. If he lost it, the bottle would be smashing against the wall in seconds flat. Then he would be hell on wheels, driving to her place to set her little fucking friend straight. *Fucking bitch.*

"Hey, Trax, man?"

He slowly turned to Gage, who had been sitting at the opposite end of the table. His eyes crinkled, and the corner of his mouth lifted. "I'm thinking the best friend isn't a fan." He grinned and snickered.

"Yeah, well, the feeling is fucking mutual." Trax dropped his beer to the table, sending a thundering clank through the room. The last thing he needed was Macy in Chey's ear, telling her he was no good for her. He knew exactly where he wanted this thing to go with Cheyenne, but knew it would be a struggle. They were different—their lifestyles, their families, and obviously, their friends. With the odds all stacked against them already, he sure as hell didn't need doubt of him put into her head. Especially from someone she trusted.

The audio installed a few weeks ago in their apartment was mainly for informational purposes. At the time, the club didn't know how honest Cheyenne was willing to be, and they needed the information on the guy who'd attacked Mick. He didn't agree with it and made it known to Kase and the other members. He was outnumbered with the decision. They viewed it as a logical move.

Now, it seemed they were getting more than they'd bargained for, and eventually, he would have to tell Cheyenne. He had no illusions of her accepting it without an argument. But with Macy, he knew it would be an all-out brawl and something that could potentially ruin a future with Cheyenne.

He stood, knocking his chair back, and circled the table. This was fucked. He was fucked. He paced around the room, trying to batten down his fury. He turned to the prospect manning the tap.

"You get anything else besides the bitch trash talking me?"

"Nothing about the driver. Mostly girl shit. And uhh…" When Trax followed his stare, Gage grinned back at him.

"Got some audio on Macy and her douchebag bitch. It's some funny shit. Let's just say our Macy is quite the actress. How the asshole didn't know she was faking it is beyond me. I'll play it back for ya."

"No," Rourke snapped.

Trax stared back at him. He tensed and cocked his brow in a sinister glare aimed at Gage.

Gage laughed, swiveling in his seat to face Rourke. "You sweet on her, man? 'Cause you heard the same as we all did. Short stack doesn't think much of us *dirty bikers.*"

Trax watched Rourke closely. This wouldn't be the first time Macy became a subject with Rourke taking up for her. He remembered exactly how pissed he'd been at Trax with the incident from the girls' apartment.

"Fuck off, Gage," Rourke said, though he never denied his interest. He hoped to hell Rourke stayed away from her. Nothing good could come from any involvement with Macy.

When she caught wind of the audio tap in the apartment, she would go ballistic. It would be more ammo to use with Cheyenne against him. But his only other option was to not say anything. It was plausible. The odds of her finding out were slim. But there was always a chance. *Fuck me.*

"I see where your mind is at, and I'm telling ya, brother, you don't wanna do it," Gage said.

Trax balled his hands and then spread out his fingers. He was so wired right now, he needed to relax, or even just calm the fuck down. "You got no idea what I'm thinking, so stay the fuck outta my head, Gage."

Gage snorted and then laughed, eyeing Rourke who stood off to the side, leaning up against the wall with his arms crossed.

"Gonna tell her?" Rourke asked, cocking a brow.

Trax stared back.

Gage shook his head. "Mistake, man. When it blows up in your face, don't say I didn't warn your ass."

Trax glared over behind him at Gage and caught Kase walking through the door, followed by a few members.

"Taking a run up to Ghosttown on Monday. Who's coming?"

"So, we're really doing this? Moving on up there? Population what, ten?"

Kase drew in a breath, releasing it with tension obvious in his shoulders. He scowled at Gage. "Just need to get the approval for the permits, and we can start construction on the rebuild to meet our needs." Kase cocked his brow. "Yeah, Gage, we'll have a fucking stripper pole installed. I also got the contractor coming up for the store. And the site for the junkyard is just about cleared."

It was all falling into place.

Another member, Danny, piped in. "Already got the permits approved for Lana's coffee shop." It seemed quite a few members and their spouses were taking advantage of branching out and making use of the commercial property on Main Street.

Kase nodded. "That's good." He eyed the group with a rare smile. "It's happening, brothers."

It had been a while since he had been up there. This was the perfect distraction Trax needed. He'd get away for a day or two.

"I'll go up with ya," Trax answered.

Kase nodded and turned to Rourke and Dobbs.

"We got the pickup, so we're out." They were headed out for another purchase of parts from a distributor that had folded. The business was continuing to go strong.

Kase waited on Gage.

"Yeah, I'll go for the ride, but why exactly are we going?"

"Wanna rush on the permits so we can get in soon. Their monthly town meeting is Monday. Figured we'd show and get in with the mayor who oversees the permits."

"The mayor? Town has twenty-two people, and they have a fucking mayor?"

Trax snorted, shaking his head. This brainchild was all Kase, and while he understood why Ghosttown was a good fit for them, he, like the others, wasn't sold on the solidarity of the small town. He'd been there a few times and enjoyed the roads, perfect for a ride, but to live out there? No, he wasn't fully on board.

He planned on keeping his house and making the drive for events and meetings. He'd spend time in the small town before he'd commit to it. Cheyenne popped into his head. She was another reason he stalled his final decision. Leaving her behind wasn't an option. She'd have to be on board with moving too. *Crazy bastard*. He knew the girl for a few weeks and was already basing his life decisions around her.

"We'll head up at two, get in by six. Starts at seven. You wanna ride back, you can. Cade offered to house your sorry asses if ya wanna leave in the morning."

Caden lived about twenty minutes from Ghosttown and had an awesome set up at his place, with a small apartment unit on his property. He'd stay the night and hang with Caden, as most brothers would probably do.

It wasn't lost on Trax that maybe one reason Kase pulled for the small town had something to do with being closer to his family.

Rourke stepped forward. "Cade commit to the deal yet?"

Trax watched Kase. His shoulders tensed, and he avoided eye contact.

"He will." It would be the only answer they'd get. All the men knew better than to push further with Kase. Trax assumed Caden just needed more time, and he understood it.

The Favor

Gage stood and made his way out of the room, followed by the prospect, Dobbs, and Rourke. Trax walked toward the door but stopped when Kase called his name. Trax glanced over his shoulder.

"Give me a minute." He jerked his chin to the door, and Trax closed it.

The tension between the two of them had been thick since the incident. He hadn't apologized for his part. Neither had Kase. Trax figured they would let it go and move on.

"We got Hades and the club visiting this weekend."

Trax immediately tensed his shoulders and straightened his back. Rourke had mentioned a visiting club, but Trax hadn't expected it to be Hades'. The whole reason behind the party on Friday was to confirm Saint's and Kase's suspicions of who'd killed Mick. Hades's club would be the last he'd expect to take out one of theirs.

Kase folded his arms. "I see where your head's at, but we don't know anything yet."

Trax shook his head in disbelief. "Yeah, but fucking Hades's club, that don't make sense."

Hades was the VP of his club and had a strong bond and connection with the Ghosttown Riders since Trax patched in. When they ran into trouble, Hades was the first man they reached out to for backup. He wouldn't betray them, or Mick, and especially not, Saint.

Kase didn't respond and walked over to the table. His silence was clear. It may not have made sense, but it didn't mean it wasn't possible.

Kase sat and leaned back in his seat. "She gonna show next Friday?"

Trax drew in a deep breath. "Yeah, said she would." He cocked his brow. "Her choice, Kase. Told her she didn't have to, and I'd back her decision, but she wants to do it. For Mick."

He raised his brows. "And you, brother."

Trax stared back, not answering.

Kase rested his elbows on the table. "Known you a long time, Trax. Hard pressed to find a brother as loyal to the club as you. Got a lot of respect for you. Always have." His brows furrowed, and he narrowed his gaze into a sinister glare. "You ever put your hands on me again, you better fucking kill me 'cause I'm only gonna let it slide this one time. You feel me?"

Trax didn't fear Kase. If they did go up against one another, there would be no guaranteed winner. They were equally as deadly. But he had been wrong. He shouldn't have laid hands on Kase. "Yeah, I get ya."

"Good."

Trax turned to walk away.

"Shoulda had you there."

Trax froze before he slowly turned to face Kase.

Kase sat back in his seat, staring at Trax. "I fucked up. Your girl, seeing her reaction to the fear, doesn't sit right with me."

"Doesn't sit right with me either, Kase."

He nodded. "I know."

Trax rested his hands on his hips. "She doesn't trust the club."

He nodded. "I'm gonna make it so she does. Just need her here on Friday."

"She'll be here." He said it, knowing it might be a lie. He could wait to come clean with her about the audio, but the longer he waited, the worse it would be. He'd explain it in a way she'd understand and forgive him. It was what he counted on.

Kase laughed, shaking his head. "Woulda thought you'd be the last one getting yourself wifed up around here."

Trax grinned. "You saw her, man, she's fucking gorgeous." He folded his arms and paused. For as beautiful as she was, there was more to her beyond her outer beauty. He sighed. "Ya know what plays over in my head when I look at her?"

Kase cocked a brow.

"She was the last thing Mick saw before he died. Her voice telling him to hang on and be strong. It was the last sound he heard. She held his hand, man." He smiled. "That shit she did for Mick, that's who she is, just good and sweet. If I didn't grab her, these assholes would be in line, fighting for a chance with her." He raised his brows. "Am I right?"

Kase snickered, which was rare. "Yeah."

Chapter 14

She clung on tightly to Trax's stomach as they made the sharp turn around the narrow bend. For the past two weeks, she'd ridden on the back almost daily and loved every minute of it. They had seen each other every day since the "kidnapping" as she liked to call it. They both had jobs and worked, but free time was spent together.

She caught some flak from Macy. For obvious reasons, she didn't exactly condone the romance. Cheyenne tried her best to ignore the snide comments.

The Friday night party had been postponed. No one was happy about it, especially Trax. She assumed he was worried she would change her mind given more time to think. She wouldn't. She had her concerns, but she trusted him. The sooner it was done, the sooner some of the guilt Trax carried would be gone. Or that was her hope.

She dodged all other invites to the clubhouse, and they spent their time at his place. He'd even offered space in his garage to house the products for their small business. It was the only silver lining, according to Macy. It would take more than a storage spot to win her over, and she wasn't sure Trax even cared to try with Macy.

She may not have any interest in the club, but she jumped at the chance to go see Meg, Mick's widow. There was something about her, an odd, eerie connection. Mick. When Trax mentioned stopping by, she asked to join him.

They pulled up to the small house at the corner. The grass needed a cut, and the trees needed to be trimmed back, but the house itself was in fairly decent shape. Trax pulled into the driveway and headed to the back to the detached garage. Two bikes were parked in front. As he parked and she dismounted, she caught sight of Rourke and Gage exiting the back door.

Cheyenne pulled off her helmet and then ran her fingers through her knotted strands.

"Gotta braid it." The deep masculine voice surprised her, and she glanced over her shoulder at Rourke. There was no emotion behind his words. She hadn't seen either man since the night when she'd been locked in the room.

"Yeah, thanks," she said, drawing her gaze to the yard.

"How's it going, Chey?" Gage came to stand in front of her with a smile. The man was gorgeous with his piercing blue eyes. His presence made her uncomfortable. They both did.

Trax had mentioned how close he was with all his brothers, especially Rourke and Gage. She knew if she was going to be a part of his life, these two would be in it. With her resistance to club parties, she hadn't spent much time around them. Unfortunately, her encounters with Rourke and Gage had not been pleasant in the past.

"Good." She felt Trax's hand wrap around her waist and tug her into his side.

The men greeted each other and walked over to the small card table. Cheyenne grabbed a seat to pull out, but Gage's words stopped her. "Babe, why don't you head inside, go see Meg?"

His tone was polite, but she didn't appreciate being dismissed. She waited for Trax to tell her to stay, but he didn't. He lifted his chin toward the house. "Gotta talk to them about shit. Go see Meg."

She stared back at him but didn't move. Where was her option?

Trax lifted his chin. "Go ahead. You'd be bored listening to us."

Rourke snorted.

"I don't mind," she said. She was challenging him. She really had no interest in anything they had to say, but she didn't enjoy being dismissed.

"Chey," Trax said, his eyes darkening. "Need you to go inside."

Dismissed.

She furrowed her brows and stepped back when he leaned in for what she thought might be a kiss. He cocked his brow, and she turned quickly. She wasn't going to kiss him when he'd obviously just dismissed her. *Fuck that bullshit.* She opened the door, letting herself in, and found Meg at the counter in her small, dated kitchen.

"Hey, girl." Meg's expression and excitement for seeing her gave just enough pause to keep her from going back outside and telling Trax to fuck off. Meg pulled her in for a hug.

"Heard you were coming. Let's get some beers and go on the front porch." Meg released her arms and went for the fridge.

"Not out back? Have you been exiled too?" She knew it was snotty and bratty, but the words just flew from her mouth.

Meg slowly stood and laughed. "God, you remind me so much of myself when Mick and I first got together." She knocked her hip into the door, closing the fridge and grinned. "C'mon. Let's go have a talk."

Cheyenne followed her out front and took her lead, planting herself at the opposite end of the porch steps. Meg sat leaning back against the column and placed Chey's beer on the step. She brought the bottle to her lips. "Tell me." She took a sip of her beer, staring at Cheyenne.

What was she supposed to say? She didn't like being dismissed? She hated there was a part of his life that would always be separate and private from her? How was she supposed to be with someone who had a life she wasn't a part of? In the past week, she noticed he left the room on several occasions to take a call. One night he'd left after midnight and hadn't returned until four in the morning. When she questioned him, he said it was club business.

Maybe Macy was right. Her best friend had sat her down for what seemed like an intervention of sorts. There was no question Macy wasn't a fan of Trax's, but she did bring up a few good points. *I do want to settle down and get married one day.* She wanted the white picket fence with a big backyard for BBQs and kids' birthday parties. They wanted different things in life. They were too different for this to ever work out. She didn't want to throw away all her dreams just to follow him on his path to achieving his. It seemed pointless to bring it up with Trax. Hell, they'd only been together for a short while. Yet, it lingered in the back of her mind because she was falling fast for him.

"I'm waiting, Chey."

She glanced up from the bottle in her hands.

"I think I want more, Meg." Finally saying it out loud had her best friend's words ringing true. Macy had hit the nail on the head. She had a plan, one she wanted so bad she could taste it. She glanced up from her bottle and caught a glimmer and a smirk from Meg before she swallowed the last of her drink. "I have plans."

"And Trax can't fit into those plans of yours?" It wasn't an accusation, but there was something beyond the seemingly innocent question.

"I'm not sure we want the same things." There was no arguing with it, and Meg would understand. She knew Trax better than most, and certainly more than Cheyenne.

"He told you that?" She angled her head and turned toward Cheyenne. "You guys discussed the future?"

"Well." She licked her lips. "Not really. Only been together a short while."

"So, you haven't talked to him about it, but you assume he won't be on board with ya?"

Her lower lip jutted out, and Cheyenne sighed heavily. "I want a family someday. I've always talked about getting married and having kids."

She chuckled. "And Trax doesn't?" She shook her head mockingly and rolled her eyes. "Strange, because I remember a handful of times him talking about settling down, being a father who showed up at baseball games and scout meetings." The corner of her mouth curled, and her brow cocked. "Might remember him saying something about not minding sitting through three hours of ballerinas if it's what his little girl wanted to do. Doesn't sound to me like a man who doesn't want a family."

"He said that?"

Meg smiled and nodded. "I think Trax would make an awesome dad, don't you?"

Cheyenne could almost picture him in the garage with small boys, showing them bikes. She smiled but cast the vision from her head. She kept hearing Macy's voice. "We want different things."

Meg sat back in her chair and smirked. "You're not willing to sit through three-hour recitals?"

Cheyenne snickered and rolled her eyes. She knew exactly what Meg was doing. Chey was grateful in an odd way. Trax did want some of the same things she wanted, but there would always be a pink elephant lodged between them. She glanced down at her glass and sighed. *Just say it.*

"I'll never be number one with him."

It was a fact, and not something Trax could even deny. She didn't need to hear it from him. It was what she'd seen, and would see for the rest of her life if she stayed with him.

"Ohhh, now I see, okay, yeah you're right, it won't work then."

Cheyenne refused to glance over at Meg. She didn't want to see the hurt that came with the confirmation. For as much as she knew it was true, there was a small part of her that wished Meg had lied and said she would be Trax's number one.

"See," she whispered.

"Not really, but I'll appease ya cause I think that's the angle you're working."

Cheyenne jerked her head and straightened her back. "I'm not working any angle."

"Sure, ya are. You won't be number one 'cause that's the spot reserved for the club, right?" She shook her head and smiled. "You have a baby, Trax still gonna be your number one? And don't lie and say yes 'cause you and I know both know it's bullshit. Your child will become your top priority, same as Trax with the club."

"It's different."

"Why, 'cause it's you versus him? Chey, I been around bikers for over twenty-five years, and while there are a few bad apples thrown in the mix, for the most part, these are good guys. And most of all, they are loyal and loving and want to see each brother get exactly what he wants and deserves. You afraid the club will come between you? If they do, it's got nothing to do with the brothers, that falls on you."

What? My fault? Cheyenne swiveled her body to face Meg and straightened her back. Getting into a shouting match with Meg was not something she planned, but this was bullshit.

"How the hell would it be my fault? That's ridiculous." Cheyenne tightened her lips to keep herself in check.

"If the club comes between you and Trax, it's because you let those two worlds collide." She waved her hand and snorted. "Made that mistake early on with Mick. Thought I could be number one in his world with his brothers." She shook her head and frowned. "Almost lost him."

"See, then you get what I'm saying."

Meg turned her head slowly and stared at Cheyenne. Her eyes welled slightly, and the corner of her lip curled softly. "Oh, I get it. But do you hear what I'm saying?" She reached out, resting her hand on Cheyenne's knee, giving her a small squeeze. "It's two worlds for him—one with his brothers where the club reigns king, and the other with you, where you reign queen. You'll be his number one, Cheyenne, just not in his club life."

She heard Macy's voice sound in her mind.

"If he goes to jail?"

She rolled her eyes and waved her hand in front of her face. "You think you marry some nine-to-five, straitlaced guy it can't happen to him?" She twisted her lips. "People go to jail all the time, not something you should base your life on."

The women, Chey, what about that?

"The women?"

Meg chuckled, shaking her head. "What about them? Look, your man wants to cheat on you, he'll do it, biker or not. Yeah, they may have an advantage with options at the clubhouse, but if you really feel like Trax would cheat," she paused and cocked her head, "then, girl, run and run fast. Now, if you're asking me, I'd tell you to open your eyes and see the man who's standing in front of you. Trax, he's a lot of things, but a cheater ain't one of them."

"I love him, and it scares me," she whispered.

"Well, yeah, it should. Love, real love, is scary, but, Chey, sweetie, it's worth it, and so is Trax. From the first time he saw ya, he was done, not another would do for him. He'll fight for ya, give you everything, but ya gotta let him be him. And if you can't, then ya got to let him go."

The silence was deafening. Cheyenne grabbed the branch from the bush next to her and picked off a leaf, tearing the petal apart. She needed something to focus on other than the thought of her and Trax.

"Ya know." Meg scooted from the other side of the porch and landed next to her, so close her thigh brushed against Chey's. She leaned on her elbows and her knees, staring out into the empty street. "I think..." Cheyenne stared at her profile and watched the corner of Meg's mouth curl before she turned to face her with a full grin. "You two will make beautiful babies."

Cheyenne chuckled and tossed the remaining leaf onto the ground. "Is this your way of offering to babysit when we do?"

Meg tilted her head and clucked her tongue. "I noticed you said when we do, not if."

Cheyenne sighed. "I love him."

Meg slid her arm over her shoulders, pulling her in for a gentle hug, and whispered, "And he loves you." She paused. "And in the grand scheme of things, it's really all that matters, sweetie." She chuckled. "I don't know much about life, but I do know love. I had the real deal for a long time, and I'm telling you, it's worth everything. The good, the bad, even the end." Her voice cracked slightly, and Cheyenne peeked up to witness her glassy eyes. "Wouldn't trade anything I had with Mick."

"No regrets."

Meg gasped and faced the road again, still clinging on to Cheyenne. "Just one."

It was on the tip of her tongue to ask what it was, but the moment seemed too personal. If Meg wanted to share, she would. Cheyenne glanced out to the road and sat quietly. She heard the echoes of the masculine voices from the yard but couldn't make out what they said.

She didn't know how much time had passed as they sat in silence, but there was something good about the quiet. A loud crack ruined the silence, and she leaned forward, watching two small boys race down the street. One faster than the other, but the little guy behind pounded the pavement, giving it all he had. They slowed their speed at the edge of the curb and fell forward, giggling on the grass.

The older boy threw up his hand, shouting, "I won."

The smaller of the two heaved his breath and rolled to his side, sitting up. "I was close."

The older boy opened his mouth to say something but stopped. He stared back at the younger one who was pulling grass from the ground, clearly upset he'd lost. She was ready to hear the older boy gloat, which she thought was his intention, but instead, he stood, turning to the younger one and offering his hand.

"Yeah, you were close. Before ya know it, I'll be chasing you."

Cheyenne smiled. Maybe the smaller boy would eventually be faster, or maybe not. But she had no doubt that one day soon, the older one would let the little guy win. And something in her heart swelled. She smiled, watching the two boys walk off.

"Just one," Meg whispered. Cheyenne peeked up and saw her attention too was on the boys, but unlike Cheyenne, she wasn't smiling. She was on the verge of tears.

Cheyenne glanced back to the boys and clasped her hand in Meg's.

Kids. Her one regret.

"I'm sorry, Meg."

Meg smiled and shook her head, still watching the boys. "I never wanted them. We had our thing, and it worked for us. But now?" Her breath hitched, and her eyes watered. "Kinda wish I had a part of him here with me."

There it was.

TRAX HAD NEVER CONSIDERED himself a pack rat. Until an hour ago. He dedicated the morning to clearing out one of the large closets in his garage for Cheyenne. He'd offered her the space two nights ago when he'd caught sight of her living room stockpiled with shit. *Not shit, product.* He smiled and lifted another box, moving it to the corner.

He had dropped by her place with take-out. He wasn't spending the night. Cheyenne had to work, but if all he got was greasy cheeseburgers in her shack of an apartment, he was going to take it. He took every opportunity he could get, and there were few this past week. His schedule was hectic between work and club business.

When she answered the door, she was disheveled and anxious.

One look in her apartment, and he knew why. The floor was covered with boxes.

"What the fuck? You moving?"

Cheyenne laughed and lifted onto her toes, kissing him. It was one of many things he'd become a sucker for. She always greeted him with a kiss.

"I wish." She sighed and pushed a box away from the entrance. "The good news is, business is growing. The bad news?" She raised a brow. "My space isn't."

"Is this shit all sold?"

She narrowed her eyes. "Not shit. Product, Trax. And no, but we've been filling so many orders, it makes sense to stock up, so our delivery is quicker to the customers."

He nodded, taking in the candle and scarf war zone.

"I got a big cedar closet in my garage. Give me a day or two, and I'll clean it out." He walked over to the kitchen counter and started taking the food out. She had been silent, which seemed odd for her. He glanced over his shoulder to find her staring at him in confusion.

"What?"

"Your closet?"

"Yeah, it's fucking huge, and just storing shit I probably shoulda tossed years ago." He scanned the room. "It's big enough to house your shit." He caught the severe arch in her brow and smirked. "Your product."

The corners of her mouth curled, and she ambled over, tossing her arms around his neck and tugging him against her for a tight hug.

"You would do that for me?"

"I'd do a lot for you, Chey."

It wasn't a big deal to him, but she was extremely thankful. She had showed her appreciation the following hour in her bed.

He shook the memory from his head. Too much time spent thinking of Cheyenne, especially naked, and he'd get nothing done today. He had been working for an hour and still had a lot to get done. He pulled out a bike, due back to its owner by the end of the week, and started working.

"Hey there."

Trax was bent behind the bike working on the engine when he heard her and glanced up from the bike. He smiled.

"Didn't know you were stopping by."

Meg shrugged and came into the garage, leaning against the frame. "Didn't plan on it, but I was coming back from the cemetery." She smiled softly and tilted her head. "Just thought I'd drop by and check on you."

Trax snorted. "It should be me checking up on you."

"You do. You all do." She paused, losing a bit of light in her face. "Mick left me in good hands. Always knew if he went first, I'd be taken care of."

Trax stood, taking in her somber stance. He saw the true magnitude of Meg's loss. It was easy to feel sympathy and sorrow for her. For most people, they mourned Mick and then moved on. For Meg, it was a road she'd travel alone. All their plans that Mick had shared once or twice, traveling and vacations, wouldn't happen.

"You need anything, Meg, you call me." It was an order with a harsh edge to it. He needed her to lean on him. She was notoriously independent. She didn't fall in line like other old ladies. Always showed respect for the club and Mick, but had her own life outside the club.

"Actually, I do need you to do something for me." She stepped forward. Trax rounded the bike, wiping his hands with a rag. The bike could wait until later. His own priority was helping her out right now. Everything would take a backseat.

"Name it."

She smiled with tears brimming her eyes. She rested her hand on his chest over his heart. "Need you to let go of the guilt you're holding on to."

Trax froze and flattened his lips in a line.

"Breaks my heart even more knowing you somehow feel

responsible for Mick." Her hand slid up his neck to cup his jaw. "It would piss him off, knowing you were holding on to this guilt."

"It was my pickup."

"Which Mick offered to do for you, sweetheart. And even if he didn't, and you asked, this still wouldn't land on you, Trax. The only person who has any blame in this is the bastard who killed my husband. Only him."

Trax drew in a deep, shaky breath. He would have loved nothing more than to let his guilt fade, but it remained, pulling him down, weighing heavily on everything he did.

She patted his cheek with her palm. "Try. For me?" She smiled, lightening the mood, though it was still dark and somber.

"Gonna get him, Meg." It was a vow, and one he had no intention of letting slide by without retribution. The man who took Mick's life would pay with his own.

"I know you will. Just don't want you to sacrifice something of yours to make it happen."

He knew what or who she referred to. He had no intention of losing Cheyenne, though some things were beyond even his control. He wasn't sure if Meg knew everything that had gone down with the club and Cheyenne, but since Nadia had been there that night, he wouldn't put it past her to fill Meg in.

Meg stepped back, walking toward the open bay door and turned. "I'm gonna give you some advice." She cocked a brow. "And if you're smart, you'll take it."

Trax bowed his head, smiling, and then glanced up. "Let me guess, don't fuck this up?"

Meg laughed. "Well, yeah, that's a given. You'll fuck up, Trax, and so will she 'cause neither one of you is perfect." She gazed off to the yard. "You'll do shit, it'll piss her off, hell, she might even throw something at your head." She chuckled. "I hope for your sake she's like me and has horrible aim."

Trax shook his head with a small snicker. He knew the story

The Favor

she referred to. Mick had shared the night he'd almost lost his head when Meg threw a cutting board at him.

"Just love her, Trax. You be faithful to her and honest with her. I know there's parts to your life you can't share." She sighed, taking on a more serious tone. "And she knows it too after our little conversation."

He flinched and furrowed his brows. Meg and Cheyenne had spent an hour together the other day. He'd assumed they'd discussed women shit like hair and other bullshit. Obviously, it was a bit deeper than that.

"What did she say?"

Meg shrugged. "She's scared. It's a different life than what she is used to and what she envisioned for herself. Can't fault her for going in cautious. But she loves ya."

"What did she say, Meg?"

She drew in a breath and crossed her arms. She was battling with herself. "I'm only telling you 'cause I'm not sure she thinks she can tell you about her concerns just yet, and I don't want either one of you to lose out on something great with each other." She paused and then broke down the conversation she'd had with Cheyenne.

Trax merely listened. They were valid concerns, but a few comments Meg made had been a huge red flag. Her best friend, Macy, had gotten inside her head. Prison, cheating, fucking biker babies. He tapped down on his temper, but some things made his blood fucking boil. She should come to him with those concerns.

"Loving, faithful, and honest, Trax. Those three things are the key to having this beautiful life with her."

"Yeah, the honest part is probably what will end us."

Meg narrowed her eyes, but before she could ask, he held up his hand. "Club business, Meg." She'd been around long enough to know it was an end to the conversation. He wouldn't tell her, and she respected that with a sharp nod.

"Okay, but if it's something that involves Cheyenne, makes it her business too. Don't discount that and put one above the other.

Because it's her biggest fear as I just mentioned." Meg sighed, walking over and taking him in for a hug. "You can't lie to her, Trax. 'Cause even if she doesn't find out for thirty years, ya never want her looking back, thinking everything you had was a fraud."

She released him and glanced up, taking a brief second before she finished. "You understand what I'm saying?"

He did. He had to be honest, and it would probably fuck everything up.

Meg took off, leaving him with a nagging twist in his gut. He wasn't supposed to see her until he got back from their Ghosttown trip. He could wait on telling her, or he could just man the fuck up and do it. He took on a whole new guilt about the audio tap in her place.

"Fuck," he muttered.

Chapter 15

Cheyenne walked to the door. It was almost a skip, but she tamped down her enthusiasm, well aware of Macy's watchful eye. They hadn't spoken much, which was odd for them. Ever since they'd had the conversation about Trax, Cheyenne did her best to avoid talking about him, and Macy did her best to avoid Cheyenne.

"Can't go one friggin' day?" Macy snapped sarcastically, tossing the paperwork on the table and heading for the hall.

"Macy," she called out but was ignored. She jolted at the slamming door.

She didn't have plans with him tonight. In fact, Cheyenne had made plans with Macy in hopes of smoothing the situation out. Her best friend could win an award for holding grudges. Trax had called an hour ago saying he needed to stop by before heading out for the next few days. The right thing to do was probably to tell him no, but she'd caved. She wanted to see him, and the idea he wanted to see her before he left was sweet. But Trax and Macy in the same room was going to be awkward, knowing how Macy felt about him.

Was it too much to ask that her best friend and her boyfriend got along? She rolled her eyes. *Yes.*

She opened the door, and her smile faltered. Trax stood in the doorway, flanked by Gage and Rourke. He hadn't mentioned they would be coming along. Cheyenne rocked back on her heels. Her past encounters with both men left her uneasy around them.

"Hey," she said.

He lifted his chin and smiled, setting her mind at ease slightly. He leaned in, pushing her back into the apartment, and kissed her. It was quick but enough to make her stomach flip and her to fall into his side, wrapping her arm around his waist. He folded her into the curve of his arm and pushed through, allowing the guys to follow.

If she expected Macy and Trax to eventually get along, then she needed to try with Rourke and Gage. After all, they were closest to Trax, just like Macy was to her.

"H-hey, guys." She stammered slightly, and he squeezed her shoulder, trying to put her at ease.

"Hey, Chey," Gage said with a grin and made his way inside the small living room. She glanced over at Rourke, who lifted his chin but remained silent.

"Need to talk. Macy here?" Trax said and then glanced over his shoulder at Rourke, who raised his brows. "Need her here too."

Cheyenne watched the small exchange. Something was going on. She silently prayed it ended differently than the last time they were all in the same room.

"Uh, yeah, let me get her." She pulled away, but Trax gripped her waist, pulling her against his chest. His left hand snaked around her neck, and his thumb caressed her jaw. *Something is definitely up.* He gazed at her with uncertainty.

"Is it bad?" she whispered.

His hard mask cracked, and he gave her a soft smile. "I hope not." He reached in, kissing her quickly. The kiss was different, leaving her unsettled when she pulled away.

She walked down the small hall and then knocked before

opening the door. Macy was sitting on her bed when she looked up.

"So Trax is here, and he wants to talk to us."

Macy's brows furrowed. "Us?"

She nodded. "That's what he said. Gage and Rourke are here too."

The sudden flash across her eyes was fast, but Cheyenne caught it. It certainly wasn't the fear Cheyenne anticipated. Slowly, Macy untangled herself from her blanket on her lap and then walked to meet Chey at the door. She lowered her voice to a whisper. "The blue-eyed guy and the big one with the tats?"

"Yeah."

Macy stepped back and looked around the room before walking to her mirror and pulling the bun from her hair. She ran her fingers through her tresses, flattening out the top and giving a shake to her dark strands falling past her shoulders. Cheyenne tightened her lips and watched as she leaned closer to the mirror and wiped the corner of her eye, which had been streaked from her black liner. She stood and did one last inspection. Cheyenne heaved slightly from her chest but was able to bite down her chuckle.

Macy turned around and walked back to her.

"Which one?" A small giggle seeped past her lips, and she smiled.

Macy jerked away. "Which one, what?"

"Just curious, which guy, Gage or Rourke, will be the recipient of all your primping." Cheyenne winked, and Macy's cheeks blazed.

"Neither." She glared. "Can't a girl fix her hair and makeup without it being about impressing a guy?" She pushed past Cheyenne and headed down the hall.

"Both, maybe?" Cheyenne teased and watched Macy stumble and straighten her back. She couldn't see her face, but she imagined a blush across her cheeks. Cheyenne followed and stopped next to Macy in the opening. Gage had taken a seat on the couch while Rourke remained standing near the door. Trax, who was leaning up against their breakfast bar, pushed off and straightened when they walked in.

"Macy." No greeting, merely an acknowledgment.

"What's up?" Her bored tone was obvious, though Cheyenne knew it was a sham.

"Need to talk to you both."

Macy crossed her arms and snapped. "Okay, so talk."

Cheyenne whipped her head toward her friend. "Macy," she muttered. The attitude was a little over the top.

Macy ignored her, not even bothering to look her way.

Trax glanced over at the guys and sighed, running his hand through his hair. There was no denying the tension. Cheyenne stared at him, trying to gain his attention, but he seemed determined to avoid eye contact. *What the hell was going on?*

"We bugged your place," Gage blurted out, and it took her second to grasp what he'd said. Trax obviously was just as surprised. He whipped his head toward the couch and glared.

"What the fuck?" His tone was sharp.

Gage shrugged. "Like a Band-Aid, gotta just rip the fucker off."

Cheyenne stepped forward and opened her mouth, but Macy beat her to it. "What do you mean you bugged our place?" She glanced around the room, and Cheyenne found herself doing the same. She couldn't miss the uncomfortable silence.

Trax sighed, resting his hands on his hips. "The day we came by…"

"When you threatened me with rape?" Macy chimed in.

Trax's jaw locked, and he scowled. "I never said rape. Fuck! Nothing was gonna happen. I told you that."

"Yeah, after, but I didn't know that when it was happening." Macy squinted, and her lips twisted. "And for the record, you apologized to Chey, not me."

Trax sighed heavily and spread out his hands. "Look, I'm…"

Rourke's movement from the door caught everyone's attention. He stepped forward, his gaze locked on Macy. "It was fucked up what went down." He paused, and even Cheyenne hung on his next words. She couldn't quite remember Rourke taking center stage in any conversations. His presence alone demanded attention. And he got Cheyenne's and Macy's.

He licked his lips. "We're sorry."

The corner of Cheyenne's mouth curled for a brief second. He sounded so damn sincere. It must have caught Macy off guard too. Cheyenne glanced her way, and Macy's bottom lip fell open. It took her a few seconds, but she veered her gaze up through her lashes and whispered, "Okay."

Gage's cackling drew her gaze away from Macy. While the apology was sweet and long overdue, they were getting sidetracked. *Trax bugged my place?* Chey stepped forward, and the second she locked gazes with him, she saw the regret, and her stomach dropped. "You recorded us?"

He moved forward, but she sidestepped across the room. She needed a clear head for this conversation. There had to be a mistake here. There was no way he would do that, right?

"Did you?"

He crossed his arm and clenched his jaw. "I needed to know what you knew, Chey."

Oh God. The pit in her stomach churned, and the heat rose up her chest. Betrayal set off a different kind of anger. It was a burning flame set to combust. She tightened her fists and gritted her teeth.

"Babe," Trax muttered, which only fueled her fire.

"But I told you everything," she shouted, unable to hold back her fury. It was an outrageous invasion of privacy. Even if she had held back from him, it gave him no right.

"I didn't know at the time. I had to be sure."

"With total disregard for my privacy?" Her body locked and shook slightly in anger.

"And mine, asshole."

Gage chuckled, and she jerked her gaze at him. He was the

only one in the room who saw the humor in this. He widened his eyes, still smiling, and held up his hands in front of his chest. "Look, it was a mistake. Trax is telling ya. If it was me, I woulda kept my mouth shut." Gage raised his brows. "He didn't have to, Chey, and you'd be none the wiser, so cut him some slack."

Cheyenne wasn't a violent person, but she was seriously considering punching Gage in the throat. Did he really think just because he'd told her now it absolved him of any wrongdoing? She was stunned silent. However, her friend was not.

Macy gasped. "Are you for real, jerkwad? Cut him some slack after he bugged our fucking house?" She snorted in pure disgust. "I can't even comprehend your level of stupidity. If you think for one second, she's gonna *cut him some slack*, you obviously know nothing about women."

Gage smirked and cocked a brow. "Oh, I know women." His tone was teasing but held a sharp edge and a sinister snicker. He leaned forward on the couch, aiming his stare at Macy. He reminded Cheyenne of a snake about to strike. "I know so much, I can get a chick to come without her having to fake it."

"What?" Macy eyed Cheyenne, but she was just as confused at the odd statement. What the hell did orgasms have to do with what had just happened?

"Don't," Rourke snapped. The warning was followed by a soft growl meant only for Gage, Cheyenne thought. But Gage didn't heed the warning. He angled up from the couch and tilted his head, staring straight at Macy.

"Sweetheart, any man who makes ya fake it isn't really a man." He winked. "Though I will say, you gave a good performance, but being an expert on the moaning of a women during a real orgasm, I call bullshit on yours."

Cheyenne gasped. *Oh God, no.* She glanced quickly at Macy, who stood motionless, not saying a word.

"Shut the fuck up, Gage," Rourke snarled. There was a hint of protectiveness in the command, which shocked Cheyenne, but she was oddly thankful. Rourke stood towering over Gage, who kept the smirk planted on his lips.

"What? Just sayin'." He chuckled.

Macy slowly turned around and walked past, her crimson cheeks blazing. Cheyenne couldn't be sure if it was from anger or embarrassment. Either way, Macy was done, and so was Cheyenne. She waited for her to slam her door, and then she turned on the men.

"What the hell is wrong with you? Why would you do that? It wasn't bad enough you bug our place, invade our privacy, but then to throw it in her face?"

Gage appeared almost surprised and eyed the guys before furrowing his brows. "What?"

"Oh, my God, what do ya mean, what?" She shook with rage. "You completely embarrassed her."

Gage flinched and glanced at the other men. "I was telling her the truth. She deserves better than some douche who can't make her come."

Cheyenne released a disgusted laugh. "Really? Is that how you saw it play out 'cause I didn't. You are an asshole, a complete and utter fucking jerkoff. Get out!"

"Fuck," Rourke snapped as he dragged his hand down his face. At least she wasn't the only one in the room who'd seen this happen. He sighed and scowled at Cheyenne. "He didn't mean it the way she took it. Tell her that." He gripped Gage's shoulder and pushed him forward toward the door but turned around halfway, glancing over at Cheyenne. "Tell her he's sorry."

"Bro, I didn't mean it, ya know what…"

"Gage, not one more fucking word. Shut up." Rourke shoved Gage out the door and let it slam behind him. It now left Trax and Cheyenne alone.

"You too, go." She pointed to the door.

He released an aggravated breath. "I know you're pissed, but let me explain."

She raised her brows. "You already did. You thought I was

holding out, right? Thought I wasn't giving you everything I knew, so you said who the fuck cares about her privacy."

"Babe—"

She pointed her finger. "No. Well, you got what ya wanted, right, so get out." She jerked her head toward the door. "Go."

"It wasn't my idea. Fuck, you think I wanted this?" He threw his hands into the air. "It was a club decision, not mine."

She released a bitter laugh. "Yeah, and they outrank me, I know."

His brows furrowed, and he stepped forward. The comment definitely struck him, but she noticed he didn't deny it.

"I'm sorry."

"I don't care. Leave."

He drew in a sharp breath and rested his hands on his hips. "So, that's it? I made a mistake, Chey." He stared at her. "Ya never made a mistake, Chey? You perfect now?"

Her mouth fell open, and she gasped.

"Don't you dare turn this on me. I'm not perfect, but I don't betray people I claim to trust. I don't trick people for my own gain."

He snorted, and his lip curled. "Fucking hypocrite. You did the same shit to me, saying ya didn't know more when you came in the club."

"I didn't know you then. It's not the same thing, and you know it."

He raised his brows. "Do I?" He crossed his arms and smiled. "And your conversation with Macy? It had nothing to do with your talk with Meg?"

She clamped her lips closed. She should have known Meg would say something.

"Ya got all these questions and doubts, talking to everyone around you except the one person you should be fucking talking to." He shook his head. "But I guess that was a mistake too, right? This whole fucking thing we've been doing is a mistake?"

He stalked toward her, and she remained frozen with her heart racing. The last thing she wanted was for this to end, but how could she be with him if she couldn't trust him? He was inches away from her, and she could feel the heat from his body. He leaned forward and whispered, "Shoulda asked me, Chey. I woulda told ya. I was set to make you my queen." A lone tear streamed down her face, and she bit her lips, wanting nothing more than to feel him against her. Then he was gone, halfway across the room with his back to her. He gripped the door and glanced over his shoulder.

"But I'm a king with flaws, and I can't be with someone who can't find forgiveness."

She was prepared for the harsh slam of the door, but instead, it closed with a soft clasp. There was no anger behind his words, just the truth.

HE HAD CHOSEN the worst time to tell her; he realized that now. He understood her anger, and a cooling period was definitely required, but him leaving town just amped up his tension. He should have waited 'til he got back.

He stayed at the clubhouse last night after several attempts to call her and some advice from Rourke. *Back off her, man. The girl needs time to cool off.* He put his phone aside. He was only aggravating the situation by his texts and calls, all of which were being ignored. This was new territory for him. He'd never tried to win back a woman.

He resisted the urge to bail on the trip and head to her place. *Give her time.* He'd fucked up almost every aspect of their relationship. If he didn't get a handle on this, he'd lose her, if he hadn't already.

He gripped his handlebars and breathed in the cool air. A ride had always cleared his mind, but it wasn't working this time. All thoughts were on her.

The ride to Ghosttown had been a smooth trip. Once they

exited the interstate, there were only a handful of cars on the backroads. They had gotten a late start, which hindered their early arrival as originally planned. They'd made it with a few minutes to spare before the start.

Getting a glimpse of the small town they planned on taking up residency in was a bit shocking. He'd been there before, but seeing it as a possible future home had Trax second-guessing his president's decision. *In the middle of fucking nowhere.* He understood the reasoning. Their current clubhouse was centered in town. The Ghosttown Riders were on display and on the radar of law enforcement. For their new venture, they'd need anonymity, and what better place than the adequately named Ghosttown. They were going back to where it all began.

As they pulled into the gravel lot, Kase, at the lead, veered around back. There were a few cars scattered along the open area with no real pattern for parking. Trax fell in line as Kase, Gage, and Saint parked. Kase's brother, Caden, waited on his bike, playing with his phone. He glanced up, lifting his chin in greeting when Trax pulled next to him.

If the club had honorary members, Caden would be one of them. Trax always found it strange he never took to club life. Kase was president, and their father, Jack, had reigned before him. The biker life was naturally in Cade's blood, but he'd taken another path.

They met up near the back door.

"Boys, welcome to Ghosttown." Cade smirked.

He greeted them with handshakes, making his way down the line, ending with Trax.

They shook hands, and Cade grinned. "Good to see ya. Heard you wifed up?"

Caden was clearly amused by the news. Unfortunately for Trax, the verdict on that was still up in the air. Trax had no intention of going into details.

Trax snorted and turned to Kase. "Pussy gossip, man. Really?"

The Favor

Kase lit his cigarette and shrugged. "Ain't gossip if it's the truth." He turned and started to the double doors.

Caden laughed and slapped him on the back. "Your prez over there said she's a good girl, helping out with the Mick thing. Look forward to meeting her."

Trax nodded.

The town hall was old but in fairly decent shape. He'd seen it a few times passing through the town on the way to the property, but this would be the first time inside. It was a converted old barn. The restoration must have taken some cash just to deem it safe for occupancy.

Cade and Trax were the last two to enter the double doors.

"You know what we should expect here with the mayor?"

Caden sighed, a strange look on his face. It was a cross between amusement and concern. "Only met the mayor once." His lips twitched. "*She* seemed nice enough."

Trax jerked his head and grasped Cade's arm. "She? The mayor's a woman?"

Cade was fighting a smile. "Yeah."

This was a good thing. Any one of the guys could have a go at her, make her see things go their way. Well, except him. He'd leave that work to Gage or Kase. Either one of them would be able to convince her to make things go their way. Trax smirked and raised his brows but faltered when Caden shook his head.

"Uh, Trax? I see where your head's at, and I'm telling ya, the shit you got planned up here?" He tapped his finger to his temple. "Not gonna fly with the mayor of Ghosttown."

Trax snorted. "Not even Kase?"

Caden laughed. "Especially not Kase. You'll see."

Trax stopped short at the door due to his brothers taking up most of the doorway. But he caught a glimpse past Saint's shoulders. Folding chairs splayed out in rows. Not all were taken, but the place was almost full. It seemed the whole town had come out for the meeting. All forty residents. From where he stood, the average age was about sixty. A young couple in the back drew his attention with their shocked stares. He cocked a brow at the man, who quickly averted his eyes.

"Holy fuck, it's Mayberry, brothers." Gage chuckled and surveyed the room.

All the men, except Kase, laughed, gaining more attention from the residents. It was as if they'd stepped back in time.

The exterior of the building may have been updated, but the interior appeared to be original. The wood finish was peeling off, the doors had cracks embedded, and paint chipped from the once brown panels. Even the long table up front seemed circa 1960s.

Kase lifted his chin to a vacant row in the back of the room, and they single filed to the back. Trax was acutely aware of all the eyes on him and his brothers. Even the room, which had the clamors of folks talking, seemed to die down. They settled into their seats. Kase in the aisle seat, and then Saint, Gage, Trax, and Cade next to him.

"Feel like I'm in an episode of the *Twilight Zone*," he muttered and caught the corner of Saint's mouth curl up. He must have been thinking the same.

The whole vibe was strange. These people and his crew couldn't be more opposite. He took a breath. He pulled out his phone and checked his messages. He had several, but none from Cheyenne. He pulled up her name and typed.

Talk to me.

He watched his message time stamp her reading it. He got nothing in return. At least she hadn't blocked him. *Yet.* He tucked his phone into his pocket and settled back into his seat. He swiveled his neck, trying to ease the tension. With everything happening back home, this was the last place he wanted to be.

He scanned the room. If his calculations were correct, almost the whole town showed. When the club moved in, they'd double the population.

"Excuse me, gentlemen?"

Trax smiled at the greeting. He couldn't recall a time they'd ever been referred to as gentlemen. Trax watched as Kase cocked his head to the white-haired woman standing in front of him. She smiled down at them, taking her time, glancing over them one by one before coming back to Kase and leaning forward. She lowered her voice.

"Might wanna grab some pastries before they're all gone."

Kase cleared his throat. "We ate earlier."

Her brows furrowed, and her back straightened. "Are you sure? They're delicious."

Trax covered his mouth in an effort to conceal his grin.

"Maybe after the meeting," Saint said.

The woman clicked her tongue. "Probably won't be much left." She leaned closer, glanced over her shoulder, and then turned back to the men. "Now, I'm not one to talk about others, but we got a bunch of scavengers around here. I swear some of them skip dinner and come here to eat." She sighed, shrugging. "Some people have no manners." She turned around and started toward her seat.

Caden chuckled. "Oh yeah, you guys will fit in."

Trax smiled and shook his head. He checked his phone, noticing the time. The meeting should have started ten minutes ago.

"When does this fucking thing start?" Gage leaned forward with his elbows braced on his knees, clearly looking at Kase for an answer. Movement from the seat in front of them had them turning their attention to an older couple. The woman kept her gaze straight forward, but the man craned his neck, looking over his shoulder.

"Meeting starts when the mayor gets here."

Gage chuckled. "Any chance ya know when that'll be?"

The older man glanced past Gage and smiled. "Here she is."

Trax, along with his brothers, looked back as a tiny woman walked in. It was actually a stretch. This so-called woman seemed more like a girl, maybe a child. Tiny in stature, bundled up with a large coat and scarf, she stumbled through the foyer and caught herself in mid-trip. This was their fucking mayor? She couldn't be a day over eighteen. She hurried past their row, tugging off her jacket, which seemed to engulf her.

"Finally," an old man with a sharp glare shouted. "Meeting starts at seven, sharp."

The tiny woman bowed her head and pulled off her hat, letting loose a wave of auburn hair. Trax heard a faint, shallow voice. "Sorry." She rushed forward to the main table set up in the front of the room.

Caden leaned closer to him and whispered, "Can you imagine Kase with her? She'd bolt the second he opened his mouth."

He was right. They were fucked.

Trax, along with the brothers, watched as the mayor settled into the center seat between the two councilmen. She shook her head, and her hair fell over her shoulder.

"Mhmmm...I like the mayor," Gage said.

Trax noticed Kase lean forward, angling his glare at Gage. "Shut up."

The club as a whole was given strict orders to not bring any unneeded attention. Hooking up with the mayor probably wouldn't fare well for them.

Gage laughed. "Just looking, man."

Trax chuckled and glanced to the front of the room.

"Before we begin, I'd like to extend my apologies to all of you." She glanced around the room with a soft smile. "Your time is valuable, and you all made the effort to be here on time. I had a..." She drew in a deep breath and twisted her lips. Trax flattened his lips to keep his smile at bay. "I had an unwelcome visitor." Her eyes widened as she sighed. "And he did not want to leave."

Trax glanced over at Caden, who seemed as perplexed as Trax felt. What the hell was she talking about?

A man sitting a few rows in front of them stood. "Was it those damn chipmunks, 'cause we get 'em all the time in our cellar."

Another woman, leaning against the side wall, laughed. "Bet it was squirrels." She shook her head. "Nothing more than furry tailed rats. Was that it, Bailey?"

What the fuck was going on here? Trax listened as two more residents piped in. He turned to catch Saint's amusement and Kase's irritation.

"It was actually an opossum."

The room clamored in echoing gasps. Even Trax inhaled a breath. Opossums were especially vicious.

"Oh, for Christ sake." An old man in the front row shot up from his seat, holding up a stack of papers. "I got a lot of issues to bring to the table here. None of which include your personal dilemmas. Now, can we get on with this meeting?"

Trax clenched his jaw. The sharp tone of the old man did not sit well with him. *Shut the fuck up, old man.* Trax's personal thought seemed to be the popular one in the room. He caught the name-calling whispers directed at the grumpy bastard. The most amusing came from the older woman seated in front of them. "How does that man sit with the giant stick up his ass." Her husband hushed her, but she continued. "Someone needs to remove that stick and beat him with it."

Trax couldn't contain his snicker. As he glanced down the row of brothers, he realized, neither could they. Even Kase had a small smirk on his lips.

"Yes, we'll begin right now. Again, I'm so sorry, everybody," she said, and her gaze filtered around the room, stopping abruptly at Trax and the club. She smiled softly. If he had to guess, it was a silent welcome.

The meeting lasted a little over an hour. It should have taken thirty minutes, tops, however, the old guy who they came to know as Arnett, had something to say about everything. At one point, an argument broke out between him and another old guy. From the shouting match, Trax learned Arnett had originally run for the mayor position and lost.

During the course of the meeting, he caught sight of his brothers. Gage looked bored. Saint was the only one who seemed interested, though he didn't think the interest had anything to do with the meeting. Trax had yet to see his vice president take his gaze off the pretty little mayor. It seemed Bailey Preston had made quite the impression on his VP.

"Thank you all for coming out. If you have anything further to discuss, my email and phone number are at the bottom of this month's bulletin. Please take one on your way out," Bailey said.

"Let's go," Kase ordered, and they followed him out. Saint came up behind him, pausing at the small table by the door. He grabbed a bulletin, and Trax glanced over his shoulder. When Saint looked up, Trax smirked.

"That for business purposes or pleasure?"

Saint cocked a brow but said nothing. He was the hardest to read of all the brothers. They filed out of the building and back to their bikes. He knew why they were waiting. Kase had mentioned earlier about talking to the mayor. The intended plan was a cash bribe. He wasn't sure how that was going to go over.

"I'm heading out unless you need me to stick around?" Caden said as he made his way to his bike.

"Later man," Trax said.

Caden got on his bike and put on his helmet. Once he started his engine, he glanced over to where the group stood. Trax watched as he stared at Kase, then opened his mouth.

"I'm in."

All the men knew exactly what he was saying. Kase's face lightened a bit, and he nodded. They all watched Caden exit before their attention drew back to the town hall steps.

Bailey came out the same as she had come in. Stumbling. She righted herself near the steps but never glanced over their way. She hurried to her car and popped her trunk.

"Hey!" Kase shouted.

She glanced around the back end of her car. Trax expected a little fear to show in her eyes, maybe some apprehension. It happened often when they were in a group. Intimidation played a big role in their life in the club. Most people approached with caution. Nothing shocked Trax more than when her lips spread into a wide grin.

"Oh, hey there." She stood and slammed her hood down. She walked over and reached out her hand to Kase. There was no hesitation.

If anything, Kase hesitated but took her hand in a quick shake.

"I'm Bailey Preston."

"Kase Reilly."

"Caden's brother, right?" She smiled. "He helped us out a few weeks back with a delivery." She pursed her lips. "He was a lifesaver."

Kase slowly nodded and eyed Saint, who stood next to him. This was not at all how any of them saw this introduction going. Even Trax expected a little caution, but Bailey seemed eager and thrilled to meet them. So fucking strange.

Trax took in the small young woman. His original assessment was off, given his closer look. She was probably in her early twenties. Something seemed off, though. She seemed too at ease among him and the club.

"Can I help you with something?"

"Just wanted to introduce ourselves." Kase glanced over his shoulder. "This is Saint, Trax, and Gage. We're leasing the McMillian property."

She nodded. "Yeah, I heard. Well, welcome to Ghosttown." She smiled with a soft giggle and stepped forward, starting with Gage and then Trax, shaking their hands. She stepped in front of Saint doing the same. This time, the sleeve of her jacket pulled up on her arm. Trax scowled at the harsh scarring on her wrist, which seemed to lead up her arm.

"Saint, it's nice to meet you," she said before following his gaze to where they all stared. She immediately yanked her hand away and stepped back.

Her cheeks blazed pink, and her lips curved. She chewed on the inside of her mouth. The silence was awkward, but Trax focused on those scars. He'd seen a lot in his time. He recognized burn marks and nothing self-inflicted. Her stare was aimed at the ground as though she was gathering herself.

Trax had had enough burns to know the pain involved. Nothing he'd ever encountered had been close to the damage on the young mayor. The scarred, coiled, reddened skin was almost painful to see.

She gasped a deep breath and smiled, though he could see it was forced. "We don't have a welcome wagon set up, but if you need anything, just reach out. We have meetings the first Monday of every month." She twitched her nose. "Except on holidays. I'm still working the kinks out on the website, but it should be up and running in another few weeks."

Kase eyed her, and for a second, Trax thought he might ask her about the scar. It was rare Trax felt sympathy for others who weren't close to him, but the little mayor seemed to bring out a side to him he didn't think existed. Compassion. Thankfully, Kase didn't mention the scars.

"The mayor, huh?"

Her pink tongue jutted between her lips in a quick swipe. Her mouth drew into a tight smile. "Write in ballot." She cleared her throat and gripped her coat at her waist. "Only Arnett was running, had a campaign and all. He worked really hard on it, posters, banners, the whole nine yards." She drew in a breath and shrugged. "Guess the town wasn't as impressed as I was, though. Apparently, they had other ideas. And now here I am." Her shoulders sagged, and she whispered, "The mayor."

Kase smirked. "You vote for the old man?"

She glanced up through her lashes, and her cheeks flushed. "Uh-huh."

"Anybody else vote for him?"

She twisted her lips to the side. Even Trax could admit she was definitely cute.

"He did."

Trax chuckled along with his brothers. "So that's it huh, two to what, twenty?"

Bailey glanced up at Trax with an amused smile. "Forty-six and growing."

Kase stepped closer to her, and to Trax's surprise, she didn't back away.

"Wondering if you could help us out," Kase said.

"Sure, what do ya need?"

"We've got the application for permits submitted on Friday, and we need to get the construction started soon." He glanced over at Saint and motioned him forward. "Just hoping we could expedite it."

Trax watched as Saint stepped forward and offered the envelope to Bailey. She tightened her brows and stared down at his hand but made no move to take it.

"Hoping this can help speed up the process," Kase said.

This was the strangest payoff attempt he'd ever witnessed. Saint stepped closer, and still Bailey remained where she stood, staring down at his hand.

"It's for you," Saint said, eyeing her with a small smile playing on his lips.

Her gaze flicked to Saint. "Is that money?"

He nodded.

Her eyes widened, and Trax bit back a smile.

She lowered her voice as her eyes grew the size of saucers. "Like a payoff?"

Gage didn't have as much self-control as the others and chuckled before pulling himself together under Kase's glare.

Kase walked up next to Saint. "Think of it as incentive to push the permits through as soon as possible."

He cocked a brow and refrained from laughing when her eyes widened and zoned back to the envelope.

The club had never offered a payoff that wasn't taken. Her hesitance was almost refreshing, but in the end, they knew people didn't turn down free money. She glanced up at Kase, and then her gaze shifted to Saint.

She eyed the envelope again, and for the first time, stepped back. She slowly perused all of them and drew in a deep breath.

"I know you're eager, so I'll make a call first thing tomorrow and see if we can get the permits by the end of the week so you can start construction by early next week."

It was exactly what they wanted to hear. Kase dipped his chin toward the envelope, but she didn't move.

Her laugh was nervous. "Look, I'm guessing there's a wad of cash in there, and while it's appreciated—" her voice lowered "—sort of." She drew in a breath and shook her head. "I'll try to get a rush on the permits for you. Marty owes me a favor, so it shouldn't be too hard." She smiled and nodded.

Saint reached out his hand with the envelope. "For your troubles."

Bailey eyed the envelope again and then glanced up to Saint. Her cheeks turned a light shade of pink. "It's no trouble, really. Just a phone call."

Saint cocked his head and glanced back at Trax with a smirk. Trax held up his hands. They were all thinking the same thing. *What the fuck?*

Saint turned to face Bailey. "You're not gonna take it, are you?"

"No," she whispered and then darted her gaze to the ground.

Kase laughed and cocked his head to the side. "You serious?"

"Yes." She glanced up and smiled. "First thing in the morning, I'll reach out to Marty. You guys have a great night, and drive safely." She walked to her car with all four men staring in disbelief. In all his years, Trax had never seen a payoff denied.

She opened her door and then slid inside. She glanced over. "Oh, and again, welcome to Ghosttown." She closed the door, started her engine, and they all watched as she drove away.

They stood silently in the empty lot. What the fuck had just happened?

Saint turned to face the brothers and quirked his brow. "Well, my faith in humanity has been restored."

Trax burst out laughing.

Chapter 16

"Where are you going?"

Cheyenne straightened her fitted shirt and adjusted her belt on her jeans. She had achieved exactly the look she was going for. She needed to fit in and blend without making herself too obvious. The outfit was days in the making and well thought out. Cheyenne turned to the mirror, giving herself one last look. *Nailed it.*

"The clubhouse." She grabbed her bag off the bed and walked to the door Macy was currently blocking.

"Why?"

In the past five days, her frustration with both Trax and Macy had her on the edge of combusting. How two people she loved could drive her bat shit crazy was beyond her comprehension. The days had been long, the nights even longer. Without interference from either of them, it gave her time to think. Really think. She'd taken what both Macy and Trax had said into consideration, and then completely removed it from her thoughts. Any decision she was going to make would be hers. Right or wrong, she was choosing her path for her future.

She tried to get past Macy without answering, but Macy grabbed the doorframe, making it impossible for her to get by unless she sucker punched her best friend. Cheyenne eyed Macy and considered the option.

"Why are you doing this?"

Cheyenne stared back at her friend. "'Cause I can identify the guy who killed Mick. And that's what I'm gonna do."

"Did you talk to him?"

Ahhh...him. Trax was referenced as only *him* or *he* for the past five days.

She hadn't spoken to Trax, but not because he hadn't called. He had. Over and over, leaving messages and texts. She listened to each one and read every message. It was a struggle not to respond. Trax wasn't giving up on her, and he'd resorted to driving past her bar, slowing down to catch a glimpse of her. His shadow was on the street when she left work at midnight. It was his single headlight following her until she made it home. Last night, she hesitated by the door, thinking he would come up, but he didn't. He waited until she was inside and then drove away. She wanted to forgive him, talk to him, and just be with him. But before they could start again, she had to do this.

"No, we haven't spoken."

"Then wait, why are ya doing this?"

"Because I have to." She pulled Macy's arm out of her way and walked down the hall. "I'm the only one who can help."

She snorted. "You're getting back with him, aren't you?"

Cheyenne jerked around, tightening her jaw. "So, what if I do, Mace? It's none of your business anyway."

She raised her brows and held her hands up in front of her chest. "Whoa, girl, I'm just asking."

"No, you're not. You're giving me a look that says, 'Don't get back with him, don't go there, he's not right for you.' Well, it's not up to you, Macy."

Macy widened her eyes. She was clearly getting the message Cheyenne tried to convey. "Okay."

"Why am I spending my time miserable, thinking about him, and wanting to be with him? Is this how I'm supposed to live?

Am I the person who can't forgive a mistake? A mistake I want desperately to forgive." She teared up and cursed herself for getting upset.

"Chey," she whispered. "Calm down."

"No, I'm not gonna calm down. He bugged my place, and it pisses me off more than you can imagine. And I hate that I can understand why he did it. Makes me feel weak not holding on to the anger." She swiped her cheek. "But all I keep thinking was he didn't have to tell me. I would have never found out, Mace. He had to know he was risking us when he did it." She shrugged. "Maybe he did it to get rid of me."

Macy laughed. "Chey, he's been stalking ya for the past five days relentlessly. You know as well as I do why he did it. He was coming clean. He didn't want a secret between you guys." Macy gently gripped her arms, and Cheyenne looked up to see her smile. "Can't believe I'm saying this…" She sighed and shrugged. "It was a good-guy move."

It was.

Macy sighed and released her arms. "Gimme ten minutes."

"For what?"

"I'm coming with you."

"You are?"

"Against my better judgment, yes." She winked and disappeared into her room.

Cheyenne leaned against the wall with her head resting back and staring at the crack in the ceiling. It had been a week, a long and miserable week, since she'd last seen him. She had no idea how the night would go down, but she was prepared for whatever he had to say. He had better be prepared to hear her too.

There were a whole new set of ground rules he needed to hear if they were really going to move forward.

THE CLUBHOUSE PARKING lot was packed, leaving the lot across the street her only option. She pulled up in between two trucks and then turned off the ignition. Damn, where was all the courage she'd had an hour ago? She peeked up past her steering wheel. People were coming and going through the main door, and a few were gathered at the entrance lot near the back.

"Ya ready?"

Cheyenne bit her lip and glanced at Macy. She was a vision of confidence. The complete opposite of how Cheyenne felt.

"What?" She furrowed her brows. "Second thoughts?"

Cheyenne sighed, slinking back into her seat. "Yes and no." She tapped her foot against the floor. Why was this so hard? She'd go in, look around, and if she saw the man from the car, she'd find Trax and point him out. *Find Trax. There lies the problem. Find him where, doing what, with whom?* All those questions currently took center stage in her mind. They had broken up. He was free to do what he wanted or who he wanted. Her stomach turned, and she felt a nauseous heated rush through her body.

"Chey?"

She swung her head back against the headrest and closed her eyes. "What if he's with someone?"

"The guy?"

"No, Trax. What if he's in there somewhere with a woman, doing…" She grunted and sat up straight, gripping the steering wheel in a tight hold. Why hadn't this thought occurred to her earlier?

"He's not in there banging some chick, Chey."

She side glanced over at Macy, who stirred uncomfortably in her seat, which only fueled Cheyenne's doubt. Macy turned and widened her eyes. "Okay, so there's a slight chance, and I mean very slight, he is in there with someone else."

"Oh hell." She moaned.

That was not what Cheyenne wanted to hear, but with Macy, she could always count on her best friend for the truth.

"But…" She grasped Cheyenne's wrist. "It doesn't change

anything, right? You said you were coming here to identify the guy who killed Mick, right? That's why we're here, Chey, so come on, let's do this, and hopefully get a free beer or two."

Cheyenne snorted and opened the door, following Macy's lead across the road through the throngs of people. She recognized a few members from the club, and as they passed, the guys gave them the once over. Some paid more attention than others, especially the man standing on the landing of the steps near the front door.

Macy reached behind her back, and Cheyenne grabbed her hand. She gazed up quickly and locked gazes with the man again. He stared back with recognition, but his facial expressions remained tight. He had been in the club the first time she'd come in. There wasn't anything distinctive about him. He straightened to full height when she passed by him. Not quite as intimidating as Rourke, but a close second. His neatly trimmed goatee and dark eyes gave him a sinister tone. Especially since his eyes shot bolts to the back of her head, and her skin chilled.

"C'mon." Mace tugged her inside. Usually, there was a bouncer or prospect watching the door but not tonight. With so many people, she couldn't figure out who was a member and who wasn't, except for their cuts.

The last time she'd been there, it had been a party, but nothing compared to what was happening now.

"Shit, it's wall to wall people." Macy, standing a few inches shorter than Cheyenne, raised on her toes and glanced around. "Let's go to the bar."

Cheyenne gripped her hand tighter as they made their way through the crowd. She was pushed and shoved and did a little of her own. At this rate, the party would be over by the time they made it to the bar. A flash of blonde hair smacked her in the face, and she jerked her head, and in the process, lost Macy's hold.

Cheyenne wiped her face and stood eye level with a set of boobs bigger than her head. She glanced up to the smiling woman. "Sorry."

"It's okay." Her body heaved forward when a large-framed man knocked into her. She stumbled backward but was righted from behind. She looked over her shoulder when strong hands curved around her waist. A man she'd never seen before smiled and winked.

"Finders keepers." He burst out laughing.

"I'm not lost." She pried his fingers from her hips and turned quickly.

"Ya sure?" He chuckled. "'Cause ya look lost."

She shook her head, trying to back away, but the crowd made it impossible. She averted her gaze, trying to find a hole to sneak through.

"Whatcha looking for, sweets?"

She shouted over the crowd. "The bar." *Oh God, where the hell was Macy?*

His hearty laugh caught her attention, and before she could move, his arm hooked around her waist and her feet left the floor. She wiggled in his hold and gripped his hands as he started to move. She stiffened when she realized what was happening. He barged through the crowd without effort because everyone parted a path for him. As his steps continued, she noticed the bar coming closer to sight.

Is this really happening?

"Over here, Chey," Macy yelled from the corner of the bar. He must have heard her because he changed direction, and seconds later, her feet hit the ground in front of Macy. *Thank God.* Her best friend eyed the man standing behind her, who had yet to release his arm from her waist.

"Hi," she said over Chey's head. "Have a drink with us."

What the hell is she doing? He chuckled, and his finger lingered over her hipbone.

"Nadia, we need a round," he shouted, getting the attention of the bartender. Cheyenne had seen her a couple of times but never had been formally introduced. Her blood cooled when she got a better look at the buxom bartender. She was the same woman who had been wrapped around Trax the night she'd been interrogated by the club.

Nadia held up her finger, gesturing for him to wait, with her back toward them. Her barely-there shorts rode up her crease when she bent over. Cheyenne's face heated. *Isn't she cold? Who the hell cares?* Cheyenne eyed her carefully. She was very pretty, and sexy. She glanced down at her own body, making a mental comparison. There was none. Seeing Nadia up close was a shot to her ego.

She sauntered over and rested her hands on the bar, smiling up at the man next to her. "How many?"

"Three beers and shots."

Cheyenne moved closer to Macy. There was no way she was doing shots with this guy, but apparently, she was the only one. Macy was practically bubbling over with excitement next to her and bouncing on her seat. Cheyenne rolled her eyes and scooted closer to her friend, trying desperately to get the man's hand off her. She wasn't going to be rude. After all, if not for him, she might still be in the mosh pit. He rested his arm on the bar, and she glanced up.

Nadia headed their way with three bottles in her hand. When she looked up, her gaze locked on Cheyenne, and the corner of her mouth curled. Then her gaze dropped to Cheyenne's hip where the mystery man's hand remained. She noticed her eyes squint slightly, but she smiled and put the beer on the bar.

"Hey, Grain, what's shaking?"

He leaned forward, taking Cheyenne with him. Her ribs pressed against the bar. He snickered. "I'm hoping you, later."

Cheyenne sighed. This man had no game. She pulled back and was able to at least move away slightly, but his hand rested on her hip. Nadia glanced over at Cheyenne's face and then lowered to her waist.

"Only thing gonna be shaking is your head if you don't get your hands off that one." She giggled and cocked her chin at Cheyenne.

"Who? My new friend?"

She grinned and shook her head. "Your new friend is also Trax's girl."

It was as though her body had become embroiled in flames. He pulled his hand away quickly and muttered, "Shit."

Nadia laughed and tossed a coaster at him. "You're lucky Trax didn't see." She pointed between the man and Cheyenne. "Ever see him mad, Grain?"

He grabbed his beer and stammered away, muttering, "Fuck me," under his breath. He scowled and turned on Cheyenne. "Why the hell didn't ya tell me you belong to Trax? Hell, woman, I don't got a death wish."

Cheyenne jerked away and watched as he turned and disappeared into the crowd of bodies.

"What else, ladies?" Nadia asked.

Cheyenne turned back to the bar just as Macy spoke. "We're good for now. Thanks."

The bartender nodded and smiled at Cheyenne, giving her a wink. She was making her way down the bar when Cheyenne called out to her.

"Uh...excuse me. Nadia?"

She sauntered back to where Cheyenne stood. She rested her elbows on the bar, leaning forward and displaying her cleavage. "Yeah, sweetie?"

"Thanks for stepping in with that guy." Cheyenne awkwardly smiled. "But, uh...we broke up."

Nadia laughed. Cheyenne furrowed her brows.

"No, seriously. Last week."

Nadia sobered up and nodded with a serene smile. "I'm sure Trax would disagree. In fact, I'd bet my next paycheck if Trax had seen Grain's hands on you, this whole place would be a battle zone." She pushed the bottle toward Cheyenne. "Drink up and stay close to the bar where I can watch ya 'til Trax gets here." She winked and then turned and headed down to the other end of the bar.

Cheyenne watched her closely, as did most of the people at the bar. She felt a nudge on her arm, and she turned to Macy.

"You heard her, he's not here yet. So stop worrying about him being with someone else and let's have fun."

Cheyenne raised her brows. "Fun? This coming from the girl who was trying to talk me out of coming an hour ago?"

Macy shrugged and chuckled. "Maybe I was wrong." She glanced over her shoulder, smiling while scanning the crowds of people behind them. "Have you seen some of these guys? I mean, they're hot. Like really hot. And they probably know their way around a woman's body."

What the hell is she talking about?

Macy sighed, swiveling in her seat, and grabbed her beer. "I could draw Jason a map, and he still wouldn't be able to find my clit." Macy whipped her toward Cheyenne and frowned. "Do you know how exhausting it is to have to fake it?"

Cheyenne giggled. "No, can't say I do." It was the glorious truth.

Macy rolled her eyes and stuck up her middle finger with a small smile playing on her lips. At least some tension between them had dissolved. It felt good to laugh together. It had been too long. Cheyenne lifted her beer, taking a sip.

Where is he?

"WHERE YA HEADED?"

Trax stopped and turned to face Gage, who had his arm slung over the shoulders of one of the regular girls. Rourke stood off to the side, smoking a cigarette.

"Beer run?"

"Yeah. Will this run take you down Northside?" Gage smirked.

It was no secret, though Trax did his best to be discreet, he was not letting go of Cheyenne. They were his brothers, they knew him well, and every night when he took off, they knew exactly where he was going. He shoved his hands into his pockets and remained silent.

"Not giving up, huh?" Gage asked, knowing the answer before Trax responded.

"Nope." Trax smiled, and Rourke shook his head, but when he turned, he saw the semblance of a smile from his friend.

"Go get her, man," Gage said right before he grabbed the girl's ass and took her in for an aggressive kiss. It didn't take a genius to figure out Gage would have this woman in his bed, ass up, in ten minutes.

He stalked down the alley, passing members of the visiting club. Chin lifts and head nods of acknowledgment was all he got, along with a contact high from all the weed being smoked in the lot. He breached the front of the house and rounded the corner, heading toward his bike.

"Trax."

He turned when he heard his name. He gazed around the crowd, searching for the source. Dobbs, a brother of his, came down the steps toward him.

"Hey, man, you going for a ride?"

"Beer. Ya need something?"

He brought his smoke up to his lips and puffed a cloud, turning back to the door and then at Trax. "No, I'm good. Want me to watch your girl while you're gone?"

Trax flinched. "What?"

"Visiting club and all. She's not patched as yours."

Trax felt the tense ripple through his spine. *What the fuck is he talking about?*

Dobbs backed away, smirking, and held his hands up in defense. "Calm down, brother, just offering to keep eyes on her while you're gone."

"What the fuck are you talking about, Dobbs?"

He furrowed his brows and tilted his head in confusion. He

The Favor

hooked his thumb over his shoulder. "Your girl. Cheyenne? Came in about fifteen minutes ago with another chick."

His heart pumped faster than it had in the last seven days. *Cheyenne is here?*

"You sure it was her?"

He chuckled and rubbed the end of his goatee. "Trax, man, I don't want a punch to the throat for saying it but…" He paused. "Your girl? Not the kinda woman a man forgets."

Trax spun around, double stepping to the door. He pushed aside a group of men from the visiting club and made his way down the hallway. The place was packed, wall to wall people. How the hell was he supposed to find her in this mess? A hand gripped his shoulder, and he jerked around. Rourke, who had been out back earlier, was now standing, towering over him with a grim stare.

"What's going on? Saw you bolt in here."

Trax turned around. "Dobbs said Chey was here. I just can't find her. You see her?"

He glanced around the room. Even at six-five, towering over everyone, it would be hard to pick out Cheyenne, or so he thought. Rourke gestured to the bar and took the lead with Trax following. Maybe she'd had a change of heart and wanted to see him, or maybe she was there to tell him to back the fuck off. He'd been watching her since their fight. He couldn't stop himself. She may have been done with him, but he wasn't ready to let her go without a fight. He'd convinced himself she just needed some time, and he would give it to her. He'd do anything to get her back.

A small opening to the bar had Trax coming alongside Rourke and a clear view of the bar with Macy chatting it up with Meg in the corner. He passed by Rourke and hurried to Macy, grasping her shoulder lightly, getting her attention. She turned.

"Where's Chey?"

Macy spun on her chair, and her gaze traveled over his shoulder to who he assumed was Rourke. The corner of her lip curled, and she darted her stare back to him. She leaned forward and shouted over the music. "Bathroom."

She grasped his hand when he moved, and he glanced over his shoulder.

"Don't screw this up with her. I know ya like her and that's good, but she's special, Trax. If you're not in it for the long haul, let her go."

He clenched his jaw reactionarily. This was her best friend, of course she would look out for her, but he didn't need advice on it. He loved Cheyenne and wanted her forever. He nodded and focused on the hall leading to the bathrooms. Where was she?

Chapter 17

The bathrooms were packed, and she was pretty sure someone was having sex in one of the stalls. As she washed her hands, a bleach blonde with a low-cut top and boobs on full display stumbled out of one of the stalls. She blinked a few times and nudged Cheyenne as she fell forward to the opposite sink.

"Sorry."

"You're good."

The woman laughed, turning to face Cheyenne. "Damn right, girl. Ask anyone in this house with a cock, and they'll tell ya exactly how good I am."

Wow, someone is completely blitzed. Cheyenne smiled and dried her hands before squeezing through the crowd and walking down the hall. She glanced back and slammed hard into a solid wall of flesh. She stumbled back, but hands gripped her arms to straighten her.

"This is what I love about this place. I'm looking for sweet pussy, and she falls right into my arms."

Cheyenne gasped, whipping her head to the man with the crude mouth. She was inches away from his cackling laugh, and the smell of his breath turned her stomach. She pulled back, but his grip was tight. She followed her gaze from his chest to his face and lost all air in her lungs.

It was an odd sensation. For all the times she'd tried to remember, she only had bits and pieces come back to her, until now. She stared longer and clarity struck, sending her heart up to her throat. She spoke without thinking.

"I know you," she whispered in shock.

He laughed. "Yeah? You sure, 'cause I usually don't forget the hot ones." He shrugged. "Let's refresh my memory."

The eyes, the hair, and more predominantly, the scar running down his forehead. This was the man from the car that had struck Mick, and ultimately killed him. She gasped for air and jutted back into the arms of another man. She froze, glancing over her shoulder and staring into the last set of eyes she'd hoped to see.

The handsome man curled his lip. "Whatcha got here?"

The man raised his brows in humor. "Says she knows me."

"Yeah?" Kase smirked, though she could see the tension in his taut cheekbones as though he was grinding his teeth.

When she moved closer, his brows drew down in confusion.

She licked her lips. This was her only chance. He was her only option. "I do know him, Kase." She grabbed his shirt in her fists in hopes he'd understand what she was trying to tell him.

He tilted his head, and the corners of his eyes crinkled.

She lowered her voice. "I. Know. Him."

She couldn't blatantly come out and say where she knew him from without tipping the man off. She jerked her head in a sharp nod when she saw Kase stare back at her with intent.

Kase slowly lifted his gaze to the man at her back.

"Kase, man, wanna double team this beauty?"

Kase stood silent, but his hold on her tightened. He laughed and tugged her closer to his chest, wrapping his arms around her waist and pulling her into his back. *Oh fuck, this is bad, so very bad.* Had he not understood what she'd said? Or was Kase just an asshole who thought to get his kicks with his brother's woman?

"Last door on the right," he shouted over the music.

Hell no.

Cheyenne dug her heels into the ground, but it was a fruitless effort. Kase basically lifted her to dangling feet and made his way down the hall. Her eyes sprang tears, and she struggled in his hold, but his strength outweighed hers as they moved closer to the end of the hall. As they passed a line of people, she recognized one of the men. Saint. He was the guy who'd promised to take care of the mess when she'd stormed the club the second time. He was talking to another guy and not looking in her direction.

She licked her lips. It was worth a shot. "Saint!" she shouted and immediately felt Kase's arm tighten against her ribs.

Her hair ruffled against her ear when he whispered, "Christ's sake, shut up. I'm not gonna fucking hurt you."

She scoffed. "Yeah right, like I'd believe anything that came outta your mouth."

Saint glanced over and shifted forward, taking in the scene in front of him. She didn't know him, but from his expression, he didn't like what he saw. *Thank God, he's gonna help me*. He stopped in front of them and eyed Kase.

"What the hell is going on, Kase? Where's Trax?"

"C-can you p-please help me?"

He glanced down at her, and his face softened.

"He's taking me in the room, and they're gonna double team me." She frantically shook her head. "I'm not a hundred percent sure what that means, but I *am* a hundred percent sure I don't wanna find out."

Saint's jaw clenched, and his features tensed as his glare slowly lifted to Kase. The last thing she expected was Kase's reaction. Her back shifted from the rumbling of his chest. The asshole laughed. Or at least she thought he laughed. It was hard to imagine he even knew how.

"It's not funny," she said through gritted teeth.

His chest rumbled again. "It's fucking hilarious, sweetheart."

"Kase," Saint warned.

Her body was pushed forward in Kase's hold, leaving an inch gap between her and Saint.

"She fingered Ron. It's him, Saint. We got the fucker."

Cheyenne watched Saint's face change slightly. *Oh fuck!* He gave a sharp nod.

She heard Kase whisper, "You, Trax, Rourke, and Gage, my room now. You tell Trax to keep his mouth fucking shut."

He dropped his gaze to Cheyenne and then darted past them. She had a flutter of relief hearing Trax's name. He wouldn't let them hurt her, right? This was just a plan, and she wasn't privy to the details. She didn't trust Kase, but she didn't have many options at that point.

Kase moved inside his room and then slammed the door shut. He spun her around with her back against the wall, caging her in. He moved closer, and for a brief second, she feared he would kiss her. He leaned in, his breath spreading over her ear.

"He the one who took out Mick?" Kase pulled back, but she couldn't answer him. Realizing quickly he was about to out her as a witness set her heart in rapid motion. *But isn't this why I came here?*

She nodded.

"Are you sure?"

"You're not gonna let him hurt me, are you?"

Kase flinched as if she'd struck him. "Fuck no. He's not gonna get anywhere near you." He seemed believable.

"You promise?" she whispered. His word could mean shit, but she needed the extra reassurance.

He drew in a breath and leaned closer, lowering his voice. "He wants you? He's gotta go through me." He paused. "And he won't get through me. Ever."

"Okay." She swallowed the lump in her throat. "I'm positive. It's him." Her eyes started to tear. She wasn't sure what got her so emotional, but the fear was more than she could take. She wasn't a hundred percent sure she could trust Kase, but she was out of options. She'd have to put her faith and safety in the club's hands.

His hands tightened on her arms, and he whispered. "Calm down, I gotcha. Not gonna let him touch ya, but I need you to play along, Cheyenne. Can you do that?"

She nodded, and he swung his arm around her shoulders, facing the man.

She trembled in Kase's hold, and he did the most unexpected thing. Kase caressed his fingers over her shoulder. He was comforting her or at least trying to soothe her. When she snuck a peek, he was solely focused on the man in front of her. Before she could think, the door opened and Trax, Rourke, Gage, and Saint walked through the door.

"Is this a fucking train, man?" The man laughed and shucked off his boots.

She peeked over at Trax, who was being held back by Rourke. Gage gripped his shoulder and stared straight forward. Kase leaned closer, but she kept her gaze on Trax, who watched through hooded lids. Kase held her against his chest and smiled at the man.

"How much?"

The man furrowed his brows. "What?"

"Just wanna know the going rate on taking out one of my guys."

The man eyed the room, clearly seeing the disadvantage he was at. Cheyenne stayed close to Kase but angled her neck, watching Trax and the guys. No one looked in her direction. They were all focused on the man in his bare feet.

"What the fuck, Kase?"

He shrugged. "You tell me. Gotta source says it was you taking out Mick on the highway. Am I wrong?"

The man's face paled, and Rourke and Gage stepped forward. The rage could be felt by all, but especially Cheyenne.

"Who?" he snapped.

Rourke made a move forward, but Cheyenne's words had him stopping and looking over his shoulder.

"Me." She drew in a deep breath. She straightened her shoulders. "I saw you. I was in the car next to you. You hit Mick and then left him for dead."

The man turned. His jaw clenched, and his furious glare turned into a predatory scowl. "The gash is lying."

She slithered back, but Kase held her in place. His fingers circled over her arm in a soothing motion.

"Okay. Where were ya the day Mick was taken out?"

Ron's gaze darted around the room, reminding her of a cornered animal. "I don't fucking know."

"You better think, motherfucker, 'cause ya ain't walking through those doors, past my guys, if you don't tell me." Kase stepped forward, blocking her view. "Now, I'll ask again, where were you?"

"Brother, I don't fucking know, it was a while ago."

Gage snarled. "You got no brothers here."

"Are you fucking serious? All on the word of some fucking slit? She's lying."

Kase stood silent, as did all the men. It wasn't lost on Cheyenne. It was her word against his, and Kase could decide to turn on her at any moment. They all could. She skirted her gaze to Trax, who stared at her.

"I'm not lying," she mouthed.

He slowly nodded and turned back to the man and stepped forward. "The seventh, Sunday afternoon. I was at the shop working on my rebuild. I remember where I was." Trax folded his arms. "Now, where the fuck were you?"

The man shifted his gaze across all the men and stammered. "Hades had me doing a run all fucking day. The bitch is lying."

Kase turned back. "Saint, get Hades."

"Yeah, get him, he'll tell ya."

She had no idea who Hades was. Trax hadn't mentioned him. She shifted on her feet nervously, staring down at the floor. She watched as Kase's hand reached behind him and grasped hers. With a tight squeeze, her body relaxed a bit.

A man she didn't recognize came through the door flanked by

two other men and wandered up to Kase. He appeared eerily familiar. She knew she hadn't seen him before, but his features resembled someone. She just didn't know who. He wore a similar cut as Trax, but his read Ghosttown Riders East.

"What's going on?" He eyed Cheyenne and then turned his attention to Kase.

Kase lifted his chin toward the man by the bed. "Ron do a run for ya the day Mick was killed?"

She read the confusion in Hades. "Yeah, all day. Why?"

"Take his bike or a car?"

"Bike, man, always the bike." He glanced around the room, his stare lingering on Saint. "What the fuck is going on?"

The man in question, Ron, lunged forward, pointing at her. "Bitch right there says it was me who took Mick out. Fucking lying whore."

Hades shifted his glare over his shoulder. It clicked in her head, while all his other features weren't familiar, his eyes were. When his brows tightened, she blinked and glanced up at Kase.

She shook her head and stammered. "Kase, I'm not lying. I saw him." Her fingers dug into the back of his T-shirt. Kase's hand reached back, grasping her hand and rubbing his thumb over her knuckles. *He believes me*. It was a silent confirmation.

Hades narrowed his eyes. "Mick got taken out by a car."

She nodded and pointed. "And he was driving. He, um, had a black shirt, and his hair was tied back in a pink hair tie. I remember 'cause it made me laugh, some big burly guy with a bright pink hair tie, it just seemed funny at the time." Her voice tapered off, and she bit her bottom lip.

Hades blinked, and his bottom lip fell open. He studied her face. Maybe he was searching for deception. He wouldn't find it. This was definitely the man who'd killed Mick. She didn't know what was happening, but he slowly turned to the man.

"He was late. Meeting up with Connors. Gotta call when he didn't show thirty minutes after the meet time. Called him, said he hit traffic. Ten minutes later, he was there."

Kase growled. "Sounds like enough time to take out Mick, return the car, and get back on the road."

One of the men who had come in with Hades stepped forward. "Or he coulda been in traffic, asshole."

Hades rested his hand across his chest, never taking his gaze off Ron. "But he wasn't." Hades stare turned into a menacing glare. "Why?"

"Hades, it wasn't…"

"Shut the fuck up," he snapped. "Man up and tell me why."

He pointed to Cheyenne. "Bitch is lying."

Hades slowly shook his head. "No, she ain't. You and I know it. Tell me why." His voice was eerily calm.

The man's chest rose steadily, but he could not hide the glint of fear in his eyes. His gaze darted across the room, and Cheyenne stepped back against the wall. Desperation made people do crazy things, and this man was desperate to get out of the room. His chances were slim to none since Trax, Rourke, and Gage had it blocked. She was probably in the safest spot she could be with Kase and Hades in front of her, but she wanted to be close to another. She craned her neck and caught Trax's profile, his cheeks hollowed from his clenched jaw. His gaze locked on the man.

"Does it matter?" the man shouted. "I'm a fucking dead man, all on the word of some worthless cunt."

She shivered and crossed her arms around her waist. She stared at Trax, and his brows furrowed before lunging forward. Rourke grabbed his arm, which Trax struggled against.

"Fucking lying bitch," the man shouted and came forward. Hades and Kase blocked him from getting closer than two feet, but it was enough to have her slide past them and barrel into Rourke, who stood on the left side of the door. He wrapped his arm around her shoulders, and she pushed at his ribs.

"Calm down, Chey, not gonna hurt ya."

"Get off me," she screamed, getting the attention of the whole room. Trax turned and rushed for her, pulling her from Rourke and curling her into his side. Finally, she felt safe. She wrapped her arms around his waist and felt his hold tighten against her body

"Get her outta here, Trax," Kase said.

"She's fucking lying." The man sidestepped Hades but was thrown back against the bed by Kase.

"You come at her one more fucking time, you'll have a bullet through your fucking head before you can even blink." Kase turned to Trax. "Take her outside. Now."

"But she..." The man, who dangled off the mattress, never finished his sentence.

Hades barreled forward, leaning over him. "Look me in the eye and tell me she's wrong, it wasn't you."

The silence was deafening.

Cheyenne peeked around Trax's bicep to see the man lean forward. The ball in his throat bobbed. "On my life, Hades, it wasn't me."

From the angle Cheyenne had, she could see him, the same as the day he'd killed Mick. It was him, not a sliver of a doubt, though he had such conviction in his lie. Speaking as though it was the truth and swearing on his own life.

"Good."

The man's body sagged in relief. "Now, you believe me?"

Hades laughed. "Fuck no, you're a lying piece of shit. But it's good we find out now before you were patched in as a brother." Hades leaned forward with a sinister smile. "Ready to meet your maker?" He turned his head and locked eyes with Cheyenne. He gave a sharp nod before glancing up to Trax. "Get her outta here."

Trax huddled her into his chest and lifted her, walking past Rourke and into the hall. The place was still packed, and from the happenings in the hall, no one had a clue what was going down in the bedroom they'd just left. He stopped at his door and shifted her onto her feet. She glanced over his shoulder to see Rourke behind him, staring down at her.

"C'mon." He shuffled her into his room and turned to Rourke. "Thanks."

Rourke nodded. "Gave ya my word." He turned to leave, but Cheyenne stepped forward.

"Rourke?"

He glanced over his shoulder.

"Can you, uh, check on Macy for me? I left her at the bar, and I just wanna make sure she's okay."

Something crossed over his features, a softness that seemed so out of place on his hard face. "Yeah."

Before she had a chance to thank him, he was gone. Trax closed the door and turned toward her but didn't come forward. Even knowing him for such a short time, she knew where his mind was, and it wasn't with her in his room.

"Go."

He stood staring at her, and she could see it. He was conflicted as to stay with her or go back to Kase's room.

"Trax, go." She sat on his bed, staring up at him. "Later on, we'll go back to your house. Just you and me." She grasped her hands on the edge of the mattress. "But right now, it's about the club. I get it." She sighed. "Go."

"I'll stay here if you ask me."

She smiled. "You would?"

He nodded.

She drew in a breath and tilted her head. "Go."

He stepped forward, coming down to his knees in front of her and cupped her jaw. Pulling her toward him, he whispered, "I love you."

"I love you too."

TRAX PULLED the door closed and pulled out his keys to lock it.

"I'll watch the door."

Trax shifted to his right to see Hades and his members flanked on either side. They stopped a foot away.

"I'll get my guys."

Hades cocked a brow. "Yeah?" He jerked his chin down the hall. "Which one of your brothers is gonna offer to stand down and not partake in revenge for Mick, all to watch the door for your woman?"

Trax sighed. He was right. No one would be willing, and he couldn't ask, it wouldn't be right. What the fuck was he supposed to do? He couldn't just leave her. He eyed Hades. He'd known him for a long time, longer than some of his own brothers. Hades had tendencies that didn't fly with him, but he'd never known him to break his word.

He pulled out a cigarette and lit it, shaking his head with a smirk. "I'm your only fucking option, man." He took a drag from his smoke. "Look, I'm offering to put pussy on hold to stand guard for your girl. Only gonna offer this once."

Trax sighed. "No one goes in there, ya hear me?"

Hades nodded. "No one, you have my word."

Trax passed by Hades but turned a few feet away back to him. "How'd ya know she wasn't lying?"

He took a drag from his cigarette. "The pink hair band."

Trax's brows furrowed.

"He stopped by my house for the delivery that morning. His band broke." He took another drag and released the smoke from his lips. "My little girl gave him the one she was wearing." He laughed, shaking his head. "Fucker didn't wanna take it, ya know it being fucking pink, but one look from me and he tied that shit around his hair. My kid offers you something 'cause she's a fucking sweetheart," he paused and his jaw tensed, "you fucking take it."

Trax was just given the confirmation he needed to enter Kase's room and do what needed to be done. For Mick. He stalked down the hall with a fiery rage in his belly. He opened the door and watched as Gage, Rourke, Kase, and Saint surrounded Ron. He'd arrived just in time to witness Rourke slam his fist across Ron's jaw, sending him across the room and falling against the wall.

"Why?" Kase growled.

Ron shifted his head. "Motherfucker deserved it." Blood trickled from his lips as he tried to stand but failed. He hugged his ribs. "Cut off my brother's fucking finger." Ron coughed.

Trax balled his fists and rushed forward, grabbing Ron by the collar, forcing him to look at Trax. "Your brother," he spewed in complete disgust. "Owed money to the club. That piece of shit borrowed from the club then fucking ran like a pussy instead of paying back what he owed." He tightened his grip. "Your brother was willing to let his fucking wife and kids take the fall for his debt." Trax was riddled with anger and pain. "Yeah, Mick cut off his finger so his wife and kids wouldn't be held liable for his fucking debt, you piece of shit." Trax grasped his neck, tightening his hold until Ron's face turned blue.

He pushed him against the wall and stalked back to his brothers. The debt in question wasn't owed to their club, but to Hades. Mick knew if retribution wasn't taken, it would fall on the guy's family. Mick wouldn't let that happen. And it wound up costing him his life.

Trax stood silent with his brothers and watched the reality resonate in Ron's eyes.

It would be the last look he ever gave.

Lights out, motherfucker.

Chapter 18

Cheyenne sat on the edge of his bed, palms tucked under her thighs and her feet tapping the wood floor. Time had stood still since he'd ushered her into his room and then closed the door behind him. She had followed him and listened to his conversation in the hall. Oddly enough, she wasn't scared with who watched the room. In fact, she wasn't scared at all, which made this situation worrisome. Was this what life with Trax would be like? A series of fights and revenge, people watching her while he went off and did God knew what?

The doorknob jiggled, and she jerked her head, watching it slowly open. Trax emerged from the hall. The low lights in the room made it hard to see anything but his silhouette. He shut the door and turned, stopping when he realized she was watching him.

What now?

She swallowed the lump in her throat and drew in a breath. "Hi."

Trax remained still for a second and then leaned his against the door, tucking his hands behind his back. "Hey." His voice was purposely soft, and she assumed it was for her benefit.

She stared back, waiting for him to come forward, but he

never did. Was he waiting for permission? Did he think she would go bat shit crazy being locked in his room, knowing what was happening? *I actually don't know, and I'm not sure I want to.*

"Hungry?"

She shook her head.

"Got some water in the fridge."

"I'm good."

He nodded with his gaze drifting around his room.

This was awkward.

"Déjà vu, huh?" The corner of her mouth curled when she saw his brows hike up through the dark room. She angled her body to face him, remaining seated on the bed. "You standing at the door, waiting for me to lose my shit." She smirked. "And me sitting on your bed, wondering what you're thinking."

"That what you're doing, Chey? Wondering about what I'm thinking?"

"Yeah."

His back pushed against the wall, and he stood straight. His arms fell to his sides, and although he didn't move forward, she sensed it. He wanted to. She could sense it, without a doubt in her mind, he wanted to come to her, wrap his arms around her, and hold her tight. *Or maybe that's just what I want.*

"I'm thinking the odds of you sticking around are probably shit after what went down here tonight. Thinking the one thing I wanted to do, keep you outta club shit, bit me in the fucking ass tonight." He drove his hand through his hair with a muttered curse. "Thinking of ways to lie to you, trick ya into thinking this won't happen again when I know my life is unpredictable and shit will go down again." He paused and then stepped forward, the light hitting his hard features. His jaw clenched, the small lines at the edge of his eyes bunched, and his lip curled. "Never have regrets living this life, but seeing you sitting here…" He clamped his lips, and her heart raced. She wanted him to finish what he was saying. He glanced up at her. "Thinking, for the first time in my life, I wish it were different. For you."

"Trax," she whispered. She needed to say something. This was not at all what she'd expected when he'd walked into the room. Of course it might be a bit awkward. They had things they needed to work out, but not this. This was an *end it all* speech. Was that what she wanted? She bit her lip.

No!

"I don't want you to be different." She made no attempt to move. She had spent the last five days going over everything in her head and finally had made the decision to be with him if they could work through his betrayal. It had been a hard few days, and she wouldn't relive it. If he was going to end it between them, truly end it, then she was leaving with closure.

"Shit will go down again, Chey." He said it as fact, without wavering. It was honest and scary.

Her gaze locked on to his stare, and she nodded, lifting her brow. "Yeah, and shit will go down in my life too, Trax. Maybe not the same kind, but things will happen, and I'd do my best to protect you from it…" She clasped her hands on her lap. She tried to hide the fact they were shaking. "That's life. You decide to share yours with someone else, eventually your crap runs into their lives."

His face softened, and she caught a faint smile. "You're worried about your shit affecting me?"

She shrugged. "Laugh if ya will, but you haven't met my mom."

The corners of his eyes crinkled. He was clearly amused. He grinned and folded his arms, cocking his head to the side. "I need protection from your mom?"

She sighed, resting her hands on the mattress and leaning back slightly. "Everyone needs protection from her. She hasn't gotten the memo yet. Ya know, the one that explains her kids are grown and capable of handling their lives without her interference."

He spread his arms out in front of his body and smirked. "Mom won't approve?"

"Oh, she'll approve. She'll charm you, and then stealthily and sneakily insert herself in your life. You won't even realize it's happening, and then..." She fisted her hands in front of her chest and jerked her fingers open wide, shouting, "Boom! You're living next to her, you're friggin' neighbors, and she's in your kitchen having coffee, unbeknownst to you since it's five in the morning and you're still sleeping. All of a sudden, you're in her book club, at her house every Sunday for dinner." Her chest deflated, and she sighed again. "Your fate is sealed. There's no way out."

She jerked her head when he burst out laughing.

"It's not funny."

"It's damn funny, babe." He chuckled. "I know you're not talking from experience, seeing how ya live in your apartment."

"My brother."

He snickered. "Maybe your brother needs to grow some balls."

"She took his balls, along with his pride. It's what she does. She's Satan in a caftan."

He burst out laughing again. He had a great laugh, hearty from the belly and gravelly, completely masculine. She drew in a breath, tucking her hands under her thighs and straightening her back.

"So ya see..."

He sobered up, and his gaze landed on her.

"My shit would eventually filter into your life. You don't see me trying to end things with you because of it." She swallowed the lump lodged in her throat. "I spent a lot of time thinking about us. Thought about you bugging my place and how it infuriated me. It felt like a betrayal." She shrugged. "But you were right for calling me out on my own shit. I shoulda talked to you about what scared me. Not Meg or Macy." She pointed at him. "You."

All traces of humor were lost, and he stared back with a clenched jaw. If this was going to end, then he'd have to be the one to end it. It was all on him. She wanted to be with him, and she wasn't going to let go until all chances were done.

"Chey," he whispered.

"Do it."

He winced and furrowed his brows but remained silent.

"Just do it. Say it's over." She paused. Her voice wavered with the last sentence, a bit shaky and filled with emotion. "This is your decision, Trax. I already made mine. I wanna be with you, good and bad shit, all of it. I want you." She pointed to him, making herself clear. "If this ends, you gotta do it." She drew in a breath, resting her hand on her lap. "So? Do it, but make it quick. Like a Band-Aid, just rip it off." She dropped her gaze to the floor and exhaled a long breath, sinking deeper into his bed. Her shoulders slumped, and her bottom lip jutted out. *This sucks.*

The silence seemed to last an eternity. He obviously missed the metaphoric Band-Aid reference. Her eyes burned, and she closed them, trying to batten down the tears that were on the verge of spilling. *I'm so weak.*

The floor creaked, and she knew he was moving toward her. She tightened her lids, squeezing her eyes. This was almost too much to take. She was tempted to haul ass to the door and run away. But then she'd be left without closure, and in order to move on from him, she had to hear the words.

She flinched when the palms of his hands curved around her knees, gripping her firmly. Without seeing him, she felt him moving into her space. His breath fanned over her cheek, and his lips skimmed her ear.

"Like a Band-Aid, right? Just say it?"

She pursed her lips and nodded slowly.

"Look at me, Chey."

Her heart pounded. She'd get the closure she needed with his words, but looking him in the eye as he said them? *Heart-ripping torture.* She wasn't a sadist. She wasn't looking for irreparable pain following her for the rest of her life. Fuck. This would be a memory. If she stared into his eyes when he ended it, it would forever be a vision she had. It would play over in her head.

"Need your eyes if I'm gonna do this," he whispered.

Her entire body tingled and heated, and the lump in her throat made it hard to breathe. This had to end before she hyperventilated and passed out. She jerked her head and blinked open her eyes. He was inches away from her, his lids hovering as he stared back at her.

"I love you."

Ah Christ, he was going to make this torturous. She gulped and inadvertently sent the threatening tears rimmed at her eyes falling down her cheeks. She waited for the rest of it. *I love you but…*

His hands caressed over her thighs, gliding up her arms and wrapping around her neck in a gentle hold. She hadn't even realized she'd spilled more tears until his thumbs brushed against her cheeks, wiping them away. Why was he prolonging this? *Just fucking say it…. I love you but…*

She was caught off guard when he leaned in, swiping his lips against hers. Their last kiss. He pulled away but stayed close.

"I love you, Chey," he whispered again, and she felt it straight to her core. She may have heard the words before, but never had she felt it, the way it ripped through her soul.

She fought against the lump lodged in her throat and swallowed hard. "But?"

She watched the line between his brows deepen.

"You love me, but?"

"I love you. That's it. I wanna spend the rest of my life with you."

"You don't wanna end it with me?"

He seemed surprised. "Why the fuck would I do that?"

She shrugged without a valid answer.

He moved closer and took a seat next to her on the bed. She watched as he leaned forward and tilted his head. "Spent the last few years saying I'd never settle down again. Fuck, I would put money on it. I'd never find a woman I wanted to keep." The corner of his mouth curled. "Then you showed up. Changed everything."

She smiled and leaned in, sweeping her lips against his. "I was the game changer?"

He kissed her, lingering against her lips. "You are my life changer."

THEY'D SLEPT in longer than he'd planned. After he'd entered his room last night, nothing could have torn him away. Being with her was his end game.

He had come out of the shower to find an empty room. For a second, he panicked, wondering if she had changed her mind about him, about them. He quickly made his way out the hall and down to the bar. He'd breached the doorway when he stopped.

At one of the tables, he caught Cheyenne with a coffee, sitting across from Saint. She smiled and shook her head.

"No tchotchkes, I promise." She giggled. "Mostly essential oils and jewelry. Candles are a big seller, and the clothes have taken off." Her eyes almost sparkled, talking about her business, which made him smile. This was her dream, and he'd do anything he could to help her reach it.

"Good for you. Keep at it. Starting your own business is hard work, but done right, it's extremely lucrative." Saint took a sip from his coffee and settled the mug on the table. "You ever need someone to look over your books or need marketing ideas, let me know.

"Do you have a business?"

He nodded. "A few tattoo shops."

Saint downplayed it. He owned three tattoo shops, which were wildly successful. He had a mind for business. He'd shared a few ideas with Trax about expanding his motorcycle repairs shop. That was who Saint was, always trying to help another brother, or in this case, an old lady.

"Damn." She sat in her seat and smiled. "I'm definitely gonna pick your brain." She laughed and caught sight of Trax. Her smile formed a grin, and Saint turned in his seat, glancing over his shoulder.

He moved toward them and rested his hand on Saint's back. "Chey, if he's offering, take him up on it. The man's a fucking genius."

Saint snorted and rolled his eyes. "I need to get going." He shook hands with Trax and turned to Cheyenne. "What went down last night? The club is grateful." He swallowed and nodded. "I'm grateful, Cheyenne. Thank you."

She smiled. "You're welcome." She paused briefly, and then her eyes widened. "Oh, my God, it just hit me." She leaned over the table, staring at Saint. "You and Hades have the same exact eyes. Has anyone ever told you that?"

Trax clamped his lips and bit back his smile. Saint sighed with a smirk.

"I've heard that once or twice." He grinned at Cheyenne and then turned to Trax. "I'm away for a while, but reach out if either of you need something."

"Thanks, man."

Saint spent a lot of time away from the club. He had legit businesses to keep up with, along with a family life, but he was always available. From time to time, a few members balked at the time Saint spent away from the club. They didn't get it. No brother was more loyal to the club than Saint. Trax took his seat across from Cheyenne.

She smiled. "I like him."

Trax nodded. "Man of few words, but Saint is a good guy."

He glanced up at the hallway and watched Kase make his way through the room, heading directly to their table. Trax lifted his chin. "How's it going?"

Kase scowled and cocked a brow. It had been a long night for all of them, but as president, Kase took on more than any of them. He stopped at the edge of the table next to Cheyenne, and Trax watched as she kept her gaze on the table. It would take some time for her to feel at ease around Kase.

Kase tossed a folder onto the table. "Here's the list. Gonna give you first dibs." He glanced down at Cheyenne and then back to Trax. "The brothers agree, you earned it."

Not him. They, him and Cheyenne, earned the first pick at properties in Ghosttown. He hadn't mentioned it to her with everything going on.

"Thanks, man."

Kase nodded, and Trax expected him to walk away. He didn't. Instead, he looked down at Cheyenne. She kept her gaze laser-focused on the table, which made him smirk. Ignoring Kase was an impossible feat, but Cheyenne was trying her best.

Kase shifted his gaze to Trax and then leaned forward, resting his hands on the table, and turned to her.

"Thanks."

Trax watched as she slowly glanced up at Kase. Her lips pursed together, and she gave a sharp nod in acknowledgment.

"It was a fucked up way how this all went down. Some of that is on me and I uh—" He sighed. "Should have fucking handled shit differently. With you." He raised his brows. "We good?"

It was as close to an apology she'd get from him. He glanced over at Cheyenne, whose face softened. It seemed she understood. It wasn't a conventional "I'm sorry," but from Kase, it was damn close.

Cheyenne smiled. "Yeah, we're good."

Kase stood. "Good." He turned toward the hallway but stopped when Cheyenne called out.

"Hey, Kase?"

He glanced over his shoulder and waited.

"Does this mean I get another favor?"

Trax burst out laughing, and he watched as Kase's lips twitched.

"No."

This was good. He leaned forward, resting his elbows on the table. She settled into her chair completely at ease. Fucking perfect. It was exactly how he wanted her to feel there with him and his brothers. It would take longer, he knew, for her to feel complete trust with them, but it would happen.

"What's that?" She pointed to the folder.

"List of properties in Ghosttown."

She tilted her head. "Saint mentioned the club moving to Ghosttown. He said it would be a good place to set up shop. Me and Macy could get a storefront real cheap and still manage online orders from there." She eyed him as if she was hesitant, waiting on his reaction.

"Sounds like a good plan."

"Do you want me there?" she whispered.

He snorted. "You in the same place as the clubhouse? Sounds fucking perfect to me."

His decision was made. If she was willing to move to Ghosttown, then so was he.

Chapter 19

Trax closed his eyes, his muscles anxiously tense as he fisted her soft locks.

If he died at that very moment, he would end it all with a grin. Waking up with Cheyenne every morning was hard to top, but this was slightly better. Her lips clamped over his shaft with a tight suction. He sucked in a harsh breath. Yeah, he'd die a happy man.

He gazed down at her, naked, her hips grinding over his leg like a cat in heat. Just the sight had him seconds from grabbing her and sinking deep inside her pussy. But he couldn't. He was immobilized with the feel of her warm mouth over his cock. He loosened his grip in her hair and weaved his fingers through the soft waves. She had the best fucking hair.

Trax flinched from the sharp graze over his length. She was far from experienced when it came to giving head, which made it sexier. She glanced up through hooded eyes. Seeing his dick slip past her lips gave his heart a steady pound. The corner of her lip curled, and she whispered, "Sorry."

His lips parted, but instead of words, he groaned when she licked his cock from the root to the crown and took him again down her throat. Maybe his woman was more experienced and just enjoyed making him squirm.

While the sex was amazing, surprising to him, he enjoyed just being with her as much as being inside her. This was a first. Even with his ex, he'd never been as content to do domestic shit with a woman. They had dates, real ones. Since his time with Cheyenne, he'd seen more movies than in the past ten years.

"Oh fuck." He grunted, grasping her shoulder and pushing her away, but she kept on him. Her tongue stroked his dick as she bobbed her head. He was giving her warning, but she wasn't relenting. His back stiffened and his legs tensed as his hips shot forward, grinding into her mouth. One last jerk and he came. She didn't let up until he softened in her mouth. *Fucking hot as hell.*

His breath labored, and he pried his eyes open to see her slithering up his body with a smirk. He'd never seen anything as beautiful as his woman. He reached down, pulling her onto his chest where she settled into the curve of his arm, resting her head over his heart. Her fingers caressed over his chest down to his abs.

"Baby, I have to get in the shower. Macy will be here any minute and trust me, ya think Gage can bust balls?" She raised her brows. "He's an amateur compared to Macy."

Trax had no doubt the fluently spoken Macy could be a real ball breaker. And a smart ass. And a bit certifiable. In the past month since all the chaos had died down, he spent most of his time with Cheyenne. And with Cheyenne came her sidekick, pain-in-the-ass, best friend.

They had spent the last few days making up for lost time. He'd had her in the bedroom, the kitchen, his shop, and the shower. They were running out of places to christen.

He grasped her hip, pulling her over his body. His hands rounded her ass, and she peered up with a smile.

"Don't want me to return the favor?"

"Nah, I'll just get myself off in the shower." She tightened her lips when he scowled. She knew exactly what she was doing.

He flipped her over, sending her bouncing on the bed with a soft giggle. "Like hell you will."

She burst out laughing.

He took her in a hard kiss, and her arms spread over his back. He could have spent the whole day just kissing her, but her grinding into his hips meant she did want the favor returned. He grazed his lips across her cheek down to her neck, feeling her heartbeat race against his chest. He'd make her wait it out a little for teasing him. He moved down her body slowly, taking her erect nipple between his lips.

"Ahhh..." Cheyenne moaned, digging her nails into his back.

He sucked her nipple and flicked the hard bead, sending her wet pussy grinding against him.

The sound of the engines gave him pause.

"Uh." Cheyenne groaned and not in a sexy mewl. "Pussy blockers."

Trax tried to hold back, but her frustrated breath sent him into a laugh he couldn't rein in. She playfully slapped his back, and he gazed up to catch her glare.

"How come they only swing by when I'm getting off? It's like they have orgasm radar or something."

Trax burst out laughing, but he was the only one. Cheyenne pushed him off her, and he fell to his side. "Babe."

She whipped her head with a strong scowl. "It's not funny. Where were they ten minutes ago when you were getting off? Is this some kind of brother thing?"

"Yeah, it's in the bylaws. Can't interrupt a brother who's coming."

She rolled her eyes and turned, but not before he caught her small smile.

"Chey, get over here. They can wait."

She gasped. "I'm not letting you eat me out while they wait downstairs."

Trax laughed. "Eat you out, huh?" He wiggled his brows. "My dirty mouth is rubbing off on you."

She twisted her lips and cocked her brow, walking back to his bathroom. "Too bad your dirty mouth isn't rubbing *on* me." She winked and disappeared into the bathroom.

I fucking love this woman.

Trax made his way downstairs to find Rourke and Gage in the garage. He had an open-door policy with them, but since Cheyenne started staying with him, they used that policy less and less. Trax guessed it was Rourke behind the decision. Gage really had no boundaries. In fact, if he had heard him and Chey? He'd have no problem teasing her about it.

He found them inspecting the work he'd done on Dobbs's bike. He gave a major discount to brothers.

"How's it goin'?"

Rourke glanced up and jerked his chin. "Fix the alignment?"

Trax strolled up next to him. "Yeah."

"Ooooo….are club secrets happening, boys?"

Trax rolled his shoulders. The sound of her voice drove a shrill through his brain. She was Chey's best friend, and he'd treat her accordingly, but Macy definitely had a personality that set people off in the wrong way. He turned and caught her sauntering up toward the door. He waved but held back on a greeting. Maybe if he didn't speak to her, she'd go away.

"Hey, short stack. What do I get if I divulge club business?" Gage passed him, and he had the urge to slap him on the back of the head. The man only thought with his dick.

"*Pfft*…depends on the secret." She winked at Gage and stopped on the edge of the garage. "I'm not trying to crash boys' tinkering time." She smirked and glanced down at the bike. "Just here to grab some inventory."

Trax pushed past Gage and walked over to the locked closet in the corner of the garage.

"You sell a lot?"

Trax eyed him suspiciously. Gage wasn't known for his small talk, which seemed odd he that he'd asked Macy anything other than her bra size. Though Trax would be humored if he did.

"Not right now. Just here and there sales, but when we open the shop, we'll be making mad cash."

Trax kept tight-lipped. They might do well if they ever opened it. Their savings were far from shop worthy just yet.

"You know forty percent of all new businesses fold within the first two years," Gage said, lighting up a cigarette.

Macy folded her arms over her chest and furrowed her brows. "No, I didn't know that, Gage, but thanks for sharing. Any more of my dreams you'd like to piss on while I'm here?"

Trax chuckled and turned to Gage. "Put the shit in her car for her."

"Uh, candles, not shit." She folded her arms and stepped back, glancing at the men. "Anyone interested in a purchase while I'm here?" She smirked. "How *about* it, Gage? You can give them to the women you bang, like a parting gift?"

A low chuckle from the corner had Trax glancing over his shoulder. He found Rourke oddly amused and staring at Macy. Trax furrowed his brows. It wasn't just amusement he saw. He'd known Rourke long enough to know when his friend saw something he liked. *Oh fuck!*

"Short stack, my seed is the parting gift." Gage reached out, gliding his finger under her chin, which she immediately swatted away.

"*Ew*, so gross. I'd much rather have a vanilla bean candle than your sperm." She grabbed the box and turned away when Gage tried to help. "I can do it myself."

It was comical watching her juggle the box that reached her chin. She rounded his bike, and Trax cringed when she came inches from knocking into it. Rourke stepped forward, but by his interest, he would probably come to Macy's rescue before Dobbs's bike.

Trax watched as she angled herself between Rourke and the bike. She stopped at the door a foot away from Rourke and turned to face him. Not many women other than those at the club, initiated conversation with his brother. Maybe it was his intimidating size or the roughness about him. Rourke hadn't had an easy life, and it showed.

She smiled at Rourke. "How about you? Interested in a candle for your girlfriend?"

Holy fuck! Trax flattened his lips and watched the show play out. Rourke merely eyed her. He had to give her credit, she had a set on her. She waited, though Trax wasn't sure if Rourke was going to answer. He raised his brows.

"Don't have a girlfriend."

A second passed before Macy nodded with a smile. "Good to know." She turned and walked down to her car, popping the trunk, and lifting the hood before bending over and placing the box inside. Both Gage and Rourke were appreciating the view.

"Damn, how have I not fucked her yet?" Gage said, and Trax punched his shoulder.

"Christ, man, not her. You fuck with her, and that shit comes back at me."

Gage laughed, and Trax ignored him as he set his sights back on the bike while Trax noticed Rourke watching Macy.

"Hey, Trax, Chey inside?" Macy shouted from the back door.

He nodded, and she walked in.

They were heading down to the club soon, and he assumed Macy would be coming along. From the stare Rourke had given her, he was probably counting on it.

SHE ANGLED her head to get a deeper kiss from Trax. It worked. His chest pushed up against her body, and she was caged in by the wall.

If someone had said she'd one day be in a biker clubhouse making out in public with her biker boyfriend, she would have scoffed at the idea. *But here I am.*

His hands reached around her back, one sliding across her ass, and she felt his erection press up against her stomach. She grazed her teeth against his tongue, knowing it was a weak spot for him. He groaned in her mouth.

"No fucking in the bar, Trax."

She froze. Trax kept kissing her, but the mood was shot. She recognized the voice and the sarcastic tone. Kase may have kept her safe, but she still wasn't exactly a fan. She liked mostly everyone she met, including the women who hung out there. Kase was hard to like. Respect and fear was a no brainer, but liking him? No.

Trax traced the outline of her lips, causing a tingling to her core, but her mind was now on who watched them. She forced a breakaway and glanced around. Not one set of eyes were on them, and from the corner of the room, she caught a couple on the verge of breaking Kase's rule. Trax turned and threw his arm over her shoulders.

"Can't believe I gave up my fucking room," he muttered.

She was now regretting the decision. Trax had given his room to Dobbs a few weeks ago. He had his place, and she had hers. Keeping it seemed pointless since she wasn't a big fan of staying there. Now would have been nice, though.

It wouldn't be long before the house closed and the Ghosttown Riders took up residency in their namesake.

She giggled and grasped his stomach. "I'm gonna go hang out with the girls."

He leaned down, taking her lips for a quick kiss, and swatted her ass as she walked away. She rolled her eyes and weaved through a small group. Just as she passed, she was tugged into a wall of flesh. Had this happened a month ago, she would probably be swinging fists, but so much had changed. She recognized the snicker and glanced up, smirking. Gage draped his arm over his shoulders.

"Chey, tell these motherfuckers about my bike." He pulled her deep into his side and leaned toward the men gathered. "Not one of you assholes gonna be able to keep up. Turn in your cuts 'cause you won't be able to keep up."

Cheyenne giggled. Trax had been working on Gage's motorcycle for the past few days. She didn't understand all the lingo involved, but from what Trax had explained, he bored out the cylinders and installed bigger pistons. He threw in a performance cam, and now the bike "hauls ass." In short, Gage got a new engine.

Gage squeezed her shoulder and lifted his chin. "Tell 'em."

"It's gonna be nice." She smiled, glancing up at Gage, who scowled. Apparently, her answer wasn't good enough. She cleared her throat. "And fast?"

"Nice and fast, that's the best you got?"

"And pretty?"

The men started to laugh, and Gage shook his head. "Ya killing me, Chey."

"What? I don't know." She laughed when his lips twisted. "Pretty is a compliment, Gage."

He released her arm. "Go, you're just making shit worse for my rep." He winked.

Since the Mick situation had been dealt with, it seemed a mutual bond had been formed between her and the members of the club. Each of them, individually, had made a point of telling her how much they had appreciated what she'd done, coming forward. Without the drama, they seemed to enjoy having her around, mostly because as Rourke had said, "You make him happy, and that motherfucker deserves it."

The club was Trax's life and so was she now. She didn't want to make him choose. Why should he? He could have it all. She'd also found an odd comfort in being around the Ghosttown Riders. These were his people, and now they were hers.

Cheyenne made her way to the bar where Macy sat on a stool. Her elbows leaned on the bar, and she was engrossed in whatever Nadia said. Meg craned her neck with a grin and winked at Cheyenne.

Things had changed. Mainly, Macy and her take on club life.

She wasn't exactly sold on the club, but she enjoyed most of the benefits.

She saddled up next to Macy and caught the tail end of the conversation.

"So, both of them, at the same time?" Macy's eyes bulged out, but Cheyenne didn't miss the glint in her eye.

Nadia giggled and tilted her head, grabbing a glass from the bar. "I'm telling ya, girl. You want a good time, Gage and Rourke together is the way to go."

Cheyenne clamped her lips closed and widened her eyes. A threesome with Gage and Rourke? It wasn't Nadia's admission that had her shocked, it was Macy's interest.

Macy sat back, sighing with a grin, and looked over her shoulder. Cheyenne followed her stare to the pool table. Trax, Dobbs, and Gage were centered around the table. Cheyenne glanced up at Macy and then realized her gaze was shifted off to the right. Not on the pool table at all, but at the table next to it. Rourke leaned his elbow on the pub table and drank a beer. As if he could sense it, he gazed over. Not at Cheyenne, though. His gaze veered to her left. He stared at Macy.

Cheyenne turned around and laughed when Nadia glanced over and winked at her. There were a few seconds of silence before Macy turned around and set her hands on the bar. "Threesome, huh?"

"Girl, ya don't know what you're missing," Nadia said.

Macy turned to Meg. "You ever have one?"

Meg choked on her beer and wiped her mouth. "I'm pleading the fifth."

Macy chuckled and shrugged, turning to Cheyenne. "And we all know you're a no. So, Nadia, were they the best? Like club-wise."

"Jeez, Mace." Cheyenne couldn't hold back. The question seemed quite invasive.

Nadia and Meg burst out laughing.

"What? She said she was an open book."

"It's fine, Chey. I don't care," Nadia said and then leaned on the bar. "They were my second favorite. Wanna guess who's my number one?"

Meg piped in. "Kase."

She shook her head. "Nope."

"Really?"

She shrugged. "Don't get me wrong, Kase is a hell of a good time, but he's not my favorite."

Macy glanced around the room with an eager smile. It was fun to watch her get so hyped about anything. Recently, she had been in a funk since her break up, and her job wasn't faring so well. She deserved better than the hand she'd been dealt.

Macy smirked as her gaze wandered the room. She shifted her gaze, and her lips pulled down into a frown. Chey looked over to where she gazed. At the pool table, and mainly at Trax. She slowly spun around and remained quiet. Of course, she knew Trax and Nadia had been together, and as much as she wished they hadn't, she couldn't fault either one. It was long before Cheyenne met Trax, and he did have a life before her, and so did she. Holding a grudge for something that had happened before they got together was unfair.

She drew in a breath and grabbed Macy's beer, taking a sip. No one said a word.

"Hey, bitch, get your own beer," Macy teased. Cheyenne glanced over and could see what she was doing, her best to change the subject and get her mind off Nadia and Trax.

"Here, Chey." Nadia placed a fresh bottle in front of her.

"Thanks," she muttered. It shouldn't bother her, but it was grating on her.

"So, I saw ya looking at him, Macy. Not impressed with my number one, huh?" Nadia giggled and started wiping down the counter.

Cheyenne felt the heat rise from her neck to her face. She wouldn't hold it against Nadia and Trax, but her throwing it in her face was fucked up and completely out of character for the usually sweet Nadia. Cheyenne gripped her beer tightly, and the small group remained silent. Even Meg hadn't said a word.

"I'm telling ya, he does this thing with his tongue." She snickered, and Cheyenne immediately glared at her. Enough was enough. Nadia surveyed the girls, losing her smile as she glanced to Meg, then Macy, and finally, Cheyenne. She was seconds from telling her to shut the fuck up about Trax.

Nadia glanced over Cheyenne's shoulder, her gaze scanning, and then locked in one spot. Her face paled and she gasped. *What?*

Nadia stepped forward, staring straight at Chey. "Dobbs, that's who I'm talking about, Chey."

Cheyenne jerked her head around to see Trax and Dobbs standing next to one another, laughing. He looked up and smiled. She sighed, relief curling up the corner of her mouth. Her face now heated in embarrassment. Of course Nadia wouldn't talk about her escapades with Trax.

She turned around, but before she could say a word, Nadia leaned into her space. "I would never talk about Trax, Chey. Never."

Cheyenne forced a smile, but Nadia wasn't finished.

"I love him 'cause he's a great guy, always been sweet, and yeah, we have a past, but hold it against me, not him."

Cheyenne shook her head. "I won't hold it against either of you, Nadia."

She smiled and breathed heavily. "Good, 'cause he loves you, and I just wanna see him happy. And you too." Nadia grabbed her hand, squeezing it tightly. "Hell, I wanna babysit your beautiful babies someday."

She laughed and relaxed again into conversation. Macy quickly got back on track.

"Dobbs, huh?"

Nadia lifted her brows. "I'm telling ya, Macy. He may not look the type, all muscles and scowls, but you want your toes to curl, come multiple times, and then cuddle all night, Dobbs is your man."

"Really?" Macy turned around, staring in the direction of the pool table again. But even from a side view, Cheyenne could tell Macy's gaze wasn't on Dobbs. No, it was on Rourke.

Interesting.

Chapter 20

"What do ya think?"

She eyed the open property. He'd taken her down Main Street, looped around the valley, and ended at the dirt road in front of the future Ghosttown Riders compound. They weren't allowed access just yet, but from the road, it looked cool. Completely off the beaten path. Large enough to house all the brothers, even giving Trax a room if needed.

With three months of renovations and a lot of manpower from the club, they'd move in sooner than expected. Trax and Cheyenne had talked about moving to Ghosttown, but not in much depth. They still hadn't decided exactly where they would live. And taking up residency in the clubhouse was out of the question. They needed their space.

For now, they spent most of their time at his house in Blacksburg, and on occasion, her apartment. Things with Macy had changed drastically, and everyone seemed to be getting along.

They traveled back through the Main Street where he pointed out a few available buildings for her shop and then veered right, down a tree-lined street. He parked in front of a vacant lot.

She dismounted and gripped her helmet, taking it off. The

street had three other homes with a large separation dividing them.

"The property is an acre and a half. It backs up to wetlands, so no one can build behind us."

"Us?"

He shrugged and glanced around. "Yeah, I mean, there are a few other homes, so it's not isolated. We got neighbors but not too close. Close to Main Street. Hell, you could walk if ya wanted."

"Did you buy the lot?"

He glanced over his shoulder and smirked. "Not yet. I wanted to talk to you first."

"What about your house?"

He shrugged. "I could sell. Take this piece of land and build one."

She slowly gazed over the vacant lot. She could almost envision a house sitting center with a large front lawn and an even bigger backyard. Her lips curled when Trax came up behind her and wrapped his arms around her waist.

"Wanna know what I see, Chey?" he whispered into her ear.

She smiled and nodded.

Trax pointed to the open space. "Two-story house…"

"With a porch?"

Trax snickered. "Yeah, a wraparound porch. We can do a garage, and then a second one in the back for my repairs. If Rourke decides to move up here, I could probably rent space in his shop, but still want a second garage." He stepped forward. "We could fence in the yard if ya want. Ya know, it's safer."

"Safer?"

"For kids, down the road."

Kids with Trax. The thought crossed her mind more than it should. She'd never spent so much time thinking of the future with any past boyfriends, but with him? It all felt right. It didn't feel like something that could happen. It was something that would happen down the road. She turned in his arms, and he yanked her into his chest. He rested his forehead against hers, and she smiled.

"You're making a lot of promises, Trax."

"And I'll keep 'em all, Chey."

She pressed her lips against his and whispered, "I love you."

"You better. I'm building you a fucking house."

She laughed, slapping his stomach. His chest rumbled against her cheek. He cupped her jaw and lifted her gaze to meet his. He stared into her eyes, and she waited for him to say something, but he remained silent. She curled her hand around his hip and squeezed.

"What?" she whispered.

"Just wanna see those eyes."

The End

About the Author

Amelia Shea writes contemporary romance. She released her debut novel in 2015 and has followed her passion for series romance ever since. Her writing style includes a little sweet, a little sassy, and lots of steam. She loves building stories with settings that become comfortable and familiar, and developing characters who feel real, and though they may be flawed, they learn and grow, and finally deserve a happy ending.

Born and raised a Jersey girl, she has settled down in the South with her amazingly supportive husband, her fabulous (most days) children, and her loyal, four-legged, furry sidekick, Bob.

Website: AmeliaShea.net

- facebook.com/AsheaWrites
- twitter.com/AsheaWrites
- instagram.com/Author_amelia_shea
- amazon.com/Author/Amelia-Shea
- goodreads.com/Amelia_Shea
- bookbub.com/authors/amelia-shea

Printed in Great Britain
by Amazon